2-01

undertow

⌐

The publication of this book was supported with grants from the Oregon Arts Commission and the Robert M. Stafrin Fund of The Oregon Community Foundation. With grateful appreciation, CALYX acknowledges the following "Immortal" who provided substantial support for this book:
Melissa L. Beal in honor of Dr. Paul B. Beal

Cover art: "Flood" by Katherine Ace
Cover and book design by Cheryl McLean

CALYX Books Prose Editorial Collective Members: Amy Callahan, Margarita Donnelly, Cheryl McLean, Micki Reaman; Senior Editor: Beverly McFarland; Assistant Editors: Amy Agnello, Laura McFarland, Teri Mae Rutledge; Editorial Assistant: Tracy Mitzel

CALYX Books are distributed to the trade through Consortium Book Sales and Distribution, Inc., St. Paul, MN 1-800-283-3572.

CALYX Books are also available through major library distributors, jobbers, and most small press distributors including Airlift, Baker & Taylor, Banyan Tree, Bookpeople, Ingram, and Small Press Distribution.
For personal orders or other information write:
CALYX Books, PO Box B, Corvallis, OR 97339,
(541) 753-9384, FAX (541) 753-0515.

∞

The paper in this book meets the guidelines for permanence and durability of the Committee on Production Guidelines for Book Longevity of the Council on Library Resources and the minimum requirements of the American National Standard for the Permanence of Paper for Printed Library Materials Z38.48-1984.

Library of Congress Cataloging-in-Publication Data
Schutzer, Amy
    Undertow / by Amy Schutzer.
        p. cm.
    ISBN 0-934971-77-3 (cloth : alk. paper) : $29.95. – ISBN 0-934971-76-5 (pbk. : alk. paper) : $14.95.
    1. Accident victims—Fiction. 2. House painters—Fiction. 3. Lesbians—Fiction. 4. Nurses—Fiction. I. Title.

PS3569.C5565 US 2000
813'.6—dc21   00-058640
                                                                CIP

Printed in the U.S.A.
9 8 7 6 5 4 3 2 1

undertow

a novel by amy schutzer

CALYX Books ⌇ Corvallis, Oregon

Acknowledgments

THERE ARE MANY thanks to give out for this book. For although the story is of my own invention and the writing of it my craft, there is the brilliance and wisdom of those who have helped me tend this book from beginning to end.

My thanks, then, to the following. Judith Barrington, teacher and mentor, whose encouragement, honesty, poetry, and insight unlocked and fostered my passion for writing. My heart is filled with gratitude to The 29th Street Writers: Anndee Hochman, Elissa Goldberg, Shirley Kishiyama, Kathleen Herron, Mimi Maduro, Mary Henning-Stout, Ila Suzanne, Kathleen Haley, Karen Brummel-Smith, Cherry Hartmen, and Janet Howey, whose artful critique and dedication to writing have been a powerful sisterhood. Tom Spanbauer, who taught me how to find the heart of a story no matter how dangerous. I have also had the good fortune of working with astute and astonishing teachers: Annie Callan, Evelyn C. White, Grace Paley, and Suniti Nambjoshi. The Astraea National Lesbian Action Foundation whose generous grant afforded me a room of my own and time to write in it. Lori, Lizzie, Carol, Jenny, Karin, Beth, Musawa, Cherie, Etta, and to all my friends who have urged me on and understood what writing means to me, you are inspirations all. My land sisters at We'Moon and to the land itself that provides me infinite poems and stories. An immense thanks to my editors at CALYX, Micki Reaman, Beverly McFarland, Teri Mae Rutledge, and everyone else at CALYX, for their wisdom and seeing the forest for the trees. Katherine Ace for her astounding art. And to the beauty of CALYX. Thank you, Margarita Donnelly, for your belief. Finally, tremendous love, thanks, and respect to Zelda and to Robert, whose support and love have never wavered.

This book is lovingly dedicated to Lori,
extraordinary friend.

part one

~

dotty and macy

falling

1995

Dotty

A MARCH DAY, I climbed up the aluminum ladder to the second story where I was painting the window trim of a house blue. Alice blue. That's the color that was picked out. A tender, creamy blue like I pictured unfolding over the prairie, a flossy bedspread in the sweet air of spring.

On each side of my ladder were holes I drilled so I could attach S hooks and hang the cans of paint and a bucket with my scraping tools and brushes and radio. The thin clouds like enticing ghosts swiveled above me. Next door a crow knocked a hazelnut against the roof. In my hand I held a brush, natural bristle, well suited for long strokes on the wide wood of the window casings. I chose the brush because of the handle's slight curve that rested perfect in my palm.

I did not pick the Alice blue. Gena, the woman who owned this place, wanted the body of the house in yellow and the trim blue: Marigold and Alice. The colors of her childhood. Like her grandfather's farmhouse in summer. Chickens. A kitchen garden. That's what she told me. Not that I asked. I didn't want to know too much about the people I painted for. It was easier that way just to unload my tools and paint. Otherwise, they would call me in for coffee or tea and want to talk, and pretty soon hours disappeared and the weather turned nasty and I'd lose half a day of painting and half a day of pay.

I didn't say anything when Gena showed me the colors.

"Don't you have an opinion?" she asked.

"I think they'll work fine together" was what I said. I didn't raise my eyebrow or twist up my mouth or anything that would give away what I thought of Marigold and Alice on a two-story fake colonial revival house.

"Fine?" she said. "More enthusiasm would be nice. But it's true you are working for me and I didn't hire you as the decorator."

As long as we knew where we both stood.

Gena co-owned a deli and catering service, and it was at a divorce party that she got my name. From Tony, who cut my hair and traded tomato seeds with me. Tony had told me there were two other women living in the house, a nurse and a substitute teacher. I saw them walk out of Gena's house to their cars on the street. Tops of their heads, shoulders, the backs of their coats and pants and shoe heels. Gena was the only one who talked to me.

Every day she'd ask me, "How much longer will it take?"

"Three weeks, total" was what I always said. Let her do the math. I'd been there two weeks brushing the Marigold yellow onto the clapboards with my black-handled brush.

"Why don't you use a sprayer or a roller?" Gena asked. Day five, after I'd scraped and puttied and primed. She was planting a flat of primroses in arcs that followed the plastic lattice edging along the path to the front door with the brass lion's head door knocker. The whole yard done up in bark dust and low growing pointy evergreen shrubs, gladioli, rosebushes, and intermittent begonias.

"I told you when you hired me that I don't use a sprayer. It's bad for the air, and a roller won't cover clapboards that good. Brushing is the best way to go; the paint sticks and lasts longer."

"It's just taking more time than I thought."

I said, "Three weeks is three weeks."

She patted the bark dust around the last primrose, both hands in sync. Took off her pink gardening gloves and looked up at me. "You're right. Three weeks is what I agreed to. It just seems like you're moving so slowly."

"It's the paint," I said. Dipped into the yellow and brushed along a clapboard, heard the sound I loved, when paint sweeps and soaks into wood.

"Is it the wrong kind of paint?" She had her hand cupped above her eyes, even though there wasn't any bright sunlight.

"No," I said, "it's high quality paint, thicker than if you'd bought the cheap stuff; it takes more time to get it right."

"Great. I want the best. By the way, the color is exactly what I had in mind. It is gorgeous. Admit it?"

"Sure," I said. She didn't say anything else to me. Walked into the garage with her trowel and gloves.

The Marigold yellow was more like a sunny-side-up egg yolk when it's over-cooked. Lurid and too bright for this double-wide shoe box of a house. Not one tree grew in the yard or along the sidewalk. Nothing to temper the Marigold, blend with it, hide it. On a farmhouse, behind some oaks and fields of wheat and corn, I could see how the color would work, fit in like a yard full of dandelions or an old, cranky, peeling yellow International tractor. But here, on this street with quiet colors, don't-notice-me greys and beiges, off-whites, lilac and slate blue trims, basic black shutters, this house was like a stinky hill of sulfur. Two weeks of Marigold. My eyes crowded with all that yellow.

But I never tired of the painting. Thirteen years, up on ladders, drop cloths, turpentine. I could paint with either hand. Didn't really care what color I painted with. I'd only have to look at it for a short time, and in that time I could think of everywhere I'd seen that color: lipstick, place mats in diners, tidal pools with their seashells and starfish. But it was the way that my body knew how to paint, without any doubts—that is what I loved. Like I was dancing the paint on. Shimmy, twirl, cha-cha-cha with the paint. Was always that way, even in my own house. When I dug into the tubes of acrylics with a palette knife, crushing the color onto small canvases like I was doing a rumba.

Painting—I was covering up and over what people didn't want to see anymore. Such an easy way to change a lie to a truth or a truth to a lie.

I started in with the Alice blue on a Tuesday. Finished the top two windows on the right by noon. Moved my ladder. Clang of the aluminum as it leaned against the house. Gena hurried up the front path from her car with a tan briefcase and four cookbooks under her arm.

"God, I'm running late" was what she said. She wiggled the key into the front door and pushed the door open and left it that way. Didn't even look up at the two windows with the Alice blue of her childhood. I looked up. Windows wideeyed in exasperation. The Alice blue the wrong eye shadow for the rouge. The house was like the face of some woman sitting too many hours in a bar drinking rum troubadours, flirting with herself in the mirror behind the rows of bottles, shocked when the bartender cuts her off at two in the morning. Like Lila. And maybe it was because I thought of Lila just then, out of the blue, that I made double sure the ladder's feet were absolutely level and I climbed up the ladder slower than usual, careful of each step.

I took out my edge brush with the slant-cut bristles. Stirred the paint. Dipped the brush into the color that Lila would smear on her eyelids even if she was wearing a red dress. Lila, all clash like this house. Maybe it was because staring at that Alice blue I could see Lila's face vividly when I thought I didn't even remember anymore what she looked like, twenty years of her being dead, that I turned on the radio and didn't notice right away that my body was hesitating with the paint.

On the radio a man was talking about NASA: how much money they spent, contracts hidden away in the cargo bays of the Pentagon, the risk and mistakes, the question of civilians in space and what can happen. I looked down at my truck with the rust polka dots. My life was in order: the dishes washed, planting time in my garden, three thousand miles from anyone who still wished to hurt me. The program on the radio replayed the morning, years ago, when the space shuttle *Challenger* exploded. The staticky countdown, the announcer describing the rocket fuel as it glowed orange and blue and lifted *Challenger*, imperceptibly at first, and then with fury, into the sky.

On the inside of the glass of the window casing I was painting, I watched dozens of ladybugs crawl back and forth, trapped and hurrying to find an exit. I could see the bed made, medical books on a tall shelf. So many ladybugs, the nurse must be swimming in good fortune. The thick Alice blue dripped onto the Marigold while I was stretching for the top corner of the window. From the radio the long bellowing of the *Challenger* explosion. My turning away. From the ladybugs, from remembering Lila's face. The Oh-No, Oh-My-God from the announcer as the rocket ship disintegrated. So many years ago. A NASA official explaining how the astronauts' bodies were completely inhaled by space and did not return, like hail, to earth.

As I reached for the rag in my back pocket, the ladder lurched from its level on the bark dust and a flagstone, tilted sideways, and then I was slipping, my body already adjusting to its new self. Hard as the earth I landed on.

Falling. Falling. Like Lila before me.

In the hospital, a nurse was there in the emergency room. Alice blue eyes above her mask. She was there later in the recovery room when I woke.

"There was no one in your wallet to notify," she said.

"No," I said.

"Dorothy," she said, "Dorothy Meyers?"

The anesthesia was a steam inside of me. "Yes" was all I said.

When I woke again, I was peels and shards held together with steel and cat-gut. It might not get any clearer. It was not just sky I fell through, but sky with the taste of flesh.

Macy

THE MEDICS WHEELED the painter in. I cut the overalls from her body. Her arms smelled like turpentine and her hair like rose water. Damp petals were balled together in her fist. In her pocket her wallet held her name, Dorothy Meyers. Dot? A hard point, she was fixed to the bed.

I had transferred to the Emergency Room seven months earlier. Wanted to see how people dealt with the shock of pain, the immediacy of it, catapulting their lives across the street, through the air, breaking the order they worked so hard to maintain.

When she came to in the recovery room, I was there. "There's no one in your wallet to notify," I said.

Her eyes were plumped up by the anesthesia, cloudy and the color of mud. Her tongue was looking for words. The IV dribbled saltwater into her arm. We were good at replenishing liquids and minerals but had no idea why the body wants to heal itself once it is so far from its original shape and pattern. How does it even know what it's looking for? Some people call it fate, God, courage. The mind's will to make whole what was broken. I think it is just simple chemistry: white blood cells, the knitting of bones, electrical impulses that snap like static across the nerve synapses. I watched her lips.

She said, "No."

I said her name. "Dorothy. Dorothy Meyers?"

Her eyes closed but then the left one opened and she whispered, "Yes."

See how easy it is to begin? There is no one. And then, bingo, I am there.

All right. I had noticed her. The painter. That's how Gena referred to her. Never her name. Every day that she painted Gena's house, the house where I lived, I would get in my car and warm it up for a few minutes and watch her paint. Her body defying gravity, up on her ladder stretching and twisting for an edge of wood. Short-sleeved shirt. The muscles in her arms, my god, all right, I wanted to climb up that ladder and feel the curve where her biceps smoothed into the crook of her elbow. Pictured myself unsnapping her overalls, crawling under that denim and cotton.

The day she started painting the trim, I combed my hair in the car, pushing my long bangs to the back of my head. I didn't even have to look in the rear-view mirror to know my hair was being defiant. Yellow hair rising like Marilyn Monroe's skirts above the subway grate blowing hot air. Jesus. Shit. I put my *NY Yankees* baseball cap over my hair to squash it down. She was standing with her legs wide apart on the rung of the ladder. Putting a coat of blue on the window frame. Ugly colors. The house looked worse than phony fiesta ware. But I was paying more attention to how her overalls were torn right below her backside, a thin rip like an incision that didn't let me see anything unless she moved. I waited until she bent forward to sink her brush into the paint can and the rip widened. I didn't think there was anything other than flesh beneath her overalls. I pictured myself standing behind her, my hand slow as a breeze finding that rip to tease her skin.

A nice way to begin my workdays. A two-week-long daydream. But then, why does fantasy have to be anything more than that? My daydreams were always pointing a finger at reality. I doubt I would have even asked her out for coffee.

Too tired. Double shifts. Another shortage of nurses. Same story, every hospital I've worked in.

Gena called halfway into my first shift, while I was filing papers, waiting for the next emergency. She didn't even say Hi, Macy, just started right in with herself.

"Why do these things always happen to me?"

"Hey, Gena," I said. "Well, you know how terrible things happen to beautiful people."

"Get serious, Macy," Gena said. "It's the painter. She fell off the ladder. God, it was a good thing I was home. I sent the ambulance your way."

I slipped the chart of Mrs. Carson with the abdominal pain into the out-patient file.

"How bad is she hurt?" I asked. I heard the siren, like a cat fight, rising howls.

"I think it's real bad," Gena said. "She couldn't move and she told me the colors I picked for the house were an eyesore."

"Gena, the ambulance is here. I'll call you later."

I was turning the painter into numbers: pulse, heartbeat, respiration. "Get the overalls off," Dr. Hale said. I picked up a pair of scissors, long blades, and cut into my daydream. She was watching my hand, her overalls being slit open. Dr. Hale saying, "Let's go, let's go, start a CBC, type and cross for two and where the hell is X-ray?"

The painter's eyes were hazel, the pupils equal. No concussion. Shock. Stunned. Her body was trying to remember what it was.

She said, "These are my favorite overalls, do you have to cut them?"

I said, "Sorry, but yes."

"Damn," she said, "maybe I can sew them back together."

"Doubt it," Lorna said, helping me pull away the overalls.

No underwear. I was right. But I was looking at her hip and her thigh. They were not joined anymore in a logical way. Her skin an ugly color that Gena would have picked out. Her eyes closed when Dr. Hale started probing. "Morphine," he said, "three milligrams." I uncapped the syringe and injected the IV in the crook of her elbow. X-ray took their pictures. Under her skin, there wasn't much of her thighbone left intact.

"It's going to be a long haul," Dr. Hale said.

Her eyes opened, staring right at me. She said, "Damn, I didn't even get my second cup of coffee."

My mother told a story. The story had no end. It started in the middle and worked backwards. There were two horses, a house on fire, and opportunity. This is all I remembered. Not the events: how the fire started or what the horses said, although the horses did speak—the mare in an Irish accent and the stallion with a stutter. My mother whispered this story to me when I was young, going to sleep. Curled herself up to my blanketed body and her smooth lips settled near my ear. I remember two lines she said: "Circumstance is a horse's behind; before you even see it, there it is in your face. But opportunity is the fire, and you have to choose whether to put it out or let it burn." Then a voice called her away, maybe one of my uncles, but never my dad, Mr. Bad-poker-luck. "It's your deal," they'd yell. And she would leave me. Opportunity a smell she left behind, like talc, vanishing as she closed the door.

Dorothy Meyers was circumstance; she fell into my nurse's hands. I went through her wallet. Found her name on her driver's license. Some grocery store receipts, a ten-dollar bill, library card, VISA, and an old clipping from a newspaper, folded up a hundred times. Which I didn't have time to unfold and read. Which, if I had had the time, I would have. Dorothy was coughing her way out of the anesthesia and I had my work to do: transferring her upstairs to a room, ordering the IVs and painkillers—morphine, to start with, then a combination of less morphine, more Vicodin. It was all there in her chart. Easy enough.

   I called Gena and told her the two things I knew for sure. One, Dorothy's thighbone was shattered and dislocated from her hip but it went back in after a few tries. The doctor had to use a steel plate and screws to set the break and she was in a full leg cast. Two, since she fell on Gena's property, Gena's homeowner's policy would have to cover all the medical expenses because Dorothy, as far as I could tell, didn't have any insurance.

   "Great," Gena said, "just what I need, hours spent tangled up in bureaucracy. Do you think she'll sue?"

   "I don't know. Do you want me to ask her first thing when she comes to?"

   "No. For god's sake, you always were a pain in my ass, Macy."

   "Well, it's nice to know I can still grab your attention. I'll see you later."

I checked in on Dorothy in the evening. Her eyes changed color to a lukewarm green and gold. The three o'clock morphine was waning and her skin twitched as if an insect—a spider or a carpenter ant—was crawling across the fine hairs.

   I asked, "How's your body? What does it feel?"

   Her eyelids were limp, having a hard time staying open. "Nothing," she said. "I am neither here nor not here."

Her body was re-creating itself. What I wanted to know was when we break or lose parts of ourselves, how do we get them back? Do we? And in what new arrangements?

But I didn't ask her any of those questions. She was staring at me like she knew who I was. She read my name off my name tag. "Macy Kahn, R.N. Does that stand for Real Nurse?"

"Only on Tuesdays."

"What day is today?"

"You don't remember?"

Her hand, with the clear and blood-pink IV tubes, touched the cast on her leg. "Must be Tuesday cause you cut up my overalls like a Real Nurse would." She smiled and her eyes closed.

"Look," I said and she opened her eyes. "There's something you probably should know about me."

"What?" Her eyes slipped closed and then opened fast, her brain's reaction to competing messages: stay open, look at the nurse, or shut out everything, sleep.

I said, "I live in the house that you were painting."

"Oh, that's why you're here," she said. "You're the go-between for me and Gena?"

"Partly," I said. "And before you ask, the other part is, I'm a good nurse and like to follow through with my patients."

She licked her upper lip but there wasn't much wet to her tongue. "Can you get me something to drink?"

"No water after anesthesia. Eight hours," I said.

"You're kidding? I've got the Sahara in my mouth."

"I'll get you an ice cube."

"That's the best you can do?"

"That's it."

I held the ice cube up to her mouth. Ran it around and around her lips. Her tongue pushed out to capture the drops, licking my fingers with the ice cube between them. She reached up her hand and circled my wrist. Pulled my hand, my fingers, closer to her mouth. She sucked on the ice cube with her eyes closed and I watched her mouth, the bend in her bottom lip, the thirst of her tongue. Her breath heating up my whole hand. I knew I could pull the ice cube away at any time before she was done. But I was a good nurse. Followed through. On most occasions. I waited until the ice cube was gone and her lips closed around my finger, a kiss, for the last drop of water.

"Thank you," she said.

There was no one. Then I was there.

Dotty

IN THE BEGINNING she was at the side of my bed, in the shadows of the room while the IV dripped like rain. Her name tag told me who she was. Macy Kahn, R.N. I woke to her eyes. To her long lips. Her hair like taffy, honey and caramel, thick in its short spikes and curls. When I woke I heard the soft creak of her breathing. She was watching me with her eyes like coals about to ignite, a candle flame's blue flicker around the iris. She asked me what my body was feeling. My body, as if it was separate from the thoughts in my head. I said, "I am neither here nor not here." To confuse her. But that wasn't accurate: I was somewhere in between. She kept on watching me as if I had another answer.

Inside the morphine daydreams I painted houses as if they were canvases. My brushes were brooms on curved sticks. I dipped them into the sky, into the rosebush, took color from the bark dust, dandelions, my truck on the street, orange as a tangerine. The houses had no roofs. There were no birds. Nothing moved except me. The houses bloomed like hotbeds of flowers and I could see all the way inside to the rooms where I could live a hundred different lives, like a doll being moved from chair to couch to bed. I painted houses of calm, of forgetfulness. Until the morphine started to wear off and the houses folded up and all my paint turned white, so much white, a brilliant electrocution of white, and I lost my footing on the top rung of the ladder and plunged into the color of bones snapping, splintering from each other.

Three days after I fell, I woke with Macy's fingers in my hair. They combed and combed. I did not open my eyes. She touched my skin with a damp cloth. Lingering on my forehead, my cheeks, the curve of my chin. I did not ask her why. I did not ask her how or where. I did not want her to stop. I wanted her there.

She came to my room the next day and read my chart, the vital signs that defined me. Sitting in the peach vinyl chair by my bed.

"You'll be dancing in no time," she said. But she didn't laugh or even smile. Her eyes rose up from the numbers on my chart and settled a humid look on me. Eyelids lowering like shades being drawn in a bedroom where someone is naked and waiting.

"Did Gena hear from the insurance company?" I talked to the left of Macy's eyes, could not look right into them. They were charms and lures.

"Yes, Gena talked to the insurance company," Macy said. She stood up and her eyes went back to being nurse's eyes. Glancing at the IV, she tapped the long tube, followed the liquids down to my hand, touched the bandage. She slipped her hand under mine and lifted it. Palm against palm. The morphine sweetened everything. A powdery sugar. I floated in her palm an hour, a minute, a second. She sat back down in the chair.

"It's all taken care of," Macy said. "The insurance will cover your medical care plus any time lost from work."

I sank my hand into Macy's hand, down onto the blanket. Hadn't I lost enough? I turned my head to the window, to the outside, where cloud after cloud mixed its grey and white and black into rain.

"What is it?" Macy said.

"When you lose time," I said, "you never find it again. It doesn't come back like a misplaced pen."

Macy said, "But you can make up for the time by pretending you didn't really lose it in the first place. Think of it more like an interruption."

"Is that what you do?"

"Depends."

"On what?"

Macy reached for the top snap of her scrubs and made sure it was closed. "On whether the time is worth losing or not. Sometimes it is."

I looked at Macy's crossed legs, longer than mine but just as skinny, down to her anklebones above the padded white nurse's shoes, not a speck of dirt on them, and back up to the curve of her hip, the length of her arm, her elbow's sharp jutting, the wrinkle lines across her wrist, her fingers bent over mine, and up to her face where that one freckle anchored just above the corner of her mouth and below the point of her cheekbone. Solid, every bone, whole, not a visible scratch or scar. Nothing undone in Macy. Yet there in her eyes, within the swirls of blue, was something broken pretending to be smooth. Her eyes were practiced at calm and indifference.

I said, "What I want to know is if you pretend long enough, does that become the truth?"

"A lie always starts with a seed of truth and then grows into its own reality and facts. Truth is never absolute and neither is a lie." Macy's hand pressed against mine while she talked. Her other hand pinched at the air, swept horizontal and vertical, then lowered to her knee. "Sometimes you have to pretend just to get through the next minute."

"So," I said, "I should—"

"Pretend that you didn't fall off the top of a ladder."

"Yeah, well, tell that to my leg."

Macy smiled, not openmouthed, full of teeth, but a careful grin, a slight rising of the corners of her mouth, and that one freckle disappearing into the crease her smile made. She leaned over my body. Pulled the sheet down past the top of my thigh. Her hand a fist that knocked a slow knock on my cast.

"Hello," she said to my leg. Her mouth blowing words onto the bruised skin below my ribs. "Listen up, leg, you need to pretend that you didn't fall from the top of the ladder and that this is just an interruption, an intermission, nap time. Okay?" Her eyelid winking once, twice.

"Sure," I said. "Come back tomorrow and you can have the first dance."

How did love begin? Was it instantaneous, all my pain replaced by the elated cloud of injected morphine? Or was it the days of quiet, noticing that what was broken was repairing but in a way not imagined, not expected? In that place of injury reduced to a false calm and pleasure by the morphine, Macy walked in and sat down. Love, I knew the fiery taste of it, the swerve and desolation. I told myself, no, this is not love. I told myself, yes. There was more: when I looked at Macy, I already knew what her mouth would do and her eyes and the way her hands would talk along with her words. I didn't know how I knew. Only that when Macy came into my room, everything about her was like a recurring dream that is both known and unknown, familiar in its repetition and unfamiliar in the details that twist into new shapes and cast a shadow of doubt onto whether it was the same dream I'd dreamed before. Love, that's what I started to call it. But why not some other word? It was too quick, sudden as falling off the ladder. One minute I was one way and the next I wasn't.

On the fourth day Dr. Madison brought crutches into the room and leaned them against the white nightstand. The day nurse, Carla Holt, with wide Popeye fore-arms, stood behind him. Tammy Irving, the physical therapist, was next to him. She carried a clipboard, and a pencil was shoved into her dense hair above her ear. Dr. Madison stared at the crutches. I stared at the crutches. Dr. Madison, with no first name on his name tag and bright red-rimmed eyeglasses like blood-shot halos around his blue eyes, would not look at me. He talked to the crutches.

"Time to get you out of bed."

I couldn't even sit up by myself.

Carla walked past Dr. Madison around the bed and slid her hand between my shoulder and the pillows. Her arm smelled of baby lotion. The tiny beads at the ends of her cornrows clicked together.

"Is this going to hurt a lot?" I asked.

Carla put her other hand on her hip and smoothed down the fabric of her uniform. Her face, her no-nonsense mascaraed eyes saying, *of course it's going to hurt.* But she said, "Nooo, it won't hurt that much."

Tammy Irving came over to me and patted the top of my head like that was how she sized up all her new patients. She said, "Don't you worry, now. You might feel a little discomfort, but we're all here to help that leg of yours get better."

Dr. Madison stepped away from the bed. The pockets of his doctor's coat were stuffed with folded bits of paper. Sunlight rounded the south wing of the hospital and gushed into the room, lighting up the crutches.

"On the count of three," Dr. Madison said. Tammy held my other arm and her hand slipped down my back until it was dead center on my shoulder blade. She and Carla pushed, and the top half of me rose off the bed while my legs stayed fixed, unmoving. Carla swiveled one leg and then the other while Tammy supported my back with her hand, and they both scooted me forward. The weight of the cast wanted to follow gravity and drop my leg to the floor, but I was still too far back on the bed and there was no bend in the plaster, no give at all. My leg sticking straight out. The morphine refused to douse the pain or color it buttercups and cotton candy. The morphine was seized and strangled. The calm stolen. And all along what was beneath the morphine was this raw hurting, predatory, like a vulture feeding off my bones and flesh. The pain didn't just stay in my leg and hip. It was like passion, surging, skipping along every nerve ending.

In fifteen minutes I learned all the ways my body didn't work. No strength, no quickness, no agility or ease. Nothing but halting. Each step a stutter of the rubber-toed crutches, and my body jerking forward. Jerking, like tug of war, my body pulled off balance, scrambling for solid ground, away from the suck of mud.

"That's right," Dr. Madison said. Standing in front of me, his foot inching the IV stand forward, his big hands directing, fingers saying, *come here*. Puny mouth talking to the crutches, not me. Carla changing the sheets on my bed, punching the pillows into regulation shape.

"I don't think I can do any more," I said. No morphine anywhere in my body.

"Sure you can, you're doing fabulous," Tammy said.

Dr. Madison's eyeglasses flashing like a stoplight. I wanted to stop. Get back on the bed. Three o'clock was ten minutes away. My afternoon injection. The vow of the morphine to make me forget what my body had become.

"Come on, now," Tammy said, "just a tiny, little bit farther." Carla walked right around me and took out a set of sheets from the closet.

Another step. I had moved three feet. How could my body not know how to walk? But it didn't. My mind could have shouted for hours at my leg to just walk, just fucking walk, and my leg wouldn't have listened. I pushed my hands against the rubber on the crutches and swung forward an inch. In my head was a tidal surge of dizzy. I stopped. The crutches rubbed against my ribs. The cast heavy as a boulder. I swayed into Tammy.

"No more," I said.

Tammy put her arm around my waist and supported me like a fence post. "Easy," she said. "The bed's not quite put back together. You're doing great. Carla?"

"Just this one more blanket and we're done."

Tammy turned me around. Carla threw the pillows into place and held up my other side. The two of them inched me over to the bed. I lay down on the stiff, new pillowcase and sheets. No softness anywhere inside me.

Dr. Madison patted his coat pockets. Maybe he was feeling for what he was supposed to say next or remembering what was written on all that paper. His red eyes focused on the knees of the crutches against the bed rail.

"Okay," he said, "enough for today, but you're going to have to do this for a longer period of time tomorrow, the day after and so on, and put more weight on your injured leg. I don't believe in babying my patients, Miss Meyers. It's counterproductive. Isn't that right, Miss Irving?"

Tammy picked up her clipboard from the nightstand and under her breath said, "Righty-O."

Three o'clock. The medication nurse, Sylvia, came in with her metal tray and my morphine. She said, "Hello, Dr. Madison, Tammy, Carla. Hello, Dorothy."

Dr. Madison tilted the crutches against the wall. Picked up my chart, shoved his hand into one of his pockets, and removed a tortoise-shell pen. "Nurse, three twenty-seven, tomorrow, a new course of medication, please check the chart."

"What do you mean, new medication?" I asked.

Dr. Madison tilted his head, but he was facing the crutches and I guess the crutches told him I hadn't just asked him a question because he set the chart down and left my room. Tammy waved goodbye and followed him out.

Carla filled my water pitcher, turned it around on the tray table with the handle pointing toward the other nurse, and said, "Sylvia, I thought you were off today."

"Supposed to be," Sylvia said, "but, you know, it's another one of those short-handed days, so I came in." The two nurses looked at each other, eyebrows rising.

Sylvia set the metal tray on the bed next to my good leg.

Carla said, "I've got to go follow Dr. M.D. I'll talk with you later."

"Uh huh," Sylvia said. Turned the small glass bottle over. The label around the glass full of words and red symbols. Could only see in the clear bottom of the bottle that there was something inside of it. A liquid like sugar water, syrup, a tint of zinc yellow. "How you doing, Dorothy?"

Doing? I wasn't doing anything. I couldn't move one part of my body. Every-where hurt.

I said, "Fine." I didn't want conversation. I was waiting for her fingers to uncap the end of the syringe. She did. It fell on the metal tray. She twisted the needle in through the hole in the rubber top of the glass jar and pulled back the plunger of the syringe. I wanted her to fill it more than the two milligrams ordered on my chart. Enough that I wouldn't feel like cement, cracked and sledge-hammered. Two milligrams. That was all. The nurse lined up the needle to the IV port. Bull's-eye. The sugar-water morphine bloomed a dozen roses on its way to my brain and then I was a field of daisies, my body like a hot, slow kiss, every-where.

I was on the phone to Jean when Macy came in, letting the fluorescent hall light into the room with her. A smudge of chalky white. No shadows under those lights. I lay in the almost-dark: dusk was watery and limp through the window.

"Gorgeous." Jean telling me about the sun in Arizona and the saguaros. She stopped talking when Macy opened the door.

"Who's there?" Jean asked. The door hadn't made any big noise. Macy hadn't said anything. But Jean could always pick up any tiny shift.

"Hang on a minute, okay?" I said.

"Sure, honey," she said, "and just put the phone to your heart so I can listen to how you're doing."

"Not a chance." I put the phone partway under the blanket. "Hey, Macy," I said.

She held the door open with her foot. I couldn't see her face with all that light falling over her. "I want to talk to you. I'll check back in ten minutes." She didn't wait for an answer. Moved her foot and the door started to close and she turned on her clean nurse's shoes and left.

"Jean?" I said into the phone. I wanted to breathe in Albuquerque. Jean stand-ing outside, watching the sky, the brush strokes of sun climbing the huge blocks of stone, the burnt sienna ground.

"So, who is she?" Jean asked.

"I'm not really sure."

"What do you mean, you're not sure? She has a name, doesn't she? And just what is she doing in your room?"

"All I know is she was there when they brought me into the hospital and she was there when I woke up after surgery. She's a nurse. Macy Kahn. Or maybe she's a morphine apparition. The perfect nurse who holds my hand."

"And?" If Jean had only one word left to use in her whole vocabulary, it would be *and*.

"I'm curious."

"Curious, huh? I think you used that exact one on me. Curious. As in I can't wait until we take our clothes off and have us a carnal feast. Is that what you mean?"

I was far away from carnal, my morphine head on top of a beanstalk. I had to touch my skin just to make sure it wasn't something else, like shellac, a shiny coating. "Yeah, can you just imagine my smooth seduction technique in this full leg cast and pickled in morphine?"

"There's nothing like a little helplessness. Some women really go for that," Jean said.

"Well, I don't know much of anything about this woman."

"Only that you're curious. And that you've been in this position before."

"What position?"

"Okay, dewdrop." Dewdrop, the name Jean had called me for over ten years, but only when she was about to tell me something I didn't want to hear. "The position of waiting. You know?"

"No." But I did. I looked at all the lights in the windows of the south wing. Light after light of sick people, waiting for pills and blood tests and doctors' proclamations. Waiting. For someone to come into their room and reverse what had happened. I didn't want to turn on my light, see my body. How still I was. Fixed. Cement. Waiting for Macy to come back in my room and soften me.

"Maybe she's the paradox that will help you stop waiting."

"Is that one of your astrological psychic twinges?"

"Yes. And let me put it this way—this coincidence is no coincidence. I've been telling you for a while now that someone is going to appear in your life. And turn it upside down. Whoever this woman is, you were supposed to meet. And it is only from this position, standing on your damn hard head, that you're going to be able to right yourself."

"Yeah, well, Jean, I appreciate your theories."

"Okay, okay. Are you going to be all right, cause I could cut my trip short, if you want me to."

"No. You and Marty have been planning this trip forever. I'll be fine. You'll be home soon enough."

"I'll call you in a couple of days. And Dotty, be cautious along with curious," Jean said. "There's nothing wrong with that. Love you."

"Love you, Jean. Bye."

Ten minutes turned into forty-five. Dinner came and went. A tray of sea-green peas, a rectangle of noodle and mushroom casserole wrapped in a sheet of crisp cheese, a plastic cup of grapefruit juice, and two oatmeal cookies. I switched the light back off after the orderly set the tray on the stand. Chewed a few peas that tasted like they were grown in their tin can. Tried a bite of the casserole—an overcooked texture, seasoning of metal and paint, the tang of nothing real, fresh, out of the earth.

Dropped my fork. Shut my eyes and feasted on the morphine—the slippery, sweet butter filling my body—and I thought about Jean. When I could climb anything and paint anywhere.

Three weeks after I moved to Oregon, Jean, the astrologer, with shiny stars painted on her walls, pushed me from her bed. "Dorothy, you are overheating on an over-hot night and I want my sleep to consider the stars. What do you want?"

"Nothing." Waiting for her to see exactly what I wanted. But she didn't.

"Come see me in the morning when nothing turns into something."

We each had a one-room apartment over the drugstore. I went back to mine, full awake. Sat on the sill of my open window. The water tower across the road the tallest structure in the neighborhood. Jean's touch still on my skin. The way she talked, running her fingers along the inside of my arm. Kissing deep, teasing, in the language of stars and planets, conjunctions, trinings, eclipses, but then stopped as if the galaxy had taken her from the carnal plane and hoisted her into orbit.

I wanted to touch Jean. Kiss her until every star was out of the sky. Love through the long groove of night. I took my brushes, my paints, heat and desire, like the suddenness when a fever comes on. Went outside, crossed the street, climbed the vertical ladder, and painted the water tower for four hours before I was spotted. On that tower they tried to disguise as some pruned perfect tree, I painted branches in fiery bloom. Apples fattening on the branches. And two women blossoming, hovering over each other, naked, every part of them nearly touching: nipples, thighs, fingers. Their faces not detailed. I was just starting on their lips when the police shined their light up at me.

I was charged with trespassing. My picture was in the morning paper, along with a photograph of the water tower that almost smelled of new paint. The moon entered Leo by the time I got home. I knocked on Jean's door.

"Nothing turned into something," I said.

"Get in here," she said.

I sat on the bed. Jean's yellow hair everywhere on the pillow like a wind had come in and shaken her head all night.

"Look out the window."

"It's too damn early to even open my eyes."

"I think you'll want to see this."

"You do, do you?" She sat up. She could see the water tower from her bed. "And you did that?"

"Yeah," I said, "and got caught."

"Shit," Jean growled, her big eyeteeth close to my face. "Drama. You've got it running all through your chart. Do you even know how to be calm?"

"I don't choose it. It just finds me."

I put my head down on Jean's warm thigh. Jean studying the water tower, ignoring me. Three weeks in this town. A night spent at the jail. What people would know of me was that I could climb and paint. Nothing else. Not where I came from. Not why I was here. I didn't tell anyone, not even Jean. I didn't need to tell anyone anything.

But Jean asked, "And just where are you from anyway, Dorothy, that you waltz up on a water tower and paint pictures like it's your own personal canvas on an easel?"

"East," I said.

"East of where?" She turned over on her side. Full sun, half hidden by the water tower. She pulled me onto her. Her breasts like moons that collided with my own. So much flesh. That plumpness of skin hiding bones. She was lush, her body soft around the edges. I sank into her as if she was peat and I had stepped off of solid ground.

"East of it-doesn't-matter," I said.

"You know, I read your tarot cards and I could not understand the placement of the deception card, but now it all makes sense."

"How?"

She said, quietly, into my ear, "You thought I was deceiving you last night, didn't you? But it was the other way around. You deceiving me. Wanting one thing but doing another."

Her hand was hovering over my heart, her fingers inciting my pulse. I couldn't move, touch her without her touching me first.

She slid out from under me, pulled a sleeveless man's shirt over her arms, buttoned up. "Not saying anything says something, Dorothy. When you're ready to ask me for what you want, then ask."

Jean in her sleeveless shirt, pulling her hair back behind her head, braiding it. I got off the bed. My hands swirled with dry paint. Stood there not looking at Jean, pretending I didn't care. Easier that way than to ask for what I wanted. I walked away from the bed, heat, and desire.

"And one more thing, Dorothy." She let go of her hair, the braid only half done, and she picked up a piece of paper from under the lamp made out of a bowling pin. "You take this. It's a forecast that came to me last night and I knew it was meant for you." She walked over to me. The piece of paper was folded small and she slid it into my pocket while she kissed my third eye. Her lips leaving a damp print that would soon enough evaporate.

"And don't read it here," she said. "I'll see you tomorrow, right?"

"See ya," I said. Went back to my apartment and waited until the moon came over the water tower again.

Waited. Always waiting for something outside myself to push me. To get me to talk. To move. Just like when I was seven years old in the field of daisies with the lightning and the rain, bangs over my forehead, over my eyes, hiding from everyone. Sitting, until Mrs. Linden, the neighbor with the Chihuahua that barked only once a day at eleven a.m., found me in the field soaked to the skin and asked why I was sitting there and I said, "Because Bell and Ray told me not to move."

"Dorothy Meyers," she said, "don't take every word they say as God's truth."

She didn't know Bell and Ray. My sister and brother. Twins. Two-headed monster, their heads always so close together, scheming. To go against what they said was to risk more than getting wet. It meant coming face to face with our father, who swore off God the day my mother died giving birth to me and couldn't conceal his hatred of me one bit. It was Bell and Ray, that duplicated wall of eyes and mouth and voice, that stood between him and me. They had seen his meanness as he shook me—he was always shaking me, until one morning, annoyed when I did not walk fast enough, he shook me by the arm until the bone snapped. They protected me. When they wanted to. Kept me like a pearl between the double image of their shells. Kept me for themselves. To play with. A toy. Amusement. "Sit there," they said, over and over. And I sat and waited.

What Jean wrote on the piece of paper, what I read as the moon grabbed hold of the water tower, was this:

To be silent is the easiest avoidance.
To lie you must be clever and articulate.
To manipulate, a genius.
To rule, all trickery and without apology.
But, to love, there is only one way,
To speak the truth no matter the risk or consequence.

Forty-five minutes turned into over an hour. The morphine like a slide show: I could see everything about Jean and me clear and warmed by that first summer, until Bell and Ray lit up the screen, their image slipping in when I wasn't looking. I didn't want to look because I knew even the morphine couldn't sweeten them. I opened my eyes and Macy was there.

"I brought you a tangerine," she said.

Macy

I COVERED THE LAMP shade with the paisley bandana I carried in my pocket. The light in the room was as pink as frosting on a birthday cake. Dorothy watched as I rolled the tangerine between my hands, loosening the membranes that attached flesh to rind, and brought it to my lips. The hospital bed was in the sit-up position, two pillows behind Dorothy's head. The tangerine was polished, speckled orange with green, an indented nipple where it once hung from the tree. It was because of the shot of morphine that her eyes were half open, shiny and constricted. She couldn't stop watching the tangerine slide across my lips.

"You planning on sharing that orange?" Dotty asked

"Tangerine. There's a big difference."

"Tangerine," she said, imitating how I said the word. Tan-ger-REEEEN. And she laughed like my mother when my mother didn't think anyone was around. Like hail falling hard and fast against glass and tin. Not like how my mother usually laughed, when other people could hear her—then it was showboating, big teeth, nearly silent, all just a big red smile with a smoky one-note tone. Almost a growl.

"This tangerine must be good medicine because this is the first time I've heard you laugh."

"There hasn't been much to laugh about," she said.

"I like how you laugh." I bit into the rind and started to peel.

"So, when do I get to hear you?"

"Depends."

"You like that word, don't you?"

"Depends on what it's attached to." I smiled but I didn't laugh.

"I get the feeling that you're always attaching one thing to another, even if they're not connected at all."

I pulled back the peel from the nipple down to the middle of the tangerine. Did that until the peels curled away like flower petals. "Everything's connected."

Dorothy lifted her arm above her head. I could see the weave of her muscles, the bends and curves, and my hands wanted to drop the peel and fruit, follow the smooth edges from her fingertips to her shoulder. But I stuck my thumb into the center of the tangerine where the sections came to a point.

"Yeah, everything's connected," Dorothy said, "but sometimes we spend too much time trying to connect the dots."

"Sometimes not enough time." I slid my other thumb in and pulled. The tangerine split in half. I took one section, held it up in the marbled light, and made it disappear. My hand folding, unfolding, the section of tangerine secreted away until I reached over to Dorothy's ear and the tangerine reappeared. But as I brought it close to her lips, her hand dropped from above her head and tugged it from my fingers.

"Christ, that's an old trick," she said. "Even on all this dope I never lost sight of it. Magician should not be your next career move."

"I thought it was damn good."

She ate the tangerine in small bite after bite. I gave her each section until there were none. Her lips and fingers were wet with all that juice. The connection I was making, what was forming between us, had a luster to it, a shiny desire. I wanted my hands to slide over skin and through to the seed, the heat, the furnace of Dorothy. I went into the bathroom and rinsed a towel in warm water and brought it out to her. She wiped her hands and face.

"Do you have family in town?" I asked.

"No family. They're all dead." Her eyes stared right at me.

"That's pretty dramatic. Is there a story that goes along with that?"

"A very boring story. Nothing to tell." She lifted one shoulder up, half a shrug, like a comma in a sentence that means there really is more.

"How about friends? Anyone who could stay with you for a while?"

"Why are you asking me all these questions?"

"Because I have a proposal," I said. "But it may not be necessary. Depends on your answers."

"There's that word again."

"So? I'm predictable."

"My closest friends are in Arizona for a few more weeks. They live in the house across the street from me. On the dead end. Besides them, all my other friends are either in school full-time or working more than one job, have a family, you know, scraping by, not a lot of extra time on their hands."

The 8:30 happy chimes rang from the intercom on the bed's headboard. Visiting hours over.

I set the tangerine peel on the nightstand. "I'm an excellent nurse, don't you think?"

Dorothy narrowed her eyes and looked at me as if I were about to do another magic trick. My hands stayed folded on my lap. The lines on her forehead deepened. Trying to figure me out, second-guess me. I knew all about the look of suspicion. The look my mother used to throw at me every day. The one that said, *something's not kosher, something stinks, someone is lying*—usually my mother, who followed the look with the giant smile that said, *trust me*. I never did.

"As far as I can tell, you're handy with scissors. You know a tangerine from an orange. You haven't pretended that I'm going to get up tomorrow and go skating. Guess that makes you as good a nurse as any. Why you asking?"

I took the washrag from her hands, draped it over the tray stand with the one cup of water, tomorrow's menu. No flowers. "Look, you're going to need some care when they release you. Here's my deal. I have vacation time coming to me and I'd like to help you. Your personal nurse, in your home."

"Was this Gena's idea?"

I rested my fingers against the pulse in her wrist. "This is an opportunity for the both of us—you need some help and I'm needing some extra cash. You could either have a complete stranger in your house or me. Doesn't it all add up? We like each other. It seems simple and right." I kept my fingers on her pulse. Smiled big. The way my mother did when an opportunity was so close at hand.

And bingo, Dorothy said, "Okay, why not."

Dotty

I FELL INTO MACY'S palm. The morphine painted a thousand luminous colors onto what she said: *simple and right*. When so much had not been simple or right. The dance of morphine in what I was feeling, the slow two-step, warmed-up words in my ears. Someone wanting to take care of me. I was ready. Didn't give it more than two seconds before saying okay. Going along to get along. And why not go along with Macy?

She slid her hand out from under mine. Sat back in the chair, the tiny squeaks of the cushion. Crossed her arms in front of her scrubs. The blue of her eyes like the first blue of the sky in the morning, after the flush of pink sunlight and the slips of clouds vanish. Blue, sleepy as houses at dusk, trim paint of Alice blue, eyelids brushed with cobalt, oceans and oceans.

"Dorothy," Macy said, "you're drifting. I should go."

"No, not yet. I'll tell you about my house. Two bedrooms up, a den, dining room, bathroom, kitchen down. Eighty-one years old. Classic, mostly. Plenty of room. Have I sold you yet?"

Macy hadn't moved. Her arms stayed crossed, her eyes watched, took in every inch of me, but her eyes said nothing. The morphine inside of me sweeping, sweeping, sweeping. What could happen? *Simple and right.* That's what I saw in her eyes. Nothing else.

"Does the den have a bed?" Macy asked. She shifted forward, placed both palms on the edge of my bed.

"Yeah, but you can have one of the bedrooms."

"Not me, you. Remember? You're not exactly going to be tap dancing your way upstairs." She tapped against my cast and left her hand there. "How far from Portland is your house?"

"About an hour."

"That's not far, an hour. We'll be country gals, right? Well, okay. Sold."

Macy stood up. Sudden, like she got the deal that she wanted and didn't want the deal to change. She said, "Good night, Dot."

"You can't call me that."

"What?"

"Dot. Dotty's fine, Dorothy, but not Dot. Okay?"

"Got it," Macy said. Her eyes like scalpels pointing at mine. She wanted to cut my name up and dissect Dot to find out what the poison was. Her blue eyes sharp and metallic as deep water. I shut my eyes. To Dot, exploding from Macy's lips like a flare that couldn't help but light up the three other people who used to call me Dot. The morphine was thick as tar heated up on the street in summer. Tar, bubbling away, enticing me to poke my fingers at *Dot* and burst the trapped water inside the bubbles. And then I was sucked in, cemented. Couldn't get myself unstuck from the tar of seeing those three shouting Dot, Dot, Dot, until Macy held my hand between both of hers and I opened my eyes and their faces disappeared. There was only Macy. Nothing else.

"Good night, Dotty. I'm going to enjoy taking care of you." On the nightstand, she left the tangerine peel shaped like a hollowed-out flower or a mouth with nothing to say but *oh*.

Macy took me home from the hospital after nine days. I was wearing a pair of her sweatpants, one of the legs cut off to fit over my cast, and a black sweatshirt that said *Rutherford Nursing School* in red letters across the back. The hop and skip of me, up the path on my crutches to the door of my house. My house. Needed paint, needed a change of color, needed me up on a ladder stroking the wood, paying attention to the detail of molding and clapboard. The elaborate order of how wood fit together and how weather fitted to wood and the necessity to paint, for me to paint. But I couldn't. Could only hop and skip; my house did not recognize me.

Macy unlocked my door with the keys I had given her, the keys taken out of my overalls along with my wallet and put in the drawer of the hospital nightstand. She followed me into my house. It smelled like old food, burnt potatoes, dusty dried spices, onions. Cobwebs arced and undulated from the ceiling like welcome home signs. Hop, skip, across the living room to the den where the sleep sofa was and all my paints and canvases. The den. The room that hooked me when I first saw the house. Because of the light coming through the southwest windows. The windows different than all the others in the house—eight feet long from nearly floor to ceiling—and I could just step into all the light coming through. My easel pushed against the wall when it should have been dead center in the room. Was always dead center. When I painted. Not now. Not for a while. Didn't know when. Didn't know if ever. In the easel's place was the foot of the sleep sofa, the sleep sofa pulled out and done up in a green fitted sheet, a yellow top sheet, blue pillowcases, the Star of Sharon quilt with a hundred interlocking stars turning colors one to the other. The sheet and quilt folded over below the pillows. Exact and smooth.

"Looks like Mitch has been here," I said. "That bed is definitely his color scheme."

"Who is Mitch?"

"Mitch is Jean's brother, and Jean lives across the street. She's the one I said was away. Mitch's been watching her house and mine."

On the side table was a pitcher of water and five roses, and against the pitcher was a picture of Humpty Dumpty: before and after.

Macy helped me lie down and adjusted my legs, my head, the pillows, the quilt. The necklace she wore, a yin and yang stone on a blue thread, swung away from the hollow between the ridges of her collarbones. She eyed the room, her hands reaching into the air, a conversation with herself, taking measure of the window, the door, the bed, me, her patient without IV or any hospital routine. Her hands fell into her pockets.

"It's quiet here," she said.

"Dead-end street," I said. "Except for the crows and wind, there's not much noise, but if you miss the sound of rush hour you can head down to the river."

"I can't swim."

"I didn't say you had to swim."

"No, you didn't." She took my keys out of her pocket, slid the keyring onto her finger, and moved her hand, the keys striking each other.

"Where is the river?" Macy asked.

"Not far. Just down that path." I pointed out the window to the narrow gate of my garden and the path that cut diagonal across the yard and into the trees. Macy watched my hand but didn't look out the window.

"It'll take some getting used to."

"What? The river?"

"The quiet. It has its own noise."

She dropped the keys into her pocket and walked over to my bed. Took it all in. Nurse's eyes rapid sweep from my head to my toe. "We need to elevate that leg. I'll go get another pillow."

She brought back the gold crushed-velvet teardrop pillow, the one Jean gave me a couple of years ago after the beekeeper left me, taking the hives and honey with her. I only went near that pillow when I needed to punch something. Macy undid the bottom and top sheets from the foot of the bed. Folded them away from my leg. "I'm going to raise it," she said. Her hand slid under my ankle, lifted slow until she could get the pillow underneath, and lowered my foot onto the velvet. She patted my cast and flung the sheets and quilt over me.

"Now," she said, "I'm going to go pick up your prescription and get a few things from Gena's house. I should be back in no more than two hours. Okay?"

"Okay."

But it wasn't okay. My leg hurt and my head. The pain was always there now, a current like electricity, sometimes weak, sometimes strong, because the morphine had been replaced by Vicodin. The Vicodin was not as soft a place. There weren't any comforting dreams: no houses or me painting the houses in odd colors. No floating above, separate from the pain. Just a lessening of the rabid screech and stab of my bones and tissue weaving back together around the pins of metal, and the threat that this artificial muting, the pill's tempering, would dissipate in only six hours. The time clock of the Vicodin.

The wind played patty-cake on the window glass. The sun was close to gone—dusk, a gathering of wisps and crooked lines of magenta and mulberry. I could see the backyard through the window—the poles for my peas, shovel stuck in the dirt where I left it, the checkerboard of beds, the pile of rotted manure, and the wheelbarrow, empty. And I could do nothing.

I slept two years, two hours, two seconds.

Macy came back and put my pills on the table. Opened the lid, tipped the bottle over, handed me the pills and the glass of water. She wore black jeans and black boots, red and ivory paisleys on her button-down shirt, and a black leather vest put on and taken off enough times that in places it was fading to grey. She didn't look too long at me, didn't take hold of my hand. We were two women in a bedroom. Undo the vest, the shirt, pants, and boots, get below buttons and her hard soles—this was what I wanted. Instead, I swallowed the pills she held out to me.

Macy planted herself in my house. Carried everything into the living room— two suitcases, a dresser, one long mirror in a gold-and-black-striped frame, an armful of clothes on hangers and an aqua-blue, wide, overstuffed chair. There were no saucepans or plates or knives or forks. She dropped ten boxes marked *books*, another three boxes marked *crap* on the floor. The front door kept opening and closing. I thought she'd bring a suitcase, two. Each thud of the boxes made me more curious about just what she was bringing into my house. Curious enough to reach for the crutches, head for the living room, and invite the pain to start its ratcheting in my leg.

The four days of crutch training at the hospital was mostly about how not to put all my weight on my good leg. Balance and smooth motion would keep my spine straight, my body from listing. But all I felt when I walked on my bad leg was the broken and ragged bones driven deeper into the hip socket. I failed the training. The physical therapist told me I'd get it eventually, when my good leg gave out and I grew tired of looking at the world off-kilter. The only perspective I cared about was the one with the least amount of agony.

I did my clumsy hop into the living room. Macy came in the front door with a coat in a dry cleaner's bag. She left the door open. The wind crawled across the room, up my crutches, into my face. April wind.

I couldn't stand for too long on my good leg. The crutches pinned me to a strange gravity. Without them, I would fall. With them I could only move by telling each part of me to move, deliberate, as if I had altitude sickness and my muscles had to be manually reminded to work. Macy squatted down among the boxes. Touched the folded cardboard lids.

I couldn't believe how much stuff she was bringing here. Like she was moving in permanent. "How long did you say you were gonna be here?"

"That depends on how fast you heal."

"What if it takes a year?"

"We'll know more after two weeks."

My good leg was done standing. I turned around and left Macy in the maze of her boxes.

Across the hall from the den and me in the sofa bed was Macy in the kitchen, moving things from the cabinets to the counter, from the stove top to the table. She brought me soup, toast, a triangle of white cheese, a tangerine. But she did not peel it. Her fingers pulled on the ends of her hair near her ears. Night brought even more quiet. She was listening to the mute dark, the air without wind, too early in the year for crickets, and even the moths with their grey ash wings flew up to the window without sound.

"I'm going to unpack." She looked around my room, her eyes squinting, as if her words did not make a dent in the quiet. "I'm going to unpack."

"Okay."

"Okay, okay, okay, okay." She chanted the word out of my room.

Up the stairs, Macy dropped and pushed her boxes across the floor in the sun porch where the beekeeper had kept her jars and mesh suit and smoker and ledgers with the names of the hives she tended. The beekeeper. A doomed-from-the-start relationship. Both of us rebounding, unable to not compare each other to the lover before. But I was willing to open up a few doors in my heart. The beekeeper was determined to keep the storm door locked. Can't even say her name without the feeling of stepping on a hornet's nest. The beekeeper and all her venom. The only thing left from her was a specimen board with dried bees pinned to the cork. Each bee labeled with the date she found it. The board itself labeled with the words *Death Becomes Us* and the date *August 1, 1991*. The day the beekeeper left. I nailed it up on the wall next to a painting I had done of the beekeeper folded inside a bee hive, a giant stinger held between her teeth like a rose.

At ten, Macy opened the pill bottle. Six hours. She was right on time.

"My mother," she said, "told me stories. There was always noise in our house. The whole house whined from age, cheap construction. She made up the stories, you know. My mother was clever. Everybody loved her. She loved everybody."

"Does she still tell you stories?"

"No, she's dead. Happened a long time ago." Macy's hands did not move while she talked. She looked at me the way she had looked at me in the hospital. Blue eyes on fire, the blue in the belly of the hottest flame.

"Tell me something about your mother."

Macy sat on my sofa bed, her back to the window and its darkness, the moths with their persistent swarming at the glass and the light from the lamp that glared almost violet off their wings.

"All right. Here's a story: the where were you when Kennedy was shot question. I was in first grade. The siren for the town was on top of the school building.

It went off for fires and at noon every day. But that day the siren started in the morning and roared for an hour. My teacher was asked to step out of the room by another teacher. When she came back, her glasses were on the top of her head and she was crying and told us the president was shot and we all had to go home. I didn't know much about presidents. I went outside. The teachers were chain-smoking cigarettes right on the front steps, their eyes on each other and the transistor radio the principal held in his hand. They didn't give any orders, any directions. The school yard was filled with kids running and yelling and crying. Mothers came in their station wagons, swerving into the parking lot. It was like an obstacle course had been set up, you know—the whole world was suddenly unable to walk straight ahead without collision. My mother did not come pick me up. I took the shortcut home. In the house my mother was dancing to *South Pacific*, 'I'm Gonna Wash That Man Right out of My Hair.' She took me by the hands and swirled me around until we fell on the couch. The needle scratched at the end of the record on the stereo, stuck there. I asked her if she'd heard about the president. 'What about him?' she asked. I told her, 'Somebody shot him.' My mother got up and lifted the needle off the record, set it down at the beginning. 'Look on the bright side,' she said. 'We can be grateful, Macy, that Lyndon Johnson is the vice president.' My mother lived on the bright side." Macy laughed. The sound of it like a heavy rusted door opening fast and closing just as sudden. Her mouth tightening.

I said, "Was your mother always so optimistic?"

"All stories are just one person's take on the world. You wanted a story about my mother. Was she optimistic? Depends."

"Christ. On what?"

"On whether you were standing in the bright side with her or in the shadow behind her."

How did love enter and converge? Was there one minute that my eyes added another color into their seeing? The darkest unpolished red? The inside of green? Macy, a patina over everything. Each day she was there, my heart was a country at war, did not want to be overtaken, occupied. I thought, no, this is not love. But my eyes knew before the rest of me, invited Macy into the territory that my heart had barbed wired, mined. I saw her inside there, the fence clipped, the land mines defused. She had appeared with a wrench and a hacksaw, pried the lock, jimmied the door, stole across the borderline, declared peace. No, not peace. My senses smashed and reordered. Stained with the color of Macy.

This was my body as Macy got to know it: its damage, its base functions. The plate in my leg kept my bones anchored. My neck was a stalk incapable of supporting the heaviness, the ache in my head. The pills took over, became bone and muscle. They lifted my head like soft hands and kissed away the pain behind my eyes. Macy touched me with a pragmatic precision and formality. She did not comb her fingers through my hair. We had routines. Macy checked my toes twice a day for swelling, slid her fingers under the cast to clear away any loosening plaster, repadded the top of the cast with strips of flannel, took my temperature, repositioned the pillows, fed me oatmeal and avocadoes and spaghetti and spinach soup and tangerines, always tangerines. Brought me a pan with warm water and a cloth but did not stay while I washed the dust that gathered on my skin like I was a book on a shelf.

We went to the orthopedic doctor. My bones were healing but the pain grew worse, traveling from hip to head, a smashup of nerves. The doctor, a knobby-fingered man with three bronze hairs on his chin and not one hair on his head, moved my neck in different positions, trying to determine the cause of my headaches. There were my X-rays pinned in the light fixture. The doctor read the clouds and puddles of bones and tissue, the vertebrae like icebergs in a cold, cold sea. He looked up at Macy who stood behind me. The plate and screws in my thigh were exactly where they needed to be and had not strayed. The cast was not too tight, no undo pressure on the hip bone. I had taken nearly all the pills from the prescription the doctor had given me in the hospital. This doctor would not give me more. This was what I knew: when the pills wore off, my body would feel itself as something foreign and dangerous. Without the pills, my body would scream at me to erase what it had become. I only knew one way. Pills.

"Three weeks," the doctor said, "is sufficient time for the pain to be manageable without the pills."

He had no explanation other than sore muscles; muscles that I hadn't used in a while were being used. "It will decrease," he assured me, "with time."

Time was Macy sitting in the kitchen like a potted plant, root bound. Watching the sunlight through the window. The radio on, the radio always on, to short-circuit the quiet. The two weeks of her vacation almost up. Day after tomorrow. But she wasn't repacking. I stood on my crutches, leaned my back against the counter. Macy did not move.

"Christ-all-fucking-mighty," she said. "How simple can that doctor be? *Time heals.* Sometimes, time doesn't do a damn thing but make it worse."

I went over to the table. Wanted to see Macy's eyes. Fall asleep in the sky of them, float on my back in that blue and forget that I was not floating, that my leg was an anchor, a ton of metal, holding me in one place. But when she did look at me, her eyes were not calm water. The blue folded over and over itself like an agitated ocean and I could not rest there. Her hands spread out over the table.

"I know one thing," Macy said. "It is not always advantageous to feel pain."

"So what am I supposed to do? Go to another doctor?"

"No." Her hands slid over the wood. Closer to where my hands were. Her fingers touched my fingers, her hands surrounded mine. "I have a way of getting you what you need."

As she talked, her hands slid across and up my arms and stopped on each side of my face and held me until I looked right into her eyes, into the clear blue after the storm, the shallow, untroubled water.

Simple. Easy. The two weeks were over and Macy did not leave. The night she was supposed to go, load all her clothes and books and boxes in her car, take my keys out of her pocket and hand them back to me, she sat on the sofa bed. In her black jeans and a grey shirt buttoned up to the neck, not a blouse, no darts and not tucked in either, although the shirt had been ironed, smelled of starch and steam. She turned the lamp off so we could watch the thin moon swimming in the twilight, the apricot and red wine sky. I could imagine she had done this before, arriving in someone's life and altering it like dusk. The someone waited, like I waited, for her to inch over me, night gliding in, overtaking sight, and when I could see, it was by the blue of her eyes and the one freckle below the point of her cheekbone, like the first star out, and that was how I navigated my way to her lips.

The land of Macy's lips. The way she kissed. An unpredictable geography. All heat, a torrid slowness, breathtaking. We kissed a day, a month, a season. We kissed a country into existence. The rules set from the start: her kiss was the wilderness and there was no map I could follow, so I followed her lips.

Maybe the kiss said everything about the two of us, who led and who waited, how long it lasted, who wanted more. But when did desire ever pay attention?

Macy stopped kissing me and turned the lamp on. "I decided yesterday not to leave. Because of the imbecility of that doctor, you'll be in a lot of pain, Dotty. You'll still need me. Won't you?"

"Yes," I said.

Macy

BINGO. IT WAS all set. Not that big a lie. Sidestepping. Go around the doctors, the machinery. I'd seen it all: one person they'd give a lifetime supply of downers to and another person not one milligram of a pain reliever. No sense to it. All right. I'll skate over the bureaucracy. Not that hard, really. I called Angie at the pharmacy and said, "Angie, you are going to do this for me, no questions asked." What could she do but pretend I was Macy Kahn, R.N., from Doctor Hasn't-got-a-clue's office. I never called in prescriptions. It wasn't my job. Angie knew. "I'll pick it up in two hours," I said.

I heard her typing the info into the computer. What was the computer going to do? Make me take a lie detector test? All it wanted to know was codes and who would pay. Nothing to it. I didn't feel one iota bad about involving Angie. Even though she said, "Goddamn you, Macy," while she clacked the computer keys. Angie, with her tiny eyes behind the same tortoise-shell eyeglasses she had worn since 1971. When I met her years ago in The Last Word women's bookstore, she still carried around a miniature Bible in her tooled-leather purse. Though she didn't get out of my bed to go to church that Sunday or the next. After me, she slept with almost every woman on the Pussycat Lounge softball team. I was just her first love. So what? She got over me in a hurry, in a giant rush of licking the skin of a dozen women, one after another, as if she were at Baskin and Robbins and couldn't decide which flavor suited her. After the last one, the big-eared catcher, she came to me with weepy, longing eyes behind her spotted glasses. I made an impression on her. I influenced her every move. At least that's what she said. I told her, "Never mind all that, I'm the friend you can count on and anyway the women's softball semifinals are next weekend. Detach," I said. "Don't get stuck on needy." The catcher finally did come back to her. Couldn't wait to get her mitt on Angie from what I heard. The two of them slick as an oil spill over each other during the third round robin.

I never did see that miniature Bible with Christ etched on the cover again. Power of first love, well, somehow that's what sat in Angie's heart and she's never refused anything I asked of her. A convenient opportunity, my mother would have called it.

Maybe that's what I saw with Dotty, a convenient opportunity. To do some good. To set things right side up. To take her pain and remove it like a splinter, tweezer it out every six hours with pills, leave behind a happy ending. I asked myself a million times why Dotty and not any of the other women I'd seen in their backwards hospital gowns, broken and hurt. Easy enough to ask questions. And that's just it. The day Dotty fell, that morning, when I got in my car and watched her painting like there was nothing else in the universe but her body and that color blue, I asked this question: how does someone know the difference between who they were twenty years ago and who they are now? Why couldn't the answer be as precise and distinctive as changing the color of a window frame from white to blue? I wanted to get inside that place where the body doesn't remember what it had been and the mind can't tell anyone what it had become. Would that place be a whirlpool of loss and confusion or the calmest seat in the universe? I was sure Dotty would tell me.

I could see how it was for Dotty—love brewing in her bones like red blood cells. Three weeks and Dotty looked at me as if I were a can of paint and she couldn't wait to pry off the lid, dip her fingers in. I sat on the sofa bed with Dotty the night I got her pills from Angie, and every one of my nerves was a shooting star. That was a problem; desire could lead to the temptation of love and I hadn't bit that apple, on purpose, for a good long time. A night with some woman, a weekend, even three months, fine, but when I started thinking in years, well, that was a challenge to me. Just seemed easier not to get to that point. So when Dotty kissed me, when I kissed her back, full on tongues and lingering on each other's lips, I tried not to think of longevity or love. The kiss was just a kiss. I stopped kissing Dotty and drank some water from the Mason jar on the night table.

Dotty said, "I finally figured it out."

"What?"

"Who you remind me of."

"Who?"

Her fingers were tracing the valleys between my fingers. That's when the weather turned wet, the rain breaking loose, and I hadn't even seen the clouds black out the moon.

Dotty said, "This lady I met in New Jersey, back in the seventies. You have the same mouth as her when you smile."

"Yeah? Do we kiss the same too?" I thought Dotty was going to start laughing, the way her lips were opening, showing all her teeth, but she swallowed that smile like it was the bitterest thing she'd ever tasted.

"I was sixteen," Dotty said, "and she was probably old enough to be my mother."

"So, you didn't kiss her?"

"No. Maybe I wanted to."

"So what. Sixteen, older women were sexy. Did she want to kiss you?"

"Not sure."

"Not sure?"

"I never got to ask her," Dotty said.

"In New Jersey, you said."

"Yeah," Dotty said. Her lips inching over mine. The charge between us fierce.

The rain didn't ease up. The busted clouds, that water sledge hammering. The urgency of Dotty's kiss. The fury of desire between us and how easy it was for me to stop desire, pull away, evaporate the wetness and curb the heat of my body. The high from the kiss. I was losing altitude. Let Dotty hold onto my fingers. I kept away from her lips.

"Where in Jersey?" I asked. I pressed my thumb along the edge of Dotty's palm. Over the calluses from painting that had softened up. Her thumb skimmed across my wrist.

"The south shore. Have you been there?"

"I grew up in New Jersey," I said.

"No shit?"

"There was lots of shit. You know, Jersey is full of it. Did you grow up down the shore?"

"No," Dotty said. "I'm from Pennsylvania."

Dotty's fingers stopped bothering mine. Her hand went palm down in the center of a black star on the quilt. She watched my lips like she wanted nothing more than for me to stop the questioning and kiss her. But I didn't stop asking. And I didn't kiss her.

"What were you doing in New Jersey?"

"*Reader's Digest* version," Dotty said. "I was working in a motel as a chambermaid."

"Summer job?"

"Turned out that way. I didn't even get through the summer. One day I bought a bus ticket and came out here. Didn't plan it. I didn't plan much of anything back then."

"Why'd you leave there, Dotty?" I said.

She lifted one shoulder up to her ear. Her fingers pulled at the points of the black star on the quilt. "Why does anybody leave?"

"Depends," I said.

Dotty looked at me, her eyes like a river stirred up. All the silt rising. "And you want to know what my depends was?"

"Yeah."

"More than kissing me?"

"As much as." I tilted my head closer. Close as the space of three words between our lips.

"The lady died," Dotty said.

The rain was a landslide of water, pushing at the house. But that was nothing compared to the wind that started up. If I could have seen the trees outside, their crowns probably looked like tops spinning in one direction and then the other. The wind whined from every side. Slapped the windows like they were tambourines. I wondered if the kiss had brought on the storm. If it was a warning. But it didn't stop me. I kissed Dotty again.

All right. We kept kissing. As if our tongues and lips had all the answers. The wind more and more furious until it knocked some power line down somewhere and the lights went out.

"Holy shit," I said. "Is the house going to lift off?"

"If it does," Dotty said, "I hope we don't wind up in New Jersey."

Dotty

IN THREE MONTHS I saw how it was—Macy and me withholding information. Talking in curlicues. Never getting too close to the past. There were years I didn't say a word about, and Macy slid easily from fragments of revelation to funny stories. When she joked, she never laughed. Just that smile. The corners of Macy's lips curved up and just kept going, like the start of a spiral. Then there was her bottom lip, the indent, the line down the center, as if the fullness had to be contained in two halves. I liked nothing better than to run the tip of my tongue over that line, that indent, when we were kissing.

Two months and we'd kiss every night. Like a bedtime story. A way of talking fairy tales and pleasant dreams. Sidestepped the circumstances, too good to be true.

Macy went back to work. Ironed her clothes every day. I smelled the starch heated up, close to burning. The routines took another shape, defined by the night, by the two of us shipwrecked on the sofa bed, locking out the larger context—the land we came from, the water we were in. We attempted a precise latitude by only the intersection of our lips. Yes, I said, this was love. Love, like the north star, the blinking dot to fix on, that points a way to somewhere known. The daytime belonged to me, but it was the night I wanted, the night that got me through the day.

The cast came off in June. Back at the hospital. The same doctor who had talked to my crutches said, "Get up on the table and try not to move." The saw opened up the hard shell. The doctor pried the cast apart, and when my leg appeared, I didn't want to have anything to do with it. The silver white skin rippled like it had been underwater. My leg did not look like the one I climbed any ladder with. A thin twig of a leg with my knee bone bulging out like some canker growth on a tree.

Macy stood next to the table. The bleached white of her nurse's uniform in the fluorescent light made my eyes sore. "Well, there's your leg."

"Are you sure they didn't give me someone else's?"

The doctor wiped the plaster flour off my skin. Pulled his mask down below his chin. Bits of plaster dotted his cheeks and his red eyeglasses.

"Your leg," Macy said, "looks very good."

The doctor stared at Macy's pockets as if she had stolen his words and he didn't have any others to replace them with. He touched my leg like it was a ham he was rubbing a honey sauce over. Bake it in an oven and maybe it would plump up. When he poked at my thigh where it joined with the hip, I slapped his hand. Not a full-out slap, more like he was a mosquito and I knew he was getting ready to bite.

"It still hurts," I said.

"Of course it does," he said, "but I have to examine the break."

"How about a shot of morphine first?"

"This won't take long. I'm sure you'll manage just fine." He kept his red glassed-in eyes on my hand while he dug his fingers into the leg that he passed off as mine.

"Start walking as much as possible without the crutches. Your leg is fine. Fine. The pain is just stiffness; it will go away." The doctor said all that to the door with the poster of the skeleton, front and side view.

Pain. How real was it? My hip scraped, sounded like windshield wipers when there's no water on the windshield. Macy and I walking down the hallway, slower than I've ever walked. Macy used to the pace of injured people. The suck and pop of the one rubber-toed crutch. Macy held the other one. She knew every nurse on the floor and said her hellos. All I wanted was for her to get me out of there, put me in a wheelchair, on a stretcher, off my feet and crutch and legs and the bone that was supposed to be in one piece but felt like splintered glass. My leg was cold. Without the cast I should have felt lighter but I didn't. I was a boulder. Macy let me lean on her arm while she talked her way from nurse to nurse down the hall with the huge squares of tile.

My broken leg was shorter than the other one. The center of me shifted. To walk I had to lift my short leg high and my long leg I had to restrain. There was no grace. Only the falling from. I limped with a sharp, choppy motion, rocking myself forward from a point left of my belly button. Each step was painful. But pain was not easy to measure. No one could feel what I felt. If the pain had no source other than stiffness, as the doctor believed, then how real could it be?

Walking down the hall, I knew I would take more and more pain pills. Macy would just call Angie. After all, I had a lifetime prescription. Macy made sure of that.

After the doctor, Macy drove to the store. I waited in her pink Valiant with the push-button gears. The car was immaculate, not a shred of paper or crumb of dust anywhere. Pasted over the horn in the center of the chrome steering wheel was a smiley face with bloodshot eyes and a cigarette hanging out of its smiling mouth.

She came out with a bag of food that she wouldn't let me see. "Surprises."

I didn't want any more. The surprise of my leg, the whiteness of it like blanched asparagus, stiff as a broomstick, refusing to bend or act anything like my other leg. I just wanted to get home to my pain pills.

At home I ignored the sofa bed for ten minutes. Used one crutch to stand in the living room while Macy went upstairs and changed into her black jeans and a yellow T-shirt. Looked like a black-eyed Susan, one delicious daisy, and I wanted her to come right up to me and help me into my room. She walked by, her hands in her pockets.

"Why don't you rest," she said. "I'm going to make us dinner."

"I'm tired of resting, of doing goddamn nothing."

"Then go out and dig up your garden." She walked into the kitchen. Started moving the pots and pans around. I went to my sofa bed and fell asleep.

On the nightstand next to my pain pills was a glass of water and in the water, stems of lilacs. That was the first thing I saw. The second was Macy. Sitting cross-legged on the stars of the quilt.

"Okay, time for celebrating." In front of her legs was a piece of my cast and on the cast, two Mason jars filled with wine. She handed me the wine and I sat up. Never even saw her take the cast from the hospital.

"To your new leg." She put her hand on my leg and it stayed there while we clinked our jars, toasted my leg, but the wine never reached our lips because our lips were together, a frenzy, wild, the waiting over.

Two months of kissing, knowing this would happen, wanting this to happen. Lovers. First time. Always a guessing game. No rules, nothing to follow except desire. The strange land of her body. Her eyes blue as cisterns, as bottomless lakes, never closed to what I was doing. My fingers inside of Macy. Macy open, so open. My fingers fast. Macy all heat, sultry, wet around my fingers. I circled my tongue around her nipple, blew on it slow until it rose up, turned ruby and fire red. I could have stayed there forever. In that fullness, her breasts exquisite, soft and then the hard nipples. My fingers and tongue wanted to slide across in every direction. While she swayed on the sofa bed. The moon bent through the beveled window and its light was a shiny mosaic on Macy's skin. The quilt of stars a constellation under her.

I kissed from one rib to the next, over her belly, to the tiny curls within the pale, straight hair. My fingers slowed, inched out, inched in. Inside Macy. She said, "More, Dotty, more fingers, all of them." Until my whole hand, in a fist, was deep, brushing the walls inside that sucked at my hand to lure me farther into her. Her voice hinged, rusty, "That's it, perfect." She watched me, my fist disappearing into her. Above her head, she seized the quilt and the sheets; she pushed against the wall behind her to move her hips, her body faster down over my hand. Her eyes half closed to that feeling of what was inside her: occupation, pleasure. Calling out "Dotty," as if she had lost sight of me, as if she was in a flood and could no longer hold onto anything. Her voice, the rise of her voice, "Dotty, Dotty, baby, more," like enormous water hitting rock. She took my other hand from her thigh and held it down under her hand over her breast. Pressed until her breast was flat and the nipple dead center in my palm.

My body trying to talk to her body, in a language of pulse and heat and wavering and wondering.

She stopped moving.

"What is it?" I asked.

She grabbed my arm and pulled my hand out from her. Laughed. Laughed. The craziness of being lovers. First time, always awkward, without knowledge of what the body needs. The blue of her eyes eclipsed by so much black pupil. Her hands in my hair, holding the sides of my face.

"Dotty, lover. Plain and simple, I want your tongue."

"Where?" I said.

She bit my bottom lip and then kissed where she bit.

"Not there, I take it?"

"No," she said, "not there."

She shifted around on the quilt. I slid my body down the length of Macy, land of uncommon wildness. My head between her legs and I brushed my cheek over the soft hair of her thigh and breathed her smell into me, took it into my heart like the first breath taken at the ocean after many years inland. I licked with the pinpoint of my tongue along the plumpness of her labia, into the heart of clitoris and hovered, like a dragonfly, just setting down, enough, a wing beat, to tempt her into slanting her body toward me. My hands on her hips, keeping her from pushing too close to my tongue. I licked and hovered. She rolled her head side to side. My tongue pressed hard, long licks getting faster. My hands underneath her, lifting her up to my tongue. Her voice saying words without sense, without meaning. Sounds strung together that could have been whole poems as she came, the pleasure of her body rocking against my mouth and tongue and her head nodding and nodding, her body leavened by something unattached to reason.

The in-between time came. My head on Macy's thigh. Macy's body selfish in its floodwater. Didn't want to give up its isolation, its own pleasure. Her body started its calming. Breath slowing. When would she reach across and touch me?

Macy's head was turned to the window where the clouds shredded and blindfolded the moon. I dipped my finger into her belly button, and she pulled me up on top of her and kissed me. Her tongue and my tongue colliding and electric as snapped power lines. Her fingers skidding down over my eyebrows, cheekbones, mixing her fingers with her tongue into my mouth. The taste of her flesh. Biting my lip, my ears. She said she would kiss every inch of me and she started with my eyelids. I wanted no other thoughts, wanted nothing else but the wetness of those kisses. Nothing else. But pain was making its own incisions, kissing from inside the healed, uncasted bone, kissing, all teeth tearing to the bruised dark lilac flesh of me. As Macy slid her lips from the hollow in my collarbone to the inside of my elbow, the pain pill wore off. Entirely. I wanted only one thing, one thing—for Macy to be the pill I took to shut out the pain. She read me with her nurse's eye and as if she saw words where my mouth was moaning, she said, "Let me be whatever you need," and I said, "I need to take my pill." She laughed, laughed like cold water and stopped kissing me. "Go ahead," she said.

The first time, lovers—how could I not overcome my pain with pleasure? Needed a pill to shift me back to what I once was. But it didn't. A moth came through the open window and banged into the lamp shade, trying to get at the light. I took the pill. Macy went into the bathroom. The moth got under the lamp shade and flew around the lightbulb, the heat, the iridescence until its wings singed, and still it tried to get closer. It was the same for me, how pain threatened to close in and claim my whole body, shake it violently until it shattered. I turned off the lamp. The moth flew to the window. Macy was singing as she walked back into the room—something she made up. A song for the moon. A song for quilts and tongues. A good-night song as she held me. A song for falling asleep together in damp moonlight, the pleasure of bodies so close, so close to the source of heat.

And the pill working its own lullaby.

In the morning with the sun's bristles in the room with us, Macy cupped around me. My leg like a third cousin, familiar by blood but not by actions. It did not move easy, was an ironing board, a countertop, no give or bend. I pulled my leg off the bed with my hands.

Macy said, "Morning, lover. Don't you want to come back here by my warm body?"

"I got to get this leg working." I could have stayed in that sofa bed forever. Next to Macy. Waiting for her, for the surprise of her every movement or word. Because her every movement and word were not the exact ones I wanted, but I believed that the next one or the next one would be. She was like another bone I was finding a place for, more crucial in its placement than a rib, a kneecap, jaw.

"You sure?" Macy stretched her arms out. "The offer's good for a limited time only."

"Then what happens?"

"We become our ordinary selves, you know, transparent." She folded her arms behind her head. Her hair kinked straight up in every direction.

I propped the crutch in front of me, leaned my weight on it, my leg shaking. Time for a pill. The morning pill, rise and shine. "Somehow I doubt that you'll ever become see-through. We don't really know that much about each other."

"Maybe that's better," Macy said, "then we won't be disappointed."

"Or maybe it's just easier that way."

"What is it you want to know?"

"Why did you decide to stay here?"

"Isn't it obvious? I like you."

"Nothing more?"

"Oh, I see, you want to know about love. Is that it? Whether I love you. Is that the only word that will do?"

I hopped over to the dresser and put a long T-shirt on, wanted to cover up all the bruises and breaks, my heart like some neon sign in the middle of the desert, begging someone to come by, notice me, an oasis, the only source of water. Looked at Macy, her body comfortable in the sofa bed.

"All right," she said, "I'll tell you what I know. I'm not sure that I love you, but it's as close to love as I've gotten in twenty years. Is that good enough?"

"It doesn't matter."

"No? I think that you love me and you want to pretend you don't. That's the difference between us. I don't want to pretend. Whether you love me does not depend on whether I love you."

But it did. It colored everything, colored another bruise I added to my collection. Macy in the sofa bed with her shut-down look, her face not doing anything, her eyes staring at me—but I couldn't tell what she was seeing. She got out of the covers and put on all her clothes like she was alone in the room. Then she left, out the bedroom door, through the kitchen, the backdoor, the screen door, the backyard, and down the path to the river, her skinny legs doing double time away from me.

Macy

I FOUND SEVEN UNEVEN two-by-fours and the tongue from a work boot on the bank. A hinge, doorknob, pine shelving, with the knots of wood fallen out. The river gyrating. Spinning over rocks. From the dark color of it, the river was deep. Not that I'd ever stick a toe in. Water held no charm for me at all.

I walked the edge along the river and hauled the debris I uncovered back to a clear space between curtains of vine maple and the water. Scrap wood, the plastic leg of a doll, a shed of tin. I was going to build a shack. One room, tiny. On stilts of birch stumps. All right. I didn't plan it, the shack, building it. Knew next to nothing about construction. But I understood how bones fit together, the angles, the joints. Stresses. Breaks. Simple enough, when I started the shack. Simple enough to make something out of nothing. Wasn't that what Dotty and I were doing? Making a house be more than a house because the magic word, love, had been mentioned? Maybe that's why I started building the shack. Testimony. Creating something tangible for the two of us.

My mother once told me she visited Carlsbad Caverns. On her honeymoon. Four other newlywed couples and my mother and dad followed the cave guide into the main cavern. Past the stalagmites that the guide said looked like the Eiffel Tower and Queen Elizabeth, only my mother said they all looked like any other rock. In the main cavern the guide turned the lights out. Which was part of the tour. In the brochure. Absolute dark. Eyes could not adjust or tell one direction from another. Three people fell over. Two had to sit down. One of them was my dad, Mr. Weak-in-the-knees. The guide turned the lights back on and my mother swears he said, "This cave is like love, overpowering. Something that makes you feel so complete that without it you lose your way and fall down." My mother swears she answered, "Bullshit." She walked out of the cavern without the other newlyweds or my dad.

That's what Dotty wanted from me. Absoluteness. Completion.

Wasn't it enough that I was there?

I didn't tell Dotty I was building a shack. Because when I went back to the house after piling up the pieces of wood I found and setting the four birch stumps in a rectangle, she had cut up a papaya and was on the bed. Naked. Waiting. All right. I was not indifferent. I slid my fingers between her toes and rubbed her feet. Kissed them, pulled each toe into my mouth. There wasn't one part of her body I didn't want to lounge over. I kissed the entire length of her. Up into her hair. Her wild black hair, curls unwinding all over the pillow.

"Macy," she said.

I kissed my name right off her tongue.

"It feels so good," she said, "but I don't know if I can do this, if my leg will cooperate."

"Your leg doesn't have to do anything." I kissed her leg.

"That's just it. My leg doesn't do anything but hurt."

I went back to her mouth. Did not kiss her. My lips close to hers. "Dotty, the doctor said to use your leg more."

"I don't think he meant in this way."

"That's because he lacks imagination. Thinks that the only exercise good for your leg is out of the physical therapist's handbook. I know better. I'm a nurse. I want you to feel pleasure, for your leg to forget all about itself. I want to be the source of that. Let me love you." And maybe I didn't mean love in the same way Dotty wanted me to mean it. But it didn't stop her from kissing me and pulling my fingers down her leg and inside her. It didn't stop her one iota.

I worked two day shifts and two swing. I was glad to get back to work, the routine of blood and sutures. Charts and IVs. The oddities of the Emergency Room. When a limb was nearly severed but the fingers of the hand were in the gesture of flipping us the bird or an eye was popped out and brought to us in a Spam container, we just went about our work. Efficient. Sharp as a wisecrack. I loved peeking inside the bodies. Into the carnal, the automatic responses of the brain telling every cell exactly what to do. Or the brain incapable of saying anymore. Death declared. Or a heart started up with an electric jolt and a bang from a fist. I told Dotty about every emergency that came in. She always asked if anyone had fallen off a ladder. No one had.

All spring and into the summer I built the shack from driftwood and garbage. The shack grew like a tumor grows, consuming the tissue without regard for anything but its own continuance. I still didn't tell Dotty because the more I hammered and sawed and set each board in place, the more I knew it was not a testimony to the two of us. Dotty was taking care of that, testifying every day to her love for me. All right, I was not unflattered or unaffected. Some days, all I wanted to do after work was to cast off on the bed with Dotty. Wrap up in those words of hers. Love, love, love. Like a wool blanket that caused a familiar itch.

When she returned from her vacation, Jean, Dotty's ex, came to the house often. Only I was at work when she was there. Dotty got stirred up after Jean visited. More hotheaded than usual. Passionate and forward. Pulling me down on the bed. Which I didn't mind, but it was as if she were trying to prove Jean wrong.

"We're good for each other," Dotty would say, or, "It is not ludicrous that a nurse and her patient are lovers."

I'd tell Dotty, "Stop defending me to Jean. She doesn't know me or like me and I don't really care what she thinks."

"Yeah, well I do," Dotty'd say.

I put off meeting Jean as long as I could. Dotty asked Jean over on my day off. For brunch. Told me that morning. What could I do? I practiced smiling the interested smile in the bathroom mirror. I'd met plenty of Jeans. Bingo. Nothing to it.

Jean didn't bother knocking. Walked right into the kitchen where I was setting the table and Dotty was sitting down. She was a tall and big woman. Every movement she made was slow and weighted as if the day were twenty degrees hotter than it was. She kissed Dotty hello, talking while she kissed, "Honey pie, you look delicious."

Her voice, heated-up maple syrup, close to a boil.

"And of course," Jean said, "you're Macy." Her eyes were busy looking me up and down.

"Glad to meet you," I said. "Can I take something?"

Jean was holding a casserole and a gallon of sun tea with huge sharp leaves floating in it.

Jean and Dotty talked about plans for Dotty's birthday. We ate the tortilla casserole with tofu and the hottest peppers my lips had ever come across. I couldn't say a word; all my focus was on how to keep the peppers from setting my tongue on fire.

Jean said something though. "Macy, are you angry that I'm here?"

I had just put another forkful of casserole in my mouth and if I was glaring at her, it was out of amazement that the peppers didn't affect her ability to talk.

"Why do you think that?" Dotty asked. Jean and Dotty had their elbows on the table, nearly touching. Jean's enormous yellow hair was also on the table, curled down and over her arm, and sat next to her plate like a napkin.

"Well," Jean said, "she's said hello and how are ya and I'll get a spatula but hasn't said another word." Jean heaped her fork and stuck it in her mouth. With a dozen red, malicious chunks of peppers.

"Christ," I said, "it's the damn peppers."

"What's the damn peppers?" Jean asked.

"They're fucking incendiary." I pushed the plate away and got up to get some water. Even though there was a glass of the tea right in front of me. The tea tasted like mold.

"Are you a Leo?" Jean asked. I was drinking the water and didn't answer. "Is she a Leo, Dotty?"

"I'm not sure."

I finished the water but the hot was still in every cell in my mouth. Bread. I needed bread to soak it up. I pulled off the heels from a loaf of rye in the drawer and started chewing.

"You don't know?" Jean asked. "Dotty, you let Macy move in here and you have no idea about when she was born or what sign she is. Even the beekeeper gave you that on your first date."

"Yeah, a lot of good that did."

I filled the glass again. Brought the bread to the table and kept on chewing. Jean picked out three peppers from the casserole. Slipped them onto her tongue and sucked them like SweeTarts. Dotty watched Jean and me, her eyes sliding back and forth, her head not moving one iota. All right. I could have left them there to finish off the casserole. Fuck coupledom and all the attendant sucker roots; the supposed-to-be not only attached to the girlfriend but the girlfriend's friend and her bitter tea and tongue-smelting casserole. But Dotty's eyes stopped sliding. Gave me a look. The lids coming down by half over the hazel, the green and brown and dark gold, the sunflower happy. Her desiring look blackening the iris. I stayed.

Jean stabbed one more pepper with her fork and held it up. "So, when is your birth date, Macy?"

"Year or day?"

"Both."

"Depends." I smiled at Dotty. Her eyelids lowered by another quarter, as if she didn't want to see me but couldn't help but peek just a little.

"Depends," Jean said, "on whether the astrological truth interests you or not."

"The truth is inherent in these dates?"

"Absolutely. And I need the time of birth too."

Dotty said, "What in hell does the depends mean, Macy?"

"It depends on who you asked—my mother or the hospital. If it was the hospital, they say it's July twenty-second. If it was my mother, then you look at where she whited out the second two on the birth certificate and typed a three. Twenty-third of July, 1957. As for the time, easy. My mother said it was noon. Exactly."

"A Leo on the cusp," Jean said. "I knew it."

"Why did she change the day?" Dotty asked.

"July twenty-second is her birthday, and she didn't want my birthday to be diluted by hers."

"That was considerate of her," Jean said.

"Yeah, real considerate." I took my plate over to the sink. Washed it with the water on full. Didn't want to see Jean speculating about me. I dried my plate, walked back over to the table. Jean was drinking her glass of tea. All of it. She watched me as she drank.

I said, "Actually, my mother changed my birth certificate because she could. And because she hated even numbers. I wonder how that figures into the astrological truth, when the birth date is a lie?"

Jean put the glass down on the table. She pointed at me with her thumb and said, "I'll let you know."

"I'm sure you will."

Brunch over. I left before I could see anything even close to love in Dotty's eyes.

On July first, the words came out of my mouth. During the barbecue, the party for Dotty's birthday, at Jean and Marty's, in their backyard with the oversized kiddie pool. Green and pink frogs and giant butterflies painted all around the wavy, corrugated sides. The water mint colored, attracting horseflies. Jean was looking at me like I was a stink bug. Her face spotted pink and red from the sun. Ninety degrees out and we were sitting in the slimmest strip of shade under a lanky poplar. Jean's eyes and mouth narrowed down to thin lines, concentrating on how she was going to pluck me off the flower of Dotty. The birthday girl sitting in front of me, between my legs, on the chaise lounge. Marty and Jean's brother Mitch barbecuing slices of zucchini the size of hamburgers. No hamburgers. Tofu patties marinated in a million hot peppers. Tony was shearing Jean and Marty's dog, Jupiter. "A dyke hairdo," she said. Shaved his belly and legs and left it long on top. All of us drinking blackberry wine over crushed ice with a shot of vodka tossed in. And a leaf of peppermint.

Tony said, "Dotty, you and Macy look good together. Like you fit right."

"You say that about everyone, Tony," Dotty said.

"I mean it about everybody too."

Dotty leaning into me, her back against my breasts. The black of her hair was threaded with silver grey, lit up by the sunlight. Her hand was on my leg, my hand on her arm, feeling the angle and arch of her muscles. All right. I was comfortable. Maybe that was what love was supposed to be: a comfort, the fitting together of days and bodies and words into a whole where even the rough edges didn't ruin anything. But comfortable was not a comfortable place for me to be. An edge had a distinct boundary, a cliff to climb up or fall off. I kept my edges away from Dotty. Kept them to myself while I tried on comfortable and Dotty loving me and love itself, which had been too big a coat for me to wear.

Jean took out some paper from an envelope on the picnic table. "I have another perspective."

"Oh no," Dotty said.

"What?" Tony asked.

Jean walked over to our chaise lounge. "I did your charts, the two of you together, to see exactly what the fit is." Jean separated the two charts, held them up in each hand. "Lots of coincidences in both. Some downright curious intersections. And the crux of the reading is that each of you is on a collision course with the other. It is in the house of communication where you hide the most."

"Goddamn," Tony said. "Doesn't sound promising."

Under my hand, each muscle in Dotty's arm hardened. "Maybe if you looked a little closer, you'd see other possibilities," she said.

"It's not a personal thing. The stars are guideposts; they lead to conclusions that we might not be aware of."

"Bullshit. Crap," I said. "It's like reducing someone to a number and that number is supposed to define the person. Astrology is a lot of guesswork and maybe it does influence us, but to say that everything is set from the second we're born is to ignore every other influence on our lives."

Jean drank half her wine and vodka. Dotty took her pill. I finished off my glass and Tony clicked an ice cube against her teeth. The sun was a highball fermenting the earth. Curling the grass blades. Yellowing the air with pollen dust. All the world sweating, living under the heat of someone else's prescription on how to live.

"It's not a matter of exactness but of currents and knowing how those currents react with obstacles and influences," Jean said. "And it's not a mandate. You either ignore what is hidden or, when it is no longer valuable to hide it, dig it up into the open and discover what you can."

"Jean, you've been pretty accurate before with readings, and thanks for doing this, but right now all I want to do is cool off in the kiddie pool," Dotty said.

Marty and Mitch brought the plates of zucchini with brown stripes from the grill and the tofu patties slick and crusted over in hot pepper barbecue sauce. Dotty pushed herself off the chaise lounge. All right. I didn't want to take my hand away from the muscles in her arm. But I did. Watched her slow walk over to the kiddie pool.

Jean handed me the charts. "I didn't mean to upset you or Dotty."

"Yeah? I'm not so sure of that."

Jean put her hand out and I let her help me up. So what? I didn't say thanks and she didn't say you're a good person, Macy. Her big body was inches away from me. She ran her tongue over her bottom lip like she had just taken a bite out of something tasty. Blinked one eye and then the other. I walked over to the kiddie pool.

Dotty was naked in the water. The kiddie pool large enough for her to stretch out head to toe. The sun cracked the water into blue and bluer shiny half moons. Dotty, on her back, under the water. Floating. Her arms out to each side of her, hands in fists around the water. The taps and clangs of the forks and knives skating across the plates on the picnic table. Mitch laughing and Jupiter barking. Dotty, her face under the water. Eyes closed. Bubbles coming out in pairs from her smile. And then, no more bubbles. I reached my hand in the water, stirred the half moons of blue into a glare. Grabbed Dotty's arm and pulled her up, until her head came out of the water.

"Shit, Dotty," I said. Water was all over the front of me, rolling off Dotty's face.

"What? What is it?"

The words came right out of every inch of me. "I love you," I said.

Her hands wrapped around my arms above my elbows. The heat of the water on my skin. Dotty kissed me. She smiled while she was kissing me. I could feel the smile curling up around my lips. Her hands tightened around my arms and she pulled me into the water. Both of our faces going under, her body turning over, on top of mine, our lips still fitted together. But only for a second. I swallowed the sun-burned water, the taste of plastic and metal. The water all around me would never let me go. I pushed against Dotty, pushed hard as if she were a door swelled up by rainwater, stuck tight. Looked past her skin and smile up to the surface with the sun glare where there was no more water on the other side, where the other side was the ground, the safety of the hard ground. But Dotty did not understand and held me for another kiss I didn't want. I rolled her over and I stood up. Spit and coughed. Dotty rose out of the water, laughing.

Dotty

THE WORDS CAME into the water. The water held their molecules, the combining, the shortness of the syllables, just three, and how could just three add up to a whole world? But they did. Macy saying, "I love you," and everyone at the picnic table turning, hearing, seeing, like an electrocution, a sudden strike of lightning, the unexpected words, shouted, as if Macy was saying SOS. When I pulled her into the water with me, the words sank, and Macy pushed to the surface and everyone at the picnic table laughed at the two of us, at love and the underwater world love reveals: swollen and distorted.

August. Passion following the weather: the one hundred degrees. Sun, no shade, every part of Macy's and my body heated through. Macy, after she got home from work, unzipping her jeans, pushing aside the rayon cotton cloth of her shirt. Stood in front of me. Directed. Told me to look, look, but don't touch, not yet, while she undressed me, circled around. Her hands undoing me, knew it didn't take much, a touch by her finger below my ear or just the faintest kiss and my body aware of every inch of itself, like being sunburned. Macy, the sun in her palms, on her tongue.

September. The light shifted, thickened, gold wavering, the temperature's gradual easing, the eye tricked by the sweetness of the light, the vividness, like the illusion of solidity far away from a pointillist painting. Macy would stop and start. Tempting me with her eyes, that want-to-love-you-entirely look, with the promise of delight, and once she had me wanting, she would lift her hand off my skin, take her kisses away. Never letting me forget I was on fire and she was the gasoline.

October. Rain without end, and then the end of the rain and summer returned for days and days, sun baked and flushed along with the merry-go-round of Macy's hot and cold. No predicting a cloud or clearing. Passion and sex were the ways she talked love to me, were how she tamed love, ignored it, controlled the weight of it. She was not without her own sudden need to be touched. Sometimes, pulling my hand right into her. Without any fanfare over the rest of her body. If I said, I love you, Macy, while my thumb circled and my fingers went in and in, she would never close her eyes to what I said but she would reply with her own, I love you, in a steady, rehearsed voice, like a bill collector.

Macy said, "I know you wait all day for this." But that's not accurate. Her saying it. She didn't. I said it to myself.

Waiting. For Macy. I added paint. My brush strokes hesitating above the postcard pieces of canvas, the pain pills slowing my hand. I worked with smaller and smaller brushes. Hills of color on the palette board. Squeezed out tubes, paint thinner in a Dixie cup. My painting's only concern was the color of desire. I said, yes, this is the heart of it, the skin of love, the untailored fit of passion, the urgency and fixation. But there was none of the fury, the unrestrained dance with the paint. I painted in stutters, each minute a deliberation, a tug of war, a meticulous rendering as if all I felt could be reduced to an ordered still life. I painted tiny bones broken and tacked together with the pure red and blue and yellow, the primary tints that every other color and shade followed, grew out of. Bones held at odd angles, misaligned, or missing altogether. Finger bones like silverware on the table. Or the collar, shoulder, and arm bones hanging off the end of a bed like a shirt just taken off and thrown there.

Macy's face, a sliver of her face, a certain angle of her mouth or eye would appear, small, so small, in the shadow of the bones in my paintings that it was hard to tell if she was really there or if she was just a smudge, a drip, a badly placed stroke of my brush.

Nineteen paintings and Macy stared at every one. If she saw herself, she did not say so.

"Is this what you do all day?" she asked. "They're awfully tiny. Isn't it tedious to paint this small?"

"Yes," I said. I did not say that each painting, each unhurried painting, was the accumulation of hundreds of minutes that I pretended I wasn't waiting for her. But mostly, that's what I was doing. Waiting for Macy to come near, to breathe into my skin, to touch down like a brush that painted an extravagant pleasure over the primary layer of pain.

I upped the number of pills I took. Refused pain, the hint of it, the wrench of my bone not fitting like it used to, perfect into the hip socket. I practiced stairs, going up and down, telling my leg, "You remember how." But it didn't. Not at first. I walked up the stairs like a kid just figuring out she had legs and they could take her places. Toddling, slow and uneven, listing side to side. One fucking step, then the next. I didn't lose the list, the crookedness, even though I got faster at going up and down the stairs.

Outside the house in the backyard was my garden of weeds. I picked up a shovel but I could not turn the earth over. No force in my leg, no balance to use my other leg. I chopped with a hoe, dainty arcs, and it took all afternoon to clear one bed. One bed. And I picked out the thistles and wild mustard from the old compost pile by the side of the house. This was what I planted: beans in the compost, tomatoes, a pepper, and zucchini in the bed. All the year-to-year flowers were surrounded by weeds and they put on tiny blooms and went to seed quick, to outrun the weeds. I threw packets of wildflowers over the weeds, but I knew the garden would do what it wanted, grow what was the strongest and most opportunistic, and I couldn't do much but watch.

August. September. October. Macy went to the river. But she didn't tell me what she did there, and I didn't tell her that I followed and saw what she was building. I hid behind trees and waves of blackberries. She never knew I was there, she never even thought to look for me. I was waiting for the grand opening, the invitation. I was sure that the strange house she was constructing was the certainty that she would stay, that love mattered, endured, and when the house was finished everything we did not say would be said. Love ripening, that was what I called it, ripening by the days and months to the point where we both would crack open and nothing would be hidden.

The collision that Jean predicted would happen. I had no doubt about that.

The middle of October. Tuesday, Macy's day off. She had been at the river. I climbed the stairs to her room. The smell of dirt and sawdust when I went by her door. Macy, on her bed, arm over her eyes. She had her shirt off, her arms and neck and face brown, her breasts and belly flour white. Freckles in wide constellations over her tanned skin. I wanted to connect the dots. Move from freckle to freckle with my tongue. But I didn't.

I walked to my old bedroom with the gold walls and the off-white ceiling. Dark raspberry on the window trim. The sheets on the bed were the same sheets that were there the day I fell off the ladder. I visited my room but did not sleep there. The sameness of it as if nothing had changed, as if I was the same, but I wasn't. My leg was more broken here in the room where I had once been more whole. I lay on the bed and fell asleep within the gold and raspberry and off-white. The sunlight woke me, falling like a river of yellow onto my face and my hands that were over my eyes. Someone was knocking. I pushed myself up and off the bed. Went to the window.

Recognition. Her left arm, crimped and shortened. This was the arm she knocked with. Knock, knock. As if it was a joke. Twenty-two years since I had seen her. She was even skinnier then. Her legs like serving forks. Rib bones you could use as toothpicks. Neck that my hands could easily fit around if I had taken the chance. She carried a bag in the other hand, pink and plastic. Pink as the scars that spiraled down her wrist and into her knocking fist. The bag had a name printed on it: *Palace of Perfumes*. I looked from the upstairs window, front of the house, from my bedroom, where I had fallen asleep after taking my pill.

"Who is it?" Macy called from the kitchen.

Right down below me in the driveway was a sedan the color of solid gold. That was where he sat. Passenger seat. I should have known. I looked down at her. The knocking arm. Grey raincoat, all the buttons open. A Russian fur hat, black as a crow, perched on top of her peach-colored hair. The same color as his. I could see the right side of his face, the jaw line crisp as a starched seam. His nose, long and slightly curved. The same as hers. She looked up and almost found me, but I backed away and she continued watching the door. The grey of her eyes was a storm approaching, drawing fuel and energy from whatever was nearby. They could disarm in an instant. They were weapons. The same as his.

Knock, knock. The door opened. She lowered her arm and raised her eyes. She knew I was here, behind the slight glass. I looked over to the car; he had found me too.

I heard the one-sided conversation.

"Hello, I'm Bell Meyers, Dot Meyers' sister … no, she didn't know I was coming … I'm in town for a conference … yes, a coincidence … is Dot at home?"

And in between Bell's sentences I tried to imagine Macy. Her nurse's eye, eyeing Bell's wrist and hand, the strange angle and bend to her arm, its shortness. The sleeve of the coat altered, the length cut away. How many inches shorter? Centimeters? Macy would do the conversion, wanting to be absolutely precise. Macy looking at Bell's eyes, the long nose, the square of the bottom lip. Meyers. There was no resemblance between us. But out in the car was that sameness: Bell's twin, Ray. He stared at Bell's back. Three crows landed by his side of the car and scrabbled for some bit of yellowy bread he tossed out the window. Bell stepped inside the house. Macy would wave her in with those nurse's hands that wanted to cut into everything. Ray smiled. The right side of his mouth veering up. The left side sluggish as if it had no intention of embracing a good feeling. Smiles were a necessary calculation. Bell and Ray, exact in their use. Ray got out of the car. Sunlight wept over him, embellished the pale reds and golds of his peach hair. His face fully in my view. The smile still there, applied for the walk to the door, to the answering of his hello, the smile of charm. But above the left of that smile was what he couldn't hide: the scars that wandered like a map from forehead to chin. Roads detouring across the left eye, over the cheekbone, forking with one spur headed for the ear and the other to the dead end, the drop-off of jawbone. This departure in sameness—her arm, the left side of his face— would bring them only closer in purpose. In thoughts, in acts, their behavior would have become even more synchronous. I knew. It was how they were, two seeds grown in the same rich earth.

Macy called to me. "Dotty, you have visitors."

"I'll be down in a few minutes." But I waited. At the top of the stairs, next to the wall. Ten minutes. Fifteen.

Let them talk. Let them talk. In a circle. Macy in the crimson chair. Bell and Ray on the couch with the dark green upholstery and the lumpy cushions. Let them fold their hands. Macy offered tea.

Bell said, "No, thank you."

Ray repeated, "No, thank you."

Politeness a trick they learned early. Macy's nurse's eyes skimming the similarities, the twins in their twinning. Bell and Ray inhaled Macy in one breath: her small body, her large hands. Looked directly into the blue of her eyes when talking. Salesmanship. That's what they were supreme at. Hooked you in with sincerity, the rapt attention, the connection, eye to eye. A few well-timed eye blinks when what the other person was saying could be of utmost importance, an insight, a profound insight. Then a few more blinks of the eyes as if tears could almost form from such truthfulness.

In a circle. All six eyes locked and maneuvering. For Macy would not look away either. She knew to keep fastened in observation, to decipher and diagnose. All six eyes, their trajectory, met above the table with the book of Judy Chicago's dinner plates opened to a yellow-as-sun vulva, unpetaled, the lips curled open, calyx, clit, a whorl of ruby and saffron. Let them talk. Let them talk. Around the obvious—why they were here.

When I entered the living room, Macy was leaning toward Bell and Ray. Laughing. She did not recognize their poison, that flattering interest, fawning over and pretending every word she said was brilliant and necessary to their lives like breath. Judy Chicago's book closed. The vulvas, vaginas, clitoris, and labias put away like the good china plates. They did not notice me, at first. I stood off to the side, hard as a wall.

"Oh my heavenly days, look who's here." Bell rose from the couch.

"Dot." Ray rose from the couch.

Both of them, on cue, rushed over to me.

Macy in her chair looking on: all is well. The picture forming, the snapshot, instant and irrefutable, of the adoration Bell and Ray were throwing at me. My face, with its suspicions and fear, eclipsed by theirs within the hug of their bodies, the stink of their overly sweet cologne.

"Come sit down," Bell said, as if this was her house.

I sat on the end of the table. Their plan was simple. They needed Macy on their side to believe they were everything they weren't so they could get what they wanted. To do that they had to keep us apart, keep us from talking. To do that they had to render me inconsequential and get Macy by herself, fill up the space of her curiosity with their conniving.

"We're here for the week," they said.

"Isn't that great, Dotty," Macy said.

"We'll catch up on all the years." Bell and Ray pressed their hands into mine. All three of them smiling.

I stood up, shook their hands away from me. "What the hell do you want?" Words like teeth that wanted to bite through bone to blood, expose their petrified hearts.

"Why Dot, we're your brother and sister. We only wanted to find you again." Ray looked over at Bell.

"Honest, honey," Bell said, "we hated the way you just up and left and have been searching for you ever since that day." Bell looked over at Macy. Those eyes, so much troubled water.

"Dotty, this is such an opportunity." Macy, stitching us all together.

"Don't try to fix this," I said.

"Maybe we should just leave," Bell said to Macy. Her hand reaching through the air between them like a rope that would tie its noose.

"Don't be silly," Macy said. "You've come a long way. It's okay. I'd love to hear about Dotty's teen years."

"You're sure?" Ray asked.

Macy glanced at me. The wink, wink of her eyelid. And that's when I saw how she was playing along as well. Not falling where they wanted her to fall.

"One hundred percent sure," Macy said. But she did not wink at me again.

She stared at Bell and Ray, her eyes penetrating as a shovel, digging, to get closer to some truth about me she was after. The truth I didn't tell. What came before the knock at the door. Mothers. Daughters. Lovers. And now: Sister. Brother.

I was hardening. One inch at a time. Soon, I would not move. Six eyes waiting for me to turn into a rock, exposed for their examination. But I got up, went upstairs to my bedroom. No time to sketch out a plan, draw a map of how to enter the living room again and not get lost in the wilderness of Bell and Ray, lost, this time, meaning they would not let me have a compass, a true direction, an escape. No time to determine if Macy would surface from whatever gold mining she was doing with Bell and Ray to see how quick they could mummify me. I went around and around in a circle. Circled back to the dresser, to the thought that love was not a reliable system to believe in. The evidence was down those stairs, in those two pairs of exact same eyes, maneuvering to hold me in place, and Macy going right along with them. Why shouldn't she? I never told her about them for one simple reason: I didn't want to bring them back into my life. As if not talking about the past could keep it invisible and disabled. I pulled out each drawer of the dresser, took out socks, a sweater, shirts. When I was done, shoved each drawer across the floor. Fourth drawer, I closed my hand around a tin Band-Aid box with money, a pad of twenties I stashed for whatever upheaval came along. I didn't picture this one. I grabbed a striped long-sleeved shirt and two bandanas, smashed them all into a backpack.

When I went down the stairs, there was no time to linger, to let Bell and Ray say one more word to me. All I looked at was Macy. Macy smiling at me as if that would lure me back. What did she know of love and hate and how much power each held over me?

Ray and Bell may have watched me leave the house. Or not. Either way, it didn't matter. It was exactly what they planned. For me to leave for a while so that they could work on Macy. Only they also needed me to come back. But I didn't.

Not right away.

part two

the story of dotty

1973

SATURDAY. MY BIRTHDAY. Bell and Ray hover. Every insect busy—the June bugs click their legs out of season, cicadas hatch out green as emeralds in the treetops and shriek. Ants hurry with their crumbs, every flower has a honey-bee in it. The yellow jackets needle into the garbage. Parasitic wasps lay their eggs in what they want to destroy. I am sixteen. Bell and Ray follow me to Bergen Park.

Pat is waiting for me by the water fountain. Pat, five feet tall—five feet even—with snake hair, Medusa hair, and a stonecutter's eyes. Eyes that will cut you up into slices like bologna if you cross her. Pat with the big Irish father, Ed, with the nickname Cook. He's one of the bakers at Sunshine. Pat's mother from down south, from one of those states with a lot of s's, like Mississippi, the sound a swamp makes. Everyone calls Pat's mother Queenie. She's got a ruby velvet chair, high backed, a throne. Queenie is six-two and needs a tall chair. Pat with the blood of someone from somewhere that no one in her family will talk about. The kind of blood that changes the color of skin. Pat is dark. Not like Italian, olivey, but of roots deep in water, rubbed to a maple sugar red brown. Pat not growing past her mother's rib bone. Where did Pat come from? Queenie sprang her loose in July, the same day I was born. I'm five feet even. Just like Pat. Pat and I see things the same way.

When I get to the water fountain, Pat throws down the cigarette she was smoking and says, "Hold out your hand, Dorothy. No, no, the other way, palm up. Now close your eyes."

I hear a horsefly's slow hum and the yellow jackets diving down to the basin of the fountain to stab at the water. Pat uncrumples cellophane. In my palm she drops something hot. Hot as in probably stolen from Globe's Five & Dime that morning.

"Open your eyes," she says.

Two earrings: black pearls, gold posts.

"These are Queenie's," I say. "You took these from Queenie?"

"Now relax. I swear I didn't heist them from her majesty. She gave the earrings to me to give to you." Pat strikes a match and the yellow jackets watch as the yellow flame stings the end of her cigarette. She lights another one and hands it to me.

"Queenie will kill you if you stole them." I inhale and blow the smoke to the side of me, in the direction where Bell and Ray wait like spiders in their swinging web.

"Dorothy, when was the last time I lied to you? Never. Right? You know Queenie likes you. She's always goin on and on about how smart you are and how artistic." Pat sketches the air with her Chesterfield King. Pat's witch-hazel eyes, half champagne, half serpent green, yellow jacket quick, land on Bell and Ray.

Bell and Ray with the Doris Day yellow hair, long legs that the rest of their bodies slouch on. Hands half in, half out of their hip hugger pockets.

"Shit," Pat says.

"Yeah, they're in a tag-a-long mood, have been all week. They're up to something. Been too nice."

Pat's eyes pick up the sun and the spokes of hazel sharpen. Pat aims at Bell and Ray. Bell and Ray keep their distance from Pat.

The first time Pat came to my house she sized Bell and Ray up in an eye blink. Bell and Ray, trying to be identical twins, but they couldn't be. Could only be fraternal sister and brother twins. They were sitting at the kitchen table eating crackers with cream cheese and jelly. Look-alikes with Barbie and Ken hair, the same pale blue work shirts buttoned clear up to the top button. They broke each bite off the cracker with their fingernail-bitten fingers. Their chins just like our father's—squared off, beveled. Each bite was small as if they measured the cracker and divided by eight. They chewed and chewed. Bell and Ray, never in a hurry. Pat coming through the house into the kitchen, watching their teeth grind up the bites of crackers. While I finished cleaning. Cleaning up after Bell and Ray who burnt the frying pan at noon grilling cheese sandwiches but blamed it on me. Our father in the kitchen doorway at one o'clock. His nose sniffing out the burnt pan. Grease polka-dotting the stove and the wall behind the stove. Our father fingering the belt with the bronze buckle that curled and fit perfect in his hand. The acorn brown leather greased down with saddle soap to keep it from cracking. Our father could remove that belt in a snap. In a hurry when he boiled over. At me. Always in a hurry, boiling over. Bell and Ray getting up from their chairs, standing in front of our father, his mercury eyes the same as theirs:

silver shifting over ash grey over smoke dark, a taunt of blue if all was calm. But not calm, our father. He was unbuckling.

"Dot doesn't deserve the belt, Daddy," Bell said.

I was squashing peanut butter with the back of a fork onto a slice of white bread. I held the fork in front of me, looked at our father. His fingers twitching, itching from the sight of me. How I was the exact sight of her, my mother, as if when she died giving birth to me she slipped herself over my bones like upholstery. Perfect look-alikes. And I just kept growing more and more into her. Her eyes, her lips with their ends like parentheses, her small body, my small body, sturdy, center of gravity low, not easily knocked down although he's tried, our father, seeing me, the slant of her nose in my nose, the hair dense carbon black surging from forehead to shoulders, the wrist bones, knuckles, kneecaps, all hers. That is what he sees, our father, looking at me. But he could not see the difference between the two of us and by only seeing her, he never saw me. He itched to erase me, the sight of me, the sight of her in me.

Bell and Ray he saw as perfect, when everything was just right, the sight of my mother with the two of them, Bell and Ray, in her arms. Me not in the picture at all. He did not see how much she lost giving birth to Bell and Ray, the spitting image of our father. But that was just hearsay, how much she lost. Our father saw what he wanted to see.

Our father took off his belt.

"It's not worth it, Daddy," Ray said.

Bell and Ray, each with a hand on our father's arm. Our father's face reddening from the sight of me, reddening like all the blood she lost giving birth to me so close to giving birth to Bell and Ray. Anemic, she was. No iron. That's what I heard, her anemia a fact. But not our father, he heard only what he wanted to hear.

Our father's face red like molten metal, eyes stiff, angry. Bell and Ray played him. Played him like an out-of-tune piano. Bell and Ray knew each note to set their fingers on, each finger sparing the sharp keys, the flat, growling keys. The melody they wanted drew his attention to them, the perfection of them, the spitting image of him and away from her, our mother, in me. They knew what our father could do to me. The slapping, kicking, belt whipping, punching in the kidneys, punching in the ribs, anywhere that wouldn't show. Bell and Ray saw his violence, learned their own brand, learned what wouldn't show.

"The belt won't teach her anything," Ray said, "because burning the pan was an honest mistake."

Bell said, "Those Jehovah's Witnesses came to the door and you know how hard it is for Dot to tell them to go away."

"Goddammit," our father said, "those people were here again? You talked to them, Dot?" His thumbs hooked the empty belt loops. The belt dangling.

"I told them we weren't interested and that you said they shouldn't come to our house."

"Then how come the pan burned if that's all you said to them?"

"Daddy," Bell said, touching his arm again, "I heard the whole thing and it was them that wouldn't stop talking. You know how they are, pushing their stupid pamphlets and books. But Dot did finally just close the door on them."

"Well, it's about time you did something right."

Our father looking for a mistake. A reason. His guts on the boil, his heart on the boil, churning like sulfuric acid, ready to cut her from me, my mother.

Ray said, "How about it, Dad, if Dot cleans the pan and all the grease from the stove? That should teach her."

Bell snapped her fingers. "The wall too. There's grease all over the wall."

Our father slipped the belt back through the loops. "I'm going over to the office for a few hours, and, Dot, this kitchen better be in order when I come home." I could hear the leather, the whine of leather being cinched up, pulled tight with his hands.

"Don't worry, Dad," Bell and Ray said, "we'll watch and make sure she does a good job."

When Pat showed up at two o'clock, I was spraying the wall with ammonia cleaner and using the spatula to scrape off the last ridges of grease. Pat watched Bell and Ray watch me.

"Almost done," I said. Bell and Ray glared at the surfaces: the enamel of stove, the yellow wall, the Medusa hair of Pat.

"Who's this?" Bell asked me.

Pat leaned in close to their chewing. "I'm Pat, and you must be those lazy, lying assholes I've heard about."

Bell and Ray stopped chewing. I shaved the dots of grease from the wall. Pat walked over to me and yanked the spatula from my hand. Threw the spatula in the bucket with the ammonia cleaner and grease and steel wool pads. Lifted the bucket and set it down on the kitchen table between Bell and Ray on their cream cheese and jelly crackers.

"Your turn now. Finish up. Dorothy and I have things to do." Pat took my hand and pulled me from the kitchen, the house, from Bell and Ray and their watching.

Pat closes my hand around the black pearl earrings.

"Come on," she says. We walk away from the yellow jackets, the water fountain, following the edge of lake. We're trailing smoke rings. Bell and Ray pursue. We cross the park that is manmade, stripped down one summer to mud. The stream that fed the marshland was straightened, the marshland dried up. They bulldozed out a lake in twelve hours, poured a parking lot, planted swing sets and see-saws, sugar maple, azaleas, stunted plants that burned brown every August. Ducks and a family of biting geese live in the park most of the year. Loaves of bread scurry across the lake like rowboats. The birds ignore the bread; too full, they plant themselves like squat bushes and polish their iridescent feathers.

In the parking lot Pat stops me. Looks behind her at Bell and Ray. Blows a gush of smoke and says, "Jesus Moses assholes."

We throw the ends of the cigarettes down on the ground with all the other butts. From her pocket Pat removes a key ring. Queenie's. Takes my hand and her fingers weave into mine. "Over here," she says and walks me with her fingers and my fingers together, locked palms together, warm. I don't say anything, not a word, not a word that could stop this, Pat holding my hand; I don't want her to stop.

Queenie's new car sitting in a parking place. 1973 Duster. Avocado green, never once shiny—the finish wouldn't take a shine. We sit on the bumper. Her fingers keeping tabs on mine. Thumbnail etching roadways and a clover leaf on my palms. Pat lights another cigarette one-handed. Her thumb rests on my heart line. We sit, smoke the same cigarette, passing the Chesterfield King back and forth.

Pat looks at me, wets her lips with the curl of her tongue. "I've got a hunger and a thirst. You're like a picnic just waiting there in the middle of a meadow, Dorothy. That's the only way I can say it so that it makes sense. Does it make sense?"

It does but I can't say anything, just nod and smile around the cigarette because I don't want a word to stop Pat, but if I said any words they'd be how she is the actual meadow, the wild grass and flower ground, what holds me up.

Bell and Ray bob like fishing floats by the picnic tables. "Jesus Moses, they don't ever quit," Pat says and takes her fingers away from mine. Stands, unlocks the Duster. "Get in."

Bell and Ray walk faster through the jimson weed.

I look at Pat, Medusa hair snake crawling out from her head, witch-hazel eyes simmering, the same five feet even as me, Happy Birthday, July first, sixteen years old. I get in. Pat closes the door. The windows cracked open to let some of the hot air out, let a yellow jacket in. The yellow jacket sizes up the back windshield, hisses and hums along the glass curve, the other side so clear: lake water, wild grasses, willow, dandelions, sky folding blue into black clouds to the east, Bell and Ray coming straight for us. Pat gets in. Jangles the keys and smiles her Queenie smile at me, big teeth in a small, plump mouth. The only thing on Queenie that's small is her mouth.

"Queenie know you have her car?" I ask.

"It's my birthday present. Queenie said I could have it for the day."

"No kidding?"

"None." Pat adjusts the pillows behind her, puts the key in the ignition, and starts the Duster. Bell and Ray peer in the back windshield. The yellow jacket peers out the back windshield. Pat starts to back up. Bell and Ray come over to my window.

"Where you going, Dot?" Ray asks.

"You know you're not allowed," Bell says, reaching for the door handle. Same smoothed-over voice—both of them talk in even-keel, sunshine tones. Pat guns the motor and flings her arm across the seat and slams down the door lock.

"Dot, you know Daddy would be angry if he knew you were doing this," Bell says.

"The aunts are baking you a cake for your birthday, and Daddy expects you to be home for dinner," Ray says.

"The cake isn't till tomorrow and you know it," I say.

"You better not go with that dwarf, Dot," Bell says. I put my hand over Pat's hand that is still on the door lock. She's wearing the ring with the sapphire eye, the ring Queenie said was her father's father's, but inside the ring is etched *1904 Thea and John Day Dix.* Only Pat's grandfather's name is Pine. Lewis Philander Pine. My palm lying over the sapphire eye, the long and short of her fingers, the color of Pat, the warm of Pat. I pull her hand away and lift the door lock up and open the door. The door hits Ray's hip. Bell steps back quick and I jump out of the car. My hand open, raising up. Ray staring at his hip, saying, "Goddamn you, Dot." Bell staring at Ray's hip and nothing to see there but his tan corduroys. They both look up at me at the same time with the same face. Fixing on me like I'm a horsefly that just landed on their dinner. Before they can step an inch, my hand arcs and slaps Bell's face and Ray's face. My open hand like it's got the sapphire eye from the ring in its palm and aims perfect. Red shape of my hand on their faces. I get back in the car, Pat reaches across me, rolls down my window, and says, "It's not polite to call people names." Pat puts the Duster in drive and we fly like a yellow jacket.

〜

To Sherwood Forest. That's where we go. We pay three bucks each. The ticket taker takes our money and looks at the black cloud grumbling half a mile behind. Lightning drops silverware from the sky.

"You ain't gonna have much time in there," he says. The exit gates stand open as families rush to their cars, thunder snapping, the air prickling with bugs.

"That's okay. We're still going in," Pat says.

We walk through the entrance of bark columns and grass fronds. Through the families: kids with soft chocolate ice cream stains, mothers with tight eyes, headaches behind the eyes, holding their babies who smell of milk left too long in the sun, dads smoking down to the filters and saying "shut up" to the whine of their swarming children. That will never be me: the mother in the middle of displeasure. Pat looking at the same scene, looking at me, taking me away from the squall of family.

Lightning takes a giant step, knifes the highway. Pat points to the right where an arrow marks Little John Way, and we turn into the forest of Sherwood Forest.

A thousand birds in Sherwood Forest. In mesh tents, in thatched huts. Walking the ground with their tail feathers fanned, combs cocked, eyes like dry beans, solid black and shiny hard. The birds come right up to Pat as if her hands in her pockets hold cornmeal, grubs, caramel peanuts. Birds with suits of gabardine, seersucker wattles, crimson feet. Pea hens, guinea hens, peacocks molting, half their feathers gone. At the intersection of Little John Way and Merry Maiden Lane, lightning sticks its fork fingers into the ground. Thunder bangs into us, thunder so close to lightning that the next strike could ignite Pat's Medusa hair. Birds scatter. We run up Merry Maiden Lane to a hut with yellow-throated warblers and dark goldfinches behind chicken wire. The birds perch on branches and do not make a sound. Each bird like a plum growing from the branch.

Pat turns around. She wears on her shirt a button with the words *Maintain A.I.M. at Wounded Knee* and the raised red fist holding a fistful of feathers. Pat red-brown as cherry bark, ruby dust, bloodroot. The color of Pat that could mean Queenie in her black velvet dress went to Louisiana or Memphis, to visit her sisters, went away from Ed the Irish man and their new marriage, and found a different color, made a baby, made Pat.

Lightning and thunder, and rain starts hitting the metal roof of the thatched hut. Pat's Medusa hair hooks my fingers, my fingers sink into her hair. Pat the red color that could mean stop, but I don't. I kiss her small lips that hide big teeth, kiss those lips that kiss mine back, and the buckshot of rain rattles the hut, the birds still not talking. I could stay here forever, Pat's Medusa hair on every side of me, electrified, crazy snake wire, and my fingers want into the current of her. We back up to the thatched wall and thunder says how it is: Pat's hands and my hands are lightning everywhere. Under her T-shirt I climb the rib ladder and her breasts are large like Queenie's, the only thing Pat has that is large like Queenie. My hands don't know how to touch anyone but myself so I touch her breasts like I do mine, curving my hands over that roundness, inching onto the spring coil of nipples, rubbing them with my thumb, Pat doing the same to me only different, the way her hand presses my whole breast and then quick lets go and hovers so close to my nipple that my nipple is growing just to reach her hand again. All that time our lips kissing lips, kissing tongues, kissing eyelids, eyebrows, ears, kissing hard, kissing up and down.

Rain slows until it is just dripping from leftover water in the trees and thunder is nearly gone. My zipper comes down and Pat rests her palm on my skin. I undo Pat's zipper, rest my palm on her skin. Our fingers settle onto the edge of pubic hair and I don't know how to go on or how not to go on, our lips kissing, tongues saying *mmm*, saying *ooo*, saying *go on*. My fingers find the current of her and go into that river of wildness. Pat does the same, dips her finger in, her finger a pulse I pull into me. Our lips kissing, tongues saying, *sweet*, sweet like birds in their dusk song.

Dusk. The yellow-throated warblers and goldfinches stop being plums. They titter and scold the thunder whose voice is apologetic, a murmur. Pat saying *ooohhh* like she has found a secret and pushing against my hand and sliding against my hand, my palm, *ooohhh*.

The ticket taker rides by on Merry Maiden Lane in a pink golf cart hollering, "Park's closing, ten minutes, park's closing, ten minutes." I pull Pat close to me, to my skin. The ticket taker passes, does not see us in the hut with its damp thatches. Our hands slipping, slipping farther into the current. Tongue, lip, sweet Pat of the Medusa hair wrapping me up in her snake-charmer witch-hazel eyes, *mmm*, her hand divining lightning, thunder rubbing color into me from her, our hands fast, fast as the warblers, the yellow throats, the wing beat crazy spiral flying behind the chicken wire now that thunder says next to nothing. Fast, her fingers fork, my fingers fork, slide so close to finding the color, the name for this. Pat reaching deep into me past all the ugliness of Bell and Ray and our father, and into the place where I am nothing else but glorious.

"God almighty mama," Pat says, and she is a thousand volts of current around my fingers.

We slide down to the ground. The warblers and finches fly and land and preen. Through the doorway, I can see the blacktop pathway, steam curling upward.

"Dorothy, Dorothy, Dorothy," Pat says, "we're definitely not in Kansas anymore."

"What do you mean?" I still have my fingers in the current, Pat squeezing every time I move them.

"Lord. You've never seen *The Wizard of Oz?*"

"No."

"Where you been?" She's sliding her hand over my hipbones and belly.

"Don't know. Lost, I guess."

"Damn good thing I found you, huh?"

"We better go," I say, but our bodies stick.

To the west of us on the street of Maid Marian, the ticket taker hollers from his golf cart, "Park's closed."

"Happy Birthday," she says. Pat takes my hand from the current, kisses each finger. My other hand touches the coil of her hair. We stand up. She pulls my shirt down and tucks it into my jeans and zips them. Buttons her own shirt, lights a cigarette. We walk down Merry Maiden Lane onto Little John Way past the ticket taker who blinks his bird eye at us.

Pat says, "Thanks a million, pal."

We drive away from Sherwood Forest into the night that's gathering like a fist over my house. Pat lights a Chesterfield King from the cigarette lighter in the Duster.

She says, "When I'm rich I'm gonna do three things: one, I'm gonna go down to the swamp where Queenie was raised by swamp crocodiles and ask those crocodiles just who Queenie is and who the man is that Queenie won't talk about. The man she made me with." The glow of the cigarette lighter red as that color in Pat. "See, those crocodiles will want to tell me cause I'll have brought them all kinds of goodies—SweeTarts, sapphires, Ding Dongs, Tupperware."

"What if the crocodiles don't care what you brought them? What if they only want flesh?"

"Then I'll bring them an arm. I'll bring them an arm from a general, still in its sleeve with its four stars." Pat is smiling, all teeth. "An arm from a general would bribe those crocodiles, don't you think?"

"It would have to be a big general with a big arm."

"Right on. Now you're talking."

She rolls down the window all the way and slides a quarter off the dashboard. Slows the Duster, but not that much, as she drives through the toll, pitching the quarter into the metal collection basket. Beats the red light before it turns to green. The smell of rain on the hot asphalt, the gush of wind through the car as she accelerates, wind all over my arms.

We smoke. I slide from sitting close to the window, from that place I always sit in any car, slide from my arm on the armrest over the pea-green seat to the middle of the seat. My thigh, my hip sliding right up against Pat's. Pat puts the Chesterfield King in her mouth and smokes it without taking it out of her mouth. Smokes it while her hand stays on my thigh.

Pat says, "Number two. Soon as those crocodiles tell me what I want to know, I'll get in my brand new Camaro and head north to Wounded Knee and give A.I.M. some money."

"Do you think your father is an Indian?"

"Don't know." Pat shifts the cigarette with her lips. "Don't think he's all Indian. Part Indian. Part black. Part white. That's my guess." Pat takes her hand from my thigh and points at her lips.

"See, I think these lips that are like Queenie's lips are from someone black and the color in my skin is from someone Indian. Queenie's got some dark colors in her but they don't show up on her like they do in me. Queenie comes from color, she just won't cop to it."

"How come?"

Pat points to her eyes, "These eyes that are like Queenie's eyes are the white part, the part Queenie believes in the most. White will get her everything she wants, like Ed, like money. Color never got Queenie anything but babies." Pat puts her hand back down on my thigh.

"Seems like she's always leaving Ed and going off and having fun. Why does Ed put up with her?"

"He's a sucker for her. Queenie's secrets excite him." Pat squeezes my thigh, looking right at me while the Duster nears sixty-five miles an hour closing in on exit 3A from the highway to my street, my house, Bell and Ray. "I've heard them fucking, you know. Yeah. Queenie's a banshee, chanting Ed's name like she's casting a voodoo spell, and Ed moves real fast. I can tell cause of the headboard knocking against the wall and then Ed will shout almost like he's in pain. He shouts and Queenie keeps calling his name and, I swear, makes him keep fucking her until she's done and then Queenie will quit saying his name and the bed will shut up and sometimes I hear Ed crying."

"Jesus Moses assholes," I say, taking Pat's words and she laughs, hearing how I say her words, deliberate and slow, like kissing someone for the first time.

"Have you ever heard anyone fuck, Dorothy?"

"No."

I only hear the word—*fuck*—in the hallways of school. It gets said a lot: "Fuck you; No, fuck you," or in the crowing voices of the girls talking about fucking and it wasn't all that good, no big deal really, and the girls who never have fucked thinking that word is a big deal, really. I look at Pat, the Chesterfield King down to a nub. I don't know if what Pat and I did was fucking. No one says fucking when talking about two girls. They say two girls is not right, is just plain nuts, is a joke, and what two girls together really need is an *m-a-n*.

"Sometimes I don't like the word fuck," I say. "It sounds like a word for when someone knocks the shit out of you, kind of hard and sharp, nothing like you and me."

"But it can be that too: hard and sharp. What we did was different, different but still fucking."

"How do you know?"

Pat turns off exit 3A, onto Prospect, past the new subdivision with its identical split-level ranch houses, no trees, lawns green and even, as if they were spray painted. The Duster at fifty miles per hour.

"I used to go with guys, before I knew that they were not the kind of candy I liked. This one guy once—long hair, leather jacket, you know, the gonna-be-a-hood kind. He was all business shoving that dick in me. It was boring. You never had a boyfriend?"

"No."

Pat takes the left fork that bends through woods and comes out on fields, a truck farm, a yellow barn. "How'd you keep them away?"

"I don't have to. Bell and Ray do."

We pass the farmhouse, the crooked porch, the field with the corn, up a hill where the trailers in the trailer park circle a boulder the size of the Duster, dropped there on an ice flow thousands of years ago. The Big Boulder Trailer Park with its haywire of clotheslines twisting out from the ends of each trailer.

The trailer park disappears. The farm disappears. We go by the gas station and the A&P and another subdivision sprouting in the knocked-down woods. Three more turns and I'll be home.

Pat's hand moves up my thigh. Her thumb on my hipbone. Her pinky on the curve that falls to the in-between of my legs. We take the third right and my house just ahead. Pat stops the Duster. Her hand in the in-between of my legs is a cook stove, a furnace, an arsonist with the secret language of fire.

My house is white, even the trim. The screen door opens and Bell walks out, looks down the street. Ray walks out, looks down the street. The Duster points at the house like a yellow jacket.

"Give me a word for that place," I say.

"Hell. Hell in a handbasket." She pulls away her hand. "I'm taking you to my house. There's no way I'm just gonna leave you with them." The Duster revs up. Pat's foot pushes the accelerator down and she shifts into drive.

"Jesus fuck-ing assholes," Pat screams. Screams are not what's heard outside any of these houses with their perfect painted armor. Inside, yes, inside is where everything is hidden.

Our father painted the house for two weeks after my mother died. Two weeks. He did not go to the hospital where my hands were pink and tiny, curled into fists. My hands opening and kneading the air looking for my mother, flesh, heat, heartbeat. I was undersized and the nurses fed me, the fluorescent lights humming. For two weeks until Satie, our father's sister, came for me, took me home to the house, white as a shroud. But our father wasn't there. He drove south with Bell and Ray to stay with his mother for two more weeks.

I know all this because Satie tells me every chance she can how I was born with the sixth sense, my mother's dying eye, and saw how everything was from the moment I arrived feet first, feet pointing toward earth to ground me but my head still anchored in my mother and not able to change a thing.

But Pat changes the direction of everything. She drives fast across town. When we get to her house, Queenie waits at the end of the long driveway. Sitting on a chaise lounge with the sea-green webbing shredded, hanging like moss. Queenie wears a silk scarf with oversize flowers of feverish orange colors. Pat shuts off the Duster; we get out of the car. For a second I think we all sigh at the same time, a gust of letdown. But the sound is the radio from the house. Just a purr of saxophone. Queenie stands. Queenie, a birch tree that can root in any soil, walks over to me, to my motherless ground, and hugs my body, a mother's hug I don't know anything about except it would have to be this strong and sure and not want to let me go.

Queenie says, "Sorry, Sugar Pie, but your daddy called and wants you home."

"Oh, Jesus camel shit," Pat says. I feel Queenie's head turn, her body shifting into its mother's hand-on-its-hip stance.

"Lady," Queenie says to Pat. Lady, like Pat's all the ladies Queenie's ever come up against. "Lady, I don't care if it's your birthday, don't use those words."

"Right, focus on the words, like the words mean more than what's really going on," Pat says, shaking out a Chesterfield King that Queenie eyes and holds out her hand for.

Queenie says, "I don't want you to say those kind of words. They're garbage. Cheap. And we are not garbage or cheap."

Pat lights her cigarette. Queenie lights hers. I stand behind Queenie while the smoke somersaults between them.

Pat says, "It's just a spit, you know. The words are just a spit and a curse to even up the playing field."

"Well, Lady," Queenie says, "the playing field is larger than you know and those words don't even up anything."

Queenie reaches her hand back and takes my arm, pulling me next to her. But how do I believe in what I don't know the first thing about. I twist out of Queenie's grip. Maybe mothering is thin as smoke, temporary, a spectacle. I'd rather believe in curses and spit.

"Let's go," I say to Pat.

Queenie looking at me with the white part of her eyes showing, the part that says hands off, each to their own, don't get in the middle, don't mother someone else's child past a fast hug. "Sugar Pie, you know I can't go against your daddy's wishes. I tried to get him to let you stay the night but he was adamant about you going home. It's your birthday, after all, and he wants you there."

"It's okay."

"No, it's not okay," Pat says, throwing her burned-down Chesterfield King hard across the front yard.

"You need to take her home," Queenie says. "There's nothing I can do." She bends close and hugs me, pulling me against her body and releasing me in a heartbeat. Quick, before the feel of flesh or heat. "Happy Birthday. I hope you like those earrings. They look smashing on you."

I step back from Queenie, from her scarf with the flowers that are too large and bright for around here. Cross my arms, hope to die, I promise myself not to believe in Queenie anymore or in anything she gives me.

"Thanks for the earrings, but I think they look better on you." I take them from my ears and drop them on the ground.

"Let's go," I say again to Pat, while I'm walking to the Duster.

I close the door. Queenie watching me from six feet up. Pat in front of Queenie, Pat's Medusa hair slithering, coiling, spitting. Pat says something to Queenie. I don't hear it all, just, "You know what they're like." Pat looking straight in the eye of six-foot Queenie and I hear Queenie say, "We can't do anything about it. Can't interfere, Patty Cake, it won't get you anywhere and it might make it worse."

Pat in the Duster, the whole dim, avocado green seat like a swamp between us. Pat starts the Duster and the Duster slides away from Queenie, from her hand closed around the black pearl earrings, from the look she gives us, the look that says *can't, can't, can't.*

We are quiet until I tell Pat, "Drop me off here." Here being half a mile from my house. Here being a handful of houses made with quarry stone on a dead-end road, and after the dead end the path through what's left of the woods before the park.

"It's getting dark."

"I've walked it a hundred times."

Pat not saying, me not saying that the danger is not in the dark but in the light in my house and who is waiting there. Pat stops the Duster.

"Dorothy," Pat says, like the first stepping stone laid down on the swamp between us. My hand crossing over the seat. The space between us, the swamp, gone, when my hand touches her hand and I pull her to me and Pat pulls me to her. We pull until we are kissing all wild, fury, our lips a three-alarm fire, unquenchable, scorching all that cannot be said. Two girls together, what two girls together do is thermal, is a fire that burns for years and years like under a coal mining town and everyone pretends the fire is not there. We are here, our lips, our lips on fire.

Pat, the same as me, sixteen, five feet even. Pat not the same as me at all. She has a mother, no matter that the mother does not understand, she is there. Pat pulls away. From me. I want her to change the direction one more time. But she doesn't.

She says, "I'll call you tomorrow. It'll be okay."

"Sure." Because I can't say what really happens, what they do, in my house. Pat is only guessing. I walk away from the Duster, from Pat.

↩

AT THE END of the street is the house with the yolk-yellow door, with the front gate made of pitchforks. The house half stone, half wood, the wood part painted in stripes: pistachio green, pink, mandarin orange, cobalt, and grape. In this house Promise sits on the organdy chair with the upholstery raised like braille. I am not allowed to be here, to talk to her, ever. Our father said he'd kill me if, Bell and Ray told me they'd tell our father if, they found out, saw me with her, the hippie witch. When I had asked my aunt Janet about Promise, she said, "She was your mother's friend until your dad came along. End of story." I never asked Promise. Never went nearer than her gate.

There are pictures I've seen of my mother that our father keeps in a box under his sweaters in the deep drawer of his dresser. A galaxy of pictures of our family. A million of Bell and Ray, a few of me. The ones of my mother are on top: her wedding, high school graduation, different summers when my mother was young, always with this other girl in the picture, jump roping, burping baby rag dolls, standing in front of a willow tree in Halloween costumes. The other girl is Promise. The two beauty marks on her chin and the crooked nose. In one picture my mother and Promise stand with their hands on their hips, wearing men's shirts and clam digger pants and eyeing the camera with the evil eye. In the wavy bottom white margin of the picture: *1953*. Two years before my mother gave birth to Bell and Ray. Four years before me. I took the picture from the box and put it under my shirt, in my waistband, to hide it in my room.

Her front door is open. Is always open. Promise has her chair just beyond the front door and her eyes watch me. Her hair in its braid is white grey, and the shirt she wears is always a man's shirt but there are no men who stay in Promise's house. She deals pot and knits sweaters that sell in Greenwich Village and craft fairs. I have stood here a dozen times while Pat went in and bought some grass. Stood here and Promise always eyed me from the house. Our father had said to me, "If I ever catch you over there, you won't know any tomorrows."

"Come in," Promise says.

"I don't have much time," I say.

"Just sit, then, for a minute. Maybe we'll talk. But sit now." Her eyes that watch me are narrow and sea green.

"I can't stay."

"Then why did you stop here?" Promise's hands unravel a sweater. She does not look at her hands. I've been told her fingers have eyes, that when you talk to Promise, it is her fingers that watch you.

"I'm on my way home, and it's my birthday, and, well, I have a couple of dollars and thought I could buy a joint from you cause I know you deal."

"I see." Promise's fingers peering from underneath the unraveling indigo and violet yarn.

Nothing in her house matches. Chairs like different breeds of dogs crouch around the kitchen table. The table is bowlegged and the feet are shaped like lion's feet. I can see the stove and on the stove is a pot and steam rises from the pot and smells like a carnival, licorice and sweet.

"A joint," Promise says, "because it's your birthday. Tell me, what will happen when you smoke this joint?"

"I won't care," I say.

"Then maybe you will never see what you need to see."

"I don't want to know the future. I didn't come here to have my fortune told. I just wanted a joint." I am sitting on the couch. I don't remember sitting but now I am, on the couch with the windows behind me, open and the night wind poking my hair.

Her fingers look at me; her fingers say you have to unravel before you can weave something solid. Her fingers pull the yarn and from under the sweater she takes out a joint.

"Here. Your birthday present. No, don't give me your dollars."

"Thanks. I'll see you." I am by the front door. I don't remember pushing myself up from the couch or walking to the door. But here I am. I step away. The air from the open door on my face, air with the static, the charge, from the lightning and thunder and rain. I turn back to those fingers in the yarn. "If you knew my mother, why didn't you ever say a word to me about her? You've seen me around here enough times."

"I saw you, yes," Promise says, "and figured when you wanted to know about your mother, you'd ask. So this I'll tell you and maybe you'll hear it, maybe not, but it needs to be said: do not wait like your mother did for what you want. Choose. Don't let the choice be made by waiting."

"That's it?" I scratch my shoes against the straw doormat. The *welcome* worn away. Promise's fingers are hidden in the wool and I look at her face, the fierce expression like in the picture with my mother. "That's all you know?"

She pushes the unraveled yarn to the floor and with her bare feet moves it to the side. Stands up and around both her ankles are bracelets with beads and tiny bells. "I can't tell you anything more."

"Your crystal ball not working tonight?" The sky is swirled blue and grey, black clouds moving fast. Cut grass smell in the air. Promise's fingers point at me.

"When your mother died, I was there, not your father. Your mother became who she didn't want to be. She tried to remedy that but your father wouldn't let her. When you are faced with decisions, Dorothy, that need to be made, sometimes you make them in haste, without awareness to what the consequences will be. Do you understand? She wanted to have an abortion. But didn't. You were born. I was there. She is dead. Whatever else you need to know, ask him."

"Right. Is that after he beats the shit out of me or before?" I walk across the porch with the broom leaning against the rail. Leave Promise in her house. I hear the bells around her ankles jingle and then stop. Maybe she is watching me go. Maybe she turned around and sat back in her chair to unravel the rest of the sweater.

In the backyard is another gate. A gate of eggbeaters, spatulas, wire whisks soldered together. The gate opens to the woods that weren't cut down to make the park. I smoke the joint on the other side of the gate. Walk and smoke. 1973. Happy Birthday. Pat wants to save the Indians. I want to make love, not war, but not call it fucking. Promise can't say why she can't say. My mother wanted to get rid of me but didn't, and she died. The clouds are rubbing each other, rubbing the moon, rubbing and fucking in the trees. I stop at an oak with a pregnant belly and breasts or one breast, one big bosom, full of milk sap. My mother should not have had me. Obvious. The smoke inside me. Rubbing.

I press my fingers into the place where Pat pressed. Into the fire. Smoke the joint and lean my back against the tree that wears the clouds like a hat. I slide down the bumps and hard edges, sawtooth bark biting into my back while I rub and rub and rub myself and this is what I know: the mammoth mama tree and the pain it causes and the pleasure my fingers find in the dark and that Pat could see into me too, into my darkness where fucking is hard and sharp, and hard and sharp is what I knew before Pat rubbed against me. My fingers press me deep into the belly of the tree, into where the bark meets skin, where it hurts but I can't stop because the hurt, the pain feels good, feels on fire, is familiar, the only thing I really know. I skid against the tree, farther down her belly bark to her legs and her feet in the ground, and the ground is wet, night wet and cool and my fingers stop thinking and I am stoned and I do not care about anything.

I walk through the woods and cross the park next to the river that was dredged and straightened and is slow as a bog and the mosquitoes breed and whine. When the mosquitoes bite, I slap my skin too late. The mosquitoes take my blood, take it into their bellies, but where do they go with it? I run through the playground and slide down the slide. The pot smoke inside, I am a transistor; I pick up signals from the swing set, the garbage can, the duck feathers floating by. The lamplight sticks to the air and the air is emerald.

I don't care. I don't care.

I bark and I oink, oink at the geese and the ducks that shit all over the grass and the Boy Scouts come and clean it up for their do-gooder's deed badge every other Sunday in the summer. Flap my hands at their soft heads. Ducks and geese stir wings into the air, rise up, and snap their beaks at me, quarreling, *just who do you think you are?* I don't know.

I don't care.

Up a hill at the edge of the park, I hold onto whatever I can, roots and fronds, and my hands claw at the dirt, dig in, and I am climbing to the moon that sits up there, above me at the top of this hill. But when I get all the way up, the moon has leapt away and dirt is ground into me, all over me.

I cut through the Manning's yard with the cherry trees covered in netting to keep the birds from eating the cherries. The trees like Afros. The Manning's house looks uptight: starched collars and buttoned clear up to the roof rafters with dull white shutters and nothing out of place. Uptight. Out of sight. Two rows of lilies on the front walk path like hands folded for prayer. Reverend Manning doesn't let any blacks into his church. No Afros. No color.

I hear the piano from Reverend Manning's house. All the windows and doors closed. I snap off a lily while the piano plays. The smell of the lily like the smell of paint. The smoke inside of me tapping against my eyes, and I drop the lily. Walk down the block, past the rolled-up water sprinklers, the boxwood hedges, the telephone poles with their creosote seeping like spring sap, the smell of hot tar rinsed with rain, around the corner, two houses and stop at the third house and come to hell.

This is what I want to tell Pat: white is the easiest color to hide in.

Dear Pat, white is the frostbite that freezes your skin until your skin falls off and reveals all the red.

Dear Pat, how are you? I am not fine. White is the color of Bell and Ray and our father waiting. I come in the door and there they are in the living room. Their eyes burned down to cold cinder ash, white, white, white.

I walk down the hall, past them, right past them, to the phone. I call Pat and I know I only have seconds and so I say, "Meet me on Monday at nine at the water fountain."

Pat says, "I'll be there. Dorothy, I never told you the third thing I'd do with my money."

"You'd take me away from here."

"Yes." My seconds are up and Bell takes the phone from my hand and Ray takes the phone from Bell and hangs up on Pat.

How my birthday ended: the three of them in the living room and me. No cake or song or happy birthday. Our father in the recliner but not reclining, the seat back straight up, our father straight up. Bell and Ray with a bowl of popcorn between them, sitting on the white Naugahyde couch. Their hands moving at the same time into the bowl, opening their mouths, putting the pieces of popcorn into their mouths, and chewing.

"Hi, Dot," Bell and Ray say.

"Have a seat, Dot," our father says and motions to the chair that was my mother's chair, a mustard yellow overstuffed chair made in 1918. The date painted on the underside of the chair. The chair no one sits in. No one. I sit down and the springs in the cushion creak.

Our father has a book on his lap. My yearbook. The yearbook is opened to the page with Pat's picture. I cross my legs. The chair's springs mumbling about no one sitting in it for so long.

Our father leans forward, holds out the yearbook in one hand. Bell and Ray watching with their blue eyes that have whitened like sky crossed with clouds.

"This the girl you been spending time with?" Our father asks, his index finger pointing at Pat.

"Yeah."

Our father asks, "Where did you two go today?"

Bell and Ray blink at the same time, popcorn halfway to their mouths.

"We went to Sherwood Forest and looked at the birds. Why?"

Our father gets up from his chair, pushes the book at me. "She's a colored girl and her mother is a whore." No mincing of our father's words, he always gets to the point with me, doesn't smooth or sweeten anything.

Bell and Ray smile. Same smile.

Our father leans over me, resting his hands on the arms of the chair, the chair no one sits in, only I'm sitting in it. I am stoned, the smoke still inside me, whirling.

"One. God. Damn. Whore. Do you know what that is, Miss Know-every-thing? No, why should you. You don't pay the least attention to what goes on. Too busy being irresponsible yourself." He is leaning so hard on the arms of the chair that the chair slices backwards across the wood of the floor. The yearbook drops to the floor. Bell and Ray chew. Our father wears cologne and the cologne is in my eyes, stinging, cloves and chemicals and the breath of his words.

"Now I find out that you are friends with the whore's daughter."

I look at Bell and Ray. At their mouths opening but not for the popcorn. Mouths opening for the lie that always starts with the same smile.

"Yeah and, Daddy," Bell says, "we saw Pat, you know, touching Dot. Kissing her." They did not see, they could not have seen, but they saw.

The chair does not make a sound. "Get the hell out of her chair." Our father pulls me from the chair. He is pulling me from the chair but I don't feel the pulling, only I was sitting before and now I'm standing.

The chair says something as he holds me up, says something, maybe *no*. But our father does not listen to the chair. Everything happens fast. Everything happens slow. The smoke still inside me confuses time, how it does not stop even for a second but plunges forward, only it has stopped, and I am looking into our father's face, into how handsome he is even like this. His arm draws back and the white of his shirt softens his arm moving back as if he is only reaching for a birthday present he has hidden behind him. His other arm, the one he holds me with, is hugging me. Our father has never hugged me. His arm comes forward, his fist. The white of his shirt a lightning strike. Fast. Fast. I watch his arm rear back. Again. Forward. His fist. The handsomeness of his face, even now. He punches me five times. I count: eye, ear, nose, breast, stomach. I count because I cannot fall or move away from him hugging me with both arms now as if he is sorry, so goddamn sorry to stop me in my tracks like this. But he is not hugging me. He is pushing me away from the chair so that when I fall I won't fall in the softness of her chair.

I am on the floor. I don't know for how long. Bell and Ray have finished the popcorn and the bowl is by my head and in the bowl are washrags once white but now red. Much redder, much darker than Pat. This red, the dark of when anger shows.

Pat, I would tell you, dear Pat, and you probably won't believe me, but Bell and Ray were my white knights who stopped our father from the sixth punch that was aimed at my jaw. Bell and Ray holding onto our father's arm, cooing to him, "Daddy, Daddy, Daddy," until he relented and his arm went slack and he let Bell and Ray lead him from the living room, their hands petting and patting and their voices like babies gurgling.

I am on the floor and Bell and Ray are on either side of me holding washrags to my eye and my nose.

"The bleeding stopped," Bell says.

"That eye is going to bruise but good," Ray says.

I am on the floor and Bell and Ray put a blanket over me. They took First Aid in health class; they're treating me for shock. My legs are raised and Bell wedges a pillow under my legs. I sleep fast and slow. They pretend to be a mother to me.

Mom, Mommy, Momma? Mother, what should I call you? Mother, may I call you? No, Bell and Ray and our father say, you have no mother. You killed her. Mommy, may I take a giant step? You took a giant step. Your feet were the first out of your mother. Stepped right out of her and took her last giant breath with you. You killed her, you killed her. Take two steps back. Mom, where are you? Stop. You may not go any farther. They keep where she is buried a secret. They keep her for themselves, our father, Bell, and Ray. Keep her for their games. They ask: Mother, may I punch her? Momma, may I spit on her? Mommy, may I cut her up with the scissors? Mom, may I kill her? I take tiny steps sideways. I'm in a daisy field. Bell and Ray take giant steps, are inches away from our mother, our father, sitting in their nest of daisies.

My mama says, "Where is Dorothy?"

"Who?" Bell and Ray and our father ask.

"Dorothy, Dorothy, where are you?" Mommy calls.

"There's no one named Dorothy here," Bell and Ray and our father say.

"Momma, may I, may I, may I?" I ask.

She steps from the nest and is a crow flying black wings over me calling, calling, "Dorothy? Dorothy?" Lands next to me and pokes with her beak at my eye, at my ear, at my nose, at my stomach and sticks her beak into my breast.

I sleep until noon on Sunday. In the living room, on the floor with the blanket over me and the pillow under my legs. When I wake, Bell and Ray are on either side of me but they have not been there all night. Bell and Ray wear their white clothes: Bell in her white denim shorts, rolled cuffs at mid-thigh, white shirt from India, collar embroidered with lotus flowers. Ray in white denim shorts, rolled cuffs at mid-thigh, white T-shirt, no pockets.

Bell says, "I think the first story is still the best."

Ray says, "It's a little suspicious. She's not clumsy and everyone knows that."

"But accidents happen all the time. She was running down the hallway to answer the phone and tripped over that loose floorboard, the one Dad was going to repair today. She fell and hit her face against the banister. I think it's perfect."

"Okay, that will satisfy the aunts, but how about when that Pat talks to her?" Bell and Ray sit cross-legged facing each other across my body. Bell is quiet, Ray is quiet, thinking up lies.

"I'll tell her...the fucking...truth."

Bell and Ray look down at me. Only one eye can open, the other swollen, my eyeball hard-boiled, my eyelid pulled too tight over my eyeball. Hurt, a color I can see. My one eye stares at Bell.

"Dot, there's no need for you to get rude at us. After all, we stopped Daddy from pulverizing you." Bell touches her throat, adjusting the truth that comes out of her mouth.

"What good will it do to tell anyone what really happened, Dot? Let's face it, you and that mulatto were not exactly being normal yesterday. We saw you holding hands in the parking lot and can just imagine what else went on." I turn my head to look at Ray. My head, inside, banging like a wrecking ball against cement. I can't breathe out of my nose.

I sit up. The chair, her chair, across the room, far away from me. "You two are repulsive. I don't care what you say to anyone anymore but I'm not going to play your game with you. And Ray, whatever you want to call Pat, say it to her face and see how far you get." My hand is on my stomach and my stomach is sore, queasy. I stand up. Pushing with my hands to steady me. I am not steady.

Bell and Ray stand up. "Don't be stupid, Dot," Bell says. "We're just trying to help you, protect you from other people and how cruel they can be."

"Oh, right, do you hear yourself? Protect me from other people, Bell? Who are you looking at that you don't see this black eye and probably my nose is broken. Just get away from me, you've never helped me in your life."

"Of course we have," Bell says. "You'd be dead by now if it wasn't for us."

"Well, that's a bonus, isn't it?"

"No need to be sarcastic," Ray says.

No need to be.

I walk out of the living room up the stairs to the bathroom mirror to look at the face our father hates.

After I get out of the bathroom and ice my eye, change my clothes, the aunts and uncles arrive at one o'clock, with six presents for me and a cake from Goldstein's Bakery. White cake with vanilla frosting—*Happy 16th Birthday Dot*—and dots of blue icing around the cake's top. The six presents they hand me as soon as they get inside the house. The uncles are just outside the front door discussing the lawn, the type of grass, how many weeds, the edging. The aunts look at my face, the black and blue of me, the new color of me.

"Oy, what is this, what happened, Dorothy?" Aunt Satie takes my chin in her hand and tilts my head side to side. Her fingernails are painted orange like sherbet.

Our father walks around us and goes outside to talk lawn with the uncles. Bell and Ray smile.

"Dot had a little fall yesterday. Do you want to tell them, Dot, or should I?" Bell says.

Satie's hand squeezes. Her eyes looking into my one eye, my other eye half-open, half-seeing. "Go on, Dorothy, tell your aunt Satie what happened."

Ray steps forward and hugs Aunt Janet, who is staring at me, at what black and blue could mean.

Bell steps forward and puts her arm around Satie's shoulders. They all wait for me.

"Our father," I say, "our father—"

"Yeah, Daddy was calling Dot to the phone and she went running down the hallway and tripped on that floorboard Daddy was supposed to fix today and she fell and her face hit the banister," Bell jumps in.

Ray says, "We were in our rooms and heard this big thud and when we looked out in the hallway there was Dot knocked out."

The aunts move in closer, the starched fabric of their dresses rubbing and squeaking. They hug me, Janet and Satie, the rose water on their skin, the smell of pancake powder and mascara I know is always there but I can't smell one thing.

"Poor child," they whisper into my ear that hears the sound of our father's knuckles meeting bone and skin.

The aunts get the truth they want; the aunts never see our father for what he is. He is their baby brother and they keep the truth of him locked outside their vision. Even when Satie took me from the hospital when I was born and our father would not come for me, Satie always said, "Your father was grieving so hard, he could not face loving you yet." Satie never saw that love never took root in his heart. But hate did. Aunt Janet lets in little gusts of what her brother does. Sometimes. But not today, not like this, my face rearranged too far from what is possible to think about.

"Our father—"

"Your father must have been worried sick," Satie says.

"I should say so. Just look at those bruises." Janet clicks her tongue three times. "Such colors like I've never seen. What did you put on those cuts, some first aid cream, I hope."

Satie says, "And ice. Or better yet, a frozen chop. Let's go look in the freezer."

The aunts move away from me. Bell and Ray follow. The uncles come in and pat me on the head and say, "Way to go, clumsy." Our father does not come near, walks around the house to the backyard patio.

Two chickens roast on the rotisserie. Highballs for the aunts and the uncles drink Pabst Blue Ribbon. Our father monkeying with the barbecue, basting the chickens, telling the uncles about a lawn mower he's seen that is electric. The aunts in the kitchen cutting up cabbage for coleslaw, putting pickles and olives in bowls, opening the containers of chopped liver and sour cream and chive dip from the delicatessen and rye bread from Goldstein's.

The TV is on in the living room and no one watching but me. War comes on: guns shot into the trees, the thick trees and green of Vietnam and soldiers run and kneel and shoot and color their faces black and blue to hide in. Smoke in the distance. Huts and shacks and animal sheds on fire.

Through the sliding glass doors I see the uncles biting the ends off cigars, smoking. The chickens revolving, the oil from their flesh slipping onto the coals and popping into the hiss of smoke.

Bell and Ray open the doors and stand there. "Come open your presents, Dot," Bell says.

I turn my black and blue face to them but they pretend it is not there. The soldiers shoot, pretending that the trees are the soldiers with the red stars. Pretend that just the wind in the leaf of a tree is reason enough to shoot. Water buffalo run around the huts and shacks and sheds on fire into the rice paddies and the rice paddies are bombed with napalm and all of Vietnam is on fire on the

TV. But Bell and Ray do not look at the TV until a commercial for lawn fertilizer comes on, the lawn greening after just one application, a lawn like the lawn at the White House. Perfect.

I sit across the picnic table from our father and Bell and Ray. All of them chewing chicken meat from the bones. The gold drops of fat pooling on the flowered paper plates. The constant shriek of the cicadas rising like piano scales and then the pause when they stop for some agreed-on second and there is the sound of our father and Bell and Ray chewing. Our father looks at me. Looks at me because the aunts tell him to.

"Look how much Dot resembles Arlene," Janet says, "even with these bruises."

"The spitting image of her mother," Satie says. "More and more, every year."

Our father looks at me. "I don't see the similarity. Arlene was more delicate." Our father stops looking. Turns to the cigar-biting uncles and asks if they want another Pabst. Their glasses are half full. They say, "No, in a little while, maybe."

Satie says, "Such a family, such a beautiful family. Luck from God was not always on your side, Morton, except with these children." Satie with the perfect wave to her hair, crashing over her forehead and down her shoulders. Her hand on my hand, patting and patting. Everything is all right. This is what she has patted into me forever. Only it is not, and in my face, my breast, my stomach is a surge of pain keeping time with the cicadas. And when it stops, the pain, the shriek of noise, I cannot feel how I was before because I don't believe there was ever a before to this. Or maybe, this time, our father punched the memory right out of me.

Janet pushes macaroni into the potato salad and leaves it there. Eats next to nothing, conducts the food around her plate with a fork and knife. She keeps gazing at me as if she can see just past the make-believe story Bell and Ray told about me falling but not far enough to her brother's fists. Uncle Will and Saul ask nothing of me, never have. They both call me "my little petunia" and always smile big around the cigars constant in their mouths and that is all they need from me, to be around the picnic table, on the periphery of their sight, a quiet girl with no demands.

Our father pulls the wishbone apart by himself.

"A beautiful family," Satie says again. No one sees the war inside those words.

The presents the aunts bought me: a cucumber green jumpsuit with elephant bells and a zipper from throat to crotch. Two dickies, in dark brown. Underpants and the aunts saying, "Oh, the men don't need to see those." A skirt made out of material like a slipcover and a pattern of flags from all different countries. Except communist. Two presents left, two envelopes, one from Satie, one from Janet. In each envelope fifty dollars. Our father eyes the money. Bell and Ray eye the money. I put the money in my pocket and hug each aunt.

"How often does a girl turn sixteen?" Satie says.

Janet adds, "And fall on her face the same day?"

Everyone laughs. Except me.

Bell and Ray hand me a present—a small box wrapped in the comic page from the newspaper.

"It's from all of us," Bell says, motioning at Ray and our father, who does not watch. His face twitching, big muscle in his jaw sticking out as he clamps his mouth tight. I rip Pogo in his swamp off the box and open the present and inside is a charm bracelet.

"Oh! Such a gift you're getting," Satie says. "Mr. Wonderful, our brother. Generous to a fault, isn't he, Janet?"

Janet says, "Your mother, may she rest in peace, adored that charm bracelet. Never took it off."

Our father hears the clink of the charms as I take the bracelet from the tissue paper. Clink, clink. Our father's face stiffening, the whole side of his face jumping, seizing up. I lay the bracelet over my wrist. The charms untangle. Thirteen charms. Thirteen silver charms. Our father opens the lid to the barbecue and the chicken fat drips and curses. Our father's face tight as the gold skin of the chicken. Smoke lurching into the air. Thirteen charms, all silver, all apples, except for one—a paintbrush. I clip the hook to the eye and the bracelet rings my wrist. Perfect fit. Slipping over my wrist bone. I touch each apple, some rounder than the others, some with leaves on the stems, one with a bite out of its side. The paintbrush has real bristles. I turn the handle over and see the word: *Promise*.

I ask, "Why all the apples?"

Janet says, "Your mother's nickname was Apple, although no one knows why. Isn't that right, Satie?"

"She loved apples," Satie says, "ate one apple a day just like in that saying."

Our father slams the lid of the barbecue down. He did not get what he wished for. I am still here, right in front of him, and I imagine Bell and Ray talking him into giving me the charm bracelet, talking fast against his objections, about how good it would look to the aunts and the uncles, until he gave in. He always gave in to them.

"Looks nice on you, Dot," Ray says. "I bet this will help you forget all about falling and hitting your head on the banister."

"That was a nasty accident," Bell says. "Are you feeling better?"

"Yeah. Sure," I say. Bell and Ray smile the smile that is all pretend and I lift my arm and the charms clink and the aunts begin to pile up the paper plates and the uncles relight their cigars while the cicadas flood the air with their urgent laments.

"Bell. Ray. Get the cake." Our father with the jumping face, the face that wants to rip her face from my face.

"Dad," Bell says, "I made a stupid mistake. I forgot the ice cream."

Ray says, "We'll take Dot and go to the store and get some. Okay?"

"That's fine," Satie says. "It will give us a chance to clean up."

Our father says nothing. Bell kisses him on his cheek, the big muscle vanishing back into his jawbone, and his twitching stops.

We walk to the A&P. Four o'clock. The sky pasty with thin foamy clouds, the sun boiling the pavement to tar bubbles. Bell and Ray in their white clothes reflecting light like tin and my black eye waters. The charms on the bracelet heating up against my skin. My skin salted, slick with the humidity, except my nose and around my eye, dry as the crackled chicken on the rotisserie. Inside my stomach is hot, where our father hit me, the muscles clamp together, hard. I stay behind Bell and Ray on the sidewalk, past the new houses without tree shade, air conditioners in windows drooling condensation onto the Kentucky Bluegrass.

"We have to go to the gas station first." Bell keeps walking, doesn't turn an inch toward me, crosses the street that takes us to the empty lot behind the gas station. Her hands in her back pockets, same as Ray. Walking their skinny fast walk up over the curb.

"Why are we going to the gas station?" I ask.

The lot smells oily and fermented. I step over beer cans, Boone's Farm apple wine bottles, little pyramids of cigarette butts, wavy pieces of bright, stiff plastic, stumpy weeds that stick their burrs to my pant legs, big humps of grass, and I want to be walking with Pat in Sherwood Forest with a thousand birds. Not here, I don't want to be here with Bell and Ray and the smell of things used and thrown away and forgotten as if they never existed.

"We have to pick up a part for Dad," Ray says.

I say, "But the gas station closes at three. That jerk won't be there." That jerk, Mr. Ned Payne, everyone calls Neddy as if he's still fifteen instead of fifty.

"Of course he'll be there," Bell says. "We called and told him we were coming."

Ray turns around with a smile on his face as if he had thrown the electric smile switch. Bell turns around and the same smile is on her face. I wish I had sunglasses for the glare. They stop walking and I stop walking and we're standing in front of the gas station.

"You know what, Dot?" Bell says. "Ray and I were thinking as long as we're here we want to test drive Neddy's Camaro. You know, the one for sale."

"You're not leaving me alone with him," I say.

"Oh, come on, Dot," Ray says. "He's a nice guy."

"Ned Payne is not a nice guy, and you know it."

"That's not true," Bell says. "It's just gossip. What did he ever do to you?"

"Nothing."

"See." Bell's looking at the charm bracelet, the thirteen charms, and her smile is gone. She knows the same stories as me. Ray does too. Ned Payne winking at all the young girls. Touching their hair and saying sweet things like "Honey" and "You're like a sweet piece of candy." Girls just trying to get a soda from the soda machine that sells the only Tab and Yoo Hoo around. Girls just waiting for their boyfriends or parents to finish filling up the car. Mr. Neddy Payne just waiting for the girls to come into the office cause their quarter jammed in the soda machine and he holds out another quarter and says, "You'd melt in my mouth just like sugar," touching their skin, a cheek, an arm, a thigh on their way out of his office. Bell and Ray always making me go buy the sodas. I usually carry spare quarters so I don't have to go in his office. But I didn't today.

"What are you up to?"

"God, Dot," Ray says. "We save you from Daddy, give you Momma's bracelet, and all you can think of is we're up to something."

"All we want," Bell says, "is for you to believe us. We're really sorry we couldn't stop Dad sooner. You know how he gets. But it wasn't our fault. Right?"

Not right.

"Anyway," I say, "Neddy's not going to let you drive that car without him in it."

"We can ask, can't we?" Ray says.

Bell puts her hand on my face, her fingers slide across the black and blue of me, her fingers cold, absorbing the heat from the bruises. "Please, Dot, please, please, please."

"Okay, but you can't be gone longer than five minutes, that's the only way I'm doing this."

"That's all the time we'll need. We promise, you won't have to wait for us more than five minutes." Ray holds up his hand like he's swearing on something, maybe the stink in the air.

The closed sign is up in the window but the office door is open. The two garage doors are shut, the stacks of used tires rolled inside. On the windows in the office are signs for motor oil and windshield wipers and car waxes, signs that cover almost all the glass. The garage is painted yellow and red like a flame but the colors are greased up, dark from exhaust. Ned Payne is standing at the counter looking through a magazine. Bell and Ray walk in. I lean against the door frame.

"Hi ya, Neddy," Ray says.

"Bout fucking time," he says. "Another minute and I'd of locked the door." He turns a page in the magazine and whistles and I know it's either a car or a girl he's looking at.

"Get us a Tab, Dot, would you?" Bell says. Bell hands me a quarter and a dime and I go around the side of the office where the soda machine is and put the money in the slot. Try to pull the Tab bottle out but it jams. Jams like it does every time, only this time I don't have any spare quarters so I hit the side of the machine and pull the bottle again and it comes out. I walk into the office; Bell takes the Tab and holds it in both hands. Neddy smiling at Bell and Ray. He's a skinny man, fits easy under cars. His neck long, his arms long, his face long but none of his bones show as if his skin was thick and his bones way down deep or not there at all. His gas station shirt has *Neddy* written with blue thread on the pocket. His hair is getting long: thin hair, fly-away, dust colored, flips up at the back of his collar. His sideburns grown across his cheeks, pointing at the corners of his mouth.

He turns to me and says, "Soda machine workin all right, yeah?"

"Yeah."

"Or maybe, ya got the magic touch."

I don't say anything. Neddy wipes the back of his hand over his chin and I can almost hear the scratch of stubble.

"Neddy's got that part in the other room, Dot. Here's the money for it." Ray leaves a ten on the counter. The cash drawer is in front of Neddy's thin belly.

"We'll go get the ice cream and come back and get you," Bell says. She and Ray walk around me to the open door.

"What about the car?" I ask.

"Later," they say.

"You can close that door when you go out," Neddy says, "so no one thinks I'm still open." Bell and Ray close the door. Neddy starts to walk through a door behind him that goes into the garage.

"Come on, let's go get that fan belt." Neddy holds the door open for me. The garage is dim like dusk, tires in stacks along one side, two cars lifted off the floor. A smell like earth gone sour, of tar on asphalt. The fan belts high up on the wall, but Neddy doesn't go there. He turns and faces me.

"You're probably sweet tasting as Dots, right, Dot?" Neddy's long arm reaches forward and circles my neck and pulls me to him and his long lips push against mine, long dry lips that push and open my lips and his tongue, thick and short, fills my mouth. The length of him bent against me and I try to pull my lips away, my body away, but his other arm reaches around and holds me like a clothespin. He touches my skin and I cannot move. His tongue like a word in my mouth, a hard, sharp word like *fuck*. And he wants to fuck me. Neddy sucks his tongue back into his mouth so he can whisper "Sweet, fucking Jesus" into the air.

"Let go of me." But he pretends I say nothing. Even when I say it again, he does not say anything back but holds me tighter. His hand like a ruler that measures me, starts at my neck and slides down my body to my zipper and he unzips me, he unzips himself. His mouth mashing against mine. I get my tongue out of the way and bite down, hard, on his. He unpins himself from me, steps one step back, and I head for the door but he grabs me, grabs my shirt and my arm and shoves me against the wall. The wall with the wrenches above me on their hooks. I face the wall. Clanging pain in my head, my nose begins to bleed. His hands squeezing my breasts.

"From the looks of those bruises, you may not be as sweet tasting as I thought. Guess I'll just have to find out."

Neddy pulls at my waistband, slipping my pants down, his hand over my ass, in between my legs, his lips whistling, saying, "Oh, fucking yeah." We hear the sound of a door closing, the sound of a car starting, close by, right outside the garage door, growl of muffler on each rev, sound of tires spinning on the asphalt, of rubber heating the asphalt and letting go in a loud, rasping squeal. Neddy takes his hand off my ass, his other hand from holding me against the wall and he is running away from me. Running and saying, "Fuck, I told them not to take the car without me." The wrenches above me jangle on their hooks. I keep my hands on the wall because I am not sure I can move but I do and spit the feel of Neddy out on the floor, and the blood that has dripped from my nose into my mouth. The charms on the bracelet have dug into my skin, left tiny dents on my wrist. I pull up my pants and hurry through the door into the office and outside. Wipe my nose with the bottom of my shirt.

Outside, Neddy is running down the street in the direction of the car, his black Camaro, shiny as night. I stand on the sidewalk watching Neddy run and I can see the Camaro is going fast, coming up on the curve that should be taken at fifteen miles per hour, that our father always takes at thirty, and Bell and Ray always screaming, happy, when he does. The sun glares on every shiny surface and I put my hand up over my good eye. The Camaro isn't going fifteen miles per hour, isn't going thirty. The Camaro's brake lights flash on just at the curve but not enough to stop it, to slow it down from how fast it's going, or keep the Camaro from flipping over three times and hitting a telephone pole, cracking it like an egg. Neddy yelling "Fuck" from three blocks away. The horn from the Camaro blaring. The Camaro squashed. People coming out from everywhere to see. I look back at the gas station and on the ground by the door is a quart of vanilla ice cream.

I walk the five blocks to the wreck. No, I don't run. My hand stays over my eye as if that will give me better vision, telescopic, and I won't have to get right up there, right next to the car and see. I walk along with dads and sons and mothers holding their daughters back and teenagers racing on their bikes, past the Beauty Shoppe and dairy store and the apartment building with the rooftop full of TV antennas like it is Cape Canaveral. The sidewalk is full of people and I am just one of them and they don't know anything else. About who is in that car. Sirens break the sound of us moving, of all our shoes moving along the sidewalk, closer, closer. The sirens pass us. Neddy is next to the car on his knees, looking in the window. I can see him knocking on the window. I stop across the street from the car and who is in it. The police come, the fire trucks come, an ambulance. The Camaro didn't crack, it wrapped its back end around the telephone pole. The blinker is on and two tires are flattened. The firemen and ambulance driver work on the car, the police talk to Neddy.

My hand over my eye still and I can hear Neddy say, "Fuck, I told them not to."

The policeman with his notepad asks, "Who are they?"

A man with a beer can in his hand and his arm over his girlfriend's shoulder walks in front of me and stops. All I hear Neddy say is "They're from around here somewhere."

Another police car comes. The firemen are working on both doors, prying into Neddy's Camaro with crowbars and Neddy puts his hands over his ears as the metal rips away from the hinges.

The police keep us across the street, walking back and forth with their arms out. No one moves. A mother with a sleeping baby on her hip asks a policeman, "They all right?"

"Not dead, that's all I know."

They get Ray out first, lay him on the ground, his head all red. His arm pointing back at the Camaro. I can see his lips talking, the ambulance attendants working on his head, bandages rolled out, Ray's head turbaned, his face covered with a wide sheet of gauze. I know what his lips are saying—they're saying "Bell." They lift Ray onto a stretcher. A policeman talks to Ray and with my hand up over my eye I picture what they're saying:

"What's your name, son?"

"Ray Meyers."

"And hers?"

"Bell, that's my sister Bell."

"Who should we call?"

"Our daddy, 231-7631."

They pull Bell from the car and lay her on the ground. Blood down the whole right side of her white, white shirt. The ambulance driver wheels the stretcher over to Bell. The firemen lift her up on it. Roll her to the ambulance, where Ray is already inside. I know I should go over there, to the back of the ambulance, and climb in because I am their sister and they are hurt bad and I could hold their hands and tell them it will all be all right. But it won't and I don't. The policeman is talking on the radio, his notepad open.

I know Bell and Ray will pin this on me, this accident, the reason they were in the Camaro, why I wasn't with them; they will invent and distort any way they can until all blame is off them and on me. Then they will watch me twist and dangle like a charm on a charm bracelet and will not stop our father this time from killing me.

～

I T   T A K E S   M E   ten minutes to run back to the house. But that is not how I do it. I can't run more than ten steps before I hold my hand to my stomach, and my bad eye is shook up to where I think it could just fall out of its socket onto the road and fry up on that asphalt. My mouth is past dry; it is a crumbled rock, sidewalk cement, and the first sprinkler I come to, I stick my head in the oscillating water and drink. A dog barks, another starts. All the way home I'm seeing the shiny points of pollen in the air. I cut through the side yard and hide in the bushes along the front of our house, thick bushes with sawed-off tops. I smell the rotisseried chicken, the charcoal, smoke, cigars. Gnats stick close to me in the cool of the bushes. Through the screen door I can hear everything: the phone being set back on the desk, the shoes on the wood floor.

Our father saying, "They're at Valley Emergency."

Janet asking, "What happened?"

I wave away the gnats, climb up on the concrete porch, and peek through the window glass and the slats of the venetian blinds. The uncles stand across from our father with the ends of their soggy cigars in their mouths, still smoking and stinking. The kitchen light on, a piece of paper in our father's hands. Janet's shoulder touching our father's shoulder. Satie has her arm through his.

He says, "I didn't get much more information from this officer. All I know is they were in an accident. Something about them being in a Camaro, and it flipped, and now they're on their way to the hospital." Our father puts his hands up in the air like he's just given up.

"What Camaro?" Uncle Will asks.

"I don't know," our father says. He looks at the aunts, first Janet and then Satie. They hold him closer, our father crying, no sound, just water from his eyes, his eyes blinking.

"It will be just fine, Mort," Satie says. "They're good kids, they'll be all right."

Janet says, "Was Dorothy with them, Mort? You didn't mention her."

Our father in the white kitchen with the swollen knuckles of his punching hand holding the piece of paper. "No, they didn't say a word about Dot and I didn't ask."

"She's probably not hurt," Janet says. "I bet she's at the hospital waiting for us."

Our father's hand closing into a fist. "Probably just waiting for us."

Uncle Saul and Will walk out of the kitchen toward the closet by the front door and I get off the porch and back down in the bushes with the gnats.

Uncle Saul says, "They don't have a Camaro. Whose Camaro is it?"

"How should I know? Why are you asking me?" Uncle Will says.

"Well, somebody should know these things."

Satie says, "For god's sake, stop arguing about the Camaro. We'll find out when we get to the hospital."

They come out of the house, the uncles in front, our father in between the arms of the aunts, and they get into the big four-door Chrysler and drive away.

There is not time. Time is fast, not slow. Time will bring our father back to the house like a lightning bolt to strike and kill the heart of me. I cannot even stop to call Pat. I cannot stop. If I do, our father will find me here, waiting.

The front door locked when the aunts closed it. I run to the side of the house, to the shed with the skeleton key under the can of 3-in-1 oil. Walk across the patio and open the back door with a string of bells tacked across it. The chicken still turning on the rotisserie, smoking and hissing and fat pops and drips, and soon the chicken will be burnt down to bone. I go in the back door and the white of the house, the white that was supposed to cover me up, paint me over, paint my mother from me, the white is dull now. Our father has not painted the house in sixteen years.

I am hurrying through the house. Hurrying and each step of hurry is remembering my father punching me, is an ice pick of pain.

Time is fast, already fifteen minutes pass just getting in the house and trying to find the red vinyl suitcase. I look in every cabinet and closet, down into the basement mess. The smell of damp spring everywhere, of the basement walls not keeping the rainwater from seeping in. Behind bags of newspapers and rags is the suitcase. I go upstairs to my room, unzip the red vinyl suitcase, and fill it with clothes I take from the drawers, grabbing at shirt sleeves and belt loops, I don't care what I bring. In the bathroom I take off the bracelet so I can wash my face, the blood from my nose. I dry my face and I imagine our father at the hospital by now, listening to the nurse tell him how serious an accident, how serious the injuries to Bell and Ray. I know it is serious. The sparks and smoke of the Camaro. The Camaro tilting, lifting into the air, turning over and over. The sound of it. Now I can hear the sound of it, the squealing and scraping, metal ripping, metal snapping against the telephone pole. I know Bell and Ray did not get out of there, did not just open the doors of the Camaro and step out. They were pulled out and laid on the grass and rushed to the hospital. This is what our father is hearing about.

I imagine that somewhere in our father hearing this, one of the aunts says, "Where is Dot? What happened to Dot?" The nurse saying, "No one else came in with them." And one of the aunts would say, "She must be at home, waiting. She must not know this happened." Our father saying, "I'll go get her, she'd want to be here." Our father pointed in my direction, a shotgun with the surest aim. I imagine the worst because that is what I've known. I run back to my room.

My room, the smallest of all the rooms in the house, tacked on next to the attic stairs with the door crooked and the window half size, the ceiling angling down from the stairs. The room painted white like all the rest but darker here without a big window and my psychedelic bright Janis Joplin, Gracie Slick and the Airplane, The Band, George Harrison posters on the walls covering up some of the white. I take my sketchbook, charcoal pencils, pastels. From the yearbook, I rip out the page with Pat's picture. I take a sweater. A wool scarf. A comb. I run into the kitchen, stuff a jar of peanut butter and some bread into the suitcase. Look at the counters, the refrigerator, stove, the white wall yellowing, the yellow flowers on the wallpaper, the sink with the cabbage hearts, the clock. The clock says they have been at the hospital forty-five minutes and I am taking too long because I don't know what I need to look for or what I am forgetting because I don't know where I'm going. But I need to hurry because time is not slow, time is fast, and our father could be on his way home in the big Chrysler, thinking, Dot did this, Dot did this to Bell and Ray.

I walk down the hall and in the mail slot in the front door is an envelope. Hanging most of the way into the house, caught by just a corner in the brass. I don't know how no one else saw it or how long it's been here. But it is here. The envelope painted with red daisies and sky, a gumball blue. My name on the envelope: *Dorothy*. The envelope Scotch taped closed and sealed with sealing wax so that no one could open it without me knowing. I hear the second hand on the clock ticking above the sink pointing, pointing, hurry, hurry. The big Chrysler could be driving down the streets from the hospital with our father willing me to be home waiting for him, the sight of Bell and Ray in his eyes with their serious injuries and me the cause, oh yes, me the cause. Time is fast. There are no extra seconds, none to stop and even take a breath with. I grab the envelope and the red vinyl suitcase and slam out the back door, taking no last looks at the white house.

↫

IN THE BUS station the man at the counter stares at me, tiny blue eyes, and his tie cinched up to his Adam's apple and his mouth tight like a line drawn on with a number two pencil. What he wants to know is why my eye is black and blue, half closed, and my nose swollen. But he does not ask that. "How old are you, Miss? … Your parents know you're going to Seaside, Miss? … What'd you say your name was again?"

"My name is Mary J. White," I say. White—the easiest color to hide in. I smile and push the bangs from my eyes. I point to my eye and nose. "Isn't it ugly?" Now that I've mentioned it, he looks away, down at the counter with my ticket and schedule, and he stamps and punches one ticket to Seaside and says, "That will be six dollars and thirty-nine cents, Miss."

From my back pocket I take out the money the aunts gave me. Separate the tens from the fives below the top of the counter, below where his eyes can see how much I have. I put two fives on the countertop and he counts back my change, out loud, "A penny makes forty cents, a dime makes fifty, two quarters makes seven, and one, two, three singles makes ten."

"Thank you."

"Your bus leaves from gate B, out that door to the right."

I lift my suitcase to go to the bus and notice there is no bracelet on my wrist. No charms. I left it. Forgot it in the bathroom.

Four hours to Seaside by bus, one and a half if I was going by car. The bus stopping in every small town, where other Misses get on with suitcases and no looking behind them, at what they are leaving. A Miss sitting next to me with her brown hair in a bun and a lace blouse and rouge on her cheeks and her eyes fixed to the window, to the moving past and the moving to something else, maybe better, maybe not. We said "hello" when she sat next to me and nothing more.

I will not call or write Pat for a year. Maybe longer. That way she won't have to lie or not lie when asked where I am. And she'll be asked. Our father will want to know where I am but I can't let him find me and I won't involve Pat.

I am in New Jersey. Crossing farms into the backsides of towns, to bus stations in gas stations and five-and-dimes or just a bench on a sidewalk. The bus driver gets out at each stop and unloads a bundle of newspapers. In Mt. Holly I take the peanut butter and bread from my suitcase and spread the peanut butter with my fingers. I didn't bring a knife. The Miss next to me watches my fingers but says nothing. I make two sandwiches and eat them both. In Wrightstown we stop for ten minutes at Kountry Kitchen and I buy a root beer. All the other Misses stay on the bus.

I go into the bathroom. In the mirror my eye and nose are turning color, turning cartwheels to pinks and scarlet, blues and violet. My ear is humming. I am running away. But that is not how I do it. Not running, I sit on the bus and wait until I'm delivered to Seaside.

In the motel time is slow, not fast. I have been in Seaside almost three weeks. Living in the last room, closest to the road, in the Sea & Sand Motel, where I clean rooms from eight to four or five o'clock. The sea and sand blocks away, smooth and whispering. I am naked in this room with the sailboats on the bedspread and mothballs in the closet. The bruise on my stomach and the bruise on my breast have widened and waned and yellowed like old fruit. Sometimes when I touch where Pat touched me, there is no fire. Where her fingers pressed and circled and pushed, finding the current to the heart, there is nothing to warm my fingers. Sometimes I touch anyway, sliding my fingers like the sea wetting the sand without any reason other than the tide moving in. I touch and time is slow, not fast.

Promise says time is a drug like any other drug. We dispense it like capsules, like speed, like Quaaludes. We measure it out, count each second instead of just living. We hold ourselves apart from time as if that would stop it or make it move any faster. Promise says all this in the letter in the envelope I took from the front door. The envelope with my name on it. I read the letter beginning with the end: *Once upon a time I was your mama's best friend and your mama and I waited for your birth with enormous joy.* The letter started: *I'm sorry. I could never change anything.*

Inside the envelope with the letter, sixteen beans, sixteen pink swirls on dark red beans. Promise says my fortune is that the sixteen beans from her garden will tell me how to stop and how to go and when it is time.

ᔄ

THE SEA & SAND Motel has thirteen rooms but the number thirteen isn't used. Sasha works the desk. She hired me, saying they were desperate for someone steady.

When she asked my name, I forgot and told her, "Dotty Meyers. I don't have to fill out any papers, do I?"

Sasha looked at me but not long. "Pay is a hundred bucks for six days work per week. Under the table. That suit you?"

"Yeah."

Her father, Carl, sits in the room behind the desk on the brown and beige couch. He yells to the guests from the couch, "I've got the cleanest motel, better than those ones up by the shore where nothing but sand is tracked in all the damn day. No way to get all that sand out of the carpeting. Here, we got rugs, they get a good shaking every day at two o'clock by the girls."

The girls are me and three sisters in their twenties who are cousins to Sasha. They share shifts and work for each other, bringing home extra money. Their husbands work on the fishing boats, taking tourists out into the ocean where the boats rock and sway hour after hour as they fish for bluegill. The sisters tell me about how the tourists are always hooking themselves with the two-pronged hooks, throwing up, and getting sunburned the color of a boiled hard-shell crab.

I clean the rooms numbered one through seven, and the sisters, taking their turn, clean the rooms numbered eight through fourteen, with number thirteen missing. Above each bed is a horseshoe. Carl is always worried someone will set the beds on fire with their cigarettes.

He yells at the guests, "We got loads of ashtrays, not like those other places that are stingy with their ashtrays and their cups and their ice cubes. Watch out you don't burn up the bed."

But there are holes in the bedspreads that we don't tell Carl about. Tiny brown spots like a blight. The guests grow sleepy and forget and their cigarettes fall out of the ashtrays or drop from their fingers and singe the red, white, and blue chenille. Also burn marks on the desks and dressers, the rugs. The rugs we beat with tennis rackets the sisters buy at a Salvation Army Thrift Store. The oldest sister is furious, left handed, pound, pound, pound, three minutes on one side, pound, pound, pound, three minutes on the other; she grunts *huh, huh* and breaks the most rackets, the heads of the rackets sailing into the brown gravel of the side yard. We don't tell Carl. Sasha comes out in the afternoons and smokes with whichever sister is there that day.

Carl yells out the office door, "Make sure you don't set the grass on fire. It's July for god's sake. Ya know how dry it is."

I keep cleaning. Take two bath towels, two hand towels, two washcloths from my cart. A set of sheets laundered a thousand times until each thread is visible like the veins in an oak leaf. Take the sheets off the bed and every day they smell different: Old Spice, baby oil, rose water, tears, and breath. Every day I smooth the night away. Every day I shake the blankets of their lint and hair. I kneel at the edge of the beds and fold the clean flat sheets over and under the mattress. How easy it is to pretend no one came before. I kneel at the toilet and Ajax the bowls with their copper and zinc stains. I kneel in the closets and find safety pins, buttons, underwear. No one knows who was here. No one cares.

Time is slow. Three weeks of slow. Wiping mirrors, sweeping, polishing the blond wood dressers. Listening to the sisters talk about fried fish and stuffed flounder and casseroles with cream of celery soup and shad. Their voices slip to a murmur when one of the fishing husbands is late getting home, his words sloshing like a sinkhole of beer, and the smell on him like a tourist. Carl anchored to that couch, a boat run aground, yelling, "Jesus, of course we got good hot water. We're not like those other places with an ash can for a water heater."

Three weeks of detergent and ammonia and rubber gloves.

Three weeks of waiting until almost midnight to run over the sand into the whispering in the sea. What the sea tells me is that I am safe. I wash back to the shore on my belly. I lie below rags of cloud and the moon is a sliver, a grin, a compass pointing at me. I am safe. The sea eddies around my legs. I open my legs, let the sea into me, let the sea push me away, let the sea pull me back.

I draw. No faces. No bodies. Just still lifes, life stilled down to an ashtray on a nightstand, a tennis racket on a rug, a bus at a red light, beans in an envelope.

When I find her, the day is the same as all the others. I empty ashtrays into a plastic garbage bag tied to the cart outside the room. Count my towels and replace toilet paper, put the paper strip that says *Sanitation Is Our Pleasure* around the toilet seat. Mop bathrooms with diluted ammonia, dust every wood surface, collect the dirty sheets. My skin filled up with the minutes of work, my heart surging to the sway of vacuuming and rug shaking, my head thinking, I'm safe, I'm safe, I'm safe. Sasha comes out in her new pair of sandals and her toenails painted and talks to her cousin on the landing above the room I'm cleaning.

Carl yells, "Don't forget my lunch, it's already noon, goddammit."

The noon whistle sounds from the Coast Guard station.

I knock on number five and no one answers. The door is not locked and I open it. A surge of bright sunlight follows me into the room. On the bed a woman sleeps on top of the bedspread with red, white, and blue anchors. The bedspread smooth, pillows on the floor.

"Excuse me, checkout time is noon." The door to the closet is open, the hangers have nothing on them. The woman is wearing a coat, wearing a sea blue coat. Her eyes halfway open and a corner of her mouth raised, not a smile, no, she is not smiling. A bottle of peppermint schnapps on the nightstand, empty.

"Excuse me," I say again. "You have to get up." She does not answer. She doesn't know that I have three more rooms to clean before two o'clock when we beat the rugs of cigarette ashes and sand. I walk to the bed to touch her arm, to shake her shoulder, to wake her. But she does not wake so easy. Another bottle, brown. I pick it up, turn it around in the sunlight to read the label: *prescription, Rx Valium*. I count: ten left.

I say close to her ear, "C'mon lady, I have to clean your room." She rubs the length of her arm over the side of her face, pressing her eye even more shut, wrinkles fanning out from the eye's corner. Her mouth starts to open and I think she's going to yawn and the yawn will lead to a stretch and she will sit up and I can get on with my cleaning. But her mouth folds and closes, her long lips slide back and forth over each other, smearing the red lipstick onto the skin below her lips. She leaves her arm over her eye.

The woman will sleep forever, wants to sleep forever. I cannot wait. She holds a book in her hand and does not fully wake, holds the book out from her coat. Out, like she is handing the book to me and I take it from her hand. This is a simple transaction.

Mother, may I? Find another to take your place? Is that what I waited for? In my ocean of being alone, of cleaning rooms, stripping beds, beating rugs, was she always on her way here for me to claim her? Tidy her up after her night of peppermint schnapps and Valium?

I get her coffee from the office where Carl yells, "The other motels don't give no one good coffee like I do. Yous remember to tell our customers that when they bitch and moan. Damn cheapskates. Rather drink packets of foul powdered instant mud than pay a couple extra dollars for fresh. Tell them that."

I take the whole pot of coffee and a Styrofoam cup. Carl watching cartoons. Back in the room, I unbutton her coat, crack the curtains and the window. "Drink this."

Her eyes coming up from an ocean of peppermint schnapps and Valium sleep. Eyes beached and sand stung and still. "What?" she says. I am lifting her hand to the cup of coffee. My fingers around her wrist, lifting until her palm touches the cup, and she says, "What the hell?" and sits up, her hand slapping at the air, almost hitting the coffee cup.

"It's just coffee," I say, "drink it."

Two swallows, her hands around my hand around the cup and her eyes crackle, jump start, see me. "You work here?"

"Yeah."

"Christ, what time is it? I have to get to Wildwood. Today. You know where that is?"

"Sure."

She drinks more coffee, her lips and tongue rolling that liquid around and around. "Can you get me there?"

I say, "The bus station's not far from here."

"You have to come with me, to Wildwood."

The sunlight has inched up closer to her bed and even though I cleaned and vacuumed this same room yesterday, dust churns in the air.

"I can't do that." I wipe off a smudge from the nightstand with my thumb; I don't want to look at her.

"You have to. Look at me, you see how I am, not well. You're the only way I'll get there. I'd be so grateful. I'll pay your way. Of course." She raises her hands and covers and rubs her eyes. When she lets her hands fall, there are no tears like I thought might be there. Her eyes, almost all pupil, are dry and plummeting again into someplace dark.

"Why do you have to go there so bad?"

"My future is waiting for me, a rendezvous, understand? My opportunity, the big one, and I'm not going to miss it this time." She shakes her red hair and lifts her arms over her head as if she was trying to pull herself right into the sky. "Honey, you can never pass up an opportunity, not when I'm holding one out for you to take. You have to take it."

This time I don't turn away. I want to see myself in her eyes, me with a sure look on my face, a just-get-up-and-go look. And why not?

"Besides, I know how to fix what hurts and I've got big, big plans you'll want to be in on." She lays her hand over my eye, the cool of her palm on the ache of my bones above and below. "Everything's going to be spectacular from now on. Everything."

"Okay."

Okay. The smile that rushes onto her face is as odd as the fact that she's wearing a winter coat in July. It is as quick as a hailstorm and then stops and settles back to that long lipsticked line.

I take the beans out of the denim bag I sewed from the cuff of my jeans. Sixteen beans in my hand. I roll them onto the floor in my room and wonder: will it always be like this? The beans scatter and pop over the carpet. One rolls under the bed, hiding. Will it always be like this? Running? Hiding? Rolling and rolling not by choice, not by design, but because I am pushed and I roll and roll, going along to get along. I have no plan. The beans tell me nothing. There is no arrow pointing south, no word formed. They do not say, write to Pat, she will save you. They do not say, call Promise, she will tell you what the beans mean in their random patterns. Will it always be like this? I scoop up the beans. Sixteen. I am sixteen, I am fucking sixteen and no one knows where I am and I cannot tell anyone where I am, cannot pretend, like the lady who wants me to roll away with her, that nothing came before this room. Cannot pretend there was no Bell and Ray, no father with his fists and belt and fury, no pushing and hitting and taking advantage of how I just rolled and rolled because what else could I do? Nothing. Going along to get along. What else can I do?

I put the beans in their bag and into my packed suitcase.

Time is nothing more than the shifting of gears, a door opening with a sucking in, a whine, stepping up the metal steps, handing the bus driver the tickets under the light where the color of his face is like baby food, stewed down to a pale yellow, and his lips say only "Next." Time is the bus slowing around corners into the town where big white houses are parked in yards of sand. The ocean always to the left of me, in the dark, no stars, no moon. The street lamps do not reach into the ocean but stop at the edge of asphalt, well back from the water, and the light sees only the sand moving and the paths of crushed seashells up to the big white houses. Time is 10:47. She is sleeping. Face curved into her hand, her hand pushed against the window of the bus. Outside the window, Wildwood.

↝

"HEY, WE'RE HERE," I say. Her mouth is open and her breath comes out in a hum. On each side of her mouth, deep lines curve up to the angle of cheekbones. She does not wake. The bus driver is removing suitcases from the hatches on the side of the bus. I see my suitcase, red, and hers, brown, stacked on the ground.

"Hey, we gotta get off the bus." I flatten my hand on her arm and push. Her body knocks against the window and the silver grey of the bus. The bus driver closes the hatches. The hollow sound of nothing left inside them. The latches scrape metal into metal as they lock. All the suitcases except ours have been carried away.

"Come on," I say, right in her ear.

She turns her head to me, eyes slow opening, hand sliding off the window, falling like it weighs a hundred pounds. "What are you doing?" Eyes wanting to close again, body not wanting to straighten itself up, stand, walk, move.

"This is Wildwood. We have to get off the bus."

"Oh. Jesus." Hand lifting up from where it just fell, lifting up to touch her face, brush the threads of hair that stick to the wetness around her mouth. "God," she says and tries to stand. She tilts back against the grey, nubby, worn seat. "Shit." Puts her hands on her forehead.

The bus driver smokes a cigarette, looking at our suitcases. The bus station has a painting of a roller coaster on its front. A roller coaster car plunges down the painted shiny track carrying families with their arms thrown over their heads, smiling. Above the roof of the bus station, I can just make out the lights from the real roller coaster and the other amusement rides, flickering pale stars.

"Give me a minute," she says, staring up at me.

"We don't have a minute. The bus driver's just about ready to get back on the bus and drive away." I slip my hand under her arm and pull her from the seat. "There. It's easy, just lean against me."

"All right, all right, all right. You don't have to help me. I can walk perfectly fine by myself." Her other hand holds her head steady as if the force of saying so many words will make her head fall off.

I walk down the aisle, hearing the scrape of her shoes behind me. The bus driver steps into the bus.

"Two more," I say.

He says, "I thought everyone was off already."

"Just about," I say. He backs up and I walk by him into the smell of ocean and bus exhaust. The floodlights attached to the bus station buzz and flicker. When I turn around, the driver is helping her off the bus, arm around her shoulder, step, stepping her into the Wildwood night. I see him looking at her, his eyes sliding up and down from the smile she's got going to the stockinged legs below her coat, looking at her, and I see she is beautiful in an unpredictable way. The curves and lines in her sharp face and the brown of her eyes and red hair add up to nothing symmetrical or even. One eye is wider than the other, her nose has a slight tilt, a knot in the bone, her hair is a tumble of waves. Add them together along with the lowness of her voice, the growl of words, and the way her lips say more than what they're saying, and I see how come the bus driver is looking at her like he is, like she is a maze that he'd like to get lost in and use every one of his senses to feel his way out of.

Her face raised up toward him. "Thank you so very very much. I'm such trouble."

The bus driver says, "Forget it. Trouble? You're no trouble. Not at all," and to me he says, "Come give your mother a hand."

Mother? Would you be like this? Hungover. Not even able to walk without me half carrying you down the sandy sidewalk. Away from the bus station. Away from the ocean. My arm around your waist pulling you along. The dead weight of you.

She is falling asleep again as we walk, her feet never lifting off the sidewalk, just scrape, scrape, scrape. Two blocks up and six blocks over, the bus driver had said. That's where the less expensive motels are. Two blocks up, six blocks over. Past a hundred tiny beach shacks, all shingled, wind scarred and blanched. Shells and pebbles and sand yards. Driftwood fences. Lawn chairs in the yards without lawns. Two blocks up. I turn for the six blocks over. Her arm around my shoulder, her arm slack, falling over my collarbone, bumping against my breast.

"Hah," she says, her finger pointing at a parked car ahead. "That's his car."

She lurches away from me, dropping her suitcase, and it slaps against the sidewalk and all the crickets, which had been sawing and clicking, stop.

"This is it—his car." She pokes the window, taps on it with her fingernail. Click. The crickets start again.

"I don't think so."

"Well, then, just goes to show how mistaken you are." Her hand rubs along the top and trunk to the other side, the driver's side. "Burgundy, that's his color." She looks over the top of the car at me. "He likes things deep and rich and full. Not pale and skimpy. Not him." She laughs, chin resting on the burgundy shine.

"Who's him?"

"The opportunity I'm here for."

I walk up to the car and touch the salt mist settled there. Wet and cool. She lowers her face to look in the window. I do the same. On the front seat there are Milky Way and saltwater taffy and caramel wrappers and crushed empty packs of Kents and soda bottles and a wad of chewed gum on the dash. On the back seat is one yellow flip-flop, a slinky, unfolded diapers, socks, T-shirts, a parking lot of Hot Wheels on the floor.

"Can't be," she says. "It looks identical. Anyone, anyone would have thought the same."

"Yeah. They would. Sure."

She comes around the car and picks up her suitcase. "Anyone." She walks away. Walking like she knows where she's going. One shoulder pulled down by the suitcase, her free arm bent at the elbow. I follow her, six blocks, to the line of motels and their vacancy signs in orange. When we get to an intersection, I look down the bigger road at the motels and fish stands and family restaurants, sign after sign, places to stop and eat or sleep or drink, all the way to the ocean, where the lights end. She turns onto the bigger road and passes the first motel—L-shaped, two stories, cinder block walls. Keeps going. No wind and still I can smell the fish fry from the restaurants across the street. She passes the second motel, painted turquoise, in a U, a pool shaped like a peanut in the center of the U. Keeps going. Waits at the corner to cross the street. I stand next to her; she turns and looks at me and the street. Eyes narrowed down, not sleepy like they were but measuring everything around her. Turns away and crosses the road.

When we're on the other side, she says, "You have to grab any chance you can by the balls. Otherwise you're dead." Says it to the left of her. Says it to where she knows I am. Following.

Mother? Would you say things like that? Out of the blue? Nothing attached to the front or end of them? Not caring if there's anyone even there to hear you?

She doesn't tip her head toward me like she would if she wanted me to say something back. Just keeps going. Right up to the next motel, set back from the road—a small L, no pool, shingled in grey square shingles. The Sea Sprite Motel, the a in the sign burned out, the other bulbs droning. She rings the after-hours doorbell. The light in the office comes on, fluorescent, shimmering bright, and the door behind the check-in desk opens.

"Yeah?" A lady stands on the other side of the door.

"We need two rooms."

"You got cash? Because we don't take no checks."

"Yes. I have cash." She holds up her suitcase as if it is filled with dollar bills.

"Okay. Come in, then." The lady unlocks the door, three locks, and walks back around the check-in desk.

"Just for the night?" the lady asks, flipping a page in the register book. "Singles?"

"No, I want to pay for a week ahead."

The lady takes the top off a fountain pen and shakes ink into the pen tip. Looks up at us. "A week."

"That's right. Is that okay with you?" She looks back at the lady who has a hair net over black wiry curlers and a burgundy chenille bathrobe.

The lady says, "Just dan-dy. You paying for two rooms for a week?"

She twists around and stares at me as if she just remembered something. Brown eyes in the fluorescence. "Two rooms for tonight and one room for a week."

"Uh huh. I'll put you in rooms one and two. Sign here."

The lady turns the motel register around but does not give her the fountain pen. Gives her a BIC. And that's when I see her name: Lila Lott. She doesn't even know mine. And I am guessing that the room for one for a week after tonight is her room, not mine. One night.

"That'll be one hun-dred sixty dollars plus eleven thirty-nine for tax. Cash. Who's she, just so's I know who's in my rooms."

They both look at me like I'm on exhibit.

"Dotty Meyers."

"Well. Dotty Neyers," the lady says.

"Meyers."

"Then, for chrissake don't mum-ble. Pro-nounce and the world will hear you, Dotty Neyers."

"Fine," I say.

Lila Lott bends down by her brown suitcase, undoes the two straps and the clasps, and unlocks the lock with a key from her coat pocket. Opens the suitcase just enough for her hand to slide in and come out with an envelope. From the envelope she takes out a hundred-dollar bill and four twenties. Slides the envelope back in the suitcase and locks it all up again. "There you go."

The lady tips her head down while she counts the money. Dyed blonde hair wrapped tight in the curlers. Gives Lila her change and the keys.

At the door to number two Lila hands over a key. "Thanks for getting me here. Sleep well, my little rescuing angel. Good night." Her eyes looking at door number one, not at me.

"Good night." I go in the room and get in the bed with all my clothes on and fall asleep.

I work eight straight days at the Sea Sprite Motel. One of the maids quit the day we came. Mrs. Modesto, the owner, took the letter that Sasha had written and signed Carl's name to. The letter that says I am a hard worker, dependable, a jewel.

"A je-wel," Mrs. Modesto says. "Seems like you were well liked at the Sea & Sand. Well, I don't care whether you like me or I like you as long as you do the work and do it cor-rect. Got it?" She slaps the letter on the counter. Three rings on her wedding ring finger, but there's no Mr. Modesto in the motel. Her hair is riding high above her head, half a beehive, teased blonde. She's fleshy and has jowls and the jowls sway when she talks and most of what I say to Mrs. Modesto is "yes."

The Sea Sprite is eleven blocks from the amusement park that sits in the ocean on stilts and piers. No pool, but clean, very clean. Lila sleeps and sleeps in room number one. The room she pays for with cash from an envelope. Her room is blue drapes and blue bedspread, blue tamped-down carpet, the same color as her coat. I clean her room, too, along with ten other rooms. Each day she is asleep when I come in and I say, "Time to get up."

She gets up. Her body in its peach nightgown, thin straps that slide down her shoulders. Satin, I think, because the nightgown doesn't wrinkle, is always shiny against her body. Her body is waiting, slow moving, a hand with a shot of peppermint schnapps in a glass raised to her lips, raised and waiting for her lips to open and her tongue to curl around the peppermint schnapps and hold onto the liquor a long time before swallowing. I see her throat, tilted back, the liquor going down. The other hand follows with a pill. The *ahhh* after all the swallowing is done. Her body waiting for what the swallowing will bring.

She says each day, "It won't be long, he's on his way, you'll see, he'll come tomorrow."

I make up her bed with fresh sheets. Exchange towels, set another glass wrapped in waxy paper on the sink.

She says each day, "This is exactly what I wanted. No one to ask anything of me."

I vacuum when I can, when she does not raise her hand and say, "Shhh, too much noise." Her suitcase and coat are on the chair. The coat smells like fried fish and lipstick. She wears only the nightgown, dimpled below her breasts, billowing big under her arms, and her breasts sneak out from the fabric. A curve, a rise, a gathering of flesh into roundness, and she does not care if they are seen. The warp of nightgown along her body, puckering and loose like drafts of air lie between the satin and her skin. Waiting in the chair until I am finished, her legs swaying together knee against knee and out again. Her face turning to wherever I am in the room. Hair falling over her eyes, hair a burnt brown at the roots, growing lighter red and lighter still toward the tips. Her eyes shiny as the satin. Waiting and happy to wait.

I am a sightseer in her room. The bottles of peppermint schnapps she goes and buys sometime during the day. The Valium behind the bottles on the nightstand. A book without its jacket leans against the lamp, green, brushed cloth. *Fear of Flying*, in gold. A playing card used as a bookmark, the queen of clubs. I look at her when I am done with towels and dusting and wiping down the toilet and bath. Hers is the last room of all my rooms. I stand and look at her full on. I don't ask permission. My eyes do not come from around the corner; I do not care that she sees me looking. She does not care that I look.

She says one day, "All my life I've been expecting one absolute moment, clear of all debris, that explains everything. He'll come, you know, but he won't have that moment. Damn it all. What can you expect from a man who carves up chickens and flank steak for a living. You know what I'm talking about?"

"Not really." I shove her wet towels into the canvas bag on the cart.

"No. Of course you wouldn't." She rubs her hand down her arm and back up from the wrist bone over the elbow to the curve of shoulder. Watching me. "Another week, another damn week. That's what he said."

"Who?"

"The man with the moment I want but don't have." Hand backing down her arm again.

"Right. Well, I'm all done. Can I get you anything?"

Each day she says, "An egg scrambled and make sure it's not undercooked. I hate runny eggs."

"Okay, anything else?"

Each day, "Call this number and tell me who answers, a man or a lady." Each day I tell her a lady answered, a lady answered, a lady answered. Each day she gets back into bed.

She kisses my forehead and says, "You're a good girl, Dotty." Her lips damp, warm, asking nothing, just marking time.

My first working day at the Sea Sprite Motel, the other maid says, "Do it cor-rect baby, cause Mrs. Mo-des-to don't give second chances, even if you is white." The other maid is shorter than me and the white of her uniform is all glare on her black skin.

"I know what I'm doing, thanks. I just need you to show me where things are, please."

"Oh. So you one of them polite girls, huh?"

"Yeah, guess so."

"Well, you just follow me, baby, and long as you don't try to take over, we'll get along fine as china." She talks fast and her hands move as fast as she talks, waving the words around in the air, punching them into her fist, throwing them over her shoulder. Her accent from somewhere in New York, some borough, Bronx or Brooklyn. Only know the sound of the leaping and swelling and crowded syllables all in a big hurry like New York.

"What's your name?" I ask.

She's getting her keys to the storeroom, jingling those keys like a doorbell. "T.K. is what you call me, baby. When I got you figured out, then I'll tell you what T.K. means."

I fill up my pale green cart with towels and sheets on the middle shelf and sanitized glasses on the top shelf along with boxes of Kleenex and paper toilet seals. I hang a plastic bag for garbage on the cart's handle, and on the bottom shelf I line up the cleaners and rags.

First day, Mrs. Modesto comes into room number ten, the room I'm in the middle of cleaning, and she's watching the bend of my knees, the way I pull the sheets off the bed, how hard I scrub the sink. "Well, you ain't no je-wel. You're coal on your way to being a die-mond. Got to get more hurry in your step and stop handling the scouring pad like it was the queen's glove."

She slaps her hand on her thigh and laughs, her jowls swinging like laundry on the line. I hear her laugh all the way down the row of rooms. But I know that this job is just like the one at the Sea & Sand and I'm good at cleaning up other people's messes. I'm learning the feel of the furniture, where the outlets are, the burn holes in the bedspreads. I slip the seal over the toilet seat and push on to the next room.

At the end of the day, in the storeroom, T.K. says, "Baby, I been done for an hour waitin on your ass to finish so I can get my good self home. Now, what is taking you so long?"

"Sorry. Just getting used to the place. And Mrs. Modesto kept popping up to rag on me." I put the last of my sheets and pillowcases into the industrial washer.

T.K. hands me a cup of detergent. "One cup and one cup only. I swear, she measures what's left in the box when I'm done. So, what she telling you?"

"Mostly, how the sun isn't gonna rise and set any different because I walked in here. And that I got to work doubly hard just like she does cause she's a wo-man alone and everyone would like nothing better than for her to fail."

T.K. watches me. Her brown eyes roll up once till there's nothing but an ice creamy vanilla white showing while I talk. The washer chugging and tugging the dirt and smells off the bedding. "That lady been speaking the same ole same ole for as long as I been here. What she know about being a wo-man alone anyhow? Her husband died and left her the motel and his life insurance. She's sitting pretty but she thinks everyone wants to take it away from her." T.K.'s fingers pretend to pinch pennies from the air and put them in her uniform pocket.

"Difference is, she's afraid we'll rise up and ask for more money, for the same wage the big motels pay. That's why she was glad Tillie left and you showed up. Now there's just me on her case, and one black girl against one white lady makes no never mind." Her hands slap together.

I fill up my bottles of cleaners from the gallon jugs. Rinse out my rags and scouring pads and pin them to the line hanging in the corner of the storeroom.

"Day is done for me, baby. Can't wait to get this ugly white uniform off my skin. Don't forget to empty the lint trap or it'll take twice as long to dry those sheets. See ya, baby, in the morning." T.K. waves her hands behind her as she leaves.

I do not open the drapes. Lila does not want to see outside. For seven days I bring her scrambled eggs and toast and the news that the lady answered the phone. Seven days we bob in our ocean.

I tell myself I will stay with her until he answers the phone, until he comes to her room and takes my place as anchor. Even though I know it will never happen, that he will never come.

I am forgetting the brush of Pat's hands on my body. Forgetting her tongue and breasts and insistence and heat. If I wrote her now, if I called her now, if I sent her Western Union, smoke signals, words in a bottle, Morse code, what would I say? Dear Pat, I am forgetting? In my bed in the room at the back end of the motel, next to the storeroom with the tart stink of chemicals and churning dryers, I sweep my hands over myself like I am making a bed. I do not feel her; I want to feel her. I tell my hands to listen, listen for the way Pat's heartbeat spoke in her fingers and her fingers talked to my body. But my hands hear only my heartbeat. I stare at the paneling on the wall, at the fake wood grain, the swirl of the grain, and my hands swirl into me. I rub and rub, a magic lamp, begging Pat to appear. But she does not appear because I am forgetting. My fingers say, *touch me here*, say, *do not stop*. I am in my room, alone, eyes shut so tight I can see colors, red and black, hovering above my hand. Jesus fucking Moses. I stop. Pull my fingers away because I am forgetting and instead of Pat, I see the ocean and me floating on my back and Lila in her satin nightgown, in room number one waiting for me to drift onto the sand, divide the day between when I am not there and when I am. And when I am, she swears I am her lifesaver. She is the mother that I save. My fingers spread over my bed. The picture on the wall not of the ocean but of a yellow field and sheep in the field, and what is this picture doing here eleven blocks from the ocean, not a sheep in the whole state.

I am forgetting everything, like how an ocean levels the sand, licks it smooth. I lift my hands up. "Pat," I say. My hands fly above me, so high above me they are sea gulls rubbing the currents of air. "Pat, come here." So far away, somewhere, she is there rubbing me. My hands rise and fall, a wave, an ocean, inching forward to the place that will not be quiet or rest and my fingers follow the tide and circle until I see Pat, over me, on me, saying, "Oh Dorothy, I want you to feel me, Dorothy," and I feel the ocean pushing until I can't stop it and let it surge out and out and out. But I don't feel Pat. Not at all.

The eighth day Lila is not in her room when I enter with my sheets and wood polish. The suitcase is unlatched, open, the nightgown thrown across it. On the nightstand, the bottle of peppermint schnapps full, the Valium not there. Did he come, then? While I was wiping fingerprints off mirrors and dusting the legs of tables, did he come to this room and take her away?

The eighth day is wind and clouds ripped and frayed, bolting across the sky. By four, I finish my washing. The clouds stiffen and barge into each other.

"You is one sorry girl. The way you waitin around. Don't think I don't see." T.K. is changing out of her uniform. Pulling on a yellow sleeveless stretch-knit shirt and brown slacks over her hard hips. Slipping on sandals and her toenails, painted red, emerge out the open end like rubies.

"How do you know what I'm doing?"

"Cause, baby, your washin been done now for a good long while and you're still sittin here. Why is that, I ask myself. Why is some cute white girl just sittin here when she could be down at the arcade being a mighty magnet for all those summer boys. Well, I think to myself, it's on account of that woman in number one, the jinxed room. You know why it's jinxed, cause only the saddest damn people stay in there and when they come out they no different from when they went in. Something about that room keeps sadness in, keeps it brewing; even the lamplight is a downer, baby."

T.K. walks to where I'm standing by the open door, the door with no number on it. The clouds getting that liver color to them. Lightning playing inside the clouds, lighting the insides of them.

"Who's that woman?" T.K. asks.

"Maybe she's my mother."

T.K. tugs at her shirt and her hands fold over her belly. Her hands are lighter than the rest of her. The rest of her is luminous like the black in my oil pastel set, indelible and brilliant. But her hands have silvered, become murky, her skin whitewashed by the Ajax, bleach, Borax, lye, carbon tet, detergent. Mud-colored hands with stand-up veins and pinky fingers that can't lay flat, that bend in the middle, always. Those hands come at me. Off her belly and in the air between us they clap together.

"If she's your mother, then I'm Nat King Cole. All I know is that you is catchin the sadness in that room. Now, get out of that nasty uniform and you can come with me and my main man Marlin down to the pier."

"I don't know."

"What don't you know? Time to have some fun, baby. That lady, whoever she is, is gonna have to do without you."

"She's not in her room."

T.K.'s hands grip my hands and pull me from the storeroom. "Well, you ain't in her room either, baby, you with T.K. now, so go get some clothes on cause we are gonna have us a time."

I speak to you in my head, Pat, because you are ocean or air or cloud or sky or sand drift or rain. Temporary, moving, shifting, warp, or kink. You are not stone or iron. Stubborn, unshakable. But I want you to be so you will stay fixed, will set up like concrete in my bones. Before I forget. Everything.

I take four hits from the bong.

How stupid to talk to you. To tell you these things, to pretend that you can hear me. You are no clearer. You are an itch, you are the heat mirages settling on the boardwalk. I talk louder to you. But you are gone and there's no point in talking to you. I'm not talking to you. No more.

Smoke rising out of the two-foot-tall bong with the face of Jesus on its base, his eyes open, rimmed red, doped up, black. Jesus is black. Marlin carved him. Marlin sells his bongs and pipes in the record store called Moby Gripe. Colombian and a sprinkle of hash. In Marlin's house on the Avenue E. T.K. shouting after every one of my hits from the bong, "You got some lungs." Marlin leaning back, packing the bowl from a film canister. Leaning back into the couch with the flag draped over it, the United States of America flag with black felt fists sewed over the stars. Fifty-two fists. In the stripes of red, Vietnam is painted over and over, rolling up and down, from the V to the n to the m, like waves. In the stripes of white, names of no one I know: Bog Cleaver, Mickey S., Ribbon Brown, Hoot, Sally, Empire Franklin. Those names touching up to Marlin's shoulders and neck, speaking in his ears.

Marlin sucks every wisp of smoke from the bong. T.K. in the kitchen turning the ice-cube tray over and whacking it against the counter. Above the trumpet jazz on the record player, T.K. saying, "I'm making lime jimmies, lime jimmies, two fingers and ice to heaven."

Marlin brings me my fifth hit. All the smoke in his cheeks, he kneels in front of the chair I'm sitting on. The trumpet jazz shouts out the window to the car traffic, to the door slamming, to the arcade across the street with its bells and sirens and the yelling of the summer boys. Marlin with his brown eyes dipped in maroon, glaring. Said two words to me this whole time: "Smoke this." Said eight words to T.K. when he opened the door and we were there, "What you doing here with a white girl?"

Marlin's face to my face. His fingers come up from the floor, wiggling, dancing up my arms to my neck. Fingers in my hair. I pull away, trying to rise out of the chair with its flower power cushions, a hundred huge Day-Glo daisies blooming on the yellow fabric. Try to sidestep away from Marlin. But his fingers spread across my jaw and cheeks and he inches me closer to his face. All the smoke in his cheeks. I say, "Marlin?" And when I say his name, his lips, with that same lick of maroon, undo one from the other and open, dime size, and all the smoke he took from the bong he blows into my mouth.

T.K. comes in holding three tall glasses, ice cubes swimming, stands over the chair, and says, "What you doin, Marlin? Trying to get that girl so messed up she won't know day from night?"

Marlin falls back against the couch, hands on his belly, laughing, wide mouth open, bazooka fire laugh, boom, boom, boom. My head nodding forward. All the smoke inside me. The room standing on its head. Parachute on the ceiling, up-side down, inside out, rip cord dangling, a hand grenade tied to its end. Posters marching up the orange walls: Black Panthers, Jimi Hendrix, Ike and Tina Turner, Sly, Mod Squad. The faces of the white Mod Squad pasted over with black faces.

T.K. hands me a glass and sets the other two on the table. "Drink this, Dorothy."

Marlin says, "Dorothy? Dorothy? Like that chick from Kansas. Well, you ain't no way in Kansas no more." The laughing from him is machetes, is aimed right at me.

T.K. says, "Marlin, I swear."

Marlin says, "What do you swear, Sugar Tee?"

"You act like you're still in the rice paddies," T.K. says.

"I may as well be," Marlin says, "with you bringing these foreign white gals into my house. This is black country here. Did you forget that?"

The ice cubes floating in the lime jimmy in my hand in the apartment on Avenue E with the parachute coming down, the green sky silk of it wrapping me up and Marlin and T.K. rat-a-tat-tat gun fire.

"I gotta go," I say.

"Now, baby, wait a minute," T.K. says. "Marlin don't mean nothin."

"I have to go outside. I need some air." The green sky parachute pressing me as I get out of the chair with the flower power cushions sticking to the backsides of my legs, follows me, wanting to push me into the wall, into the poster where my face could be inked out. And my face could be a face he could see. All the smoke, all the color getting in our way to seeing.

"Yeah, you just get along now, little white gal," Marlin says.

"Hush up already, Marlin. Goddamn you're mean." T.K.'s hands, slowed down by the hits from the bong, come toward me, palms up. "You gonna be okay, baby?"

"Yeah. Yeah. Thanks. I'll see you at the motel."

"Not tomorrow. That's my day off. So you take care. Go meet some pretty boy at the arcade. Okay?" T.K. touches my arms with her palms, smoothing down my skin.

"Sure."

↬

FIVE HITS FROM the bong and I walk out of Marlin's apartment building. The sun orange and sunk halfway into the clouds. The clouds sag in the ocean. I go up the sand-draped ramp to the boardwalk, holding on hard to the round railing, five hits and I move so slow and when I stop moving I'm standing between Frank's Hot Dogs and the rifle-shooting booth. Across the boardwalk from me rubber ducks float in a duck pond, plastic fishing poles used to hook the ducks and win a troll. I stand there because I can't tell my feet how to walk any farther along this wood into the commotion of wheels of fortune spinning and rows of stuffed blue bears and three-foot-long felt bananas hanging from the awnings of the booths. Radios erupting rock and roll, all tuned to different stations. Whistles and bells start the wheels whirling, the clack of the rubber tongues on the wheels slowing to land on a number or letter, and the shouts of winning and losing, and the summer boys in their booths yell, "Take a chance. Only one buck for a chance."

Shit. What chance do I have in this hand-is-faster-than-the-eye place? Rubber ducks bouncing in the water, too far away from the hook on the plastic fishing pole in the hands of a crying kid. Under the blinking of lights, I blink and within the blink everything changes. Like a fist in the eye I see what is really there. Like how the fist was first just a hand, the hand of our father, fingers open, curling my wet hair behind my ear, squeezing a rubber duck in the bathtub that I shared with Bell and Ray, looking the same because they were five-year-old twins, and all our hands splashed in the water until his hand helped me out of the water while he cried, looking at me in the big towel. His finger touched my nose and ear and eyelid, him saying, "How could this happen?" The fingers of his other hand closing into the palm, into a fist. Not to hit me, that first time, but to hit his own thigh. Three times. "Why? Why? Why?" Bell and Ray splashed in the bathtub with the upside-down rubber duck and yelled, "Why, why, why."

I blink. Staring at the flashing row of blue and red lights. Someone hooks a yellow rubber duck and it swings in the air above the water. The kid won't let go of the plastic fishing pole, he wants the rubber duck, not the troll. He waves the plastic fishing pole up and down, saying, "No"; the rubber yellow duck falls off the hook back into the sapphire water.

Bright pink hot dogs turn on spits under the heat lamps. Sea gulls wait on the roof of the rubber duck pond for a hot dog bun to drop to the dark pitch wood of the boardwalk. I blink. My eyes, are they as pink as the hot dogs? Five-hits-from-the-bong pink? I don't care.

On the other side of me three men in Bermuda shorts shoot the rifles at the ten tin Indians in war paint and buckskin. Bows and arrows in their hands, hiding behind fake rock and cactus, swiveling and jumping up, running from rock to rock on tin legs. The three men set their rifles on the wooden fence and aim. Ten tin Indians fall down as the bullets hit their hearts. Indians being shot at because they're Indians. They don't stand a chance. Men in Bermuda shorts reach into their wallets for another round.

I tell my feet, go, and I walk into the take-a-chance-winning-and-losing, but I don't take a chance. I walk paying attention to the walking, to not having anyone notice that I am paying attention, telling my arms and legs to be natural, normal. I keep in the middle of the boardwalk. Past the arcade and pinball and skeet and a palm reader. Into the booths of food and everyone eating saltwater taffy, cotton candy, snow cones, pretzels with mustard.

I think I see her in a pink, sleeveless blouse and a black-and-white-flowered skirt. Lila? I'm not sure I can tell it's her without her peach nightgown. She sits on a bench, legs crossed at the knees, one leg swinging. Licks a soft ice cream dipped in chocolate, a man next to her. A man in a shirt and tie, his blue suit coat folded over the back of the bench. Reaches over, his hand wide and gliding around her hand. Pulls her hand and the ice cream cone to his mouth, to his lips sucking the soft ice cream. Her eyes watch those lips.

Is it him? Did he come, then? The man with the moment? I stop in the middle of the boardwalk and everyone has to go around me, saying, "Jesus Christ, get out of the way." I tell my feet to walk closer to get a better look. But I don't. Not right away. Lila, her hair in red waves around her face. The man next to her, thigh to her thigh. They lick the ice cream cone at the same time. I take a chance, walk over to her, my hands reaching out.

This is how it is, five hits from a bong, looking at the lady who could be my mother but is not. Her eyes all brown sugary from staring at the man's lips so close to her hand. The charge between them is red blue white green lights flaring, bells and sirens, wheels of fortune stopping on their number. If I stuck my fingers into the space between them, I would get a shock. I would be electrocuted.

"Hi, Lila."

"Why, Dotty, what a nice surprise." Her eyes change from brown sugar to mud. She has colored over the paleness of her skin from eight days of waiting. Colored in suntan and everything is fine. Put on a short skirt and sandals and just like that, she chooses to be different than she was. "I was just celebrating my new job with Mr. Cole, who manages the amusement park."

"Hello, Dotty." Mr. Cole not taking his hand away from her hand. They hold the ice cream cone between them, a torch, burning up and melting.

"Hi." They look at me like I am a three-foot-long stuffed felt banana hanging from an awning: win me, take a chance, only a buck. But they want to move on, past the looking at me, back to the lick of their tongues. I can't move. I can't stop staring at her, at how easily she has gone from needing me to not needing me.

"So, Dotty, Mr. Cole and I have to finish up talking about my employment. I'll stop by your room later and fill you in." Just like that, she turns to Mr. Cole. The wheel of fortune hitting me on the head: you lose.

I walk underneath the boardwalk. Underneath the pier that holds the big amusement rides. I look up through the spaces in the wood planks. Up into the Octopus throwing its black arms above its head. On the end of each of its arms, held in its suction cup chairs, couples scream against gravity, scream into the sky that has emptied of orange sun and cloud and is dusk, polished as the Octopus. I sit in the sand with my back against a leg of the pier. Five hits from the bong pausing between fucked-up and straight and back again. The snap and tumble of the water slides closer to my feet while the lights, all the prancing, uncoiling lights on the arms of the Octopus, drift down through the spaces in the wood.

When she does not come to my room, when it is after midnight and I can't sit on the floor cross-legged anymore with my sketchbook and my pastels, not drawing one recognizable thing, just light and dark and spinning, I go to her room. Not a bit stoned anymore, I'm all straight edges. The icemaker chirps and cracks fat ice cubes into chips. A thousand moths circle and cling to the heat of the floodlight above the icemaker. Her room, lamp lit, curtains closed. The parking lot full of cars and everyone in their rooms using the towels and glasses and emptying their shoes of sand onto the carpet that I will have to clean tomorrow. I go over to her door but I don't knock. I hear her and him, their bodies talking. The bed's clank and thin squawk moving in its bed frame. I want to ask her if this is one of those opportunities she's been waiting for. But I won't. In my room I sketch a wheel of fortune on a background of red and white stripes and black stars, no arrow on the wheel to stop anywhere.

I have on my housekeeping uniform. She has on a dress. Both are white and zippered down the front. Her eyelids tinted grass green, mouth lipsticked in pink, skin pancake powdered, all the lines around her eyes and mouth filled in and smooth like dough. No more waiting in her eyes.

She says, "When you're done with work, come to the boardwalk and we'll get an ice cream. I want to talk to you."

"What about?"

"That can wait. Just come to the offices below the miniature golf course and ask for me."

I cross my arms in front of me. Small, I am small, five-feet-even small. She is not as tall as Queenie but she leans over me and she could be six feet taller than Queenie, the way she leans over me and with her pink liar lips kisses my forehead as if she is my mother.

"What if I don't come?" I ask. Pulling away from her lips.

"That would be a shame. You'd only be shooting yourself in the foot." She crosses her arms in front of the lowered zipper. "Friends are hard to find, Dotty. I'm your friend and want to help you. You've helped me so much already." Her grass-green eyelids fluttering. "So?"

"I guess so."

"Good. I'll see you later." Her hands wave down the length of her dress. "How do I look for my first day?"

"Fine."

"That's it? Just fine?" Her hands still waving. "Dotty, fine should only be used to describe the fine print when someone is trying to take advantage of you. I'd say I look smashing."

"So *you* say it."

She turns on her high heels, picks up her white patent leather handbag from my chair, and walks out of my room. Girl walking, hip and butt swaying and rolling with each step. Her dress higher than mid-thigh. A thread dangling from where she just hemmed it.

☙

ALL DAY I CLEAN. Room after room, the same set of furniture in each room: three-drawer dresser, nightstand, desk, all the wood stained phony hickory. Oval mirror without a frame tacked to the wall. All the walls painted eggshell white but grainy and raised in sandy bumps in swirling patterns that come to quick dead ends. Two lamps, one on the desk, one on the nightstand, both with pleated lamp shades and shiny yellow pear-shaped bases. The carpet is the same blue in every room.

I vacuum all the carpets with the canister Hoover that clogs every other minute with sand and hair. The Hoover whines and whistles when it clogs like a teakettle come to a boil. I undo the hose from the canister and, holding both ends, I beat the hose against the floor until the clumps of hair dislodge and the sand pours out. In room seven I beat the hose against the floor and in the hair and sand that comes out is a cuff link. Square and flat and black with two lines of gold that cross and where the lines intersect, a round red stone, a ruby or maybe just glass. I put the cuff link in the pocket of my uniform. Supposed to turn it in to Mrs. Modesto. Supposed to turn anything in that might have some value, that someone might call about. Supposed to. But I don't. The things I find I've been keeping in the wrinkly satin pocket of my suitcase. So far I have a corduroy eyeglass case, tweezers, a postcard from Georgia with a picture of a peach tree and only the words written dead center in the blank space, *I'm glad you're not here*, no address or anything. I have half of a Barbie doll, the top half, nipples drawn on the Georgia peach-colored breasts. A silver watchband scratched up and the links all loose. A keyring in the shape of a dollar sign and a tuning fork that hums forever when I hit against my knee.

All day I clean.

At 4:30 I unzip my uniform and put on my tank top and cut-offs and I look like the lamp base, a shiny pear with short legs. My hair grows and grows; I do nothing with it and it thickens and sticks out in every direction. The salt air from the ocean makes it worse, frizzes the curls. I have no iron to iron my hair straight or giant curlers to tame the curls. I don't care. I will never look like all the other girls on the boardwalk. Looking in the mirror, I twist a rubber band once around my hair and pull it back into a ponytail. My face comes clear and I see the pout of my lips. What do I care if people think I should smile? I don't want to. I stick my lower lip out further into its pout. My nose has a bump below the bridge, a bump like a knuckle, like the knuckle of our father's fist slamming into my nose. The bruises are completely gone.

In the bright sun of morning hardly anyone puts down a buck for a chance at the wheels of fortune. It is only when the light shifts and dims and swells orange that the chance seems more appealing, seems easier to believe in, that you could really win, like the boys who spin the wheels don't have a secret switch that makes you lose. Lila puts a buck down on a three of clubs in the dusk coming down over us. The boy with his long hair and wiry new mustache grabs the wheel and lets it fly. The rubber tongue clicks.

Lila says to the boy, "Don't let me lose." She smiles, crooked smile, pink lipsticked lips. Grass-green eyelids one wink, two, at the boy who shakes out a Marlboro and lights it and puffs smoke at the wheel spinning.

"Not a chance you could lose, lady." His hand drops below the counter. The wheel slows and stops on the three of clubs. "See? You got the luck."

She winks her eye. My pout is as big as the wheel. Lila bends forward, hands spread open on the counter, the zipper of her dress unzipped a few inches, four inches, five. The boy grins and smoke comes out in a sheet.

"So, what prize do you want?" His eyes moving from her wink to her zipper.

"I know what I want," she says, "but you have to lean over here so I can whisper it to you." He leans across the counter and she whispers through the long hair that covers his ear. He leans back and looks at her steady, takes another cigarette puff and looks at me.

"Have to think about it," he says. Puff. Puff. Hands Lila a stuffed five-foot-long Kool-Aid blue snake.

She takes the snake and wraps it around her neck a few times. The snake's head sits in the opening of her zipper. "If you have to think about it, you're not worth the wait." She turns and walks away.

In the haze of night lowering, of pollution from smokestack cities to the north, welding the colors red and orange to the sky, a seam of gold between the ocean and the night.

My soft ice cream is strawberry. Lila's is vanilla. Both sunk into warm melted chocolate that cools the instant it touches the cold ice cream and wraps around the peaks and curves.

Lila says, "I want to help you. I want to help you because we're in the same boat. Do you believe me?"

I want to believe what Lila says. I shouldn't. It is so simple not to believe. It takes more work to turn a lie into a truth, but that's what I want to do.

The red, the orange crawl into Lila's hair. Her tongue is quick, dipping into the ice cream. Lila licks her ice cream until she has nearly licked all the way through. Her eyes ringed with eyeliner like Cleopatra. I don't want to watch her, but her eyes stare at me, staring without a doubt as to what my answer will be.

"Sure, I believe you." My strawberry ice cream tastes like nothing could ever be a lie. Tastes like there is no forward or backward, just here, my hand holding the cone up to my mouth, my legs crossed at the ankles, resting on the pitch dark boardwalk, my hair pulling out of the rubber band and uncoiling to hang over my eyes that watch Lila bite into her sugar cone. I want to believe.

"I knew you were a smart girl. I knew you were a girl not afraid of taking chances. You can't just settle for anything. If you do, you'll pay the piper, you'll absolutely die. Got it?" She eats the last bit of sugar cone and wipes her hands in the square napkin. "Now listen. We're two girls out on our own. We don't have to answer to anybody. We're liberated ladies. But we have to play our cards right, even if that means cheating a little. Understand?"

"You mean we shouldn't trust just anybody, right?"

"And you know why? Because no one is going to give us a damn anything without wanting something in return. And I'm not about to give anything away for free. Not anymore."

The wheels of fortune are spinning double time. Dusk gone. Night here and the boardwalk lights crackle red, green, blue, white, and buzz. People line up three deep to slap their dollars down and dream while the wheels spin. Dream of being the one, the only one to win, singled out by luck and fate. Their skin is burnt from hours of doing nothing but lying in the sun with their children yanking on their hands to go. But they don't go. The rubber tongues click, so close to their number.

Lila unlatches her pocketbook and pushes Kleenex and her comb around until she finds her lipstick. There's a toothbrush and a map and scissors and the Valium bottle in her pocketbook. She draws the pink on her lips while looking in a small round mirror glued to the inside flap of her pocketbook. I bite the point off my sugar cone and suck the strawberry through the hole. Lila blots her lips on the napkin twice, and the pink of her lips is plump and smashing and I want to believe everything her lips say.

"Mr. Cole found me an apartment and I'll be moving at the end of the week. Now, it's not like I'll just forget about you. You can come over whenever you want. It's temporary, you know. As soon as my fiancé moves here, which is soon, very soon, we'll get a house and then you can live there with us. Won't that be super?"

She smacks her lips again and looks in the mirror, erasing with the tip of her pinky finger the excess pink that escaped over the edge of her lower lip.

I want to believe her. Believe pink lips that are moving away at the end of the week, waiting for the man who will never come.

I suck from the tip of the cone. The wheels of fortune stop and everyone loses and the summer boys scoop the dollars off the counters and yell, "Better luck next time, and next time you'll win, guaranteed, put your dollars down, you can't win unless you play," and the people leave their lost dollars and new people take out their wallets and believe in the impossible.

"Lila," I say. "I'm going to the West Coast, so you'll have to live happily ever after without me."

"I see. When did you decide this?"

"I've been thinking about it for a while. Soon as the summer's over I'll have enough money for a bus ticket and some extra for when I get there."

"Do your mother and father know you're going?"

The bells cling and the sirens go off at one of the wheels—a winner, a lady in a too tight red-checked halter top with her breasts squeezed out the scoop neck, her belly perched on the waistband of her white shorts, throws her arms around her boyfriend's neck, screeching, "I won, I won, I won," winning a carton of Kents, and her boyfriend pats her on the head and tucks the carton of Kents under his arm.

"There's no mother, no father."

"So what you're telling me is that you sprang out whole at age sixteen, that's how old you said you were, isn't it? Sixteen? Sprang out of the ocean, I suppose?"

"It doesn't matter."

"No, it doesn't matter, except you're full of shit about the West Coast. Know how I know you're full of shit? Because you don't know the first tiny little thing about how to lie without it showing."

She takes out the Valium bottle from her pocketbook and unscrews the lid. Taps out two pills. "I gotta find some water. You should take one of these, Dotty. It'll relax you." Holds out the Valium. Blue sky pill.

"I am relaxed."

"Then why is your forehead all puckered up like that?"

"Is that how you think you can tell I'm lying? By my forehead?"

Lila taps her knuckles against the top of my head, her smile growing into its curls, a few teeth showing. "Think? Honey, I know you're lying." She stands up and cups her palm around the curve of her hair-sprayed hair.

"Take this." Lila holds out the pill again. Hands me the lemonade she bought.

I take the pill because it doesn't matter, because I'm going to the West Coast, because Lila can't see what my forehead says. I want to believe in one thing, even if it's how a pill takes all my thoughts and makes them relax.

We walk down the boardwalk, past the 5 Balls for a Dollar, knock the milk jugs down. Ring toss. Dart throw, pop a balloon. Win, win, win.

I ask, "What did you whisper to that boy when you won the snake?"

Lila is swinging her pocketbook, smiling at everyone who passes. "I said that you were a catch in a million and he should ask you out because he wouldn't be sorry that he did."

"Jesus fucking Moses."

"Dotty. No need to swear about it." Her eyes focusing hard on me like a teacher's eyes when you say the wrong answer.

"You shouldn't have said that to him."

"Look, you need a boyfriend, Dotty. That's your problem in a Grade A nutshell. Sixteen? That's all you think about, right, a boyfriend, someone to hold your hand, buy you a soda, kiss you."

"No, I don't want a boyfriend."

"Oh, come on. That's what every girl wants. Trust me. You get yourself a boyfriend, and I can help you do that, believe you me, and you won't have any time to mope around."

"Like Mr. Cole helped you?"

Lila stops in front of the carousel. Grass-green eyelids blinking. Hand patting hair-sprayed hair rising up from her forehead like the carousel horse's plaster mane. Pink lips curl up, curl down, settle into a smile, a Valium smile. "Got to hand it to you, Dotty, you're not as dumb as I thought."

Her hand comes to my face. Tap, tap on my cheek, like a mother's hand, saying *how smart, how clever,* and her Valium smile that knows exactly how perfect and sweet it looks while her hand is tap, tapping but wants to tap harder, tap the smart and clever right off my face. I move away from her hand. Turn from the carousel and Lila. Coming down the boardwalk, coming right at me, are T.K. and Marlin.

T.K. and Marlin, and everyone on the boardwalk watching them because no one else is that color, and everyone shaking their heads thinking what are they doing here and everyone sidesteps out of their way. T.K. wearing a loose-knit red and yellow low-cut top, no bra, and her breasts dancing up and down. Red shorts high up her thighs and no shoes. Walking like her feet knew the pitch dark boards when they were trees. Walking like she cut and nailed each plank. Her feet slapping solid on the wood. She walks right up to me and says, "Dorothy, baby, you have to come with us."

Marlin looking Lila over. Standing behind T.K. A foot taller than T.K., his Afro another half a foot. Wearing coveralls that are cut off to above his knees, the cotton frayed into fringe. A tool belt around his hips filled with wrenches, a can of oil, a screwdriver, a hammer, and a yellow rag. Looking Lila over like he can tell that smile she has is manufactured, nothing sincere, a by-product of a pill. He keeps on looking and Lila stares back, grass-green eyelids, one wink, two.

"Where you going?" The Valium has taken my words and pushed them from my mouth slow motion.

T.K.'s breasts stopped their dancing up and down when she stopped, but her hands are doing that same up and down that her breasts were doing and she says, "To the new roller coaster, baby. Marlin been working on it all spring and summer. They cuttin the ribbon right now for its first night."

Lila says, "I love roller coasters." One wink, two at Marlin, who chews on an unlit cigar, rolling it around with his tongue.

"Nothin I like better then to hear a bunch of white ladies screaming when they go over the top of this motherfuckin roller coaster." Marlin walks around T.K. and pokes Lila in the arm and says, "Come on, then, I'll put you right up front in the first car."

T.K. grabs my hand and pulls me along.

Valium is taking the edge off the sharp razor look in Lila's eyes. I'm seeing round and smooth and I'm going along to get along and I don't care, nothing matters and I am solid, right on. I could stop at each wheel of fortune and win, win, win. Marlin leading us, his tool belt bouncing against his legs. Afro halo lit by the thousand flickering lights. Taking a right off the boardwalk onto the pier with the big rides. The Zipper, zipping and unzipping: dimes and quarters and pennies and combs and cigarettes falling from the upside-down people in the upside-down cages, swinging loose everything from their pockets. Tilt-A-Whirl, bottom falling out, gravitational push and pull. The Matterhorn, round and round and round on the tilted track, faster and faster, while The Doors roar from the speakers and then the sled car on the tilted track stops and reverses. Marlin snaking us through the lines of people. People stepping out of his way. We come to the corner, the far end of the pier that sits in the ocean, and on this corner is the roller coaster. The roller coaster called the Speed of Light.

⇔

VALIUM SITTING PRETTY in my heart and I want to be right next to Lila and right next to T.K. in the first car. Marlin walks to the front of the line to the ticket taker, a guy in a white T-shirt and black hair oiled back.

"Hey, Brother Mouse." Marlin raises his fist in the air.

Brother Mouse grins, a grin with four teeth missing. "Brother Marlin, the beast is purring like a pussy cat."

"That's cause I know how to treat a woman." Marlin raises his hammer in his fist and Brother Mouse laughs.

One of the roller coaster cars is rattling along the far curves of the track.

"Ain't this just bitchin?" T.K.'s hands are doing their up and down, in front of her breasts doing their up and down, her whole body in motion. "Baby, we're in for it now."

"I got three VIPs need to sit in the front car next time round." Marlin points us out, Lila, T.K., me.

Brother Mouse nods at Lila and says, "Ma'am." Sees T.K. and says, "Sister, sister, you're gonna ride the twister?"

T.K. says, "Mouse, Mouse, I'm gonna let the cat loose in the house." They make fists and tap knuckles together.

The roller coaster car gets closer, rattling like buckets of pennies. Screams getting louder. Lila unwraps the stuffed snake from around her shoulders and hands it to Brother Mouse, who stashes it by his feet.

When we get in the roller coaster car, Lila wedges her white patent leather pocketbook between her hip bone and the side of the car. Smooths down her white dress with the flat of her palm over her nylon stockings in the shade of tanned skin. Pats her hair-sprayed hair. I'm in the middle, T.K. on the other side of me. All our thighs touching, tan, white, black. Lila turning her head to where Marlin is standing. Grass-green eyelids, one wink, two. Marlin, arms crossed over his chest, at attention, Army man, sees everything.

"Why isn't your boyfriend coming along?" Lila asks T.K.

T.K. leans forward, hand sliding along the black front of the car. Her eyes pinpointing Lila. The glossy car, the polish looking all wet, looking like a mile down in the ocean. The black of the car against T.K.'s hand and arm and I see the chestnut and violet and grape colors in T.K.'s skin.

"My man," T.K. says, "doesn't believe in doin what everyone else is doin. Especially when the everyone is white."

I turn my head, and behind me in the roller coaster car, we are all white except for T.K. I stick my hand in my back pocket and get a piece of Juicy Fruit.

Lila says, "Don't chew that while you're on the ride. You'll swallow it and choke to death."

"Shit, lady," T.K. says. "You ain't her mama."

Lila's grass-green eyelids don't wink. Her smile is one lip up, one lip down. She doesn't say, yes I am. She doesn't say, no I'm not. "Sounds like to me your m-a-n is too scared to ride the roller coaster. Would rather watch. Yes, he seems the type that likes to watch."

"Seems like, this is close as you've ever been to a black person but you trying to tell me what you know about Marlin based on what you know about white men. That's like saying black-eyed peas are the same as Boston baked beans. You don't know the first thing about black or Marlin or me so just ride the ride and don't be in my face."

"Fine by me," Lila says. "If you want to be on your high horse, just get on and gallop."

"Lady, when the revolution comes, the horse gonna gallop right over you." T.K.'s hand slapping out each word on the black metal of the car.

An old man with a tattoo of a sinking ship on his arm comes up to us and unfolds a metal bar from the front of the car and puts it across our laps and latches it. He knocks on the side of the car and yells, "All set."

T.K. says into my ear, "Baby, you don't have to pretend nothin. She ain't your mama. She's trouble, I can tell you that. I see into her heart and what is there is a month of Sundays of trouble. I'm telling it like it is. Don't get fooled, baby."

The roller coaster car jabs forward. Metal toothy chain hooked to the underside of the car pulls us up the first hill. Lila waving her arms in the air, waving at the ocean. The moon stepping up from the water—half moon, sliced in two. T.K. rapping her knuckles on the outside of the car, keeping time to the toothy chain rattling us up the first hill.

Valium saying, I could get to the top of this first hill before we rock over and plunge, and I would never be happier, getting that far, to the top, how slow to get to the top and finally see everything.

The car chirping and squeaking. Already someone is screaming. Screaming, "God, I want to get off this thing." Almost to the top of the first hill and we are high up above the ocean, the moon, the thousand blinking lights on the boardwalk, corn dogs, Marlin, the solid ground, wheels of fortune. T.K. swaying her head, short Afro catching hold of the moonlight, gold in the black curl. Her hand finding my hand. Her fingers opening the fist of my hand on my thigh. Opening each finger with such a slow pulling and when my fingers are open and flat she rests her hand over mine, her fingers entering the spaces between my fingers.

Almost to the top.

T.K. yells, "This is it, Dorothy. Halfway between your greatest fear and your greatest joy. Hang on, baby."

Lila still waving her arms over her head. She wants to stand up. She wants to lift right off the car seat and at the top of the hill fly into the moon. Lila saying, "Yes, yes, yes."

Valium a tide in my blood, calm and perpetual, carrying me to the top.

The top.

I see everything. All the way to China. All the way to Bell and Ray in the white, white house with our father forgetting I was ever there, and me forgetting too. All the way to Promise whispering to her beans that grow into the trees and the clouds. All the way to Lila's grass-green eyelids one wink, two at the lucky man who comes and gives her that one moment, that one definition, and happily ever after. All the way to California where I will plant sixteen beans and never leave and send for Pat and we will live, two girls together, and everyone will know this is the truest thing, Pat and me. T.K. and me. Me. I can see all the way to my mother.

And after the top, I fall.

What I remember is the smell of Lila's hair and T.K. pressing my hand and the moon back flipping and the ocean above me when it was supposed to be below and the upside-down and the screaming, thousand lights of the boardwalk coming close and whipping away. A million minutes at the speed of light snapped me into fear and I couldn't find the joy of that hurtling down, acceleration, car on its side, car twisting and leaping until I closed my eyes so I wouldn't see where I was, where I didn't want to be.

What I remember is the sound of the Speed of Light, ocean in my ear, a tidal wave, sand and wind blown against skin, toothy chain gnawing the metal, all the screaming, "God, I want to get off … God, faster, … Stop this thing … Yes, yes, yes." Lila sucking in all the air, T.K. beating the side of the car, Valium not saying one word to relax me.

The Speed of Light came to a stop. The car plummeted down the last hill of the roller coaster track and the toothy chain quit its dragging and propelling, just let the car crawl back to the beginning and stop.

Marlin not there.

The man with the sinking ship on his arm knocking the side of the car and saying, "All done." Unlatching the metal bar. T.K. pulling her fingers from my fingers. Lila standing up, quick, first one off the car and down the stairs, going right up to Brother Mouse to get back in the front of the line. To get right back on the Speed of Light.

T.K. holding me up, walking me down the steps on the other side of Brother Mouse. I remember seeing Lila waiting, swinging her white patent leather pocketbook until she sat in the front car again, and how Marlin came out from underneath the roller coaster tracks slipping a wrench back into his tool belt and saying to Brother Mouse, "That'll take care of it. Chain was built in goddamn Japan and you know that's the whole problem."

What I don't remember is me sitting down on the wood pitch of the pier. But I am sitting. T.K. with her hand on the top of my head, saying, "Breathe, baby, just breathe."

The Valium breathing. I watch the roller coaster car go up the hill, Lila waving her arms at me. I lift my arm, my hand. Lila turns to the ocean, grass-green eyelids, one wink, two. The roller coaster car goes down the hill, down and down, traveling the speed of light, breaking its chain, the barrier between it and the ocean.

⌒

I CUT OUT THE newspaper article with blunt children's scissors. Red plastic scissors. The thumb hole and index finger hole the same small round size, size of a quarter. *The Ocean County Newspaper* had printed up extra copies of the morning edition, and the story, front page with three accompanying pictures, was picked up by other newspapers and was retold on radio stations and TV newscasts up and down the east coast and over to Chicago and Ohio and on to California.

When I finish cutting and lift the article away from the rest of the paper, the shape of it, the shape of the paper, the story, is the shape of a boat, like a child's drawing of a boat before the child drew on a mast or sail, just the hull, large and bottom heavy. The first picture riding like cargo on the deck: the roller coaster lit up by searchlights and the moon. People running, caught and frozen between strides. Hands pressed to faces, the shock of the faces, staring toward the camera as if the camera could tell the faces something about what happened. But the camera only captures what is: night, the Speed of Light roller coaster, the ocean beyond the roller coaster, Coast Guard boats, searchlights, the moon almost perching on the first hill of the roller coaster. A perfect half of the moon. In front of the roller coaster, one girl sits cross-legged on the boardwalk, while the people run on either side of her and the people hold the shock of their faces in their hands. She sits, eyes not looking toward the camera, not looking at her fists resting on her thighs, not to the left or right, not at the roller coaster or the ocean and what it holds, not looking. Her eyes closed. She could be meditating. Saying *ooooooom*. Listening for the arrival of peace.

The second picture fits under the prow of the boat: a two-inch square of a woman, an employee of the Wildwood Amusement Park, taken the day before for her personnel file and ID card. The woman has the smile of someone who knows how to smile when she is told: one, two, three, smile. A smile that is too big, not usually there, taking up so much space on her face. Her eyes do not smile, do not hold delight in what they see. Her eyes are narrowed down and contemptuous of the quick snap of the camera lens trying to pin her down. The quote of a Mr. Cole, manager of personnel at the Wildwood Amusement Park: "This is a tragedy for everyone and we are deeply saddened by the loss of one of our employees."

The third picture follows the stern like a lifeboat. Rectangular, long, riding steady in the wake. The picture could be morning or night. Could be the cameraman set up a flock of stage lights and pointed them at the ocean. Could be that morning had come, dark and grey, and wasn't going to get much brighter. The ocean. Four-inch rectangle of it in the picture. A quiet ocean, the waves barely cresting, just swelling and sliding forward over the sand. The ocean. Could be a lake, how still it is.

On the ocean, in the picture, that is why the picture was taken. What washed up, was pushed in toward land. At first it is hard to tell what is here. Could be a tide of jellyfish or simply foam. But it isn't. What the ocean is delivering are pocketbooks, sandals, loafers, eyeglasses, sunglasses, a wig, combs. Crawling onto the sand, a sweater and a stuffed banana. Caption below the picture says: *Lost and Found.*

The headline above the boat of words and pictures is colored red. Sunset or sunrise. What is the difference? The outcome is the same. *Killer Roller Coaster Goes Beserk 17 Die.* Below the headline in smaller letters, black letters: *Chain Snaps, Car Sails off Track and Plunges into Ocean.*

I put the scissors away. Take the rest of the newspaper and crush it into the wastepaper basket. The cut-out story with the pictures rests on the floor. I stand above it, looking at the words and pictures anchored to that spot, captured, held down, drowned words and pictures, never to move past that headline, past the *17 Die,* and the one who will never surface and walk up to me and tell me the real story, the truth, the reason for it all.

This is the last thing I do with the story: fold it up into a square, take out my wallet, and slide the square story into the slot under the coin pocket. I close the wallet and sit on the bed holding it.

part three

the story of macy

1973

I GOT INTO NURSING school only because of my mother. Okay? I am not straight-A's, study all the time, never cheat. That's just what my mother wanted the family to believe. My mother? She's like pearls. Or an ice pick. My mother lies. To everyone but me. In front of my dad, Mr. Factory-floor-manager, she's like oleo. Spreads herself over him, pretends to do everything he says. Butters his bread so thick he doesn't see the mold underneath. Only to me she's oleo gone rancid.

"Macy," she says, "be grateful, you little shit, don't make me look bad in front of the family."

I got into nursing school with a solid C average and the strings my mother yanked. Got it? I'm no teacher's pet, first with my hand up, extracurricular activity seeker. I did summer school twice. The same day I received the acceptance to Rutherford Nursing Hospital, I was sending in my application to the art school on the matchbook: if you can draw this you can be an artist.

All right. My mother lies. "Today I'm going to be different," she says on the day I turn sixteen. Which is July twenty-third, 1973. My mother bakes a cake even though the house is sweltering, the walls so hot my hands stick to them. The cake is seven layers tall. But because the oven is ancient, the racks bent by years of heavy roasts and chickens, the cake leans a couple of fractions of an inch off center. I know. I measure it. I can tell by an eighth of a teaspoon what kind of mood my mother is in. With a sieve or a spatula I can size her up. My mother is Avon blush, too thick. My mother is drunk on my birthday. My mother is quicksand trying to pull me in.

The radio on the shelf is tuned to WNEW—the gush of violins and a harp, salted voice of some old man singing. My mother puts the cakes in the oven: three on the bottom shelf, four on the top. Every year, the same thing. The three on the bottom burn and the four on the top don't bake all the way through. She says, "It balances out in the end." And, "Be grateful you're getting a cake." And, "You little shit, another year older." The windows are open, two fans turning high speed. She says, "Come here."

"What?" I say. I'm studying the Sam Goody's advertisement, deciding between Led Zeppelin or The James Gang, on sale through Saturday.

"Dance with me." She unties her apron and drops it to the floor. Blinks her eyes. This is one of her old games. Dancing the funk away. She has me for the whole damn morning because it's my birthday, and because she is responsible for it being my birthday, she thinks she has the right to torture me with her dancing. There's no getting out of it. She'd just keep bugging me till I give in. Easier just to get it over with.

When I enter the wingspan of her arms, I hold my breath. I don't want to smell her right away, the soap and hair spray, the five fingers of liquor over ice she rocks in her hand.

"An occasion, to drink to the birth of my daughter. The one, the only Macy, juvenile delinquent, sweet sourball, holiest of holy terrors." She swallows two and a half fingers, the ice sliding to her lips. "And now a toast to me. Right? To my being gutted open like a damn fish sixteen years ago." The glass empties and she dances me into the living room, around the cube-shaped tables, gliding next to their shiny plastic corners, leaning her head to the side and smiling, rubbing my palm with her palm.

I could say I am taller than my mother by half a head, taller and leaner, my bones wrapped with tight muscles. But in that dancing she leads me as if I were six and not sixteen. Her arms, covered with moles and freckles, have muscles bigger than mine; her biceps rise up when she spins me out and pulls me back at the end of the song.

I could say I am faster, smarter, more with-it, righteous, got my act together. Not going to be like her. Better believe it. But she has me jammed next to her, feeling the way her hips know every note and her feet follow. Her eyes don't even have to look for her to move perfectly with the beat, while I have to eye the walls, count the one-two, one-two-three of my feet moving, trying not to step on her feet.

I could say I look like her. But I don't. Not the flushed auburn hair. Not the dark eyes under heavy lids, shaded with number five eyeliner to make them heavier, droopier, sexy, falling. No. Even the mouth that everyone says is the same is not. She knows how to use every inch of her mouth, every curve up or down, every lick to her lips, every grimace, grin, pout, kiss. My mouth has outbursts.

She spins me. Dips. Stretches my arm out in tango. Laughs the laugh, which is like mine—part cruel, laughing at. All in the throat, pitched low, like a stinging fastball right at the heart.

I ask her, "Why do you have to be like this?" Every year on my birthday, getting drunk as if it is a day to be mourned.

"I could ask the same of you. But it's really quite simple. I made you, you made me."

She laughs. I don't.

What version of the truth do we tell?

My mother says, "Today I'm going to be different." She's been telling me she was going to be different forever. Been saying it since I was five, starting kindergarten.

Walked me to school with my feet in their yellow boots, real rubber. Up the boots, clips, that's what I called them. "Buckles," my mother said. She walked in her high heels ahead of me. I was pleased at the way my yellow boots left puddles of gold wherever I stepped. We cut across the parking lot at Shop Rite, behind the Laundromat and Chinese restaurant and Discount Millie's. We walked a long time and crossed over into the nicer part of town. "Hurry up," she said, "be grateful you've even got a mother who'd do this." Her raincoat, black, unbuttoned, flapped around her as if she had broken wings. "Be grateful," she said, "because this is the last day I'm doing this. Better stop watching those boots and pay attention to where you're going." She had her head swung sideways, surveying me with one eye, and I looked around. We were on a street with wide trees touching red leaves one side of the road to the other. I saw a house with a birdbath in the front yard. The statue's arm was cracked off at the elbow, the basin on the ground full of leaves. Someone in the house at the window had on a hat of feathers.

I made pictures in my head all the way to school. A map of pictures: the house with the birdbath and pin-striped awning, turn in the direction of the fire station, stop at the corner with the crossing guard. My mother had taken my hand in hers and told the crossing guard, "First day of school for the little one. We're very excited, but I bet you've seen this a thousand times?" Crossing guard in his blue pants and a yellow coat. Not as yellow as my boots. He had old white hair sticking out from under his cap, and he held a cigarette in his mouth. His voice sounded like the cigarette burning. "Cute little girl you got there," he said but he wasn't looking at me. No. His eyes were on my mother, on her dark red lipstick and pink dress. The dress she wore to go out to play cards with my dad, Mr. Poker-player-never-wins. "She's a doll, isn't she?" my mother said. The crossing guard let out a smoke signal, yes. He stepped into the street, stopping the traffic with a salute to the cars, and we crossed.

On the other side I made more pictures: fence with a pointy top, a fire hydrant, a house with five dogs, their hair curled and bows on the top of their heads. A gully. A house with bushes like lollipops.

"Turn down this street," my mother said, pointing at the street sign. Her high heel caught in a deep sidewalk crack. My yellow boots were solid on the ground. My mother pitched forward, her arms waving at the air, hands trying to grab the air, good luck. My mother fell. Her coat and dress slid up, her slip slid down. She was on her hands and knees in the grass between the sidewalk and the street. The grass where the dogs did their business, and my mother checked her hands and knees for any business. "Shit," she said. "Goddamn it. I hate this street. Carp Road, more like crap road. Look at these houses, will you?" She stood up and looked at the houses. Putting her hands on her hips as if the houses made her fall. The houses with their lost paint were tall and pointy. "They've been here so long they don't give a good goddamn." Each house had different colored stairs—blue, red, green—and each house had a swing set. "Catholics," my mother said, "be grateful you don't live there in those houses where they make their children live in the basements."

She picked a couple more pieces of grass off her leg and we walked to the end of Carp Road, where the school slouched low to the ground on red cinder blocks. A flagpole in its front yard. My mother said, "This is it, Macy. Be grateful you're getting an education." Her slip still showed but I didn't say anything. I added the picture to my map: my mother in front of the school, stains of grass on one knee, her red mouth, shaking her head. She said, "You've got it made, brand new school, not like what I had to put up with." I drew two more things on my map: devil horns on my mother's head and me alone, walking into the school door.

But my mother walked with me through the door. When we got to my classroom, my mother held my hand again. She bent down and said in my ear, "Today I'm going to be different, Macy, remember that." Her mouth breathing into me. Different. I stood there seeing her being the same, whispering promises to me that no one else could hear. She put her hankie with the bluebird stitched in the corner, small and ready to fly away, in my coat pocket and said, "Here's my advice: do everything the teacher says, sing when she says to sing, draw when she says to draw, be a good good girl, don't do anything that would make me look bad. Be grateful, I love you, I'll be here at noon."

Be grateful. I love you. I'll be here. My mother turned around and left, her slip back where it should be. Invisible, gone.

My mother wasn't there after I sang and drew and was a good good girl. In the hallway, the red bell rang. The school doors opened. Mothers waited under their umbrellas to collect their children. The rain fell against the leaves and the soggy leaves fell against the street. There were two of us left. With no mothers.

I said, "I've got a map."

The other girl said, "Yeah?" She didn't have boots, just some polished Mary Janes and dull anklets.

"Yeah," I said. "My mother is always late because she's a nurse and has to help sew people up."

The girl said, "My mother never goes out of the house."

The rain landed on my head and bounced off my nose. I pulled the hood of my raincoat up but I couldn't remember how to tie the strings into a bow.

The girl watched my fingers and said, "I can do that." She did. One, two, three, a bow.

I asked, "Where do you live?"

"One one nine Water Street."

"Where's that?"

"I know where it is. It's got a birdbath in front."

"Oh, and an awning?"

"Yeah, green and gold."

"I passed there on the way to school."

"Good, then you can pass it on the way home. Come on."

"Okay." I followed the map in my head, backwards, and the girl with the Mary Janes walked past the bushes like lollipops and the gully filling up with mud. The rain stung my hands.

The girl asked, "Does your mother cut people open?" She had on a sweater with daisies around the buttonholes under her raincoat without any clips that closed. Her hair was pigtailed, rubber banded at the ends. In her hand she carried a blue felt bag with a drawstring. Her face was thin. Like there wasn't enough flesh to go around. Her bones stuck out below her eyes and her chin and her cheeks, drew her face in like the drawstring of her bag. Her eyes and nose and mouth sat really close together.

I said, "My mother has six hearts from dead people she operated on and she keeps them in the kitchen cupboard in mayonnaise jars."

"Yeah?" she said.

"Yeah." I told a lie to see what it would do. I followed a map in my head with my mother crossed out. In her place I drew the girl who lived in the house with the birdbath and the mother who never left. "My name is Macy."

"I'm Maybelline Blue."

She knew there were no hearts in the cupboard but she didn't say so. I saw her eyes squint when I told my lie as if she were trying to read something far away.

"Your mother forgot about you," she said.

And I knew what a lie could do was show the truth.

"I got cat whiskers in my bag," she said. "Want to see?" We stopped at the house with the five dogs but the dogs weren't in the yard. The yard was all dirt. The rain made the yard melt and rubber bones rise up from the mud. Maybelline Blue opened the bag and said, "Look." I looked inside and saw the whiskers, wiry threads of white. She said, "My mom hates cats but my dad doesn't. My dad built a house in the backyard for the cats. There's little beds and sometimes he sleeps out there. My mom's allergic to cats. When my dad comes in the house, she sneezes."

She closed the bag and we walked to the street with the crossing guard but he wasn't there. The cars going by wiped the rain from their windows. Maybelline Blue moved her head left to right, right to left, and stepped into the street when there were no cars on our side. She said, "Come on," and raised her hand to the cars that were coming the other way and they stopped. We stepped up on the curb and Maybelline Blue waved at the cars.

When we got to her house, she said, "My dad's a detective. He could put your mother in jail."

"No, he can't."

"I'll walk with you again if you want."

"Okay."

In her house, her mom pushed the curtain aside, knocked on the window, and on her shoulder sat three little birds. Maybelline Blue lived on the block where the houses had no stairs. Brick below the windows, brick walkways from the driveways to the front doors, and brick patios. Lime-green lawns were always mowed and edged. Caterpillars hung on their threads from the maples. I walked and counted eleven more blocks to my house. All the houses on my block were thin, two stories, beige with small windows, and tied to one another by telephone wires.

My mother wasn't home. I made a mayonnaise sandwich—white bread and Hellman's—and sat at the kitchen table with the Lazy Susan and nothing on it, turning it around and around. Watched the clock with its arrows pointing at the time I was learning to tell: 12 and 3 and 6 and 9. The little arrow moved from 12 to 3 to 6. I moved from kitchen to sofa to watching out the window with its pane cut into smaller panes by strips of black metal to the TV with the one pane.

When my dad got home, Mr. Galoshes-without-clips, he said, "Where's Mom?" No smell of dinner, no radio on, no calling out, Honey Bear, is that you?

"I don't know," I said.

The galoshes sucked the shoes off my dad's feet. My dad pulled the galoshes from his shoes. Put them on newspaper in the closet, put the shoes back on his feet over his grey socks. A cloud of mustache under his nose. The mustache moved when he talked. "You don't know where your mother is? Didn't she pick you up at school? She hasn't been here all day? Did she go out? Did she say when she'd be back?"

"No," I said.

He said, "You don't know anything, do you?"

"No." I still had my yellow boots on and he was staring at my boots.

"Jesus," he said and went to the phone; his finger stabbed into the holes below the numbers, the numbers circled faster and faster. After he made the phone call, he said, "Your mother is at your aunt Barbara's," his mustache moving up and down with each word. He smiled really fast as if Aunt Barbara had told him, make sure you smile.

I went to the refrigerator and took out the Hershey's chocolate syrup and milk. Got my glass. I stirred more and more chocolate syrup into the milk until it was nearly black. My dad, Mr. Still-smiling, drank it all.

"Macy," he said, "you're a good girl."

My mother was nowhere and then was back. I thought my dad was never going to stop beating the kitchen counter with the soupspoon. Probably all the noise he made woke my mother up from wherever she'd been sleeping like Sleeping Beauty for three days. But when she came in the front door she had not been sleeping. Not for a long time. She wore a new coat, bumpy and blue, with fur around the collar. My dad was sitting in the kitchen chair. I was on the floor with the coloring book my dad had bought me, coloring in a picture of life in colonial days: Indians in buckskins, squaws with baskets on their heads filled with Indian corn. Colonial dads in knee-high socks, holding muskets across their shoulders. Colonial moms wearing big bonnets and stirring the kettle in the side yard while their children in smocks and suits with short pant legs laughed and played in the wheat, never thinking, my mother ran away.

When my mother came back in her new blue coat, her brother was right behind her. He stood there and said, "Ira, it's not what you think. She's got an explanation. A good reason." Her brother, my uncle Mel, saw me looking at them, holding out my orange crayon that I used to color in all the big smiles in colonial life. Uncle Mel shoved his head to the side, like he was shoving what he just said away from my ears.

"Macy," my mother said. No smile. Nothing but my name.

"Go play in the other room," my dad said. I stood up and dropped the orange crayon on the coloring book.

My mother knelt down next to me. She said "Macy" again; this time the end of my name rose up. I didn't want to smell her new coat. I held my breath and counted one, two, three. I didn't want to smell her hair, all messy and falling over her eyes with the mascara smudged and runny. She threw her pocketbook down and pulled me into her arms and squeezed, and I had to take a breath, a huge breath of her until she let go and I could run to my bedroom.

My uncle Mel went home. I came out of my bedroom and squinted from the hallway at my mother flattening the truth into something else, something yummy because my dad was smiling. Even though she had been gone for three whole days and came back with a new coat with a thin fur collar, my dad let her talk in his ear. She put her one hand on his heart, the other held onto his belt buckle. He didn't yell. Didn't say a word. She stepped right on the colonial life in my coloring book. When she kneeled down, her high heels divided up the crayons and shoved them across the floor. Red and yellow rolled under the refrigerator. My dad put his face in her messy hair. I couldn't hear what she said but she was talking a mile a minute. Her hand was smoothing his heart and her other hand was undoing his belt buckle, unzipping his pants, moving inside his underwear until she brought out a piece of him I'd never seen before. A part of him that was pointing right at her. My mother, whose mouth had been busy talking in his ear, saying all he wanted to hear, bent down and licked. She kept licking until he sort of jumped. After that he said, "God, I love your mouth," and she said, "Yeah, well, don't get too attached to it." She went over to the kitchen sink and spit. Her coat all buttoned up.

"Your mother ran away," Maybelline Blue said when we walked to kindergarten the day after my mother was back.

I told my dad, Mr. Not-really-listening, that he didn't have to drive me to kindergarten because Maybelline Blue and her mom were going to walk me there. Wasn't that different from the truth. Really. Maybelline's mother would watch us walk as far as she could out the picture window. My dad said, "Okay." He couldn't find the sugar but he stirred his coffee anyway. Mr. Not-asking are you sure you don't want me to take you? Mr. Not-saying your mother ran away. He stirred his coffee. My mother still sleeping, her new coat lying across one of the kitchen chairs.

Maybelline and I walked to school with her two sisters, Tiny and Tina. They were in second and third grade. Tiny was bigger than Tina but younger. Tina walked pigeon-toed, following the edge of sidewalk to keep her from walking into Tiny. Tiny was tall and plump and wore dresses with cross-stitching and lace. Her feet were small and she took twice as many steps as Tina.

"Your mother ran away," Maybelline said again.

Tina said, "Maybelline, shut up."

"Why?" Maybelline asked.

Tiny said, "If you don't have nothing good to say, don't say it."

I said, "My mother didn't run away, she was at my aunt Barbara's."

Tiny, Tina, and Maybelline stopped at the corner with the crossing guard who wasn't the man with the old hair under his cap. The crossing guard rubbed his hands together. He was shivering, wasn't wearing a raincoat, and the drizzle stuck in his hair like soda bubbles. He waved us forward, holding one hand above his head like the skeleton of an umbrella.

On the other side, Tiny and Tina skipped up ahead.

Maybelline said again, "Your mother ran away."

"How do you know?" I asked.

"My dad said so. He works at night at the police station. He has a bullet stuck forever in his shoulder."

"But how does your dad know my mother ran away?" I asked.

"She told him."

"I don't believe you." The rain was pouring down. We were yelling over the rain.

Maybelline said, "She was drunk and disorderly and he took her to the jail and your mother told him who she was and said she had every right to run away from home. My dad wrote it down in his book."

⟿

WE DANCE. ANOTHER tune. "Sixteen is for the birds," my mother says. Her feet say *bossa nova, cha, cha, cha.* She smells like fingernail polish remover. Cotton balls steeped in the stuff congregating like clouds on her dresser. She paints her nails especially for the day, Congo Rubine: color of birth. I make a birthday wish. I will never have babies, I will never be a mother. My mother pulls me closer, her hair dyed a bright red, her lips smeared with the lipstick from the tube called Sunset. The top five buttons of her sleeveless crimson dress undone, her breasts hilled up in her bra. We dance.

The house is dim, the shades down, the sun kept out, but the heat wells up inside anyway, comes right through the cheap walls. The houses are pressed up against one another. I can reach my arm out the window in my bedroom and pass a joint through the air to the house next door, to the bedroom where Hissy waits with her fingers in their roach-clip pose. Hissy once said, "The houses were built this way, all the same, just like how the days in the factories were all the same."

My mother dances, pulling me along. The house ninety degrees inside. The cakes hot and swelling in the oven. My mother humming into my ear.

I say, "I'm meeting Maybelline and Hissy at two." My hand sticking to the flesh over her shoulder blade.

"Oh, and just where do you think you're going?" she says.

"Out," I say to the back of her head, to the bright red, the bloodshot hair.

My mother pushes me away. Hard muscles even in her hands. My shin hits the corner of the plastic cube table. She walks back to the bottle of liquor on the kitchen counter. "Good, go. Just as typical as you can be, Macy."

"Yeah, how typical this all is. Do you think you're Cleopatra? What the hell's so different about you? Nothing. You're not a molecule different."

"Here's what's different," my mother says. "I don't care, have never cared what you think, even though I'm supposed to. Written in stone somewhere: mothers have to care. Supposed to give a shit, capital S."

In the dimness of the room I can see how her mouth works, faster than the words she is saying. Her mouth stops moving and still words come out.

She says, "Be grateful, I'll be leaving soon."

The oven timer goes off. My mother refills her glass.

To be different you have to be different from something else. My mother was not different from herself. Not with me. With my dad, my mother was a smooth sheet, Woolite, a lullaby. Here's how it worked. My dad, Mr. Nose-to-the-grind-stone, wanted one thing and one thing only: security. Worked six days a week. Believed with his whole heart in appliances. Saved money in a tin box in enve-lopes marked *dryer*, *upright vacuum cleaner*, *dishwasher*, *electric carving knife*, and one more envelope marked *Macy*.

He lectured. Liked to lecture, to hear his voice get going and rehash the same words over and over: "Macy, buckle down, do your homework, stay out of trouble, don't become one of those hair-to-your-ankles flower bums, hitchhiking to San Francisco." "Macy, pressure is what kills people, you've got to stay calm and steady and work, work, work." He worked. My mother met him while he was working; Mr. Delivery-man had a truck and a route. He liked what he saw: my mother, a good worker, a nurse, calm and steady. Marriage. Baby. Pass it on. Like a factory. My dad, Mr. Beginning-middle-end, knew about raw material to fin-ished product. He thought my mother was there to help him manufacture Macy into calm, steady. And she was convincing. He believed what she said about me. He just forgot about quality control.

I have a picture of the three of us ice skating on the frozen duck pond. My mother had told my dad the night before the picture was taken, "Macy got all A's on her report card." My dad, Mr. Didn't-ask-for-the-evidence, said, "Great, let's celebrate—we'll go ice skating tomorrow." There we are circling each other. Hot chocolate waiting in a thermos for me and a thermos of coffee with whiskey for them. C's and a D lined up on my report card with the words, *doesn't apply herself*.

It wasn't his fault that he couldn't see my mother entirely. My mother was hooks and eyes, venetian blinds, Halloween. He liked her dressed up and taking the dress off. He just never got beneath the pretend. Or didn't want to. Or wouldn't. Sometimes the perfect fit comes from not looking at how it doesn't fit. My dad didn't look.

My family does not say that my mother ran away. They call it my mother's vacation. My dad, Mr. Always-whistling-the-same-tune, said, "Sometimes pressure builds up too fast, too much and blows. When it blows, you gotta go."

My mother blew and went twice more.

The next time was the day the mothers came to school in third grade for Show and Tell. She picked out our clothes the night before: black stretch slacks and yellow-and-black-striped stretch tops. We looked like bees. She said, "Today I'm going to be so, *so* different, Macy, you won't recognize me." She took out her eyelid colors she kept in her dresser drawer. Leaned on the dresser top and smoothed on yellow with a tiny brush. Mascaraed her lashes until they poked straight out like bee stingers. Her lips she colored in red mixed with a dot of black until they were two identical archways. My mother hummed "Night and Day." Teased and hair-sprayed her hair. "Let's go," she said. Brought a bag with her like we were trick or treating.

The other mothers shifted from foot to foot when they saw my mother. Their hands skittering to their mouths and brushing invisible lint off their dresses. The teacher, Mr. Lofitt, came over. Waved me to go sit down. He had ice-cold hands that slapped your wrists if you did anything bad and he made you go sit in the hallway. When I got to go there I was glad.

"Mrs. Kahn," he said. My mother blinked her stinger eyes at him. "It is not Halloween until next week," he said. The other mothers nodded.

Maybelline Blue passed me a note: *Roses are red, bee turds are yellow, I think your mom's brain is made out of Jell-O*. I peered over at Maybelline, my eyes blinked and I shrugged my shoulders.

"Big deal," I said. "So what?"

"So what," Maybelline said.

I folded up the note to add to Maybelline's other notes. All the notes that told the absolute truth.

"Children," my mother said loudly, and the whole class watched my mother. "Your teacher says that today is not Halloween and that is true." She walked to Mr. Lofitt's desk, the black board behind her with the words WELCOME MOMS outlined and shaded in with chalk.

Mr. Lofitt said, "Mrs. Kahn," in his I-don't-like-what-you're-up-to voice.

My mother raised her hand into a stop sign and Mr. Lofitt stopped, his mouth closed, lips pulled together in a thin, straight line. I sat in the middle row in the middle of the room. Mr. Lofitt turned and stared at me as if this were my doing. I wanted to go sit in the hallway like I usually did twice a week. "Causing trouble again," Mr. Lofitt would say to me. And I'd say, "Guess so," stand up before he had a chance to say stand up, and go into the hallway. I wanted to go sit at the desk in the hallway with the smooth top and put my head down and sleep.

Maybelline tied her braids together under her neck. The other mothers stood by the globe with America upside down. "Children," my mother said, "today is no different than any other day. The sun rises. It is not Halloween. But why must we wait to do and try something different? That is the question I bring with me for today's Show and Tell."

"Mrs. Kahn, please," Mr. Lofitt said. "This is all well and good but we have not said the Pledge of Allegiance yet."

My mother said, "I'm sure one morning without the Pledge of Allegiance will not harm the children. In fact, they will appreciate it all the more tomorrow. Don't you agree, Moms?" My mother looked in their direction, at the moms in two rows like a pack of crayons waiting to be taken out and colored with. "Well," one mom said, and my mother said, "See? All agreed. Now, children, let me begin.

"There once was a farmer in New Jersey, Who was always in too much of a hurry, He made a mistake, Fed his vegetables his steaks, The next morning the cabbages mooed like Guernseys."

Under the tight stretch knit of my mother's shirt there was no hiding the edges of her bra. Or that the flatness of those black and yellow stripes on her shirt was lifted into two definite pointed hills. Mr. Lofitt's arms were crossed. His fingers pinched the grey fabric of his suit coat while his eyes looked everywhere except directly at my mother. My mother was not finished. Mr. Lofitt didn't know how to get her to stop.

She looked out at the class and said, "That was a limerick. A crude form of verse that I'm sure Mr. Lofitt has shared with you."

Billy Rubin next to me said, "Your mom is nuts."

"Yeah," said Susie Buccino, "nutty nut nut."

I lifted up one end of my lip in the sneer my mother said would freeze on my face permanently. That shut Billy and Susie up.

My mother clapped her hands and opened the bag. Maybelline passed me another note: *Want to come over today? Cat had kittens.* I nodded. All of Maybelline's cats were named Cat. Maybelline tapped her pen on the desk and that meant good.

"Now," my mother said, "let me illustrate how a nurse, like myself, uses imagination. In the operating room you need to picture all sorts of things." She rolled a cabbage out of the bag and asked, "What do you do with cabbages?" She answered, "Coleslaw, of course. But today this cabbage will show the art of scalpel work. Who knows what a scalpel is?"

Lawrence waved his arm and stood up when my mother pointed at him. "A scalpel is a surgical knife."

My mother said, "Right you are, little man." She took a scalpel out of her purse. I squinted at her, and her eyes were like two black holes with all that mascara and eyeliner. She was smiling the whole time. Teeth showing. Like she enjoyed this, instead of what she said while she had picked our clothes out: "Be grateful that I'm even going to do this dog and pony act. Show and Tell. What a bunch of crap."

Tommy Esposito asked, "Can I hold the scalpel?"

"Holy Mary," one of the other moms said.

And my mother said, "Not today, sonny." She set the cabbage on the beige blotter on Mr. Lofitt's desk. "First I'm going to make an incision in the cabbage. I'll cut one small hole out and then another. Mr. Lofitt, perhaps we could all sing a song while I'm doing this. Macy, what songs are you learning?"

I touched my knees with the black stretch slacks too tight over my skin. My hands and arms were useless. No bee wings to fly out the window.

Carla DiCarlo mouthed at me, "Not the spider one."

"I don't know," I said.

My mother did not look up at me. "Macy, what was that one you were singing the other day, about a spider?"

Mr. Lofitt said, "Fine, we'll all sing, and then Mrs. Kahn should be done and we can say the Pledge of Allegiance and the rest of the moms can share what they brought." Mr. Lofitt pulled his pitch pipe from his pocket. Blew C. We all hummed C and on the third snap of Mr. Lofitt's finger, sang. At the end of the song the moms clapped. One mom bumped the globe. My mother kept looking over at Mr. Lofitt. Her scalpel dug into the cabbage. The pieces of cut-up cabbage she put right into the bag.

"Done," my mother said. She turned the cabbage around to face us. The cabbage was a face. Nose dented in at the middle. Mouth in a thin-lipped frown. Lines carved in deep rays from the sides of the eyes.

Maybelline said, "It looks like Mr. Lofitt."

And it did. But no one else said it did. No one said anything. Mr. Lofitt's cabbage face stared out at us. For as long as it would have taken to say the Pledge of Allegiance, the cabbage face watched us. Mr. Lofitt went over to my mother, took the cabbage, and dropped it into the bag by her foot. I heard the cabbage hit against the floor.

My mother walked back to my desk, left the bag with me, and said in my ear, "Be grateful, Macy, that I'm different or you'd grow up to be just like Mr. Lofitt." She kissed me on my cheek. I could feel the slide of lipstick on my skin.

Billy Rubin said, "Yuck."

My mother stood up and said, "Goodbye, class. Good luck, Mr. Lofitt." She walked out the door, everyone watching the swing of her hips.

At Maybelline's, the kittens had holes in their necks. Five kittens with five holes. The holes were close to their neck bones. When I dipped my finger into the hole, I could feel the kitten's bones moving when the kitten moved its head.

"Inbreeding," Maybelline said.

"What?" I asked.

"Inbreeding means the breeding of closely related individuals. They are all related to one another. Like in the Bible where it says you shouldn't marry your brother or cousin because then the babies would have deformities. Like the holes."

"How come you know so much?"

"I'm smart. My mother says I could be a genius. I don't want to be one but my mother says I might not have a choice."

"So smart your brain would explode?"

"Not likely."

"Good. I wouldn't want to scoop it up and put it back in your head."

My mother was not home when I got home from Maybelline's. She disappeared for four days. "Vacation," my family said on Friday night. Uncle Mel sat at the table, his mustache waxed and as black as the little remaining hair on his head. He was working on biting his fingernails without Aunt Selma catching him. Aunt Selma was counting plates and silverware and arranging them on the kitchen counter.

Aunt Barbara sat at the edge of her chair, legs crossed. She said, "Funny time to take a vacation."

Aunt Toby wet her finger and wiped a dot of stray lipstick off Aunt Barbara's skin. My cousin Julie, who thought she looked just like Jackie Kennedy but didn't, was chewing gum. Wrigley's Spearmint. The only kind she liked. But once she started chewing, her teeth couldn't stop. Her mouth was in motion until she pulled the gum out and wrapped it up in the foil sleeve. She was in secretarial college and was engaged to get married. She didn't pay much attention to me except to give me a stick of gum if I left her alone. Uncle Mitch was shuffling a new deck of cards.

My dad, Mr. Let's-just-play-poker, said, "Deal already, for chrissake." Coffee bobka on the table, along with the red, white, and blue poker chips and Southern Comfort in shot glasses.

Everyone sat down and Uncle Mitch gave the deck of cards to Aunt Selma. He said, "Vacation or not, it's not our business."

Aunt Selma said, "Whaddya mean it's not our business, she's my little sister."

"Not so little anymore." Aunt Barbara recrossed her legs and picked up each card as soon as Aunt Selma laid it down.

"The point is," Aunt Selma said, "I went to Myra and said, 'Isn't my sister supposed to be here today,' and she said, 'Why no, Selma,' in that squeaky voice, 'no, Selma, she took today and the next three days off.' Raised her eyebrows like she was one up on me." Aunt Selma moved the cards around on the table. Each of her fingernails was long and pointy like a surgical instrument. Aunt Selma was a surgical nurse. She always gave me a quarter when she came over and sat me on her lap and told me about diseases.

Aunt Toby said, "Myra only got that job because her uncle bought the pediatrics wing."

Aunt Barbara said, "She's a terrible nurse. You ever have to work a shift after her? It's a stinking mess."

Aunt Toby nodded and Aunt Selma said, "That's the god's own truth."

Aunt Barbara was in her favorite card-playing outfit, pale pink blouse, semisheer, and I could almost see through it. I was always trying to see through it to what Aunt Barbara called her underwire bra, which I pictured as a telephone wire strung from arm to arm holding her breasts up. Her breasts, much larger than even my mother's or Aunt Toby's or Aunt Selma's, rested on the kitchen table. Her cards fanned out in an almost straight flush before her. She wore blue stretch pants and her pink mules. Always, first thing when she came in the door and took off her coat and we all could see her card-playing outfit, she would say, "I'm just like Ann-Margret in this get-up." Her hair was just like Ann-Margret's, flipped up in the back, bangs to her eyebrows, rinsed with as close as she could get to Ann-Margret's hair color.

My mother and her sisters, all nurses.

Uncle Mel said, "Can't you talk about anything else but the hospital?"

Aunt Selma said, "I was speaking about my sister, for your information, Mister. I was saying how she arranged for the four days off."

I was sitting with my back against the kitchen door. From there I could see their legs shifting. Shoes sliding an inch forward, an inch back. The run in Aunt Selma's stocking, up her shin. Worn-out edge of Uncle Mitch's pant cuff. My dad's work shoes, polished every other night, like mirrors, and I could see the underneath of the table where Uncle Mel stuck a card in the leaf hinge.

The linoleum lifted up from the floor next to the wall. Under the table where all those shoes were moving, there were pieces of the linoleum rubbed away, pieces of the mustard and ketchup colors and the bits of blue. Not like at Maybelline's, where the floors were shiny and lay flat. No one at Maybelline's lied or cheated at the kitchen table. Her whole house was modern and matched. Not bits of this and that, rummaged from a dark, moldy second-hand store, like at my house. Even my family was like that: mismatched, as if we came from a bargain basement, all argyle and plaid and polka dots clashing but pretending we didn't, that we really just had style.

I saw Aunt Toby patting my dad's arm, saying, "It's just another vacation, Ira. She needs them. She works so hard."

No one looked at me so I crawled under the table and took the queen of diamonds from the leaf hinge.

My mother came back after those four days with a transistor radio and rabbit fur mittens. Twirling around in the kitchen with the mittens over her head. She made lasagna and apple pie. Picked me up. Kissed my cheek. Set me in the kitchen chair and said, "Life is one wild ride after another." She stood the rabbit fur mittens in the center of the table. Lit candles beside them. Called me "My little rabbit, my peach, my seashell." Her smile was huge, miles of teeth. She said, "Let's get ready for Daddy." Took my hand and we ran through the house to the bathroom. Called me "My biscuit, my rum cake, my gold nugget girl."

"Mom, I got a gold star in reading."

"Gold," she said. "Do you know the butcher has gold eyes?"

"No."

"Silly me, of course you wouldn't. Now hand me the bubble bath." The water filling up the tub. Hot and foggy in the bathroom. My mother clearing the fog from the mirror with a washrag. Looking at herself, tilting her head side to side, pouting up her lips, winking.

"Mom," I said.

"Not now, Macy." She was touching her face. Her fingers curving over her eyelids, her nose and ears, pinching the skin on her neck, putting her whole hand over her mouth. "Get in the bath," she said. "Don't come out until I say to." The front door was opening.

My dad said, "Macy? Sweetheart? Sweetheart, are you here?" My mother lowered her hand from her mouth and the smile, the huge smile, was back in place.

I stayed in the tub. The bubbles rose up into clouds around my neck and knees. My mother laughed. The radio came on and my mother was shouting, "Oh, I love this song, it's our song, remember, Ira, remember?" I stayed in the tub. The bubbles floated and banged into each other, broke apart, combined into bigger bubbles that sank into the water. My mother said, "Dance with me, Ira, please Ira, please, please, pretty please?" My dad, Mr. Velveeta-melting-cheese, said, "Where have you been?" My mother laughed and laughed and said, "Oh Ira, let's just dance, forget all that." I stayed in the tub until the bubbles disappeared and I could see my skin pink as a skinned rabbit. I got out. Put my clothes on. Climbed up on the edge of the bathtub and opened the medicine cabinet so I could see in the mirror. I tried on my mother's huge smile but it didn't fit.

The living room was dark. I walked barefoot across the scarred wood. My feet left wet prints, two heels and ten toes. When I got to the doorway, I squatted down. On the radio I heard a trumpet like wind, violins, a man singing. In the kitchen my dad and mother danced. No fox trot or waltz. Nothing with any steps they had to count. Just the two of them close together, moving their hips and knees. Noses touching. Foreheads. Both her arms pulled behind her, caught in one of my dad's hands. Holding her. Her breasts mashed into my dad's shirt. My mother saying, "You're hurting me." Dancing, but they hadn't moved an inch from where they started. My dad saying, "I never hurt you, nothing I do makes a ripple. It's the other way around." "Oh Ira," she said and she kissed his eyelids and right below his eyes like there might be tears there. But if there were, she took them away. She said, "Stop talking nonsense." Slid her lips down to his mouth and kissed my dad. With her lips working their charms, he couldn't say a word. He let go of her hands.

I saw that my mother was stronger than my dad. Watched her kiss him and maneuver him into a corner. That's where he lived, in the smallest corner of her heart. But watching him, his hand smoothing down her hair, fingers touching down on her ears and neck and shoulders and back, I knew he thought he was dancing in her whole heart. That was the game she played and won, getting him to believe the opposite of what was true. Not me. I knew she ran away; it was no vacation. I just didn't say so. I was learning from her. Don't reveal the truth too quickly. There's more opportunity in turning your cards over one at a time.

↪

MAYBELLINE SAID, "YOUR mother ran away with the butcher."

"You're lying," I said. Three of the five kittens with the holes in their necks had died. The other two walked sideways past us.

"No, I'm not," she said. The cat house had green carpeting and a window seat. We sat on the window seat. Twenty-two cats in the cat house. "My mom heard it from Mrs. Linn on Saturday and Mrs. Linn is the butcher's best customer."

I said, "Mrs. Linn is ancient and she makes things up."

Maybelline said, "The butcher's wife told Mrs. Linn she didn't know where the butcher was and Mrs. Linn said to call my mom."

"Did she?"

"Yes. My mom talked to the butcher's wife who wanted to know if she should file a missing person report with my dad."

"Then the butcher was missing and not with my mother."

"No, he was missing with your mother." Maybelline's face had sprouted freckles over the winter. All of a sudden they were there. I watched how they shifted and slid over her face when she talked. Her hair was turning orange. She had been blonde that fall. Her eyebrows were still blonde, but when she turned nine her pigtails and bangs ripened like a pumpkin. Her eyes and nose and mouth were getting smaller, closer together, and she was almost as tall as Tiny.

"Did your dad find the butcher?" I asked.

"Yes. He found him at the butcher shop on Sunday grinding pork into sausage casings."

"My mother came home on Monday."

"I know," Maybelline said.

"She was on vacation."

"No, she wasn't," Maybelline said. "She ran away with the butcher. My dad said the butcher told him."

The two kittens with the holes walked sideways into the wall, stopped, and lay down. "Let's go inside," Maybelline said.

"Wait. If my mother ran away with the butcher, where did she go?"

Maybelline looked at me, her face scrunched up, squinting like she was working on a math problem. Eyes, nose, mouth so close to one another they could almost trade places. "I don't know exactly," Maybelline said, "but it was somewhere near the ocean."

"My mother hates to swim in saltwater."

"They probably weren't swimming."

"Then what were they doing?"

"Hanky panky."

"What's that?"

"Suspicious activity, like pretending not to be married when you really are married to someone else."

"Oh," I said.

"Oh," she said.

Inside Maybelline's house Tiny and Tina were singing a Beatles' song. Maybelline and I were in the utility room with the washer and dryer and the pantry full of Campbell's soup. She opened the door and we went into the back room where the parakeets and love birds and canaries flew around in their big cages. Maybelline's mom was scooping feed into a bucket. The birds flittered their wings and sang. The cages were taller than me. Once a day, Maybelline's mom let some of the birds out and they circled her. A yellow and green and pink and white and red hurricane. She was always showing us something about the birds and writing things down in a notebook with graph paper.

Maybelline said her mom was recording her observations and didn't even have to go outside to understand nature. "She's going to write a book."

"Why?" I asked.

"People like birds," Maybelline said.

"I don't."

"Hello, girls," Maybelline's mom said.

"Hi, mom," Maybelline said.

"Hello," I said.

"Macy, would you like to stay for dinner?" Maybelline's mom asked.

"I guess so," I said.

"Fabulous," she said. "Now girls, come look at this." She lifted a solid blue shawl from a smaller bird cage and inside two eggs were cracked. Two ugly baby birds without any feathers, their throats bobbing up and down, cried at their momma who sat on the perch picking at her feathers. "*Conuropsis carolinensis,* Carolina parakeet."

"Great, Mom," Maybelline said.

"Isn't it?" her mom said. "I've been trying to breed these Carolinas for over two years." We walked through the room, across the sheets on the floor, feathers floating in the air like snowflakes.

Upstairs Tina said, "I want to be Paul."

Tiny said, "You're always Paul, I want to be Paul."

"Tough," Tina said. "You're too tall to be Paul. You can be Ringo."

"Yuck," Tiny said. "I'll be John."

We walked into the bedroom. Blue walls and a white ceiling, pink dressers, three beds on pink iron frames. The bedroom took up the whole upstairs. There were six rectangular rugs that didn't even cover the whole floor. The middle of the room was empty and my bedroom could have fit right there.

Maybelline said, "I'll be Ringo and Macy can be George." I looked at Maybelline, who smiled her crooked smile at me, just half of the top lip twisted up into her nose. She knew I liked George the best.

"Okay, great," Tina said.

Maybelline turned the wastepaper basket upside down and pretended to play the drums, while Tiny, Tina, and I grabbed anything that could pass for a guitar and strummed. The four of us being boys, singing "Yeah, yeah, yeah." Being boys in our jumpers and blouses. I tried to stand the way I saw George stand on Ed Sullivan, straight and skinny, moving my fingers up and down the yardstick I had, watching my fingers and the other boys and not the audience. Tina shook her hair like how Paul shook his hair, smiling the whole time she sang. Maybelline beat and tapped on the wastepaper basket with her hands and looked like she knew what she was doing. Tiny imitated Tina and sang louder.

Tina said, "You're too loud, John."

"No, I'm not," Tiny said. "You're hogging the microphone."

Ringo kept beat. My fingers slid over the yardstick and I watched Tiny and Tina in their jumpers and knee socks pull each other's hair. Ringo sang, "Yeah, uh-huh, yeah."

Tiny and Tina stopped and shouted at Maybelline, "Ringo never sings."

"Girls," Mrs. Blue called.

"What?" the girls all said.

"Come down here this minute."

Tina said to Tiny, "Nice going stupid, now we'll probably have to listen to another one of her bird songs."

Downstairs, Mrs. Blue stood in the back room. She held a coaster in her hand. The birds perched and cleaned their feathers, turning their heads all the way around to dig into their backs. Cooing. Mrs. Blue pointed into the kitchen. She asked, "Who let that beast in here?" A cat sat on the counter licking its paw, smearing the paw over its face.

"Not me," said Tina, Tiny, and Maybelline.

Mrs. Blue sneezed five times in a row and said, "Macy, that leaves you. The cardinal rule of this house is no cats, remember? I've told you before."

"I don't remember letting the cat in."

"But you don't remember that you did not let the cat in, do you?"

"No," I said.

Mrs. Blue sneezed again. She put her finger up to her nose to try and keep the sneeze in but it came out. "I'm sorry, but you'll have to go home, Macy. I'm sure the next time you come over you'll remember to keep the door closed." She turned to the kitchen and hurled the coaster at the cat. The cat jumped from the counter but could not get a good foothold on the floor that Mrs. Blue waxed every week. The cat skated and ran in place until it kicked its legs against the base of the counter, pushed off, and ran out the door.

Maybelline walked me home. She gave me the answers to the spelling homework from her three-ring binder. She gave me the homework because I said, "Maybelline, give me the homework for spelling and grammar. I didn't have time to do it because my mother took me to the hospital to see the two-headed baby."

Maybelline kept walking. Her three-ring binder bumped against her thigh. Her mouth pushed out like her mom's did when her mom was chirping like the birds. "Uh huh," Maybelline said.

"Really," I said, "I'm not lying." Maybelline walked fast with her long legs. A lot of my lies to Maybelline were about the hospital and what I imagined my mother did there in the hours she spent in her nurse's uniform. Medicine interested Maybelline. "The two-headed baby sucked both the mom's breasts at the same time. The two-headed baby had four different colored eyes. One head slept while the other one stayed awake."

Maybelline asked, "Will they cut off one of its heads?"

"Of course."

"Good," she said.

She gave me the spelling: *planet, percent, polliwog, poison, prey, quake, queen, quest, quick, quote.* Memorize them. Use them in a sentence. Extra credit: write three more words beginning with Q. Bonus points for definitions. Maybelline wrote small, her letters compact, clipped to one another with right angles. The letters never went off the lines. They ended well within the margins. Like her eyes, nose, and mouth, the words stayed extra close to each other. The words had colons next to them and the definitions were arranged under *a, b,* and *c*'s with plurals and past tenses added. I folded the homework and put it in my book bag. Later, I would take it out and try to make my letters stay on the line, but they always strayed. Bumped into the words above. Inched past the pale red margins. The definitions were too much like Maybelline, brainy and neat, and I knew the teacher would catch on if I copied them. So, I left out some of the *b*'s and *c*'s and never wrote down past tenses. Sometimes I did the extra credit words. If I thought I could get away with it.

We stopped at the corner of my street. The air smelled of fried fish and sausages browning in already used oil. Maybelline did not come to my house. Did not walk down my street. Yet. She was getting closer. But there was too much on my street she didn't have definitions for: the turned-over garbage cans, the houses without lawns, the houses with cracked foundations, windows fractured and taped with masking tape, sidewalks heaving up, signs above doorways that said *Ironing* and *Home Sewing* and *Engine Repair*. Shops on the first floors of some of the houses that sold *Used TVs, Radios, Furniture. Knife Sharpening* in the middle of the block. *Palm Reading* on the end of the block where the wall of cement was six feet tall. Beyond the cement wall the bank of ragweed that tipped down to the highway. I knew this street like Maybelline knew her street with its lawn after lawn, houses sitting in the center of the lawns, each house waxed and polished. Smelling fresh and new from the lilacs and rose bushes and Tidy Bowl and Lysol.

Maybelline turned around, facing back to her house.

I asked, "Why doesn't your mom go outside?"

Maybelline said, "The last time she did, she was hanging up the clothes on the clothesline and my dad got shot."

"At your house?"

"No, my dad was arresting somebody when another guy came out of a bathroom and shot him before my dad could shoot back. My mom thinks that she disturbed the air when she went outside and that led to my dad getting shot. She thinks if she goes out again, he's dead for certain."

"That's crazy."

"Maybe it is, but my mom says if you believe something you have to stick with it no matter what."

We were standing next to the dry cleaner's. Hot air with the smell of ripe bananas leaked from the side vent. We could see into the back through an open door where three ladies were pressing pants and shouting at a man who stood in front of the presses with his arms crossed. Steam jumped into the ladies' faces every time they opened the presses. Their hair was wet and stuck to their foreheads and ears. We couldn't hear what they said but their mouths were wide open. The man just stood there shaking his head while they scooted the pant legs into the steam.

Maybelline asked, "Why do you think your mother runs away?"

"I don't know. You're the only one that says she runs away. Everyone in my family says she's on vacation."

"I think she runs away because she wants to disturb the air and see what happens."

⇝

MY MOTHER BANGS the cake pans on the kitchen counter. I dial Maybelline's phone number on the phone in my parents' bedroom.

Maybelline says, "Hello?"

"Guess what?" I say.

"What?"

"My mother's freaking out because she gave me life sixteen years ago."

"Is she drunk yet?"

"Yeah, surprise, surprise. Look, I'll be there in about half an hour."

"Okay," Maybelline says.

I go into my bedroom. Over to the open window. Just the skimpiest breeze coming in. All of it hot air. I yank on the Gumby that's tied to the string that hangs down along the window molding. The string goes out my window, across the two feet of air, and into Hissy's window next door. I can hear the tiny brass bells jingling in Hissy's bedroom. There are bells on my end of the string too, but I hold them in my hand so that my mother won't hear them ring. Hissy throws back her curtain. She isn't wearing anything and is brushing her teeth. "Jesus, Hissy," I say, "don't you know Mr. Tanner just bought a new telescope that sees around corners? He's been trying it out, aiming right at your window."

Hissy leans out the window and spits toothpaste down to the alley. "Fuck you, Macy," Hissy says and leans farther out, her breasts big as boulders. "And fuck you too, Mr. Tanner, you perverted dick brain." She rests her breasts on the windowsill.

"So," I say, "you aren't dressed yet?"

"Nah, it's too fucking-A hot. I don't want to wear anything."

"They'll love you at the quarry."

"Yeah, yeah."

Everything about Hissy is overheated. Her skin, her hair, her eyelids, even her nails are a glossy red like she's in a perpetual blush. She works in the Pabst factory and smells fermented. Bees follow her the second she steps outside. She started carrying one of those Chinese fans, four for a buck, from the variety store, to keep the bees from landing on her.

I say, "I'll meet you outside in fifteen minutes and don't forget to bring my present."

"I'm weighing it up right now," she says.

"Okay."

"One more thing—your hair looks like crap. Come on over here and Betty'll even it up for you."

"That's okay," I say, "you know what happened the last time Betty worked on my hair. Just go get ready."

"All right," she says and unsticks her breasts from the windowsill and the curtains fall back into place.

I don't even have to get the mirror out to know how crappy my hair is. Dishwater blonde, that's the color my mother calls my hair, only I've never seen dishwater this color, sort of like a lawn that never gets watered and has dried up. A muddy blonde with a hint of Palmolive green—maybe that's where the dishwater comes in. Thick, crappy hair with a temper. Sticks right out whenever it wants. There's no controlling my hair. I've tried. So has my mother.

When I was thirteen my mother cut my hair because Betty, Hissy's older cousin, cut my hair. Only Betty's haircut wasn't cut like you could see it. The cut was a trim and that was the problem; my mother couldn't see that Betty had done anything. All right, she probably hadn't. Maybe Betty trimmed a bit in the back, but she was stoned and was digging on my hair and telling me, "Macy, your hair is gango." Gango, the word she said she got from Lou Reed in the Village.

Hissy said, "Betty, Lou Reed would never say gango."

"Au contraire and spile," Betty said, "Lou Reed invented that word." But it was probably Betty who invented that word because Betty invented lots of words and added them together into poems that she wrote down in a composition notebook.

Betty lived with Hissy's family. In the basement, which they tried to fix up like it was just a regular room with windows, but it wasn't. The basement was dark no matter how many coats of white paint they used. Betty didn't care. She always had lots of candles going, which she got at the store that sold Catholic things. A gross of votives went for five bucks. Betty went through a gross in less than three weeks.

There were shadows all over those white walls while Betty was cutting my hair. Mostly, she just felt my hair, holding clumps of it in her hand. Hissy was rolling a joint, which usually took her forever. I said, "Christ, Hissy, any time now."

Betty said, "Sinko, Hissy." Which Hissy and I thought meant hurry up but Maybelline defined as ditto. Maybelline was reading one of Betty's books. Betty had a whole wall of books and magazines. Shelves on cinder blocks.

Maybelline said, "This book says that birth control is fundamental to understanding our bodies . . ."

Hissy said, "What the hell are you reading from?"

Maybelline said, "*Our Bodies, Ourselves*, and listen, it goes on to say that deeply felt attitudes and shame about sex prevent many of us from seeking information."

Betty said, "That book is nen, I mean, they analyze the important health issues of women's lives but are very down to earth and poss, not at all out-of-reach academic. It should be every woman's bible." Betty tugged my hair a little and I heard the scissors open and close but I didn't see any hair fall to the floor.

Hissy lit the joint. She could suck down half a joint in one suck. All the time hissing but a backwards hissing, on the in breath, not the out. None of us could hiss on the in breath. We watched Hissy to see if we could get how she did it, but we couldn't. The way she sucked in seemed just like how we all sucked in.

"Fuck," Betty said, "you better start another doobie, you hog."

"Yeah, yeah." Hissy passed the joint to me.

I took a drag and Betty put her hands on my head. "Macy," she said, "I can feel your mind expanding."

"Uh huh," I said.

"Inf, inf," she said. Which I was sure meant yes but Maybelline said it was one of the few words that Betty had shortened from a real word, the word infinity.

Hissy asked, "How do you get that it's infinity?"

Maybelline said, "Because Betty is into that cosmic thing of all being connected and it makes perfect sense when she's in agreement that she says infinity."

I was convinced Maybelline would wind up a brain surgeon, but Hissy said, "Not a chance. She'll be one of those weird math teachers."

Betty clipped the shortening joint into the end of a bobby pin and passed it to Maybelline. Maybelline sucked little sucks like she was sipping something too hot. But then she could hold it in her lungs forever.

Maybelline read us more about birth control—"'. . . an egg in a follicle . . . .'"

Hissy cracked up. "Egg in a follicle. That sounds like a two-for-one special at Howard Johnson's."

Maybelline said, "You should pay attention so you know what's going on with your body." I was smoking the last of the roach and Betty had her hands on my head again, which I didn't mind, the feeling of her hands, the weight of them keeping my head from floating off my body.

Hissy was sifting more pot on the James Gang album cover. "I know all I need to know."

"Oh yeah," I said, "so what kind of birth control do you use with Patterson?"

"We use a rubber, okay?"

"A rubber, that's it?" Maybelline said. She was turning pages fast and said, "The book says that in actual use, a good-quality condom's failure rate is quite high."

"Lookit, Maybelline," Hissy said, "I don't care what that book says, I just know I haven't gotten knocked up, so maybe they don't know everything."

The shadows from the candles were calm on the walls. Maybelline said, "Well, if you went on the pill, it'd be more reliable."

"Yeah," I said, "especially since you and Patterson are screwing every time you see each other, which is like every day."

Hissy said, "And just who's gonna get me the pill? My mom would cut her right hand off and place it on the altar at St. Bartholomew's and commit me before she'd let me go on the pill."

"Betty could do it," I said.

Betty took her hands from my head and picked up the scissors again. She said, "I could and I will because, nuck, I don't want you to get pregnant, Hissy."

We had asked Betty a few months before what kind of birth control she used. Betty had said, "I don't use dick." Literally. Which answered the question we really wanted to ask, which was did Betty go out with guys. Hissy said she'd never seen Betty with any. But we didn't ask the other question, even though Maybelline would have.

Maybelline had said, "In mathematics there are no mysteries because everything is questioned and put into terms of an equation, and that way you can always understand how it all adds up."

Hissy said, "Well, Betty isn't a fucking-A number, Maybelline."

"Hissy," I said, "Maybelline's just making a comparison. If we don't ask the question, we'll never know the answer."

"Well, I don't care," Hissy said. "No one's asking Betty anything."

The question didn't get asked. Hissy gave us updates on who Betty was hanging around with. No guys, of course. In fact, Hissy's whole family was always talking about Betty. They were serious when they gossiped. They mostly hated the truth because that put an end to their speculations. If Betty just walked in and said, I'm a lesbian, it would've taken all the fun out of guessing. They would have been pissed.

Hissy was chewing on the pot seeds. She was convinced they made her more stoned. "Hey Betty," Hissy said, "Patterson's coming over. Is it okay if I roll a joint for later?"

Betty said, "Only if you come with me on Wednesday to Planned Parenthood."

"Jesus Christ," Hissy said, "this whole fucking family loves to blackmail. Yeah, I'll go with you."

Betty snipped with the scissors but she was just snipping in the air. Over an hour went by and I don't think she cut more than a split end.

And that was the trouble. Because when I went home, my mother cut my hair with the scissors she kept in the kitchen drawer, along with the dried-up airplane glue, matchbooks, coasters, rubber bands. Half the scissors' blade had cracked off and the edges were dull from coupon cutting. My dad was sitting in his chair polishing his work shoes. My mother said, "Just a trim? Come on, Macy, what do you take me for, an idiot? Betty didn't do a damn anything. And if you don't sit down in this chair and let me cut your hair, I'll make an appointment at the beauty salon for a permanent."

"Okay," I said, "but you better not cut too much."

"Don't worry."

She sprayed my hair with water from the spray bottle she used for ironing. My mother said, "You're thirteen and just look at your hair. Do you think you're still ten years old? Christ, what a hassle to untangle this mess." She brushed my hair like she was brushing a dog, scraping my scalp and pulling my hair the whole time. "You should be grateful I'm going to get rid of these split ends, then maybe you'll look halfway pretty."

My mother? She's a fun-house mirror, a kaleidoscope, a guillotine.

The pot was wearing off but I was seeing the real her, good at playing house and wife even though she had told me a million times how much she hated it. She wore an apron with white and blue checks but she wasn't doing any cooking. Dinner was fish sticks and Tater Tots that she took out of the freezer, shook out on one of the black cookie sheets, and stuck in the oven. The tartar sauce and the plastic lemon filled with juice were already on the counter. I didn't want any fish sticks. There was something strange about them. I just knew when I put a fish stick in my mouth I'd be thinking about what was in it. Did they use the whole fish? Bones and eyes and scales put in some giant blender and then squeezed out into slabs that were coated with bread crumbs and cut into rectangles? At least the Tater Tots sort of looked like a potato. I could deal with them.

My mother stood in front of me to work on my hair. She said, "Keep your head straight, Macy." That meant I had to stare right at her breasts pushing out the words stitched on her apron—*Kiss The Cook*. Her hair bobbed past the blue-and-white-checked collar of her blouse. This month she was dying her hair Southern Mahogany and it had a car-wax sheen. She was letting her hair grow.

My dad, Mr. Never-change-a-hair-on-his-head, looked up, saw the scissors, and said, "You both look like goddamn peace hippies with your long hair."

I said, "What's so bad about peace?"

"Macy," he said, "use your brain; peace is not a natural condition of the world. Look around, why don't you. Wild animals are always hunting and killing. Why would it be any different for man?"

My mother said, "Oh Ira, I'm just keeping up with the fashions. Just because my hair is longer doesn't mean I've stopped believing in Richard Nixon, for god's sake."

"You'd better the hell not," my dad said. "Nixon's the best president this country's ever had."

Yeah, well, my mother believed in the underhanded, the roundabout, the two-faced. Why shouldn't she believe in Nixon? She kissed my dad and he said, "It's about time you cut her hair."

I said, "Well, I think Nixon is a creep and he should have to wear a sign that says *Warning, Dangerous Liar.*" I swung my peace medallion on its long silver chain.

"Macy, don't irritate your father," my mother said and jammed the comb in my hair and snagged some knots and pulled.

"Shit, owww," I said.

"Macy, don't use that word," my dad said. "You see what happens when the world loses order; you kids go crazy and don't respect the President, much less your parents. Well, you'll see. Richard Nixon will prove you all wrong. We'll win the war and get back to how things should be." He took out the brush with the brown, thin bristles that looked like his own hair and buffed the shoe polish on one of his shoes to a high shine.

The scissors clicked like cicadas right before they start their screeching. My hair was coming off fast, falling in clumps. I tried to feel where she was cutting, but she slapped my hands away from my hair. "Stop it, Macy," she said. "Can't you sit still for ten minutes? Christ, you were a restless baby and you haven't changed one iota."

"Just don't cut too much off."

"Macy. I'm doing a fine job, aren't I, Ira?"

My dad said, "Doesn't look like you've cut very much off at all. If I had those scissors, it'd be snip, snip and she'd look like Julie Nixon."

She cut around my ears until I could feel her breath with its little ending hum. "Take these," she said and handed me the scissors. She ran her hands under cold water and combed them through my hair. "There," she said. She took the towel from around my neck and said, "You look absolutely liberated."

My dad stared and said, "Not bad."

I touched my ears and could feel the space where there was no hair above them. Inches of my hair were on the floor. I did not want to look in the mirror. Halfway pretty. Yeah, right. I went into the hallway to the closet. Inside the closet was a full-length mirror with my mother's coat hanging over it. I pushed the coat to the side. My mother had cut five inches off the left side, six inches on the right. She cut my bangs on the diagonal, starting at the bridge of my nose and clipping a severe angle to each side. "Holy crap," I said, "I look like a Vulcan." My hair was pointy, all angles.

"Oh, Macy," my mother said, "you're exaggerating, as usual."

I let the coat fall back and said, "Exaggerating? I look like a cross between Dr. Spock and Mr. Spock."

She was sweeping up my hair. "It's fine. You look just fine."

My dad rubbed his shoes with the cuff of his work shirt and said, "Pretty as a picture."

I stole barrettes from the drugstore. Eight to a package: four fake gold, four tortoise shell. I slipped the package of barrettes up my coat sleeve. Maybelline talked to the druggist about the prescription for Tiny and Tina. I pushed a comb up my other sleeve. Black comb for men.

The druggist told Maybelline to make sure everyone used their own towels, that pink eye was highly contagious. Maybelline said, "I never get sick." I slid Midnight Mascara and Autumn Blush fingernail polish next to the comb and went out the door. The door tinkled its jingle bells.

Maybelline came out and said, "Okay, what'd you take?"

"What do you mean?" I said.

She said, "It's not too obvious."

We walked across the street past Rosemary's Beauty Salon. Rosemary had her scissors in her mouth, getting ready to cut a fingerful of some old lady hair. I said, "I needed a few things." We walked behind the post office and I shook out the barrettes and comb and mascara and nail polish.

"You don't even use mascara or nail polish," Maybelline said.

"Yeah, well I needed these barrettes," I said.

Maybelline's freckles had multiplied every year and the spaces between the freckles were disappearing, the freckles melting together like chocolate chips in a cookie. Except for her nose. Her nose didn't have any freckles, which made her eyes and nose and mouth appear even closer together than they were. The other Blues had round faces with broad, brown eyes that kept their distance from their noses, and their noses, small and narrow, kept the right amount of distance above the mouths.

Maybelline was ugly. It was no secret but everyone at school acted like it was. Like Maybelline didn't know she was ugly. They passed notes about it and waited until she walked down the hall before saying anything. They'd say, "God, that girl is ugly." But when Maybelline was standing next to them, they pretended she was just like them. Pretty. Maybe being ugly made her more honest or maybe being smart made telling the truth easier. Whichever, Maybelline always told the truth. Like a razor blade. She could cut the thoughts right out of you without you even opening your mouth. She could see things, like a finger tapping a desk or an eye blinking four times, and say exactly what those things meant. They were signs from the psyche, she said.

I stole and Maybelline knew I stole and I lied and I cheated and she told me so. I told her she was ugly. "So what," we'd say. So what.

She asked, "Why'd you take the man's comb?"

I said, "It looked like it would work better in this fucking hair." The sky was lowering, drizzle sitting in the air, not falling, just sitting. We followed the alleyway behind the post office and lamp shade shop till it ended and became a dirt path. The path thinned as it went into the woods. On a tree was a no trespassing sign that had been gouged at with jackknives until all it said was *o ass*. Maybelline's hair was more orange than any of the leaves on the trees. I tried to find the color of her hair but it was not here, outdoors. It was a thin orange and cloudy. A color created under fluorescent light in a test tube.

Maybelline said, "That comb won't work because the teeth are too thin."

I said, "Then I'll have to go back and get a better one." She didn't say I should stop stealing or lying or cheating. She didn't say this was good or bad or that I should be different. I didn't have to pretend. And Maybelline didn't have to pretend she was not ugly when she was with me. It didn't matter that Maybelline's face was as pointy as her mom's mynah bird's. Or that her eyes were like vegetables steamed too long, dull grey and milky. She was ugly in a way that pretty could never be. Pretty was always measuring up to someone else's standards. Ugly had no standards, was one of a kind, never imitated anybody. I was halfway pretty, which meant I was halfway ugly. But my ugly was wearing off as I got older. It would wash off. Maybelline's wouldn't.

I clipped my bangs to the side of my head with the barrettes.

Maybelline said, "Nothing's going to help your hair."

"In case you hadn't noticed, I'm not trying to be beauty queen."

"I noticed."

"Good," I said.

"Good," she said.

The path in the woods was marked with piles of cigarette butts and beer bottles. Other paths angled off the main path. We took one and walked single file, Maybelline in the lead. The sky cracked like eggshells, bits of yellow in the cracks.

Maybelline said, "There's three boys up ahead by the swamp."

"Who are they?"

"I don't know. They're facing away from us."

"Let me go first." I knew that boys had to be met head-on like a collision. That I had to say something to them before they even knew we were there or else they'd start throwing wisecracks and put-downs at us just to impress each other. And Maybelline was to put-downs like shit is to flies. They came to her by the truckload. She could return an insult as furious and fast as a hardball. But that was in school or on the street where there were precise borders and limits to the hallways and homerooms and houses. In the woods by the swamp was not neutral ground. Was not our ground. The boys owned this place because they hung out here, pissed here. Would stay hours pitching their cigarettes into the green, slimy water. Rolled their joints and smoked them until their eyes got roasted. Drank beer they stole from their dads or the A&P. Girls could visit but could not stay.

My mother said this to me about boys: "Macy, when it comes to boys, you have to be a snake charmer and then grab them by the balls."

We walked right up to them and I said, "Hey, you got an extra cigarette for me and Maybelline?" The boys turned around. The three Mackeys—Bruce, Bill, and Marcus. Bill was in my homeroom and Bruce in Maybelline's.

"Hey, Macy," Bill said. "Sure I got a cigarette, but I didn't think Miss Skunk Face did anything but kiss the teacher's ass." The boys laughed and Bruce made kissing noises with his fat lips. Maybelline's face was sharpening, drawing a bead on Bill.

"Don't," I said to Maybelline, and to the boys I said, "Do you got a cigarette or not?"

"Yeah," Bruce said, "what's your big rush?"

Maybelline said, "We're heading over to the hospital to schedule your lobotomy."

"Great," I said.

Bruce said, "Well, maybe you'd like some bodywork done on you, right here and now." He rotated his hips and made his hand into a circle that went up and down near the zipper on his jeans.

I said, "Look, we really are on our way to the hospital because I've got to meet my mother there; she's a nurse, you know, and just happened to tell me your sister had a miscarriage. Is that right? I thought your sister was having her appendix out." Bill took two cigarettes from his pack and threw them at me. I picked them up. No one was supposed to know about their sister. I gave Maybelline one of the cigarettes. Marlboro. "Hey, Marlboro Man," I said, "got a match?"

"Fuck you," Bill said. But he came over and lit my cigarette anyway and blew out the flame with a quick breath from the same fat lips all the Mackeys had.

"Now hers," I said. Maybelline put the cigarette in her mouth, and it looked like a flagpole stuck in the peak of a mountain. Bill struck the match and held it up to her cigarette. His eyelids were lowered. I could hear the breath out of his nose, cranky one-note. Marcus not looking at us. Bruce rolling up some rope, tying the end into a series of knots. Maybelline's cigarette not catching fire.

Bill saying, "Jesus, fucking drag on it already."

Maybelline looking into his eyelids. "Thank you, Bill."

"Christ," Bill said. Let the match burn down to his fingers before spitting on it.

"See you in history," I said to Bill. Maybelline and I walked through some skunk cabbage and I heard Bruce say, "Fucking ugly bitch." Maybelline kept going, the cigarette in her mouth flaming like a birthday candle.

What my mother didn't tell me was that she knew everything about being a snake charmer with men, and she could let the snake wrap completely around her body and never get bit. She could rub the snake on its diamond scales or sing one word into its slit ear and the snake would fall under her charm. That's because my mother was half snake charmer and half snake.

I saw this for myself. Maybelline did too. My mother was always talking about opportunity or the circumstances of her life, but what about coincidence? When we got to the edge of the swamp, where it became the outer parking lot for the hospital staff, we saw my mother and the butcher get into his 1970 Cutlass Supreme. Maybe coincidence is where opportunity and circumstance intersect, and my mother was right there. I tugged Maybelline's coat sleeve and stepped back into the woods behind three birch trees.

"She didn't see you," Maybelline said.

"I know," I said.

"Don't you want her to? I thought you had to get some money from her."

"I want to see what she's doing."

"Why don't you just go ask her?"

"God, Maybelline, don't you see who she's with? It's the goddamn butcher. She's up to something and I want to find out what it is."

"Whatever shape you make is the shape you occupy."

"What the hell does that mean?"

"It means that if you're being a spy, then you're being deceitful and underhanded."

"Then I'm being deceitful and underhanded. Okay? You don't have to stay."

"I'll stay," Maybelline said.

The shape I occupied was rectangular, a rolled-down car window like a picture frame. This was the picture. My mother singing "Moon River" in a bad French accent to the butcher while he's yelling at her. "I can't stand this," he said. "There's got to be an end or a beginning," he said. "When are you going to make a decision already," he said. "Someday," my mother sang. "Someday, some-day." Closer to his ear. "I won't wait," he said. My mother sang charms into his ear. Snake charmer soothing the snake. Snake wanting to bite. But the butcher stopped yelling. Just closed his mouth. She kissed his face, his eyelids, his fore-head. The snake bit his tongue and my mother made her strike, her lips sliding over his.

Maybelline said, "The shape you make both contains and keeps out."

I looked at her, her thin orange hair sticking out from her head like a million antennae. Maybelline's eyes as sharp as I'd ever seen them, focused on my mother kissing deep into the butcher. I said, "What do you mean?"

She said, "It's like a Venn diagram—two circles that overlap."

I closed my eyes. "Maybelline, I hate math and you know it."

"Just listen, it will make sense, I swear."

"Damn. Go ahead."

"The butcher and his life are one circle. Your mother and her life are the second circle. When they intersect, the area that overlaps contains parts of both circles, but it also keeps out the parts that don't overlap."

"I don't see it."

"Yes, you do."

"No, I don't."

"Yes, you see it because you're looking right at it." Maybelline's nose pointed at the car. "Even if it is only a coincidence that you're seeing your mother and the butcher, you are seeing. If you hadn't come here, you would never have known they were overlapping. Your mother and the butcher thought they could keep you out of the intersection by keeping the knowledge from you. Now they can't."

"How do you remember all this math shit?" I asked.

"I just do," Maybelline said.

My mother was the shape of the butcher, of his arms coming around her. Of his hands rubbing all over her, unzipping her uniform. Of his body sinking down with hers onto the seat, disappearing.

I turned around and walked until I found another path that cut through the woods away from the swamp and ended back in town. Maybelline followed me. "Tell me this," I said to Maybelline, "what would you do if you saw your mother in a car with a man not your father?"

"My mom doesn't go out of the house, remember?"

"But if she did."

"But she doesn't."

"Shit."

"Look," Maybelline said, "you can only look at the shape that's in front of you. That's how it goes. One of the rules in mathematics is that we are not working on infinity with each equation, but with each equation we are getting to infinity."

"Jesus Christ, Maybelline, just tell me what you'd do."

"Depends on what you want to happen."

"I want my mother to leave and never come back."

"Really?"

"Really."

"Be careful what you wish for."

I didn't turn around to see Maybelline watching my back, watching the way I hurried, watching what I wished for. I was too busy wishing.

My mother? Here's her rap:

She said that if you don't recognize opportunity, then you're too stupid to deserve it. She said, "Here's how you distinguish opportunity from circumstance. Circumstance you just happen into. Like being the thousandth customer to walk through the door at the grand opening of an A&P and win the dessert of your choice in the frozen food aisle. Opportunity, on the other hand, you see coming and plan to meet it at the corner, shake its hand, and sign on the dotted line."

⤙

CIRCUMSTANCE: I BECAME a candy striper when I got caught stealing the mood ring, two days after I saw my mother with the butcher, which was two days after she chopped my hair off. I took the bus to the Plaza with Gimble's on one end and Macy's on the other. I picked Macy's. The store my mother loved. Yeah, the store she named me for. Where she always headed to the shoe department first and would try on a hundred pairs of shoes. She'd listen to the salesman with the shoehorn tell her about each shoe's heel and arch and leather while he held her foot, pressing and stroking his thumb into her flesh.

I passed the shoes by. The pajamas. Housewares. In jewelry I looked for the mirrors and how many sales ladies were there. Two. They were each helping customers pick out watches. I knew where the mood rings were displayed. Third counter by the cheap clip-on earrings of fake gold and pearls. The mood rings were in little plastic bags with a piece of paper inside that told what each color meant. The plastic bags dangled on a T that stood on the counter.

I pretended to examine the chokers and ID bracelets. The sales ladies never looked at me. I took a mood ring off the T and slid it right up my coat sleeve, all in one motion. I was smooth. The mirrors were pointing away from me and the sales ladies didn't even know I was there.

Across the aisle where rows of bell bottoms hung on round racks, I found my size and held a pair of crushed velvet emerald elephant bells up to my waist. The bells were huge. All I needed were some ornaments and I would have resembled a Christmas tree. I kept on walking through the young misses department touching velour floor-length vests and corduroy hip huggers. The mood ring up my coat sleeve reading my mood. Yeah, I was fucking-A clever. Wait till everyone saw my mood ring; they'd be green for *envy*.

See, I have nothing to hide. I know how to evade, get around the obstacles. I learned from Maybelline to have an answer for everything. But my answers were not the facts or the truth like Maybelline's were. Mine were slanted, polished up. Looped in barbed wire.

But the day I stole the mood ring, when I walked outside Macy's, the security guard came up behind me and took my arm to steer me back inside the glass doors and the answer I had for why the mood ring was in my coat sleeve didn't keep them from calling my mother.

My mother would have to come to Macy's and pass by all those shoes.

The guy who was not a regular guy but a modified undercover store pig wearing jeans and a red-checked shirt said, "I know there's something up your coat sleeve." He said, "Shake your arms."

I shook my arms and for a while the mood ring didn't budge.

The guy said, "Keep shaking." Old lady shoppers came into the aisles and stared at me like I had ruined their day of shopping. The mood ring slid out from my coat sleeve onto the floor. "Knew it," he said.

"I don't know how it got there," I said. "It must've come with the coat."

"Right," he said. He held onto my arm and pulled me all the way through the store and up to the second floor. Red-checked shirt smelling like Irish Spring.

In his office, the assistant store manager, Mr. Wert, didn't say hello to me but said, "Fine job," to the guy who left after shaking Mr. Wert's hand. Mr. Wert had the shortest neck I'd ever seen. Almost like he didn't have one. His earlobes touched his shoulders, that's how short his neck was. He sat down behind his metal desk and I sat on the other side. The mood ring sat in the middle of the desk, the stone black for *hard to read*. "You are in a great deal of trouble. What is your name?"

I didn't say anything. Didn't know if I had to say anything. If he didn't get my name, what could he do to me? He opened a desk drawer and removed a file. From the file he took out a form called Incident Report. I unbuttoned my black pea coat. The office was hot and too green. The walls were painted a pea color.

Mr. Wert kept peeping at his watch while he wrote on the incident report, as if each of his thoughts had to correspond to the minutes. He set his pen down. Stared up at me. His eyebrows bent up at the ends like those tildes in Spanish. His stomach grumbled. What he wanted was lunch. But first he had to fill in the incident report and talk to my mother and yell at me. When he yelled at me, I could see his thick tongue forming the words in his mouth.

"Okay, Miss Jane Doe," he said, "I have the power and authority to turn you over to the police for shoplifting. Do you know what that could mean for your future?" He slipped the mood ring onto his pudgy index finger, barely past the nail. It wouldn't fit any farther than that. When he shook the ring at me, he said, "And all for this, this bauble, this trivial indulgence. If this report went to the police, it would stay with you your entire life. Did you think about that?"

What I thought about was not what he wanted to hear. What I thought was that he was like the pudgy, picked-on boys in school who spent their days plotting how to get revenge. They got even, all right, by growing up to become the pudgy assistant store manager with an incident report in front of him and a mood ring on his finger. Thinking to himself that he had the power. But the mood ring said otherwise. The mood ring turned brown for *nervous, tense.*

I said, "I'm aware of all the possibilities. So what?"

Mr. Wert pointed his finger with the mood ring on it at me. The mood ring's brown color swirled with green for *irritable, anxious.* "You don't have the slightest understanding about your predicament," he said, "and your impudence will only dig you in deeper. If it was up to me, I would not bother to call your parents first. I would personally drive you to the police station. Unless you tell me your name this instant, I'll do just that."

I tried to raise one of my eyebrows like Mr. Spock. Interesting, I wanted to say. Your logic is illogical. What's in a name? But I knew. Everything was in a name. "My name," I said, "is Macy."

Mr. Wert started to write that down but stopped. He said, "You think that being a smart aleck is going to prevent me from finding out who you are?" He clicked on the intercom to his secretary and said, "Dorrie, get me Sergeant Blue's number."

Maybelline's dad.

Mr. Wert was bluffing. I was sure of that. No kid I ever knew who got busted shoplifting went to the jail. Mr. Wert was nothing but a pudgy, hungry, nervous assistant store manager, irritated that he could not do what he really wanted to do. He was not the boss. Even though he was trying to get me to believe he had power, his hands were tied. My punishment was not up to him. My punishment was somewhere in the *Store Policy Manual* he had sitting on his desk.

The intercom buzzed. "I have that number for you," Mr. Wert's secretary said. He looked at me. "Either you tell me or you tell the police."

The office had no windows. I was sitting next to the wall with the baseboard heating, the heat rolling out like it never stopped. There was a fan in the room pointing right at Mr. Wert, blowing cool on him while I was burning up. I wanted out of that office. I said, "My name really is Macy, Macy Kahn."

"Good," he said, "Miss Macy Kahn. Now, I need your phone number so I can reach your mother."

I gave him the phone number. He clicked the intercom on again and told his secretary to call my mother. She did and buzzed Mr. Wert back saying that Mrs. Kahn was on her way. Which I figured meant ten minutes tops for her to get into her Nova and gun it onto Route 17 to here. He said, "Let's continue. How old are you? Your address? What grade are you in? What school do you attend?" He filled in the boxes of the incident report. Blocky letters, no frilly loops. The letters lined up, little soldiers all at attention. The intercom buzzed three times. He got up out of his chair and said, "I'll be right back." I looked around the office. I wanted to steal something from Mr. Wert and throw it into the quarry water where it would never surface. But there wasn't much of anything on his desk that he would miss: paper clips, pencils, a box of thumbtacks, and a hole punch. Across the room on a filing cabinet was one of those beer mugs with a lid and next to it was a baseball cap, *NY Yankees*. On the wall were wood plaques and pictures of baseball players. On a shelf below the pictures were two baseballs with signatures in red and blue, which I figured were New York Yankee signatures. I went over to the filing cabinet and just like that I stuck the baseball cap in the inside pocket of my pea coat. Nothing to it. The fan was on a smaller filing cabinet, and I turned the fan so it would blow a little on me while I waited for my mother in the chair next to the hot air.

Mr. Wert came back with a cup of coffee and a Danish. Half of it was gone already and Mr. Wert put the rest of it into his mouth. His cheeks puffed out. By the time he walked around the desk and sat down, the Danish was all chewed up and swallowed. Mr. Wert said, "You're a smart girl, Macy. It is always best to cooperate." He sipped his coffee and reread each box in the incident report. When he was done, he turned the report around and pushed his ballpoint pen across the desk. "Sign this," he said. His stomach let out a huge farty sound.

I laughed and said, "Not without my mother."

The mood ring was turning colors again as he waved his finger in my face. He said, "Now you listen to me, you insignificant piece of nothing, I've had—"

Mr. Wert's secretary opened the door for my mother. "Mr. Wert," my mother said, "I'm Mrs. Ira Kahn, and you can imagine my shock when I received the phone call about this."

The mood ring was settling on red. Red as my mother's hair, red for *spontane-ous combustion*. Mr. Wert stood up, brought my mother a chair from the corner of his office. His shoes were the color of butterscotch. When my mother sat down, she knew what my punishment would be. Nothing in that store policy book. She had dreamed it all up by the time she was on the escalator to the second floor, rising above the racks of shoes.

"Mrs. Kahn," he said, "this is not a pleasant job, but it is an important one. We have the opportunity to help your daughter."

My mother said, "I fully understand, Mr. Wert. The telling of bad news is not easy for anyone. I should know, I'm a nurse." My mother pulled her chair closer to the desk, her nurse's uniform tight up on her thighs. I counted to myself, one, two, three, and on three, my mother smiled. The big smile. The fucking jumbo smile. The one she pulled out on special occasions. Like a once-in-a-lifetime opportunity. Mr. Wert swallowed that smile like a Danish.

"Good," Mr. Wert said, "then you are in agreement with how serious this situation is and that appropriate remedial action needs to be taken."

"Of course," my mother said. The smile still taking up half her face. Lips in their perfect curl. My mother fucking Mr. Wert's mind with her smile. Yeah, his eyes didn't stray one iota from that smile. The mood ring on his finger jumped from red to purple for *confident, cheerful*. "I appreciate your integrity in this mat-ter. And also that you see this as an opportunity because I feel the exact same way. My motto is to never pass up an opportunity, isn't that right, Macy?"

"Yeah," I said, "my mother has that motto framed above her bed."

She looked at me for the first time since coming into the office. Not the eyes looking at me but the smile. What she really wanted me to see was the price I'd pay for her being here in this shitty little office, playing nice to the shitty little man without a neck.

"Let's get down to business," my mother said. "I see it this way. We need to teach Macy responsibility."

Mr. Wert nodded his head and said, "That is true, Mrs. Kahn, absolutely true." He twisted the mood ring off his finger and set it on the desk. On a pad of yellow paper he wrote down what my mother had said.

My mother put her folded hands on the desk and leaned forward like she was confiding in Mr. Wert. "I promise you that my plan will turn my daughter around. I promise you that this will never happen again." Mr. Wert's head continued to nod to each of my mother's promises.

Mr. Wert asked, "What do you have in mind?" He glanced at his watch and wrote the time on the yellow paper. I read the time upside down—*12:47 p.m.* The next word he wrote was *Decision*.

My mother said, "It is so simple really, Mr. Wert. Work is the key to good habits. That's what teaches responsibility. When we leave here today, we're going straight to Rutherford Hospital, where I work, to sign Macy up as a candy striper."

"Macy Kahn, candy striper," my mother said. "Has a nice ring to it."

I could just picture it: me in that bubble-gum-colored uniform, smiling over a bedpan. We were in the Nova, cloverleafing from Route 17 to Route 3. My mother laughing, the window open, blowing her laugh right at me. My mother had the mood ring on her finger. Her finger curved over the steering wheel above the horn. The mood ring was fucking *happy*. Mr. Wert never even realized she was shaking his hand with the mood ring on her finger. Slid it off his desk while he wrote, *Decision: candy striper.* "Your father will be so proud of you," my mother said. "We'll tell him you volunteered."

She was so happy that she went to the store, bought a loaf of white bread, and drove to the duck pond. There were so many ducks in that pond that I couldn't even see the water. The ground next to the asphalt path around the far end of the pond was nothing but grey and green duck shit. When my mother walked down the path with her loaf of white bread, I swear the ducks heard the plastic bag knocking against her leg. The ducks followed us over to a picnic table. "Here," my mother said, "feed them." She gave me half the loaf of bread, kept the other half for herself. We broke the slices of bread into small pieces and wadded the pieces up into spongy white bread balls and threw them at the ducks. They squawked and flapped and pecked at each other to get at the bread. I started throwing whole slices at them until the bread was gone.

My mother said, "What you haven't learned, Miss Know-it-all, could fill that duck pond." She opened up her handbag, took out a Pall Mall. This was a smoking occasion. My mother didn't smoke all that often, only when she wanted to linger over the taste of something like Macy Kahn, candy striper.

"So you're so smart, what haven't I learned?"

"First, you're sloppy. You think you've got all the bases covered and then you get overconfident and forget to check behind you. If you're going to make shoplifting a hobby, then don't forget there are people who make catching a shoplifter their career." She blew smoke out of her mouth like she was blowing a kiss across a room, the Pall Mall filter resting way up between her fingers next to the *happy* mood ring. "Second," she said, "consequences. Always know what the consequences will be. You went in there thinking only about wearing this ring home on the bus and never considered what would happen if you got caught. If you know the consequences, it makes you much more careful." She tapped the ashes onto the picnic table.

I said, "You're not all that careful."

"What do you mean?"

I pulled the cigarette from between her fingers and took a drag before she remembered who she was and who I was. Cheating, lying mother and her klepto daughter. I blew out the smoke.

"You're adding smoking to your repertoire?"

"Only on special occasions."

She shook another Pall Mall from the package, lighting it with matches from the Colony Inn, with the swimming pool and two phony palm trees. "Let me guess that the special occasion is that you think you know something about me?"

"Yeah, that's right."

My mother was sitting at the duck pond smoking, her eyelashes curled with the eyelash curler and tarred with Revlon Midnight Mascara. Her lipstick, one of three shades of red that she used. She tweezed her eyebrows. Dyed her hair. Went to the Colony Inn when no one was looking. My mother, with her perfect makeup disguises, pretending to love what she hated, pretending so much of the time. I didn't want to be like her. I sucked on the Pall Mall, and more than anything else I wanted to know if I would be like her. I already knew we had more in common than I wanted. The mood ring was settling down onto *confident*. My mother was ready.

"I want to know about the butcher," I said.

My mother threw her cigarette on the ground, where it smoldered. She opened her pocketbook and found her compact, eyed her lips in the mirror. Uncapped the lipstick and added more red over her red lips. "I'll tell you, Macy, don't ever confuse love with opportunity. Don't ever think the one will become the other. The butcher? He's like a guest who's dropped in and you have to pay attention to—happy when they're there and usually happier when they leave." My mother turned to me but all I saw was camouflage, big smile surrounded by red.

I said, "I saw you with him in the parking lot at the hospital."

"And?"

"I want to know— "

"What? If I love him?"

"Yeah," I said.

My mother smiled, but not the fake one. This smile had as much sad in it as happy. She was looking right at me, looking like she was seeing something she hadn't seen before. "Macy, I once took you to the quarry, oh, when you were about four. It was hot, days of hundred-degree heat, and all I wanted was to get into the water and stay there. But I had you with me—you with your wanting to be loved, no questions asked, as if love was your birthright and I had no say. The perfect mother would have carried you with her into the water and let you splash and laugh and float in the safety of her arms. But I sat you on the dirt beach and told you not to go anywhere. And you didn't. You just watched me swim. All I wanted was to keep going. Leave you there."

She leaned her head back. Big hoop snap-on earrings were caught up in her red hair. The sun was setting behind the clouds, like glare on water. "Don't you see, sometimes love and opportunity are equal burdens, a long list of obligations, that suddenly you're supposed to follow. I never wanted that. The butcher loves me like a four-year-old."

I kept holding my Pall Mall even though I was done smoking it. All the ash curled up from the filter as my mother told me what she saw that day. That day when I lost her to the water. Sitting on the hard brown sand, the sun like an umbrella I was holding just inches from myself, heat and more heat, and I sat. The water nothing but shine. No mother. And with my finger I drew a circle that curved behind me and met up with the beginning where I had first dug into the dirt.

My mother touched my hair, the hair she had chopped into this shape of hard angles, no place to rest in soft or round. She touched the V of my bangs with her thumb, and her thumb slid down to my skin, my forehead, my nose, over my eyelids. I closed my eyes to her touch that was telling me that love was not a safe place to rest in.

My mother hid the mood ring. After the duck pond, before we got back into the car, she took it off, but I didn't see her take it off. I noticed it missing when we got home. My dad was in his chair and my mother swooped down. A noisy, red-feathered bird, kissing his cheeks and lips. I opened the refrigerator and took out an apple, while my mother told my dad that I was going to sign up to be a candy striper. She was sitting in his lap and her hands were around his neck. There was no mood ring on any of her fingers. Just her wedding band, silver with a ruby chip set in a raised silver circle.

I bit the apple. My mother stood up and smoothed her uniform down. My dad kept his hands on her hips and she raised her eyelids—her eyes so sharp, they could take a bite out of his eyes. His thumbs waited on her hips, his hand rested on the curve above her uniform's pockets. My mother didn't smile; her eyes did all the talking.

I bit into the apple again and chewed and swallowed. The look between them lasted that long. My dad didn't see anything out of the ordinary. Didn't see anything beyond where he looked. He didn't see my mother giving the butcher the same look. I walked with the apple across the linoleum. On my way to being a candy striper.

My dad said, "Macy, it's good to see you following in your mother's footsteps." His hands still on her hips.

"Yeah," I said, "just what I always wanted to do."

My mother stepped out of the hold of his hands, stood in front of me, smiling a victory smile, and kissed the corner of my lip like she always did when she was one up on me.

My dad said, "What a beautiful sight, my two favorite girls. Baby, you've done a fine job with her."

"Yeah," I said, "I'm a masterpiece."

My mother said, "We waited a long time to have Macy, Ira, and she's our prize." My mother turned around and put her hand on my dad's heart. My mother? She was precision timing, a tuning fork, the snap when the mousetrap gets tripped.

I turned the TV on. Nothing there but a laugh track and stupid jokes and a silly, never-in-a-million-years-would-this-happen story. I was following in my mother's footsteps and I wanted a punch line to get me out of her shoes.

↶

"A LIE IS TO the truth as deadly nightshade is to the tomato," Maybelline said.

We were sitting outside the cats' house. She was tagging the cats with collars she had made out of white shoelaces. On the ground was Maybelline's red marker and a clipboard holding unlined white paper with a list of numbers.

"Okay, I give up. How is a lie to the truth the same as deadly nightshade to the tomato?"

Maybelline squatted. I was sitting on the bench above Maybelline, looking down at her, at her eyes with no space between them. "They are both from the same origin only they appear different. The tomato and the deadly nightshade both come from the same family, Solanacea. One is poisonous, the other edible. The seed of a lie originates in the truth."

I was wearing my best imitation Janis Joplin outfit. Big bells, a tight, shiny green long-sleeved shirt. Thirteen of my bead necklaces around my neck and thirteen of my bracelets piled up on my wrist. A gold vest with a bunch of feathers I'd glued around the neck like a boa. Granny glasses. No mood ring—my mother still had it. But I had other rings. Two poison rings that I could open. Another ring like a daisy that covered two fingers.

Maybelline scratched a cat below his chin and asked, "So why do you look like Gypsy Rose Lee?"

"Christ," I said, "this is pure, undiluted Janis Joplin. You're so out of it, Maybelline."

"So?" Maybelline said.

"So, do you think they'll take one look at me at the hospital and declare me unfit to be a candy striper?"

Maybelline let go of the cat and looked at me. "You could use more makeup if you really want to give them the wrong impression, but maybe it wouldn't be so bad to be a candy striper."

I held my arm up. My bracelets slid to my elbow, knocking into each other. The sun had been warming the wood shingles of the cats' house, and the warm was jumping off the wood into my hair. I didn't want to go anywhere, especially not anywhere near the hospital. "Maybelline, I don't want to be like my mother."

"The interesting thing I've discovered is that the more you don't want to be, the more you are."

"Thanks."

"You're not welcome." She walked over to the cement fish pond. There wasn't any water in the pond. Just the cement, cracked and chipped. A bunch of cats were sunning themselves. Maybelline picked up a white cat with black spots.

"What are you doing?" I asked.

Maybelline said, "I'm studying this group of cats—specifically, the recessive male calico gene and how often it shows up in a generation."

"Jesus, don't you ever get tired of being so smart?"

"I never think of it as a deficit, Macy, it's more like an urge. You know how Tiny and Tina get excited by spending most of the night in some boy's car parked by the quarry, and you get a thrill from stealing? I get that from figuring out the mathematics, the probabilities of a question."

"I wonder what you'd be like on acid? You'd probably rewrite the law of gravity."

Maybelline said, "I'm not opposed to trying LSD."

"You're kidding," I said.

"No, I'm not. I'm not a prude. I have enormous curiosity, it just comes out in a different way than yours." She took out a measuring tape and measured cat number five's length. "Too bad I don't have a scale. The study would be more accurate."

I lay down on the bench and looked at the sky. I'd never seen one bird fly over Maybelline's yard. But I could hear birds, off in the trees, like a warning system not to go near this place.

Maybelline said, "You know what, Macy, I've never seen curiosity kill a cat. I think it's the opposite that kills—stagnation, refusing to let your mind explore."

"Shit, yeah." I opened my beaded bag, the one with the drawstring and the peace sign branded to the bag's side, and took out the bottle of Arabian Musk. Tipped out some drops. Dabbed them on my neck, on the inside part of my arms. Reached down inside my shirt where there wasn't a bra, just my breasts, and ran my finger with the musk over each one. The rest I just rubbed in my chopped-off hair. "This ought to do it."

"Smells good to me," Maybelline said.

"Well, you aren't the candy striper coordinator, now are you?"

"No," Maybelline said.

The Janis Joplin didn't work. The musk didn't work. Nothing deterred Mrs. Lamphere from hiring me. She was at least a hundred years old, couldn't see, couldn't smell, but her hearing was perfect. Even in her office with the paintings of girls playing nurse with cats and dogs, she pointed her chin at the closed door and said, "Two ambulances arriving at the same time, that's a big accident for certain." I hummed rock and roll but all Mrs. Lamphere said was "I like a girl who hums; it shows a fondness for the beauty in all the arts."

I had to put on the bubble-gum-colored uniform. I grossed myself out just looking at it. Hanging there to the middle of my calf, with darts that tried to arrange my breasts into two neat points. Two pockets below the waist. A zipper down the front. I was in the bathroom by Mrs. Lamphere's office, the bathroom marked *Private*. One stall, a full-length mirror on the pink wall, a round mirror above the sink. On the sink top some air freshener stunk up the air, overpowering the musk. Even without looking in the mirror, I knew I looked like a jerk. Like someone who'd never heard of Janis Joplin.

Mrs. Lamphere, outside the bathroom door, asked, "How does it fit?"

I said, "It's too long. I'll bring it home and hem it."

"That's fine, just fine," Mrs. Lamphere said. "We want your uniform to be comfortable as well as let the patients and staff know who you are."

Yeah, they'd know who I was all right. I freed my necklaces from inside the uniform. Pulled the zipper down so I could see my breasts. Shook my bracelets. Gave the mirror the finger, both hands.

"Remember, Macy," Mrs. Lamphere said, "a candy striper is plain for a reason—to give the appearance of comfort and calm. Therefore, no jewelry or makeup. You'll find that in the handbook under Personal Hygiene, Chapter One."

I had to learn the rules in the handbook. Brought it home with its pink cover. All the rules started, *It is in the best interest of the patient . . . if you are always friendly, if you always smile, if you get them water (but only after checking with a nurse to see if that is allowed), if you always tie your hair back, if your hands are always clean and manicured.* There were pictures of candy stripers doing their thing. Smiling like they were in a commercial and not with some sick person. All the sick people smiled back and looked as if they could pull out their IVs and skip home. The candy stripers in the handbook smiled while they fluffed up those thin hospital pillows, handed over a *Reader's Digest,* or opened the curtain like the sunshine was just what the doctor ordered and the candy striper could deliver it any time of day. Rule number twenty-seven: *It is in the best interest of the patient if you do not wear rings.*

My first day, Mrs. Lamphere told me the patients I had to visit. She showed me where the magazine and book cart was kept, in storeroom F, which was nothing more than a bathroom. The sink was still there but no toilet. Six shelves of books and boxes of magazines. She said, "A candy striper is an essential part of the patient's recovery. Don't be afraid of the patients."

I asked, "Why would I be afraid of them?"

"Some of my girls have gotten queasy being in the presence of an illness or an injury. We all have our different tolerances, after all." Mrs. Lamphere pushed the book cart out of the storeroom and into the hallway with its glossy light and no shadows anywhere. She said, "Take this up to the third floor, start at room 3A, and visit every room that has a blue dot next to the number on the door. Reserve the copy of *Newsweek* for Mr. Pine. Change the water in the flower vases. Extra pillows are kept on the shelf in their closets, and, Macy, don't forget the most effective aid you can give to their conditions is your smile."

Room 3A, blue dot. I picked out a *Ladies' Home Journal* with fifteen fruity dessert recipes and how redecorating could spice up your love life. The smell in the room was chocolate from the cup of pudding on the tray stand that swung over Mrs. Grear's stomach. A breaded cutlet and peas and pears in a runny syrup were on the plate next to the chocolate pudding. When I went into the room, I had to hold Mrs. Grear's hand. She motioned to the chair next to the bed and held out her hand in the air like this was the routine and I had to go along with it. Her hand had only three fingers. I didn't smile, and Mrs. Grear with her bandaged eye didn't smile either. Mrs. Grear fell asleep about five seconds after I touched her hand. I could've just switched the water in her flower vase and left. But I didn't. I looked at the places where her fingers were missing: the pinky and the ring finger. I didn't mind looking. It didn't gross me out. The stitches no longer there, just red shadows. The skin smoothed over the dents where the fingers had been as if nothing were meant to grow out of those places, as if the doctors had told her hand what it had to be now and the hand believed the doctors. I smiled at her hand.

Room 3G, blue dot. I had to raise the glass of orange juice with a straw to the mouth of Larry Morgan who had broken both his wrists falling off a beam at a construction site. In between sips he said, "Here you are, a real living doll, and once my hands are back to normal, they could caress your skin until you shined like a penny." That's the word he used: *caress*, just like the soap. "The only thing your hands are good for is to get in the prayer position and pray that god will touch your puny thing, cause your hands are so broken up you won't be able to for years." I held the straw a few inches from his mouth. Made him lean forward to take a drink instead of doing what a good candy striper was supposed to do and bring the straw to his mouth.

Room 3H, blue dot. Mr. Pine. Around his neck was a thick, wide beige collar with metal bars coming out the top. His jaw was wired shut. I put the *Newsweek* on the stand, but he opened and closed his hand really fast—that's the way he talked now. So I brought the *Newsweek* over to where his impatient hand was. He grabbed the *Newsweek* and checked the date and fanned through the pages. Probably making sure no one else had seen it first. His whole face was puffy and his skin was swirled red and pink and white like a parfait. He stuck the *Newsweek* under his blanket and snapped his fingers and pointed at the window. I said, "What do you want?" He snapped faster and his other hand flapped. "Open?" I asked. "You want the shades open?" He snapped and pointed at me. The cord that opened the shades was stuck all the way up at the top of the window. I had to stand on a chair and untangle the cord so that I could pull it down. When I got the shades open, all I could see was the other wing of the hospital, more rooms with more decrepit people. Mr. Pine was reading the *Newsweek* but looked up at me when I came by the bed. "Anything else?" I asked. His eyes were as puffy as the rest of his face, like two Ping-Pong balls. He snapped his finger, pointing to the door. I stared at his Ping-Pong eyes and I didn't smile. He couldn't smile and probably never did anyway.

At the end of all the threes with the blue dots, I went into the bathroom and that's when I saw it. In the mirror: the way I stood like my mother. My body shaping itself to the uniform, the job, the way I could walk into any room and demand attention and get it. Even my hair with its sharp edges fit the picture— I looked sure of myself. Like I had chosen the perfect hairstyle for the job. In the mirror, my eyes were just like my mother's, tilted up, making nasty demands. Serious mind fucking. I closed my eyes. I didn't want to see.

The whole year boiled down to the color I had to wear twice a week. Pink. Like Pepto-Bismol. I didn't follow the rules in the handbook. I hemmed my uniform high up my thighs, four inches higher than the handbook said. Wore an earring.

Just one tiny black pearl. Mostly I didn't smile. A smile wasn't what everyone wanted. Sometimes it only made their conditions worse. When I did smile, none of the patients jumped out of bed. They didn't put on their shoes and coats and dance down the hallway and out the door. They stuck to their beds, watching *One Life to Live*, and waited for the doctor to tell them what he would do. And they waited for me.

My mother said that there's an opportunity that comes only once in a lifetime. She was waiting her whole life for that one, that only opportunity. But me? I could see how opportunity could come in parts. Like Maybelline said, to get to the whole you have to add one thing to another. So I added. Pink uniform to my wardrobe. One patient's condition to the next. Each of their surgeries, heart attacks, broken bones. Pills, anesthesia, casts, and crutches. Every pain, cramp, bloodstain. All opportunities. I didn't know what they were adding up to. But I was liking my two shifts a week. Did a good job, no one ever complained.

I went into the hospital rooms and turned off the TVs and asked my patients to tell me about their conditions. Everything. Every skipped heartbeat, every sliced-up-and-sewn-back-together tendon, every tongue-bitten seizure. I saw foot-long scars and how the IVs snuck up their veins. They talked and talked. But I wasn't interested in comforting them. I never said, it'll be okay, or, you'll be better in no time. I wanted to see the fresh stitches, the bandages gumming up their skin. But mostly I was fascinated by how willing they were to give their bodies over to the doctors and nurses, no questions asked.

I took my mother's *Surgical Nursing* and *Practical Nursing* textbooks. In my bedroom, I looked up the diseases and the procedures I heard about. The correct order of surgical instruments. Latin for the parts of the body I'd known by simple names: fingers, *metacarpals*. Heart, *ventricles*, *aorta*, *atrium*. The vocabulary came in handy.

Like the day I dropped the formaldehyde in first period science class. Formaldehyde preserving the dead peace of the frogs. The teacher said, "Pair up, two to a scalpel." The kids all groaning. Monday, nine a.m. Dead frogs. No one even wanted to open the lids. We all knew the sour, sharp smell. I dropped the jar. "On purpose," the teacher said, and maybe it was. I was sick of hearing the whining from the kids whose houses had exhaust hoods over the stoves and central air and cleaning ladies and room purifiers. Not like at my house where the fans rusted in the windows but still turned. Pulling in the odor of thousands of gallons of Pabst Blue Ribbon fermenting at the factory a quarter-mile away. Dead hops. Dead frogs. The formaldehyde reeked. Long after we were through with the tiny hearts of the frogs and had latched onto DNA, the boys said, "Smells like Macy in here." Most of the girls laughed and held their noses. The girls were dipped in White Shoulders. I didn't smell like formaldehyde, but something close. Clothes hauled up from the damp basement, resurrected from thrift shops, and no matter how many times they were washed, they still had a stench to them, a mold that lived inside the threads like DNA. That's when I called Patty Crane, the head cheerleader with the horse laugh, a hematoma. And it caught on. Even though no one knew what hematoma meant, it sounded like the perfect put-down. You're such a hematoma.

Maybelline said, "A hematoma is the blood pooling between the brain and the skull due to a blow to the head."

"Christ, Maybelline," I said, "is there anything you don't know?" We were sitting on the floor in my bedroom. She was cutting up an orange into twelve wedges with a penknife.

"Sure," she said, "lots of things."

"Name one," I said.

She put one of the orange wedges in her mouth and moved it around with her tongue. When she pulled it out, the juice was all gone. The orange skin was a couple of shades lighter than her hair, which she still wore in two braids. She stared at me. I picked up a piece of orange, peeled the skin back from the corner, and pulled all the flesh of the orange off with my teeth. She said, "I don't know why you like me." She stuck another whole wedge in her mouth.

I knew why. The ways that we weren't the same were what I liked. When I lied she saw right through it. Like she was in my head, adding all the pieces of me up. She saw all of me and didn't try to make me into a fraction. I swallowed my orange and, with the tips of my fingers, I touched right below Maybelline's lip where juice from the orange seeped out and pooled. She took the orange from her mouth. I kissed Maybelline. Just leaned over and my lips were up against hers and her hand was at the back of my head, in my hair, pulling me forward into the kissing. Then we stopped. We wiped our hands on each other's jeans.

We ate the rest of the orange and didn't kiss again until she was about to go home. I threw the orange peels into my wastepaper basket. When I turned around, Maybelline was standing there, book bag in one hand; her other hand reached up to my face, and her fingers touched my lips. She said, "The eyes might be the windows to the soul, but I believe the eyes can easily lie. But a kiss always tells the truth."

I kissed Maybelline. She kissed me. Her tongue was skinny and pointed and skated around mine. Like Peggy Fleming doing a hundred spins. I held her face in my hands. My lips were jumpy, humid, thrilled. The look between us, sticky. I sucked the short line of her lips. Maybelline leaned back against my bedroom wall with the poster of The Rolling Stones. Her eyes closed, my tongue just reaching in to sting hers. Maybelline moaning. I saw how a kiss could tell the truth. I wanted to keep hearing Maybelline liking what I did, but I also wanted to stop so that she would want it even more. These were the fractions of me that Maybelline didn't see. The ones that added up the opportunities. Even though I didn't want to, not with Maybelline. Her tongue started to slide into my mouth, but I stepped back from her lips. Pulled away. She opened her eyes with their constellations of freckles. We didn't say, this will never happen again. We didn't say it would.

"A kiss is just a kiss," I said.

"Okay," she said.

"Okay," I said. But when she had gone, the kiss was not just a kiss. Maybelline went home and I lay down on my bed.

I touched my skin, touched my vagina, *labia majora* and *minora*. I knew all the parts from the nursing books, the names dressed in Latin. Whole clitoris with the shaft, glans, and crura. My fingers followed the crura, dividing from the glans like a wishbone. I wished by placing the tip of my finger on the glans and circling.

I lay in my bed and invented a doctor. A doctor at the hospital asking for a volunteer. For a nurse, and I raised my hand because I was in the candy striper waiting room of soon-to-be nurses. The doctor said, "Yes." I was asked by the doctor to lie on the operating table. "We are here today," the doctor said, "to put to rest the notion that girls can satisfy their own desire. It will become clear that girls are natural liars when it pertains to their own pleasure." *Not so,* my fingers said, circling.

There were interns, bird-eyed boys in their thin hospital greens, in a horseshoe around the table. There were nurses behind the interns, quiet and masked. The interns looked on while the doctor cut away my half-candy-striper, half-nurse's uniform. "This is a young nurse," he said, "nurse *juvenile.*" The interns wrote that down. "Juvenile and virginal," the doctor continued. Virgin, from the Latin *virgo*, a word with no traceable meaning. Virgin here meaning untouched. My fingers slowed in their circling the glans. The blood hurried, rushing and waiting at the same time.

The doctor said, "You cannot do that."

My finger slipped past the hymen into the introitus-vaginal opening. Inside, my finger was surrounded by tissue, walls, fluid—sticky, warm. I said, "You can't tell me what to do."

"See here," the doctor said, "the hymen can only be broken by force. Force of nature, the nature of a girl, force of habit, force becomes a habit." The interns wrote that down, *force*.

I pulled my finger out. Back to the clitoris, where the truth was unmistakable. I tapped slowly, teasing arousal, pressed harder. Pleasure cartwheeling on the tips of every nerve ending.

The doctor and the interns scratched their balls. They didn't write anything down. They watched my hand sweeping over my breasts, pulling at my nipples. The motion of my fingers alone said *pleasure is my root*. Doctor, I don't need a thing from you.

The doctor added up his figures of pulse and heartbeat. The interns saw my temperature rise on the monitor. They stepped closer, not believing how good one finger, two fingers, three, could feel to a girl. The nurses behind the interns said, "Keep your distance from the patient." The interns watched. The doctor watched. I lifted my hips and swayed and pushed at my fingers.

I could taste Maybelline's orange tongue. The doctor said, "Her respiration is increasing." I sucked Maybelline's lip. "More blood is getting to the epidermis," the doctor said and pointed at my nipple with a ruler. "See," he said. My nipple was sticking out, fattening up. The interns stepped closer. They wanted to enter me, force their way in to see if I was telling the truth. The nurses said, "Do not get too close to the patient or you will be expelled from medical school." They could only watch me. That was what I wanted. They had no choice. I was in charge. They couldn't stop me. My finger sliding over my clitoris, seeing Maybelline's lips where my fingers were, pushing her tongue into me and out. Everything so fast: her tongue, my fingers, and I came rolling over on my bed, my hand pressing into me.

My pulse backed down from its high altitude. My hands rested on the bed-spread. The interns disappeared. The doctor disappeared. Maybelline. The operating room faded. Except in the corner of the operating room, one nurse was lowering her surgical mask: my mother, nurse *maturus*. "Be grateful," she said. "I taught you everything you know."

⤚

THE CAKES ARE cooling on the racks. My mother has the electric mixer on high, whirling together sugar and butter and some fake food coloring. I stand in the kitchen watching her drink from the tall glass while her hand pulls the mixer in circles through the frosting. She pours some of her drink into the bowl. Mixes it in and adds some more. The secret to her frosting recipe is to add what gets her through the day. My day, my birthday. She isn't dead drunk yet. She's still ready-for-anything, stand-up-straight-and-stubborn. There's no sway to her back, no slouch. The liquor hasn't reached all the way in yet. Soon she won't care. It's the same way every year on my birthday. It takes until late afternoon for the two or three or four more glasses to get all the way under her skin. She'll say how grateful she is that I am her daughter. She'll pick out the candles that I just blew out and say, "I hope your wish comes true, Love." The only time she says *love* like it's my name, only soaked in a bottle of liquor.

She turns off the mixer. Bright pink peaks of frosting follow the beaters. She hands one of the beaters to me, like she knew I was there all the time, behind her back, watching.

I say, "I want vanilla ice cream tonight, not that strawberry you always get."

She turns around. Licking the other beater. "Fine," she says, "you'll get everything you want, everything you've always wished for." Winks her eye at me. Cocks her smile. Makeup perfect on her face. She turns back around, taking another lick of frosting, taking another drink.

My mother? She's my full-length mirror.

I make a vow—I will never bake a cake. I make another vow—I will forget when my birthday is. And one more—I will never, ever be like her.

I go into my parents' bedroom. The bookcase full of my mother's books. The books she reads with the bedroom door closed and locked. Going in there in the afternoons after her shift, walking past me, slamming the door. The high-back chair angles in next to the bookcase, a floor lamp with a ratty yellow shade next to the chair. On the opposite wall is the water stain from the peak of the roof that leaked and my dad, Mr. Know-it-all, said he fixed. The stain grows and grows. Seeps downstairs onto the wall by the front door. I open his dresser drawer with the tin of money and take twenty bucks. The envelopes have the things he bought crossed out and the things he wants written below: *electric can opener, trash compactor, family portrait.* The envelope marked *Macy* I never steal from. There's only twenty dollars left in it anyway. My mother takes from that envelope and tells my dad that she puts the money in the bank so that it will earn interest.

On the second shelf of my mother's bookcase is a small cedar box. I know the key is in my mother's makeup drawer, under the Tawny Rose pancake powder. I unlock the box, pick up the prescription bottle, open it, and tap out six Seconals. Another prescription bottle has diet pills, amphetamines, in it, but I leave those for another day.

Downers and Uppers. I know what they are. The bottles are not marked but I had brought one of each to the hospital library a couple of months before. After my Tuesday candy striper shift, looking like I belonged there in that library with the interns and nursing students. Asked the librarian for the *Physicians Desk Reference* and sat at the farthest away cubicle with the uneven desk leg that seesawed every time I touched it. I paged through the book. All the pills lined up on the shiny paper like Good & Plenty candies. Looking for the colors to match, the shapes to match, the letters and numbers to match. Seconal. Dextroamphetamine. Brought the book back to the librarian. She said, "Did you find what you were looking for?" I said, "Yeah, thanks." She said, "That's what we're here for. It's nice to see a candy striper taking a further interest in medicine."

I put the Seconals in my pocket. Lock the box, slide the key under Tawny Rose. I look in the mirror above my mother's makeup dresser. My mother once told me a mirror can suck you in if you stare too long into your own eyes. She said, "Be grateful, Macy, I'm telling you this, when you look in a mirror, look quick and don't wait for the mirror to say whether you're beautiful, say it before you even sit down in front of the mirror, like I do. Yes, you'll see how it is, Macy, just you wait. You'll understand all too soon."

I look in the mirror. Seeing my mother. Seeing my mother in me. Three Seconals in my pocket. Happy fucking birthday. On her makeup dresser, under a scarf of pink and lemon, is a new camera, not the Brownie my dad has.

In the kitchen the cakes smell like nutmeg. I ask, "So where'd the new camera come from?"

"What were you doing in my bedroom?" She sets her glass down and watches me.

"I was getting the tweezers. I had a splinter, and there was the camera."

She twirls the ice in the glass. "Got it with S&H Green stamps, fifty-nine books. That's four years of collecting the damn things, pasting on the strips of stamps, while you're off in your room listening to some screeching crap on the radio and your dad is telling me for the hundredth time how the union is as corrupt as the owners of the factory and he's caught in the middle and on and on and on. Jesus." Clink, clink. Up goes the glass. "Four years of toilet paper and baked beans and corn flakes and tuna and Velveeta and corned beef hash."

"What are you getting at?" I ask.

"Four years. I figured I would buy something with those stinking stamps that could record what four years amounted to—a camera. I'll bring it to the supermarket and take pictures of everything I buy for the next four years. That's exactly what I'll do."

"Have you tried it yet?" I ask.

"Today," she says, "I'm going to use it today."

"Well, I'll see you later."

She says nothing. The fan in the window pulling in hot air, the stale summer smells of the sunburnt grass from our backyard, the wood rafters under the blisters and peels of paint, and the Pabst Blue Ribbon beer. The tar on the asphalt bubbling up. On my mother's finger, the finger she taps her glass with, is the mood ring. I never could find it after the day she hid it, even though I went through the drawers and closet in her bedroom. Sticking my hands under slippers and through the half-slips and bras, unrolling her socks, checking every pocket and cuff. Nothing. No mood ring.

She taps the glass and the mood ring is turning from black to gold. There was nothing on the piece of paper that came with the mood ring that said what gold meant.

She says, "Goodbye."

Hissy sits on her front step. Her hair a frizz, a long cloud of pale red. She says, "Bout time."

I say, "You know how it is, my mother's an obstacle course. I remind her of her lost youth and she likes to have me around so she can suffer properly."

"Yeah, my mom's like that. Wants me to believe she's a saint." Hissy stands and adjusts her paisley halter, too small for her breasts. Paisleys swirling around her nipples. Hip-hugger blue shorts and a wide brown belt that Patterson tooled, a diamond-backed snake slithering along the leather. Her name hissing out the snake's mouth.

We walk into town the short way, down the alley with the giant dogs barking behind fences. Hissy sucks on a cigarette, walking her summer walk, slow, like she's battling gravity. American flags hang outside every store. Red, white, and blue crepe paper is strung in twists above doors. July fourth is over but all the decorations stay up until Halloween. I take out the NY Yankees baseball cap from my bag and put it on my head.

"Where'd you get that?" Hissy asks, her cheeks all splotchy red like a firecracker had gone off.

"I stole it. I forgot I even had it, but I was looking for some rolling papers in my closet and there it was."

We pass by Mandee's Apparel Shop, which has the ugliest clothes. Racks of frilly blouses and stretch pants with elastic waistbands in shit brown and beige. This is the place all the mothers like to bring their teenage daughters and all the teenage daughters hate to go. The sales ladies are mean and snotty when you go in by yourself but really pleasant when your mother is with you. Mostly the mothers buy stuff for themselves: big cotton panties, summer muumuus, raincoats.

"Jee-sus," Hissy says, "look at that mannequin, will you. What is she trying to be, the Statue of Liberty?" The mannequin holds a sparkler above her head and wears a white shiny sleeveless dress that goes all the way to the floor. Around the mannequin's waist is more of that crepe paper, only with red, white, and blue stars. "If you ever see my mother taking me in here, shoot me."

"Will do," I say. We walk across the parking lot of the A&P. "Why'd you leave your car here?"

"Shit," Hissy says, "I locked my keys in it for the third time this month. It's Patterson's fault. He's got me thinking about him when I should be paying attention to the damn car."

"What else is new?"

"Shut up."

"Is Betty going to the quarry?"

"Yeah, yeah, didn't I tell you? Betty's said she's got a big surprise for your birthday."

"What is it?"

"Don't know. All Betty would say was that it was a secret and a miracle she got it."

⤻

A SINKHOLE FILLED WITH black and blue water. A mud cake underneath. That's the quarry. We set down our towels and bags at the end of the beach. Near a willow. Hissy takes out her Tab and Kents, sticks the can of Tab into the sand. Betty sits on an India-print bedspread with a pink tree and green flying monkeys and red pears. On the other side of the quarry the grey rock rises up in giant steps. The scraping steam shovels left behind teeth marks in the rock. No streams go in or out of the quarry. The water is all from rain and percolation—it collects and darkens. Nothing shows in the water, not the skinny sky or the trees or the black-eyed Susans climbing up the giant steps.

Maybelline sits behind me. I can feel her shadow like it's something I can pick up and hold. Betty's friend, Pam, lies on the India print next to Betty. Pam has a boy's haircut and wears sunglasses, the aviator kind with dark green glass and chrome rims. Can't see her eyes at all. Maybelline, Hissy, Betty, and I squint at the sunshine shooting its rays off the tin box Betty hands me.

Betty says, "Happy Day, Macy." I unknot the shoestring bow and stick my thumbnail in the dent under the lid to open it.

"Careful," Betty says, "don't tip it over." Inside the tin box is a beige powder on blue tissue paper.

"What is it?" I ask.

"Crystal meth," Betty says.

"Shit," I say, "I've never done that before."

Betty opens her hand in front of me and I put the tin on her palm.

I say, "It looks like the talcum powder my dad puts in his shoes."

Hissy says, "Well, I don't care what it looks like cause I hear crystal meth is a real trip and a half."

Maybelline says, "Hissy, you wouldn't care if dope came pickled in formaldehyde; you'd ingest anything that was put in front of you."

"Yeah, yeah," Hissy says, "up yours and so damn what?"

From her red straw handbag, Betty lifts out a spoon, a three-inch paper straw, a saucer. She says, "My gift to you, Macy, is to experience your birthday in a new way just like when you were born." She dips the spoon into the crystal meth and makes a short, plump trail of it on the saucer. She hands me the straw.

I look around the beach to see if anyone is watching. Three mothers in skirted bathing suits are on the other end of the beach chasing after kids, who are wearing nothing but the slippery water. Two old ladies sit in lawn chairs, reading. Both have on identical jumbo-size blonde straw hats with a seashell dangling from the top. Behind them a group of young girls, all on their bellies, arms out to their sides, wearing bikinis and baby oil, shine like gold crosses. None of them looks at us. No one else is on the beach. The boys are up on the rocks around the corner from us in the quarry's side pocket, where the steam shovels had started to dig the quarry bigger but then abandoned the whole thing. The deep pool is over there, and the boys jump off the giant steps into the water, one after the other, like lemmings.

I hold the straw and Betty holds the saucer. I say, "So what do I do?"

Betty says, "You snort it up one nostril, keeping the other nostril closed."

"Why don't you go first," I say.

"All right," Betty says. I give her the straw. "It's really kay."

"What?" I say.

"Simple," she says and takes in a breath and lets it out. Puts the straw above the crystals and the other end a little ways into her nose and vacuums up the crystal meth in one quick snort. She pinches her nose and keeps breathing the crystals in. "Gango," Betty says, when she lets go of her nose.

"Okay," I say, "dish me out some." Betty scoops more onto the saucer. I do what Betty did, breathe in the crystal meth. As soon as it gets into my nose, it flies everywhere in my body, a tingling tidal wave.

Betty says, "The world will open and you will be at the center of the world and everything will be in its correct place." She puts more of the crystals on the saucer for Maybelline and Hissy.

Hissy says, "Fucking-A, I can't believe you got this." She grabs the straw, which I am holding in my hand without even knowing it. Hissy's frizzed-out hair falls around her face when she bends over the saucer, like she wants privacy as she sticks the straw up her nose. "This is very, very righteous."

Betty laughs, her teeth all showing. I have never felt my teeth like this, the edges curled and sharp and all of them humming.

Maybelline looks at the crystal meth and then at Betty, who is scooting more into a straight line on the saucer. "What is crystal meth?" Maybelline asks.

Betty says, "Ask Pam, she's the big mama of biochemistry at NYU."

Pam turns on her side, picks up the tin box, looks at Maybelline. "If you want to know the chemical structure, well, sister, I can tell you that. Molecule by molecule. I know you'd understand. Science is your thing, right? I can explain what will go on when the crystal meth hits the brain. But the important thing, sister, what crystal meth really is, is a key to a thousand doors opening and you being able to experience everything—every smell, the touch of the sky, the tiniest decibel of sound, bend of light, shade of color, in each of those thousand doors at the same time."

Betty says, "That is pure poetry, darlin."

Pam pushes the aviator sunglasses higher on her nose and her lips look like they are about to kiss Betty, but she turns her lips to the saucer and says, "I'm ripe for that." She snorts the neat line. And then there is just Maybelline.

Betty holds the saucer closer to Maybelline. Maybelline tilts the straw down and sucks up the crystal meth, slowly, with her eyes closed. When she is done, she opens her eyes, blinking, and says, "My thing is mathematics."

Pam says, "Cool, sister."

The crystal meth enters my brain like doors unlocking. Doors and doors, with red knobs and keyholes the shape of Maybelline's mouth after she kisses me. The hinges on the doors resist, the brass metal knifing into the wood, leaving dents and scars. But the crystal meth keeps pushing. Unlocking. Hand to the door knob, pulling. I look at Maybelline and she looks at me. The meth crystals grind into my bloodstream. One plus one, the doors open into infinity and Maybelline, the way she's staring at me, I know she can see it too. How we are at the center of the world, together, and everything is in its correct place.

Maybelline rubs suntan lotion onto my shoulders and back, her hands slick over my skin and bones. The crystal meth is coming on and on. Maybelline's hands are going right through me to my heart, latching onto the crystal meth's hurry.

Hissy says, "My body feels like it's a sunbeam." Betty and Pam are lying on the India print, thighs touching, the green monkeys flying, the pink tree birthing a million red pears. Pam's aviator glasses are off and her uncovered eyes are looking in two different directions at once. Her whole face is different one side to the other. Her smile rises up higher on the left, her nose bends to the right, one eyebrow is straight across and the other arches. Maybelline quits rubbing. Takes her hands away. I can feel her hands backing up from me like they have strikes of lightning in them.

The crystal meth speeding into every moment, every moment getting wider and longer. In my mouth, my tongue clicks against my teeth. I see Pam's pinwheeling moving eye looking desire at Betty, her hand just an inch from Betty's hand. Only a monkey's tail between the two hands.

"Candy striping," I say, "suits me." Don't know why I say it. My mouth just needing something to do with its tongue and teeth. My tongue points each word out of my mouth, telling them to get out, fast. "I mean I can go into all these rooms, where people have lost their hands or a spleen or have a million stitches or old people with all their organs winding down; Mr. Garland with the appendicitis thinks it's because of the penny he swallowed when he was a kid, forty years ago. I mean there's a different condition every day I'm there. They tell me everything, just so I won't leave right away and they'll have to be alone. Sick people hate to be alone. I think I'm going to go to nursing school, what do you think?"

Pam's pinky is on top of Betty's pinky. Betty says, "Nursing runs in your family, Macy."

Maybelline says, "That's true, Betty, but it's not like that facet could be inherited."

Pam watches me watching her pinky, waiting for me to raise my head. When I do, her good eye is not moving one iota away from the stare she's got going into my eyes. Her other eye is fixed to the right of the willow. Still staring at me and not Maybelline, Pam says, "Well, sister, sounds like you know something about genetics, but I have to challenge your conclusion based on the research I've seen. The aptitude for nursing or any occupation, for that matter, that many relatives in the same family hold in common could very well be inherited."

Pam taps the side of her head with two fingers. The dark shine of her hair. Sparkle of a few white strands. I push my feet deeper into the sand of the beach. Pebbles between my toes. Trying to hold myself still. The rush of slow and fast of the crystal meth. Pam points two fingers at me and says, "What interests me, Macy, is the fact that what you like about candy striping is the power you think you have when you go into those hospital rooms. It doesn't sound like you care one way or another what happens to any of those people. Is that inherited too?"

I stare back at Pam with what I know I have inherited: my mother's look, the nothing-is-going-to-get-my-goat, screw-you look. Pam and I keep staring until I say, "So Pam, what the hell is wrong with your eye?"

Pam puts her aviator glasses back on and says, "To know about my eye you have to know something about the heart, and I don't think you'd understand that."

The crystal meth coming on and on. I turn an inch and I can see all of us and how we are tinted the pale green of the willow leaves. Covered in dots of sun.

Betty laughs but this time her mouth doesn't open to show her teeth. Laughing to herself. She says, "The heart is never black or white and that's the complication, isn't it? To walk in the in-between and not know where the heart will take you. Some people run from that and some people don't." Betty rests her hand over Pam's hand. But only for an instant.

Hissy says, "I don't get what's going on between all of ya. I thought we came to party, have a good time."

I say, "I'm having a good time, Hissy, all right?"

"Yeah, yeah," Hissy says. "Well, look, I've got presents for you." She shoves the Kent into her mouth and the smoke clouds over her hair. Her toes wiggle out of the sand as she twists to reach for her bag. She hands me two packages, wrapped in pages from a magazine. The first package I can tell is an ounce of dope. Underneath the wrapping there it is, with two packs of rolling papers, the usual Zig Zag and another kind with pale butterflies skidding into each other on the double wide papers. Hissy says, "Colombian."

"All right," I say, "someone roll one up in the butterflies." Betty takes the baggie and starts sifting the dope on the saucer.

In the other package is a belt. Yellow jackets are tooled into the leather and my name is on the back part of the belt. Hissy says, "Patterson made it, but I told him what to put on it because of that day you walked right through all those yellow jackets in the woods and didn't even get stung."

I slip the belt through the loops of my shorts. "God, Hissy," I say, "thanks, and tell Patterson he's back on my good side."

"Yeah, yeah," Hissy says, "that'll last, what, four minutes?"

Betty lights the joint. Pam holds onto it for three tokes. Lying on her back, aviator eyes to the sky, one arm stretches out over her head. Smiling her short, lopsided smile, not aware of anyone else. The crystal meth is a frantic river I can't stop and everything floods into me, through the open doors. The heat is like hands all over my body, itching and fiery. Each breath releases more of the crystals. Willow leaves spun in see-through petticoats by the caterpillars blow in the puffs of wind. Pam's odd eyes beneath the green glass. Betty sits up, her black hair glazed with the yellow sunlight. Hissy is smoking the Kent, the smoke, frizzy as Hissy's hair, going nowhere in the muggy air. My body is rushing and waiting at the same time. Pam lets go of the joint and Betty passes it to me. I suck the smoke into my mouth. The outside of my body is an outline, a stick figure, and the inside of my body is hollow, and the smoke, a crayon coloring me in. I turn to Maybelline to give her the joint. Maybelline is watching the water. I could watch Maybelline's face for my whole life and never get tired of it.

But the crystal meth is pushing at me to ask the question that's still sitting on my tongue. "Pam, I really do want to know about your eye."

"Why?" Pam asks.

"I don't know. I guess I'm just curious."

Pam slides her aviator glasses off. "Another condition?"

"Yeah, maybe it is just another condition, but what I didn't say about my candy striping is that I like going into all those rooms because I want to know how their bodies get used to their conditions."

Hissy says, "I can't believe this. Did you become a philosopher all of a sudden? I'm going to the bathroom." She gets up and takes her Tab and another Kent with her. Maybelline is still watching the water.

Pam says, "Okay, Macy, it's like this, see if you can follow. I got in a fight, a screaming match, both of us drunk and arguing . . . it went on a long time. I was trying to make the most convincing point, sway the outcome to my side. But it didn't work that way. At some point she just stopped arguing and laughed at me instead. That was her strategy. Pissed me off. More than I've ever been. I left and got on my motorcycle and ten minutes later went through an intersection on a yellow light while a car was turning into my lane and that was that. Broken nose, crushed cheekbone, and my eye lost. The doctors put in a glass eye."

"Christ, so that's why your eye doesn't move."

Pam puts her green glasses on and says, "Yes, that's why it doesn't move."

I reach over and pull a Kent out of Hissy's pack and light it with a match from the Colony Inn book of matches I carry around. Maybelline puts her hand on my arm and says, "I want to go in the water, okay?"

"Okay," I say.

I look in the water and I see only water. Not me. Nothing of me comes back from this black shine. Or Maybelline. Both of us are staring into the quarry, down around the corner where the path to the cliffs starts. I don't care that I can't see myself. The water is my mother's ground. Not mine. The water smells of oily weeds, elastic bathing caps, nickel in the rock, snake grass rubbing the edge of the water and rotting. My mother is at home here, swimming away from the rock and ground and the life she never wanted. Lost in the water. I can't even swim.

Our feet slip into the washbowl of mud beneath the water. I scoop some mud and draw a line down Maybelline's arm. Maybelline does the same, drawing a line down my arm to the tip of my finger. My hand slides under her hand and back until just our fingertips touch and the mud line matches up. Clips us together. We walk up the path, my hand in her hand. The sun is glue on my skin, pollen from the ragweed sticking to me.

Maybelline says, "Do you think we'll always be on the same line?"

"I don't know," I say. The path steepens, cuts back into the trees then winds close to the edge again. The water down below gets blacker, looks almost solid. Ash trees tethered in the granite cliff.

Maybelline runs her finger down the line on my arm. She says, "It does all come down to odds and probability."

"So, do you figure out what the best odds will be or do you just wait and see?" We stop by two oak trees. The sunlight is like steam rising from the leaves. On the other side of the oak trees is a ledge of grey rock. I can see some of the boys up on the high pink and grey rocks across the quarry from us, swinging out on knotted ropes over the deep pool and dropping. Long seconds pass before I hear the splash of their bodies.

Maybelline says, "I always know the probability."

I step in front of her. "What's the probability that I'll kiss you?"

"In my favor."

I kiss her and she opens her mouth and the kiss goes everywhere in my body, turning the kiss into nothing else but the kissing of Maybelline. I don't want to stop or make her wait. There is no more that I want. Just Maybelline.

I sit on the ledge. Maybelline sits on me, straddles me. She unbuttons the white blouse I wear over my bathing suit. She says, "Your skin is on fire." My breasts are in her hands. She pulls my nipple, a detonation of pleasure. My fingers follow her spine up and down, over her shoulder blades. My palms rest on her ribs. She says, "This is what I think about all the time. You about to touch me." My hands turning the corner from back to front. Across the fabric of her bikini top. Undoing the hook and eye until there is no fabric in the way and my hands are over her breasts. Nipples round and deep orange. We are pushing our bodies into each other. I kiss a line across her face, over the closeness of mouth, eyes, and nose. To her ear. My tongue skims the opening of her ear. She is leaning her head toward my tongue. I pull back. Her hand is on my other breast. I bite down on her ear, her neck, her lips. My hands pulling her body closer. She says, "A kiss is not just a kiss."

I say, "Maybelline."

Kissing Maybelline, a thousand more doors open. But in each of those doors a hundred questions sit on chairs, fill up soup bowls, pick up knives, want to be asked. A hundred thousand questions but really just two: does Maybelline love me and what does that mean? I let go of Maybelline, my hands, my lips, my tongue. Maybelline, the ugly beauty of her face. The melted, runny rust-red freckles shadow her eyelids. She leans back from me. I undo her braids, pulling her thin orange hair out of its pattern of over and under. I love what doesn't pretend to be anything else.

Maybelline takes my hand and turns it over, kisses my palm. "The truth is, Macy, I think it is better to believe in circles, and the ability to bend back around, than in straight lines." She puts her hand in her pocket and brings out a blue felt bag. "This is for you, for your birthday." She takes out a necklace, and on the string is a circular stone: half black, half white. "It's a yin-yang charm, two separate things connected to make a whole." I put the necklace on over my head. Maybelline looks right into my eyes and says, "I love you."

Maybelline leans back, taking a breath in, letting a breath out, smiling at me. She touches my lips with her finger. "I'm really warm, blow some cool air my way." I blow on her neck and belly, breast and arms. She stands up and shakes her head, orange hair dusty in the sun. I can hear the boys yelling chicken at each other. The heat rushes off the rock. Maybelline turns and looks out across the quarry and walks out on the ledge. The water is black and cold below. "I am so hot, it must be the drugs," she says. I stand up, wanting more than anything to kiss Maybelline again. She is watching the water. She takes her shirt off and drops it on a rock.

She faces me. "Macy, there is only one version of the truth worth telling. Sometimes you need a different vantage point to see it. Today, I saw it."

"What?" I ask.

Maybelline's pale eyes are like the white yin stone with the black dot. "You don't have to be like your mother. You don't ever have to run away, Macy, like your mother, in order to be loved."

"What are you talking about?" I take a step toward Maybelline.

She waves her hand in front of her and says, "I saw your mother before I got here. She was talking to the butcher at the bus station. She had a suitcase and was getting on a bus. She's running away."

"Oh," I say.

"Oh," Maybelline says. She takes two steps backwards, turns around, and says, "I'm going in the water now, to cool off."

"But Maybelline, you can't. It's too high up."

"It's okay. Come with me." She puts her long arms over her head and dives.

I look in the water and I see Maybelline surfacing and floating. Not swimming like my mother swims. Not one part of her moves. Her face is up to the sun, to the squall of cicadas. I run down the path, all the way to the water. Betty and Pam are wading, bringing palmfuls of water up to their arms. "Maybelline," I say. Say it loud, say it louder than just calling someone, scream it. Betty and Pam look at me. The smiles slip off their faces into the black water. I am pointing and stepping into the water, mud sucking my feet, trying to hold me in place. I can hear Betty and Pam pushing through the water, following me around the rock into the quarry's side pocket. Maybelline is floating by the rocks below where she dived. The boys across the quarry are still yelling and swinging off their ropes. Not noticing us. The water is up to my waist—broken, jagged granite pokes out from the base of the cliff. Red in the black water, floating next to Maybelline. Pam swims past me, cutting the water like she's a knife slicing through a chocolate cake. I can't go any farther. The water is just below my chin. I can't swim. I can only watch Maybelline floating, Pam hooking her below the breastbone, swimming backwards, pulling Maybelline with her. The red in the black water following them like a string. The crystal meth so fast inside of me, I'm seeing it all. Experiencing everything: every bend of light, touch of the hot sky, tiniest decibel of sound. Pam's breathing is like a hurricane as she kicks through the water, pulling Maybelline out. Maybelline lies on the sand. Betty crying. Smell of the bitter water over us. All colors, red. The red of Maybelline's blood over her face, floating out of her head. At the center of the world, just me alone, looking down at Maybelline, and every one of the thousand doors closes and locks.

part four

~

dotty and macy

remedies

1995

Dotty

IN MY HOUSE, Bell and Ray stunk up the air with their perfumed talk, Oil of Well-Kept Secrets. The cork, jimmied from the champagne Bell brought in her shiny pink shopping bag, popped like the snap of a thick bone as I walked out through the back screen door, my leg full of ache. I was crooked, nauseous tilting, lopsided, the world lopsided.

"Dotty, where are you going?" I heard Macy ask.

"She'll come back," Bell said.

Ray said, "Let's have a toast."

"To what?" Macy said.

I stopped outside the screen door, down the two steps, next to the pile of old compost. All the windows in the house opened to the last warm October days. How could I not hear the toast they made? My cheek against the bean trellis stuck in the compost pile. The purple-podded beans grew up the trellis next to the house where inside Bell and Ray and Macy tipped their glasses.

Did Macy lean toward Bell when Bell said, "Let's toast to today and finding Dot."

Did Macy look at Ray, at his mismatched face, as he said, "And to the kindness and generosity of Macy."

Would Macy hold her glass back for just a second or two as Bell and Ray brought theirs to the center, to the meeting, to the no coincidence that they had tracked me down and were toasting spells to charm Macy.

The glasses tapped and murmured together, soft, like a good-night kiss.

Macy did not come out of the house to find me, to talk to me. She sat in the living room where Bell and Ray were descending, an ice age of glaciers sweeping over all feeling, freezing anything related to love. I pulled nine dry bean pods off the vines. Walked away from the house, down the path to the river. Past the brambles with their seedy blackberries. I took the beans out of their stiff jackets. Pink swirls on red beans and I slid them into my pocket that held seven pain pills. I had enough tears to fill up a pond but I didn't let even one condense and fall. The thing I knew about Bell and Ray was that they could smell weakness; it was the perfume they loved the most.

I stood at the door of the house that Macy built. That odd little house. I had watched the piece by piece of it, the gathering of the driftwood in a pile, the imprecise fitting and nailing together. There wasn't two the same of anything. Macy had no plans, no blueprint. She built the house in forty-one days, her body a flood of purpose. The house was singular, a monument, peculiar as what she yelled at it as she constructed. In a voice like a child mimicking her parents, she'd say, "If you don't obey me, you'll be sorry" or "Be grateful you're even getting a roof over your head."

The floor of the house sat on four birch spines. The walls rose up, twisted and warped limbs, their serrated and kinked ends sawed off, hammered into place, not measured first for where each board should fit. Macy made them fit. Pounding with a mallet, the boards splintered, sheared off, slid in and rubbed their pitted and rough edges together. When she was done, what gaps were left were thin as paper, would not let any eye see in. The roof was just a flat top. She set two small windows side by side in the wall facing the river and painted the glass milk white and grey.

The door had bobbed down the river the first week of October and popped right out of the water onto the ground. The door was a three-by-five-foot board, a sign, the skin of paint leached from red to pink. I had watched Macy set hinges in the door, screw the door into place, and go inside, closing the door. The house that Macy built was done.

I had never even peeked inside until today. When I pulled the handle, the door was light, as if it was nothing but sawdust beneath the faded paint. It smelled like oil—burned, rancid. I went into the house and lit a beeswax candle that was on the uneven floor. There were smells there: salt, peppermint, and alcohol. Shadows entered the house, sat on the edge of the table, and waved at the ceiling. My leg ached and I leaned against the wall but nothing was solid; the boards moved. I put my weight back on my leg and closed my eyes for a moment, wishing the pain away, but it would not leave.

When I opened my eyes, what I found was Macy's mother. Lila? I brought the candle over to the table and there she was. In a photograph framed in beveled wood, the date written across the bottom corner in red: July 23, 1973. Macy's sixteenth birthday. Written in black in the top border of the photo: Lila B. Kahn. Macy's mother. Lila? It couldn't be, but it was. She was holding the blue coat in the picture. The same coat that hung behind me from a wire in the ceiling, an empty blue skin, pocked by years of moths and the pinholes of their chewing. The same coat that I found her in on the bed in the motel room. Lila?

She was approaching a door when the picture was taken. Turned her face to the camera. The sky was shut out from the house by the curtain over the window in the door. The light in the hallway was on and she narrowed her eyes with their heavy coats of eye shadow. She did not smile at the camera but winked a slippery wink. Lila?

But Macy had told me that her mother died in an accident on Macy's sixteenth birthday. The same day Lila checked into the Sea & Sand Motel. Macy told me her mother was on her way to the butcher's shop to buy a London broil for Macy's birthday dinner. The house smelled like frosting. The cakes cooled as her mother prepared for Macy's birthday. She left the basement sink filled with bleach and undershirts, that's what Macy said. *Happy Birthday* streamers arced across the living room. Sixteen red candles waited in the box with the see-through window of cellophane. She died that day, that's what Macy told me. Died, quick, no pain were the words Macy used. No pain. But she did not die that day. That was the lie that hinged all the other lies together, mother to daughter, daughter to mother, both of them to me. Lila.

I sat on the apple crate. My heart scorched. Goddamn. Why didn't Macy say anything even approaching the truth?

I rubbed the part of my leg where the metal occupied the bone, the pulse of ache, that metronome, throb, seizure, the daily timekeeper, pain. I picked up the 1945 high school yearbook that was on the table, opened it, and followed the alphabet—but Lila's last name wasn't Kahn yet. That's why I didn't know, didn't connect the smile to the name, the daughter to the mother, because Lila didn't use her married name. I looked at the first names because I didn't think I'd recognize her, but I did. It was the familiarity I noticed when I looked at Macy for the first time. Knowing how her eyes would flame and cool and how her smile would form. I found the picture with the name of Lila Lott underneath. It could be Macy. How similar they were to each other. Down to the slight exaggeration of their long lips, that slow promise of a smile whose intent I was never sure of. Because I never looked past the promise.

Lila Lott, you had no nickname, didn't belong to any clubs. Your future wish was to be a nurse. And the quote they used to sum you up was from Shakespeare, *The Winter's Tale*: "I think there is not in the world either malice or matter to alter it." But that's a lie. She knew how to take the world and crumble it with the wink of her eye.

In the framed photograph, she isn't waving goodbye because her hand holds a highball glass filled to the top with its stinging medicine: peppermint schnapps, no doubt. Hair in its raisin-red twirl. She said nothing to the camera when the picture was taken. Lifted an eyebrow. Her lips luminous and wet. I know that face—eyes half closed, mouth curled, slightly open. Even in tasting death, the same face. I knew, I saw it.

Did she look? Underwater? In all those seconds when oxygen was still in her lungs? I imagined she did. That there, under the surface of things, where the green was lulling and the light wavered like eels, she watched how her body was caught in the clutch of the chrome bar. Her arms and legs, heart and lungs were synchronous and could move easily, could swim. But she could not get herself out right away. Then it was too late, the oxygen gone. When she floated free from the roller coaster car, the water kept her for days. I knew. I walked and waited on the beach for Lila to wash up, wash in.

The third day, the current brought her to shore with her half-open eyes. Dead fish eyes staring, black, the whole of the iris black and no longer shiny, like dull buttons sewed on a rag doll. She wore what the ocean gave her. Sea whips with their bulbous anchors, a dress of seaweed wrapped around her. She left behind her shoes. Shells looped in her hair. She was folded up on the shore. The waves had bent her knees and elbows, and the water, the three days of water, pleated her skin in a rippled pattern. Her face not softened from its anger at having been caught and held and killed. And then, stared at by the crowd that surrounded her, pointing like she was a whale that beached. Lila.

I picked up the photo of Lila that leaned against a tin coffee can and laid it face down on the table. I thought about how I had become more and more like her. Putting pills in my mouth every day. Telling lies when it suited my purpose. Only the truth showed up anyway, in its own time, in the middle of the hour on an ordinary morning. On a Tuesday. Even when it seemed impossible that the truth could ever dig itself out from the twenty years of debris we piled on top of it, here it was. Lila. Bell and Ray. And Macy? Now I saw how much of Lila was in her, that need to conduct, to orchestrate, to keep everything within a certain distance but not too close, unless close was advantageous, an opportunity. And was that what I was, nothing more?

Love. The paradox of wanting the very thing that can hurt the most.

I opened a cardboard box marked *crap* next to the table. Inside, on top, the front page of a twenty-two-year-old newspaper. I picked up the newspaper, took a step across the floor, toward the blue coat. How did Macy get the coat? Another step. Another. Until I could smell Lila there in the fabric—the charm, the seductive breath, the mysteries that lies brewed like perfume. Another step and I could have taken her coat in my arms, pretending that she was inside it, waiting there, harmless. But I didn't, and she wasn't, and never was harmless, was she?

I walked past her blue coat and sat on the cot covered with a flowered bedspread. Peonies of bright pinks and white against a light green. Lit more candles until there were many shadows and enough light to read by. Unfolded the newspaper and I found a picture of Macy: her eyes silver snaps and a tiny dot of black in the center of each, her lips swollen, moist as if she'd been kissing for a long time. But that was not accurate. She had done CPR: her lips opening and pressing breath in through the lips of someone else. Her hands busy counting out the beats of the heart, one, two, three, and the lungs, breathe, breathe, breathe. For four minutes—until the dead girl was living. That's what the paper said.

Macy Kahn, Candy Striper, Revives Girl. A picture of the girl: not dead, not coming back to life, but years before, a childhood snapshot, the girl with cock-eyed braids, sitting in an empty fish pond, surrounded by cats.

Fast Thinking and First Aid Saves Friend's Life. The life of Maybelline Blue. That was the girl. Who was, in the words of her high school principal, a genius, scoring perfect on every test she had ever taken. Her life saved by the breath and the measured beats of Macy's hands against Maybelline's heart. Hit her head on a rock after falling or diving—it wasn't crystal clear—into a quarry. She underwent surgery at Rutherford Hospital. Macy Kahn was to be given a certificate of bravery by the mayor at two o'clock, August 4, 1973.

The photo looked like Macy could have been watching TV. Nothing was getting into those eyes or face. Not the shock of Maybelline falling or of Maybelline dead and then alive. Nothing was getting through.

Then I cried. For all of the damaged stories that had been told or held captive behind the eyes. But the eyes told the stories anyway. My hands pressed over my eyes. My nose ran and I wiped it on my shirt sleeve; I didn't care. A wet growl came out of my mouth. I'd had too much of all those salt tears turning into stone. But it wasn't because we looked straight into the pain that we turned into stone, it was because we looked away. And that was all I wanted to do, look away. From all of this. I could have just taken another pain pill and not felt a thing. But I didn't. I saw how the pain pills were my blindness.

I found the hammer and saw in a bucket, along with a tape measure, nails, pencil, and square, but I was not adding on, shoring up, patching. Before I left, I dismantled the house that Macy built. Not all of it. No, it would be like the houses we all live in: full of holes, impermanent, penetrable, the sanctity of secure isolation a terrible facade. The great gusts of lies that churned like tornadoes in kitchens and bedrooms, those I let out from the eleven boards I removed. Splinters everywhere in all our houses that caught us by surprise, punctured, wounded, and hobbled, remained under our thin or our thick skins and pointed their sharp memories at our hearts. I whacked the hammer against the wood, pushed out the boards from their roots in the floor. I pulled nails, twisting them side to side and yanking until they gave. Eleven spaces in the walls. My eyes scratched from crying. I blew my nose on the corner of the bedspread.

I took the furnishings outside. They were just scenery, props as the damage unfolded. The last to go was the door. Doors that we thought we could bolt and lock and they'd be dependable defenders from intrusion, interruption, unwelcome news. But it all got inside. The doors held it in and we feared the unbolting, the opening of the door where the world peered in at the secrets that flourished. Nine brass screws. I unwound them with a rusted screwdriver from the hinges—how little kept the door in place.

I put on the blue coat. On the floor, in the center of the empty house, I placed a teacup that had sat on the table. Took the seven pills from my pocket and dropped them in the cup and put it on top of the picture of Lila. Leaned the story of Maybelline against the box. I opened my wallet and unfolded the clipping I'd saved from the *Ocean County News*, Lila's accident, the pictures of the ocean and the pier, all of it in black and white, creased and tearing. I set it on the teacup. I left my omissions and disappearances with Macy's.

When I was done with the house, I nailed the eleven boards to the door, tried to get them snug, square, watertight. Seven boards down the length of the door and four more on one end, to raise it up. Used the sixteen-penny nails from the bottom of the bucket. I tied down a pillow on top of the four boards and dragged the raft to the green river. My leg, crazy with pain, almost wouldn't move. So I moved slow. I shed my boots with the worn-down waffle soles, peeled my socks from my feet and balled them up inside the boots. Stepped into the water. Skating bugs angled away from me in geometric leaps. The current of cold water matched the cold in my heart. The cold of the terrible power of taking a step and I knew with absolute certainty, without a single doubt, that this step was the one that would change everything.

I pulled the raft into the water. Climbed on. The raft lurched, tipped, and I sat on the cushion. Didn't move. What I knew was to remain still, to not disturb, agitate, take a step unless told to take one or forced to. But I picked up the paddle I made, hammering together one of the table's legs and a piece of board. The water bugs came back and skated around the raft. When they moved, they knew everything about that current, shifting in all directions with ease. I didn't know if I would float or sink, but I pushed the long end of the paddle into the bank and the raft inched forward into the current. My shadow slanted onto the ground, distorted, crumpled as the pain pills had left me, as Bell and Ray had made me, as Macy had devised, as I had done all along to myself.

Macy

What I was not was a doormat. But I could tell Bell and Ray were accustomed to welcome mats and red carpet. All right. I could put on the hyena's smile. Plumped up some pillows. Carried in one hand a tray of assorted crackers and perfect triangular slices of cheddar cheese, the mold cut off, no one ever knew. Whatever Bell and Ray were after, whatever they wanted from Dotty, would be harder to get than they thought.

The first bottle of champagne was their idea. Bell lifted it out of her pink plastic shopping bag and presented it to me like a trophy. Champagne. A happy drink. Easier than an IV of Pentothal. But longer to administer and the results weren't as predictable. All right. I could do the slow dance to get at the truth. Unfolded their napkins. Handed them plates. Held out the tray and waited while they took their sweet damn time choosing the sesame cracker, the butter cracker, the round rye cracker, and forked the appropriate number of cheese triangles to go with the crackers. Smiled. How wonderful to serve you. I brought in the glasses. Translucent pink, ribbed, bloated on short stems. I cut the foil, removed the wire cage from around the cork. All this while Dotty was upstairs in her bedroom. From the sound of it—the wood scraping wood, grinding a shrill groove—she must have been dragging the dresser from one side of the room to the other. Bell and Ray never even looked up at the ceiling.

I rocked the cork out of the bottle. Dotty came down the stairs in her almost quick but cockeyed step. Backpack over her shoulder. Straw hat tight on her head. Bell and Ray didn't turn around. They pretended to watch the bottle in my hand but it was my face they were really looking at. Dotty stared at me too. Waiting for my face to do something unusual. Only Bell and Ray wouldn't know what my unusual was. Dotty did. I smiled at Dotty.

"Join us," I said.

Dotty said nothing. It was the silence that got me. Her not saying one word. Made me smile as big as my mother used to smile, the jumbo smile with teeth. Her eyes nearly closed to the whole scene of Bell and Ray and me. Like she couldn't stand to have any of us in her line of sight. She limped through the living room and kitchen and pushed the back screen door open. I knew she wanted the screen door to smash against the house. To rip right out of the hinged sockets and sail across the yard. But the door had a thick spring and before it could hit the house, it came back with as much force as it swung out.

"Goddamn stupid door," Dotty said. The door opened again, with the whine of its unoiled hinges.

Bell and Ray: they're like two pockets in a frayed vest, teacups from the same set, only chipped, scarred; left ventricle, right ventricle, but I don't think they added up to a full heart. Sat like dominoes on the couch. Dotty wasn't back. A polite hour had gone by. I learned not one iota about why they came. All right. I brought out the second bottle of champagne.

"Gracious god," Ray said, "we're having a party." He slid his hand over his prickly hair. Pale yellow like phony pearls. Long in back and ponytailed. The same haircut as Bell. Temples exposed. Two tiny protruding veins bridged each of their left temples and wiggled when they talked.

Bell touched Ray's knee with just her index finger. Code. They spoke in code. A touch, a look, a motion of hand or head or foot, no words necessary. And— bingo—just like that, the first mention of Dotty.

Bell and Ray spoke one after another, fast.

Bell said, "Dot is an odd bird, leaving like that."

Ray said, "Always was."

"Full of imagination."

"And loved a good joke."

"She was a prankster, oh, the stunts she pulled. Like tonight. What was that about?"

"Unbelievable. Her deceptions."

"Well, deception is a bit strong."

They reached out their hands to the glasses of champagne and drank.

"Tell me a story about Dotty," I said.

Bell said, "Really, there's so many, I wouldn't know which to pick. Why don't you tell us one. About how you met each other."

I leaned forward, cutting the distance between us in half. My smile parked on my face. Like it was always there. I sipped more champagne to dull the ache in the muscles that propped up my smile. "I'd rather hear about the time when Dotty left home."

I stared at Bell's ash grey eyes. Her pointy, mascaraed lashes, lids tinted a faint blue. Her short arm rose from its resting place on her waist. The crooked, unopening fingers of her hand, almost a fist, touched her breast bone, anchored there above her heart. It was a simple movement but one she wanted me to watch. She sunk her other hand into the shopping bag and there, in between her fingers, was a photo of Dotty: a black and white rectangle, the kind taken at a photo booth in a drugstore. Only there's usually four in a long strip and here there was one and this one was cut in half. Dotty's arm removed, sliced off with whoever was in the other half of the photo.

"1973," Bell said, "a week before Dot's sixteenth birthday."

Ray said, "Cute kid, always was a darling."

"Breaks my heart to see her limping, so obviously in pain."

"What happened, Macy, what happened to our Dot?"

Bell and Ray talking. A perfect, practiced modulation, one finishing up where the other left off. The tone waxy, sweet, a slight melting to the vowels. Salesmen voices. I finished my third glass of champagne. Listened carefully to their voices. The words almost incidental for that was their sleight of hand, wasn't it? To be charmed by the voice, to not notice the insincerity of the words until even the most obvious lies could sound convincing.

With my feet, I scooted the coffee table closer. Set my glass down. Ray immediately poured more champagne.

I said, "Why did Dotty tell me all her family were dead?"

Ray laughed. A laugh like dust, irritating the throat. But he didn't spill any champagne. "Dead, gracious god, that's a new one."

Bell said, "Families. You know how little squabbles get exploded into wars in the mind. Dot has resentments. Who doesn't?"

Ray said, "She is priceless. Crown jewel of the family and she says we're dead. Well, here we are in the flesh to prove her wrong."

Bell said, "Everyone has their own story. Ray has his. I have mine. Dot has hers. Sugar and salt. What I remember might not be the same as Dot. But you, Macy, you could tell us a thing or two that would help us understand the turmoil Dot is in."

The porch light flashed through the window, dimes of yellow light bubbling on the floor. Bell and Ray used their voices like levers and crowbars. Dynamite. Nearly two bottles of champagne and their bodies were no looser. The unpredictable weather in this house and what they saw was my calm and Dotty's winter plunge. All right.

"I was Dotty's nurse after her accident. Now I'm her lover."

"How much love factors into it?" Bell said. "Why would she just leave like that and not come back?"

"Maybe," I said, "the more important question is why did she leave when you arrived?"

Ray set his hands on the table, thumbs hooked under the lip of wood. Turned his head toward Bell so that I was staring at the scars on the right side of his face.

"Bell, we're here as Macy's guests. It's not our place to question their arrangement."

Decoy. Yes, I knew all about it. Bobbing wooden mallard in a cold pond. Look at those scars, two hundred stitches, at least, maybe three hundred. Not a great job, but not bad considering how many lacerations. Four hours, minimum, of sewing.

"Macy," Bell said, "you have to overlook my stupidity. It's the champagne, I swear."

"She gets like this every time."

"But only with champagne—any other drink, I'm a pussycat."

"I bet," I said and smiled at Bell. The medium smile, not many teeth showing. "So, tell me what it is you want and why you're here."

"Important family business," Ray said. Uncrossed his legs, inched to the edge of the couch.

"And what would that be?" I extended my smile into large. More teeth, more curl, this was all just fun, the pleasantest of pleasant small talk.

"It's complex, and strictly a family matter." Bell matched my smile. Every one of her teeth showed: the pointy incisors sharp as switchblades. Her smile as fake as wax Halloween teeth.

All right. Champagne was not an efficient truth serum. Bell and Ray gave me one stitch in the whole seam of why they were here. Family business. Could mean anything. We finished the champagne, the bubbles ricocheting down my throat, my bloodstream overloaded with the carbonation, and I was drunk. The living room wasn't blurry. Just the opposite: crystal clear, in a one-dimensional way. Bell and Ray like life-size cardboard car salesmen waiting in the lobby of the showroom to snag me. I was partway to signing on the dotted line. Buying into these charades. Bell pulled her earlobe. I was tired of looking at them so comfortable on the couch.

Bell and Ray got up, put on their coats. Bell stopped smiling. The champagne did that, restored her mouth to an open belligerence.

"Where is Dot?" Bell's words were loud, exploding the quiet of the polite hours of maneuvering. She pointed to her watch, ten o'clock, no Dotty, no more cheese and crackers. Ray buttoned his coat. Bell left hers unbuttoned. The sleeve of her left arm was hemmed to fit the arm's shortness.

I pushed myself out of the deep cushions, planted my feet on the floor so I wouldn't sway. "I don't know where Dotty went."

Bell said, "When you do know, you call us. Immediately. Hear?"

Ray pulled out a zippered leather daybook from his coat pocket. Undid the zipper. Removed a pen velcroed to the inside spine of the leather and wrote down the name of the hotel and a telephone number on a blank piece of beige paper. Tore the paper out of the pad and handed it to me. The numbers were three inches high.

Ray said, "That's where we're staying. We will be in town for a week for the National Perfumery Convention. Make sure Dot calls." He zipped up the daybook and dropped it into his pocket.

"You tell Dot she cannot run away from this." Bell's finger made a stab at me. A charm bracelet full of silver apples slipped out of her blouse's sleeve to her wrist. Bell bent her arm up so that the bracelet slid back into her sleeve.

I said, "I don't tell Dotty what she can and can't do."

Bell leaned closer to me. "Oh, but I think you do precisely that." Her short arm swayed away from the grey of her coat and tapped into my arm. There was little weight to her arm, as if the bones had been removed. But I knew: her arm had probably been fractured in several spots, tendons ripped beyond repair. The doctors cut away the unsound, functionless places to save the rest and sewed it together with fancy stitchery.

"I'll tell Dotty exactly what I know."

Bell says, "Which is?"

I pushed Bell's arm off mine and stepped back. Tilted into my drunkenness and smiled for real. Like my mother smiled after her night and day of drinking. As if we knew the inside of other people's heads and had everything the way we wanted it and nothing could spoil it. "That whatever it is you both want from Dotty, it is not to forge brotherly and sisterly togetherness. Dotty's the key to an opportunity that will benefit you, at her expense."

Ray cupped and clapped his hands. Laughed, two quick barks. Bell kept staring at me and laughed just like Ray. They walked to the front door. Ray holding the pink plastic bag that Bell carried in. Ray opened the door and stepped onto the porch, under the light that flickered.

Bell turned around and said, "Macy, don't try and come between Dot and us. It absolutely won't work."

Dotty

AT NIGHT, THE women carried houseplants across the courtyard. Except the one old woman who pushed an empty wheelbarrow over the wide cracks in between the pale red stones without once catching the wheel. The wheel ticked like a clock and that was how I told time.

I didn't ask their names. They didn't offer them to me when I ran aground on their small beach. The front of the raft clipping into the river like a shovel, the surge of water onto the boards, over my feet, while I had paddled as fast as I could in the gold light of October dusk, trying to get far away from Bell and Ray and Macy. But I didn't paddle even half an hour, steering in the fast current, before the raft began sinking. My feet bronzed with the gold of that cold dusk light swamping the river. I saw the small beach and dock and the backside of the hotel, and there was the choice of just sinking or stopping there at the dock with the sign under the Iris Hotel sign that said *Eleanor Roosevelt Slept Here*.

The courtyard was a neat square in the center of the Hotel Iris: two stories, four sides; each side, four rooms. Two outside lampposts, the lightbulbs circled by yellow glass, the yellow glass thick with the last of the summer insects. Their shadows were long and simple, revolving like second hands. With the shutters of my window opened, I set the point of my chin on the edge of the windowsill and watched the women, their brown shoes with twine laces, dark freckled arms bent at the elbows, houseplants in stained clay pots held against their bellies and breasts or pulled on a low dolly. The old woman in wool sailor slacks pushed the wheelbarrow from the yellow door to the green door, number three to number eleven, turned the wheelbarrow around, and pulled it into the room. For three nights, this was the time I knew, the emptiness in the wheelbarrow moving counterclockwise around the square, the emptiness never decreasing.

I came down from my room after four days of no pain pills. I was a slip knot; one pull and I'd come apart. Toxic as the Love Canal. With my arms crossed over my breasts and my hands squeezed under my armpits, I held my rib cage in place. Leaned against door number two, the orange door, to keep my legs from forgetting they had any bones at all. But it didn't stop the shaking. The whole of me shaking—it started in my ankles and rumbled through my veins, set off a knee, then a wrist, elbow, my belly, shoulders; nothing could stop my head from nodding and my teeth from clicking.

I was one rattling shiver leaning against the orange door. My temperature was a furnace, a tar boiler, a smelting oven. Yet my skin refused the flush of fire or heat. My skin was as white as a flour moth. Humidity inside me, four days of steam, fever growing like poison ivy, the itch of wanting a pain pill. I wanted a pain pill, fuck, I needed a pain pill, and there were none because I had left them all behind.

The women came out of the other room. They saw me and put down their potted plants, wiped their hands on their clothes as they walked to where I was standing. They didn't notice the shape of me right away, the enormous disarray. Used to being friendly and of service, they all said their hellos and I said mine back. The old woman was wearing the same sailor slacks as the first night but had a house dress on over them.

She said, "We didn't hardly get a chance to meet you the other day. We're so busy clearing out the old greenhouse, moving everything to the new one. You're Dorothy Meyers, that's right, isn't it?"

"Jesus, Nora," the woman next to her said, "you know that's her name; we only have three paying guests and she's the most recent."

Nora didn't turn to the woman but her eyes looked sideways and darkened—or that could have been just the shadows of a moth's wings passing over us.

"Don't care if there's three guests or thirty, I still like a proper introduction."

She offered their names to me like confetti: strings of names thrown in the air, riveting together as they fell in place.

"That's Marjorie Delores Kopetski," she said, pointing her thumb at the woman next to her. "Del, for short. She's Sandra Rae Kopetski. Sunny. That's what everyone calls her. And I'm their momma, Mrs. Nora Rye Kopetski. I don't go in for formality, so you just call me Nora."

I looked at them through the strips of shadows. The limbs of the black cottonwood tilted and the wind loosened handfuls of dry leaves from the branches above us. They all had blonde hair, platinum, polished bright as mother of pearl. Nora's hair was set in curlers that formed waves across her head. Their noses had a similar bump at the bridge. Their bones were big and apparent in their wrists and cheeks. The daughters were not young, forty to fifty, but the way they stood just a little behind Nora, I guessed that Nora ran the show.

I said, "I'm Dorothy. Thank you for the lemonade and biscuits you left outside my room yesterday. I haven't been feeling very good." The words shaking out of me, popping like firecrackers.

"Very good?" Del said. "Shit, I'd say six steps from death's doorway."

"Five," Nora said.

"Anyway, thanks." The shaking surged and climbed up my bones. My hands clapped against my rib cage, until there was nothing I could do but slide to the stone and stare up at them. They stared down at me. All of them with the polished brown eyes, dark as ground cloves. Eyes cut deep into their faces, a fierce look, sizing me up.

Nora said, "Sunny, go fix the tea that's in the lime jar."

I tried to stand up. My hands pushed against the stone, but there was nothing but shaking in my arms, no strength, and I couldn't move.

"Help her up, Del, and take her to her room."

Del lifted me and she smelled like potpourri, but not overly sweet, like all the dried flowers were roses. There was something underneath the sweet—decay and dirt. She held me up beneath my arms. Sweating for four days, my armpits wet, her hands damp and I said, "I'm sorry."

Del said, "Never mind about sorry." She walked me up the stairs to my room, chewing gum and cracking the gum in time to the slap of her feet on the wood floor. "Almost there, you just hang on."

My hip was shaking and my leg useless, just dragging behind me as she carried me down the hall with the yellow-and-white-striped wallpaper. The pain in my leg was strong, but I didn't know if it was as strong as it was when I first started taking the pain pills. There was no comparing the worse or better of the pain since I'd kept it under wraps for months. Nothing like this hammering where the metal plate joined my bones. The hammering went all the way up my spine into my head, the pain like a rasp trying to level down wood. Inside my room, Del sat me on the bed but I fell right over.

My body didn't know what to do without the pills and doused the trouble of my thoughts in sleep. If there were dreams, they were submachine gun fire: quick, brilliant explosions that hit no target, just shots into the night, glimpses of a dark world made light for a second. I couldn't remember what I saw within the boundary of sleep though I knew I was looking.

I woke. The lamp was on, a pink glow through the hourglass lamp shade. Yellow light outside the window could mean morning, could mean night falling: sticky light, soft and fattening up the world. No clock. I could have been asleep a year, a day, a minute. No six-hour alarm of take-a-pill. No pills. My legs were bent over a pillow I hadn't put there. The chenille bedspread was folded at the foot of the bed. A cup of tea on the nightstand almost gone; I didn't remember drinking it. Across the room on the four-drawer dresser was a spider plant with a dozen babies on long stiff stems. Above the dresser, hanging on a picture hook on the pale green wall, was a photograph of a woman in a well-fitted, full-length dress holding a bottle of champagne. She was about to crack the bottle against the prow of a war ship. *Eleanor Roosevelt 1944.* In a *U*-shape around her stood newspaper photographers and the bright winks of their flashbulbs.

I fell asleep again, slept that whole day, and woke long after dusk. I knelt on the bed with my chin on the windowsill. The moon had split in half, lacquered its light over the black cottonwood tree in the courtyard. I was neither there nor not there. I was Eleanor Roosevelt's arm lifted forever with the weight of the champagne bottle, the weight of almost setting something into motion, suspended, caught between moving and not moving. I had taken one deliberate step, but could I take another?

I watched Del walk out of the office pulling the dolly with a rex begonia, two dumb canes, a tall corn plant, and a wandering Jew with hundreds of branched stems. I stood up. The pain in my leg swelled and ebbed; it was losing its constancy and fury, yet it reminded me of how careful I needed to be when I took the next step.

I put my hooded sweatshirt on and walked down the hall. A slow limping across the creak of wood and the slight pop of my hipbone as I stepped and shifted my weight. Down the stairs with the cherry banister, the smell of bees-wax. Into the courtyard. The air had winter in it. I sank my hands into the pocket of the sweatshirt and went up to Nora.

"Do you have a phone I can use?" I asked.

"Yes, darlin dear." She said in her holy-water-and-rock-dust voice. Cigarette-burned southern accent and her words were slow. The wheelbarrow she pushed was not empty. It was filled with dirt, the same black as the metal. Dirt so rich it smelled like forests that had never been cut into, the ground a thick sponge, a box spring. "Is it a local call?"

"Yeah," I said, following the wheelbarrow across the stone to door number eleven.

"Phone is on the front desk, next to the Boston fern." Nora stopped, set the wheelbarrow down. The dirt was salted with teeny bits of pearlite.

"You're feeling better tonight," Nora said. Her voice didn't rise; it wasn't a question she was asking.

"I'm doing much better," I said. Only I wasn't. My body didn't know how to align itself without the pills. But I smiled at Nora. "That flu really knocked me out. I hope you don't get it."

Nora said, "I doubt it." But what she was looking at was my leg, not my smile.

I asked, "So, about the phone, do I need to dial nine or something to get a line out?"

"You just dial direct, darlin."

Sunny came out of room number eleven and stood in front of the wheelbar-row. Her hair was damp, kinked up. Dirt on her face and hands.

"What are you doing?" she asked Nora.

Nora stared up at the almost six feet of Sunny and said, "I was talking to Dorothy here and I was about to ask her a question, okay with you?"

Nora didn't wait for Sunny to answer. "Now that you're feeling so good, how long you planning on staying?"

I said, "I did pay for a week, didn't I?"

Sunny said, "Yep, you're paid up."

I said, "I'm not sure."

"About staying or leaving?" Nora asked.

"Both," I said. "Either one."

"Maybe when you're all through being sick, you'll know." Nora buttoned her blue sweater up to her neck. Her hair was short on the sides and angled away from her face. When her fingers were through with the round silver buttons, she looked at me and said, "Maybe you won't."

Macy

WHERE WAS DOTTY? In the bed, the grainy lamplight sawed over the covers in a jagged stripe. I had fallen asleep with my clothes on. And the lamp. Champagne, like a rolling pin, pressed each thought of Dotty thinner and thinner. I had no idea where she was. Outside the window the wind fidgeted in the bean stalks. Dotty and me. All right. I never promised complete salvation, did I? I eased her pain, made it bearable. Said I loved her.

I pushed the covers off me, put my feet on the floor. The bursts of sunlight coming through the window said it was noon. I put on my jeans and red sweatshirt. In the bathroom, I shook my hair into place. The champagne had turned to vinegar in my head. Without even looking in the mirror I knew my face was tallow, slack, my eyes a watery blunt blue, baggy skin below, my lids heavy as brocade drapes. Crappy, cheap, worn.

In the kitchen I switched on the front burner of the electric stove. Set a pan of water on it. I washed the dishes in the sink, the sponge squeaking on the pink champagne glasses. No Dotty. Not one word on the answering machine. I dried my hands. Wrote *lightbulbs* on the backside of an envelope below *sesame oil, coconut, jelly, eggs,* which I'd written two days ago. A mild hangover. Livable, functional, I could get through the day. Easy.

I called Jean. "Good morning, this is Macy. Can I talk to Dotty?"

"She's not here, Macy. Everything okay?"

"Sure." I didn't wait for Jean to ask questions. "Must've misunderstood her. Thought she said she was walking over to your house but she must just be taking a walk. Thanks anyway. Bye."

I poured water through the coffee filter. Forgot to put in the coffee. Started over. Two heaping scoops. Ran cold water over my hands. Rubbed my palms against my forehead. I couldn't believe Dotty had not come back. Should have gone after her. Left Bell and Ray on the couch like two buoys on a calm sea. That's what Jean would have told me. Fuck Jean. I measured out three teaspoons of sugar. Added lots of cream but burned my tongue anyway. Threw the spoon at the refrigerator. I should have gone after Dotty.

I shoved my feet into Dotty's rubber boots and took her gardening jeans jacket off the hook by the back door. Walked outside into Dotty's garden. Dotty couldn't bend or kneel for more than a few minutes at a time, which meant the weeds had overtaken the vegetables, left them stunted, bearing miniature tomatoes, peppers, flowers. Everything hurrying to set seeds and let them fly before the weeds smothered them. All except the beans. They grew up to my window, pointed their curly suckers at the glass, looking for a place to anchor. They waited until I opened my window, and then they climbed in. I pushed them back out. Dotty said they were magic beans and they would bring us good luck. Yeah. All right.

My mother didn't believe in good luck, only bad. And I was the same. Bad luck, the story that followed me. The story I most wanted to forget, the one I could never forget. How many good-luck stories could I even name? Not many. A reminder from my mother—good luck was not the same as a good opportunity. With opportunity you had control. With luck you didn't.

I carried the empty champagne bottles in my hand, candles in my pocket. Down to the shack. Today was my mother's real birthday. Two days before Halloween. Not July like I told Dotty. Every year since I was six, my mother did the same thing on her birthday: woke me up at five-thirty when the sky was dark, light just a dream behind my eyes. She'd say, "Macy, get up, you're wasting the best part of the day and we'll be late." I'd hear her strike the match against the black strip on the matchbook. My room would flare up in shadows of red. She'd light a candle, hold it in front of her face, and say, "I don't look one iota older, do I?" In that light, that blush, her face was so soft, her eyes sweet, untroubled. Only the trouble hid in the red shadows. Behind the fancy smile on her face. Her voice came out fast as a lightning strike: "Get up, Macy, you will not ruin this day like you try to do every year." And every year, she flung back my covers and I had no choice. I put on my thickest clothes, a hat, gloves, and got in the car. We went to the quarry. The black water even blacker in October. She'd wear her bathrobe and a pair of my dad's pajama bottoms. The morning light grew wavy yellow and red. She'd park the car on the pebbles, the tires crackling over the rock. "Come on," she'd say, "take off your boots." "Can't I wait till we're down there?" I would say. "No, you can't wait." We carried our shoes from the car and walked onto the rough sand to the water. She set down a blanket and relit the candle she'd brought into my room. She'd say, "Hurry, 6:47 is in two minutes." I'd say, "Do I have to?" "Don't argue, don't pull the same damn act every year. This is my birthday, Macy. When will you get it through your head? God knows I'm trying to pass along the importance of this tradition to you. Be grateful, Macy, you have a mother who knows the difference between tradition and crap."

I gave in, every year. I unbuttoned my coat, threw my hat on the blanket, my shirt, my undershirt, my dungarees, underwear, gloves. My mother only had to take off the pajama bottoms and undo the tie around the waist of the bathrobe. She wore nothing else. Her skin was like the cream color of the sky. She grabbed onto my hand, looked at her watch, and ran me to the water. Into the water. Up to my ankles, knees, ribs, and I went under and she let go of my hand. She'd scream into the quiet of the morning. I'd fling around in the cold water like some bird shot down from the sky. My legs scissoring, pointing my toes to reach the ground, my breath making embarrassing sounds. Like what comes out during a deep weeping. But I pretended I wasn't crying, that it was just the water splashing on my face. I tried to run, once I found the muddy ground of the quarry. But I couldn't, could only walk with the cold weight of the water on me, back to the blanket and the towel and my clothes.

My mother would swim. Not for a long time, but she swam across the stillness of the water. When she came out, she was the red blush of the sun pushing up into the sky. She shook the water from her hair and opened her arms to the air before drying off with her towel. Her face was bare of makeup. A surprise, astounding in its beauty. I could not imagine that she wasn't cold or miserable like me. She waited a minute before putting the pajamas and bathrobe on. Tied the bathrobe. Looked down at me on the blanket. Her eyes beginning to focus. To return from the aloneness of the water, of her body occupying an enormous space in the world, free of everything and everyone. She said, "Jesus, Macy, you'd better learn to swim already or you'll probably die by drowning."

The last thing she did was throw her pair of short-heeled shoes into the water.

Later on, after we went home and ate the eggs and toast my dad made and she drank coffee with thick cream, she'd get back in the car. Drive to Macy's Department Store and buy new shoes. And later, the kitchen table would be covered in stacks of poker chips. Baskets of pretzels. Party mix with the sesame sticks and salted nuts and my mother would drink peppermint schnapps or Southern Comfort, depending on her mood. The makeup would be back on her face. She'd be in a red dress, clinging and low cut. Sheer stockings and her new shoes, high-heeled, shiny red as the sunrise. My aunts and uncles would arrive with more bottles and a sweet cake, topped not with frosting but with crumbled sugar and nuts. Then it was all noise: toasting my mother, shuffling the chairs in and out from the table, dropping poker chips into the kitty, dealing wild cards, cracking the ice from the ice trays. My dad, Mr. Good-luck-with-a-royal-flush, pulled my mother onto his lap. She looked almost happy.

The champagne bottles tapped against my legs. I walked past the tumbled waves of blackberries. Some of the big blackberry vines reached across the path, and no matter how I tried to avoid the thorns, they grabbed at me. Stuck into my pants, looking for my skin.

"Fuck off," I said. Sidestepped a few feet and I heard the thorns pop out from the denim. The blackberries were dried into hard, seedy sour balls. Beyond the blackberries, the path narrowed between the alder and cottonwood trees and circled a small empty space where no trees took root. This was where I had built the shack. And today I was coming to light a candle for my mother's birthday and burn the whole thing down.

The shack was where I put my mother. No, I didn't put her there, she walked in and took over the place. Because she knew it would have to come to this. Build her a monument, manifest her everlasting skeleton, the house of her body. No forgetting. The power of first love, Macy. Even if the first love was the worst. All right. This was the shack I built for my mother. When I finished the roof, nailing down the corrugated metal and the flattened tin cans, smearing roof tar over it all, I brought her books here. Robert Frost, *Surgical Nursing*, her yearbook. I didn't have a shack warming.

When I walked up to the uneven steps, it was not the same as I'd left it yesterday. The shack had come undone. Boards pushed out. The door gone. The cot and table and crates and chair were in a heap on the ground. Light flooded into the shack. Light that was never meant to peer in now surged over the floor, eroding the dark. I stepped over the boards with their bent nails and splintered edges.

Jesus, shit. In the center of the floor was a teacup and in the cup Dotty's pain pills. The box of crap was open and the newspaper about Maybelline leaned against the box. All right. All right. Dotty had met Maybelline. The picture of my mother was under the teacup. Another newspaper article lay on top. I unfolded it and saw it was the same one I had cut out when we went to Wildwood to identify her, my mother, bring her back, bury her. I dug through the box until I found the newspaper, front page story. The exact same one. And something else I pulled out of the box. A pale letter-sized envelope. But there's no letter. A postcard. That's what she sent. The last of my mother's words on the back of the postcard with the picture of the beach, the ocean, the sun rising out of the water.

I read the postcard a hundred times the day it came, twenty-odd years ago, nearly three weeks after my sixteenth birthday, the day my mother ran away for good. Studied the postcard, then, not because I wanted to find out where she was. She didn't say. The postmark was faint as if the ink in the machine hadn't been changed for years. It could have said NY or NC or NJ. But I didn't care. I read it because she had exchanged lives. Her new life fit, without any complication, entirely on a postcard. I could have recited it by heart back then.

Macy,
Happy Birthday. Better late than never, right? By now you must know I'm not coming back. You'll do fine on your own. Mothers were meant to be dispensable, after a time. Just look to the animal kingdom for the evidence. And don't

mope around, for chrissake. Grow up and do what you want. Look at me,
that's exactly what I'm doing. Selfish, some might say, but I'm happy. I landed
a new job and will be moving into a darling apartment tomorrow. I've made fast
friends with a girl your age, Dorothy, sweet as pie, a real honey, who never
knew her mother. Life is like that: a swift kick in the you-know-where. I'll write
again. Don't bother to show this to your dad. I'll be dropping him a note in a day
or two.
Always be grateful. Your Fabulous (ha ha) Mother.

My fabulous mother. "The lady died," Dotty had told me. New Jersey. Dorothy. What's in a name. Everything. It can't be. What were the chances. Do the
math, Maybelline would have said. But I wouldn't. I hated math. I turned around.
My mother's blue coat was gone.

I went outside and sat on a crate. The river was foamy with silt and fallen
leaves. I lit the candle. The bits I had told Dotty about my mother were the ones
I wanted to believe, the lies I'd told myself, that my mother loved me. Maybelline
once said that when two lines intersect it created a tension that could be measured. The stresses adjusted to hold the lines straight and plumb. If I had said, how
do I adjust to the intersection of my mother and myself, Maybelline would have
said, you will lie to keep the stresses under your control, just like your mother did.

I blew the candle out. Why bother burning the shack down? It would fall
apart on its own, each remaining board loosening and opening like a poppy. And
when Dotty came back, I would take her here and say, look inside, who do you
see? Lila Kahn. My mother. Me. We are the same. Opportunistic as bees in a field
of flowers.

And I would say, which are you, Dorothy, a flower or a bee?

I went back into the shack with the champagne bottles. Turned the teacup
over into my palm. Seven pain pills. I put one in my mouth and swallowed, to
quiet my hangover. I threw the rest outside. I never said goodbye to my mother
and she has never left. I kept listening to her crap: Be grateful, Macy, that you
don't have the slightest idea what love is. All right. Well, the thing I learned
from her was I knew an opportunity when I saw it. I raised both champagne
bottles over my head and hurled them across the room at the part of the wall that
was still standing. Shards of glass flashed as they broke apart and ripped through
the sunlight. When the pieces of glass stopped falling and piled up on the floor,
they were like the ocean after a storm and all the blue and green colors were
chopped into bits. That was how I started to cut my mother down to size.

I walked away from the shack carrying the box of crap with the picture of my
mother, the postcard, and the newspaper articles shoved inside.

Dotty

THE HOTEL OFFICE was humid, overheated, the air steamed by all the orchids sitting in their pots of moss and pebbles on the shelves under the grow lights. The top of the shelf draped with sheer scarves of cinnamon and goldenrod and eggshell. I picked up the phone. Held the phone in my hand. Could not bring it to my ear. I turned around. The orchids raised their waxy mouths to the light. They flourished in here. Their stems swelled, and they bloomed brilliant violets and pinks, sultry flowers, wildly opened. But it was artificial, all this climate control. No bees or insects crawled into those flowers. If I switched off the grow lights, they would pale and shrivel and die. They were not where they're supposed to be—under ferns and thick-barked trees, flowering their exuberant flowers.

The deep shaking came from trying to believe I did not need the glue of the pills. I dialed the seven numbers. Staring at the orchids. Shaking. When Macy answered, my mouth was the mouth of the orchids: bright and open, so open to the artificial light.

After Macy said hello, I said, "Hello." Quiet. As if that one word could undo every other word.

"Where are you, Dotty?"

"I am in a room of orchids."

"Where?" I heard Macy walking across the kitchen floor.

"In a hotel. I've been sleeping in the bed that Eleanor Roosevelt slept in."

She tapped a spoon against a pot. "So, you've been sleeping with presidents' wives now. Dotty, what hotel?"

"Are Bell and Ray still there?"

"Yes. No, not here in the house. They're staying at the Rose Motor Inn downtown but they stop by every damn day to see if you've come back. Dotty? Jesus. Why didn't you call? When are you coming back?"

My shaking increased. "The day after tomorrow. Pick me up at the off ramp at Fourth Street and Park at two o'clock. I'll be up at the top, on the right." I didn't wait for her to say anything else. My back to the orchids, their whispered smells of strange ripe fruit fallen to soften on hot ground. I hung up the phone.

I leaned against the counter, stared at the orchids. Shaking. My hands on the countertop, holding me up. Five days I've been gone. Five mornings. I can picture Macy in her bed, reading the newspaper. Looking for information. Facts she could use to explain my absence, a missing person. The obituaries first. Then, local crimes, into the business section, mergers, real estate deals, mutual funds. The world with its wars and starvations. She'd look for me in the ruin, in the unfathomable national debt, the comics and their unending childhoods. Page one: my family that should have stayed dead but didn't. The long lost sister—me—missing again. Macy interpreting everything. It all fit together, perfect. Almost. It could take her all the days I've been gone to figure out I never wanted to be found. Not by Bell and Ray. But by then, Bell and Ray could already have remade the world.

All I wanted was to call Macy back, tell her where to find me. But I didn't. My head was dizzy, headache jumping from eye to eye. I was in no shape to dig into my heart and show her what grew in there.

On the paneled wall behind the office counter, two dollar bills were taped to blue construction paper and framed in a black wood frame. Above the dollar bills was a square photograph of Eleanor Roosevelt standing in front of a house, the wood siding bleached to the same dimmed color of the dust fields around her. There was no beehive of photographers. No harbor, no ship with its steam stacks and guns. Nothing but the terrible sun and a father and mother and three children who had nothing to offer the president's wife except the thin slant of shade on the porch of their house. Eleanor Roosevelt didn't wear a hat. It was in her hand. The sleeves of her blouse rolled up past her elbows, up to the puff and billow of the uppermost part of her sheer sleeves. She held a square basket filled with fruit out to the mother. The mother with the thank-you smile, her dry lips curling up as if they still remembered the feel of rain and the oceans of wheat and corn, sour apple trees, and flowers' enormous faces. The father looked at the dusty ground, hands in his back pockets. The children, three girls, holding hands and their eyes watched Eleanor Roosevelt as if she was a rain cloud.

Nora opened the door into the office, walked behind the counter, and pulled a pair of scissors out of a drawer. "You just imagining making a phone call?"

My hands were still wrapped around the phone, my palm was hot, and my fingers curled up tight. "I already made my call. I was looking at the picture."

"You know about Eleanor Roosevelt?" Nora asked.

"Not much."

But I wanted to know how Eleanor Roosevelt kept on going when all she saw were the troubles and the terrors of people living through impoverished days when the weather turned unfamiliar. Or when war took whatever it wanted: limbs, eyes, whole families. I wanted to know if she closed her eyes, showered it off, turned stone hard. Or did she bring baskets of fruit wherever she went and that was enough to forget what she saw?

Nora cut an unraveling thread from her sweater. She put the scissors down and from the drawer pulled out a cigarette and lit it. "We had lemonade the day she came."

"That's you?"

"Middle girl. Imagine that, she brought us lemons and sugar and a damn block of ice. A hundred and god knows what degrees, the whole world fried up like a fritter and my father chipped off splinters of ice from the block. My mother dropped each piece into whatever cups and glasses were clean. I stirred the juice of the lemons and the sugar and it was like I was diluting the sun."

"Where was this?"

"Texas. Border of Oklahoma." Nora twisted off a dried frond from the Boston fern next to the phone. Her lips colored a pale peach, leftover from morning lipstick.

"Then Eleanor Roosevelt didn't really sleep here?"

"She did." Nora leaned her elbows on the counter, cigarette propped between her thumb and index fingers. "Happened by accident. Eleanor Roosevelt was heading to the shipyards in Seattle. The big push was on to build ships fast. I'd owned this place a year and did a damn good job. In those days, the train ran close by and everyone traveled that way. Not so many cars. Business was ready-made for hotels close to the trains.

"Eleanor Roosevelt came here by an act of God, or so the newspaper said, but really it was because the train couldn't go farther. Day after spring began, we had a snowstorm that stopped everything. Even the newspaper was two days late in re-porting the fact of her visit. Eleanor walked here from the station in her pointed boots with the buttons up the side and fur around the top. There were four of them: press secretary, two bodyguards, and Eleanor. One of the bodyguards walked right across the floor without stamping any of the snow off his shoes and said, 'Turn on the No Vacancy sign.' 'What for?' I asked. He said, 'Don't you know who's standing there, in your lobby?' 'Course I do,' I said. 'That's Eleanor Roosevelt, but we're not near filled up.' Eleanor Roosevelt walked over to the desk and said, 'I'd most appreciate your hospitality and a room that is warm. Don't bother about the sign.' That's what she said. The bodyguards sat in the lobby all night. I gave Eleanor Roosevelt the room you're in. Put the press secretary three doors down from her. I never got her name, only what Eleanor called her: My Dear. They were here a night and most of the next day. The snow melted and they were gone."

Nora tapped her cigarette against the metal rim of the plaid beanbag ashtray. Looked at me in the same way that Macy looked at a cut: appraising the severity, the methods needed for cleaning and stopping the blood. I was shaking again. Didn't notice how bad until Nora looked at the jump of my shoulders, the shiver in my hand on the counter. The pain blossoming its thorns and thistles in my leg and head. I'd been standing too long, jamming my hip, and my hip sparked against my leg bone, the wildfire bursting up my spine and no pills to stop it.

"Come with me," Nora said. She walked out of the office to room number three next door. The cigarette in her mouth, angled sideways, burnt to a long ash. I followed Nora into a room filled with plant stands and shelves and grow lights hanging down from the ceiling. Behind this room was a door leading into a greenhouse. There weren't many plants left but I could smell the wetness of dirt, of watering, a room full of plants and on the walls were the dark green wisps of mildew climbing like morning glory up and up. On one side of the room two yellow chairs and a red couch, all smooth vinyl, circled a wicker table.

"Sit down," Nora said. She went into another room, her shoes leaving dirt prints across the floor. I didn't sit—my hip and leg warring all the way from the office—I fell on the couch. The vinyl was cold and I pressed my whole left side into a cushion with three recessed buttons. I could hear what Macy would say if she was there lying next to me. This is the kind of couch I've always wanted, and then she would touch my hip and my leg and say, We could do some serious loving on this couch, Dotty, and her hand would hush all of my pain and her lips would slide into her smile that was real, without any pretend to it, and there on that couch I might even believe love mattered.

But the pain didn't quit and the cold of the vinyl warmed from the heat of only my body. Nora sat in one of the chairs and the chair cushion let out a grunt of air.

"Can you sit up?" Nora asked.

"Sure," I said.

"You said that a half an hour ago, and you still haven't moved a hair. You need to drink this tea. It's lukewarm but that doesn't make a difference. It'll do the job."

Nora was reading *Better Homes and Gardens*, a cigarette in her mouth, and I wondered how her plants thrived so well with her smoking nonstop. But that's how it was: we adjusted and settled in with what was at hand.

Macy

DOTTY CALLED, TALKED about orchids and Eleanor Roosevelt and not one word about love. Figured. I was getting attached to the word and now it was gone. I went outside and looked at the house with the trellis of lucky beans that grew two stories tall. As if good luck were nothing more than having your feet in a compost pile.

That's when it came to me: I'd been refusing to see what it was I wanted Dotty to show me in the first place. Why all this started. How I ended up at this house. Not because she fell off the ladder and I wanted to see how her body adapted to its new state. That's just what I kept telling myself. Look, I was a nurse. The body adjusted. I'd seen it a hundred, a thousand times. The body got on with it.

But the mind didn't always cooperate so easily. Refused, sometimes, to fix what was broken. Or couldn't. Or wouldn't. What I wanted Dotty to show me was how to believe love was possible when everything said it was not. The more Dotty showed me about the capacity to love, the more I looked the other way. Love—that fury, unrelenting. Dotty's point exactly. The heart tried despite the possibility of damage. My heart. Was trying.

Bell and Ray were sitting in the driveway in their rental car. Low-slung four-door sedan. Gold, like a dress of shiny lamé. I was walking out of the garage and could have gone in the back door of the house and pretended I wasn't home, but I walked up to the car. To Bell's window, where I could see across the seat to the good side of Ray's face. She rolled the window down.

"What do you want?"

Ray leaned over, sliding his hand along the seat top and said, "We knocked but no one answered."

"That's because I wasn't home."

Bell looked up at me with her sharp grey eyes. "We saw your car, thought you were here. Where were you?"

"At the ocean."

"You're a bit inland for that."

"And who the hell are you to even ask where I am or what I do. So again, what do you want?"

Bell's lips curdled, went sour, and then straightened back out. "I don't care what you do, Macy, I just want to know if Dot's come home yet. It's been five days."

Ray adjusted the rearview mirror and I glanced behind the car but there was nothing there but the pear tree Dotty planted and the mailbox.

"No, she's not back. Are you trying to meet a deadline?"

Bell said, "It's urgent. Yes. It's a legal matter that we can't clear up without her."

Ray looked away from the mirror at his hands on the steering wheel. On his finger was a gold ring with a deep red stone set between two diamonds. "Dot's dad died."

Bell swerved around at Ray and said, "Don't say another word."

Ray stared at Bell. "Why not? What does it matter?"

Bell looked at me. "The only thing you need to know is that it is crucial for us to talk to Dot. Ray, let's go." Bell pulled Ray's hand from the steering wheel and placed it on the keys in the ignition.

He turned the key and said, "You have to find her, Macy."

"I really don't know where she went."

"Then look everywhere." He backed the car out of the driveway. Not in a rush or a roar but at a slow, slow speed. Bell's hand was on his arm and she was talking. Her mouth moving fast. But Ray did not look at her.

Inside the house it was quiet. Nothing moved unless I moved it. The houses I'd lived in were full of noise, not this dead silence. "Dotty," I said. But Dotty was not here to take away the quiet with her crooked walking, her whispers of love words. The picture of my mother and the newspaper articles were on the kitchen table. I picked up the phone. Dialed each of the numbers I'd known for thirty years.

"Hello."

I sat in the kitchen chair, and out the window the bright sky chased after the wiry tails of clouds.

"Hello," I said. "Mrs. Blue, this is Macy."

"Macy. It's been quite a long while since I've heard your voice. Is everything all right?"

"Yes." The last hint of cloud disappeared. A crow crossed the polished sky. "How are your birds?"

"Fine and good. Two new peepers last month and the albino is pregnant." Her voice chirpy as the parakeets, her words a bird singing to morning.

"Sounds like you have your hands full. As always."

"I love these birds. They're never too much. You know that, Macy."

"Yeah. I read your articles in the *Audubon* magazine. They're very funny."

"Thank you, Macy. When did you become so interested in birds?"

"I'm not. I just like to read about your birds. Because I can see them perched in your room. You and your pillowcases of feed. And everything else."

"Macy, do you want to talk to her?"

"No. Yes." I unfolded the newspaper clipping. The picture of Maybelline, eleven years old, the fall her hair turned to orange like an oak leaf.

"She's doing fine, you know. She helps me with the birds. Writes down what I tell her to—their weight and color. Sometimes she even draws pictures of them."

"She just can't draw any conclusions about the information."

"No."

No. The condition of Maybelline was not reversible. Her body healed perfectly but not her mind and her mind didn't know the difference. The before and after.

"Put her on the phone," I said.

"Macy, you can't change what happened. You know that, don't you? After all this time. No one blames you, least of all Maybelline."

"How could she possibly blame me. She doesn't even know what happened."

"No, she doesn't. But you have to understand she's not suffering."

I pushed my fingers through my hair and over my face. A soft rain was falling, looked like it'd last for days. I sat back in the chair. "Thanks, Mrs. Blue. Let me talk to her, okay?"

"Macy, don't wait so long to call. She misses you."

The birds chittered when Mrs. Blue called Maybelline. Her hand wasn't completely covering the mouthpiece of the phone. "Maybelline," Mrs. Blue said, "there's someone who wants to talk to you on the phone."

"Who?" Maybelline asked.

"Macy," Mrs. Blue said, "remember?"

"Macy." The birds chimed in louder, their wings sizing up the air, the den, Maybelline. "Birds."

"Yes, honey, it's close to their feeding time. Do you want to talk to Macy? She's on the phone."

"I don't see her."

"No, she's not here, she's on the phone."

"On the phone."

"Yes, Macy wants to talk to you."

"Macy, my nurse."

"That's right," Mrs. Blue said, "go ahead."

Maybelline said, "Okay, hello."

"Maybelline," I said.

"Maybelline," she said.

"This is Macy. Do you know who I am?"

"I know."

"Who am I?" I said.

"Who am I?" Maybelline said.

My hands were cold. I stretched my arm out on the table. Rested my cheek on my elbow. The picture of Maybelline an inch away from my eye. Too close. Her face, unclear, disintegrating into the dots of the newspaper ink.

"Macy is my nurse," Maybelline said. "She sews people together. Macy hates math."

"Yes."

Maybelline said to her mother, "Don't feed the birds without me." Her voice pitched high. A child's voice. A five-year-old. A kindergartner, for chrissake.

Mrs. Blue said, "No I won't, honey, you just talk with Macy."

Maybelline said, "You ran away."

"I didn't run away, Maybelline. I took a job in a hospital in another state. That's all."

"You ran away," Maybelline said, half sang. "Macy ran away like the cats."

The dots in the picture were biggest in Maybelline's eyes, big as keyholes, big as quarries. Holes bored into the skull, into the brain to relieve the pressure, drain the fluid, save the body.

"I didn't run away, Maybelline. I stayed with you after you got out of the hospital. I took care of you. When I was in nursing school, I lived in your house. Remember?"

"Mmm," Maybelline said. I heard her palm slapping her chest, not hard, just steady, calming. "You tied my shoes. Your bed was in my room. You combed my hair. You kissed me good night."

"Maybelline."

"Maybelline," she said.

I wanted to hang up the phone, stop listening. I wanted to get on a plane and rush to her house and hold onto her. I wanted to make everything right. But I couldn't because I saved her life and now her life was this. "Maybelline, tell me what one plus one equals."

She whistled like one of the songbirds. "I know that. That's easy."

"What is it then?"

"One."

"Oh," I said.

"Oh," Maybelline said.

"I have to go now, Maybelline. Do you want me to call you again?"

"Macy. Don't run away."

"Okay, Maybelline, I won't. I'll just say goodbye and you hang up the phone. Okay?"

"Okay," Maybelline said. "Okay, okay, okay."

I walked out of the kitchen pulling my sweatshirt and T-shirt over my head. In the living room I kicked off my shoes, stepped out of my jeans. I was in my blue underwear and no bra, not one scar on my skin. Nothing ever broken or cut too deep or anything removed, nothing diseased, cancerous. Whole. I was in one piece. See? Maybelline did not affect the way I stood. Got it? My mother had not changed how I moved one damn bit. My body did not remember any hurts on the surface or in the bones. My body forgot everything.

I went into Dotty's room, lay down on the sofa bed. The green bedspread pressed swirls of dents into my skin. In that room, Dotty touched me with her fingers and love words and kisses and I hushed their effect. Did not want one visible mark left on me. Not a gesture or an intonation. Nothing that would stick, everlasting. But Dotty had gotten in. Her touch was in the touch of my palm, there, on my belly. An invisible pattern seesawing over and through the patterns of Maybelline's equations and my mother's opportunistic incisions and disappearances. No matter what I told myself, my mother and Maybelline were permanent patterns, fixed stars in a constellation. Dotty, the inconstant light of the moon.

Dotty

NORA, DEL, AND Sunny stood next to the dry fountain, said nothing, didn't move. The moon settled in the black cottonwood tree. Clouds came by and dressed her up fancy, but the moon went nowhere. My chin and hands on the cold windowsill. The wheelbarrow was turned upside down. All the plants had been moved to the new greenhouse.

Nora said, "Well, that's that." Her voice like a small wind talking in a tree. She kissed Del and Sunny on their foreheads. Walked to the office, her hand rubbing the small of her back.

Sunny pointed at the sky. "Star shooting. Make a wish."

"Fresh out," Del said. "Make one for me." She shoved a pair of gloves in her back pocket, headed over to door number four. Sunny followed, long arms folded in front of her.

I lifted my chin from the windowsill and closed the shutters, refused to wait for any movement out there—of light or a word—to direct me. I drank the last of the tea Nora brewed, and it sailed fires down every capillary and I was contentious, hungry. Ready.

Seven a.m. In the office with the orchids, Nora was smoking while she dusted their leaves. Del and Sunny loaded up the station wagon with houseplants. All night, I watched out the window. The tea inside me like a crowbar lifting up the edges and underneath was the problem of Bell and Ray. All night the problem of Bell and Ray would not let me sleep. But that's not accurate. I slept an hour, a minute, a second. Bell and Ray vanished, and I saw nothing in front of me but fields of snow, the snow undisturbed. And maybe it was that simple—to create a different land overnight. To change the face of the world. One minute everything was a snowfield, paralyzed, waiting for the breath of springtime, and the next minute the ice was melting, a flood. Nothing to hold the water back. Ready. For Bell and Ray.

The straw hat was on my head and Nora said, "You look like a scarecrow I used to know in Oklahoma." And I knew that what she said was true. I had thinned down to the bone. Leaching the pain pills from me. My body occupied with nothing but loss.

That close to the bones, I saw that despite everything, I would always believe in love. Not the constant deluge. Nor the absolute calm. Somewhere in between was what I was aiming for: love as solid ground, leveling, with mole holes and wild violets.

Nora was still watching me. I was not doing a thing but standing still. Ready. Nora blew curls of smoke and said, "You have to let go of what's tearing you up."

"And what do you think that is?"

"Could be anything, but it's all the same. Poison is poison. You have the look of not enough and I hope you find what will satisfy you." She put the cigarette in her mouth for a long inhale. Hardly any smoke came out when she said, "I was like you. Did my leaving on a river. Walked half a day just to get to that water. And all I did was go from one side to the other, but that was all I needed to get myself untangled from what I didn't want. Course, didn't know that's what I was up to. Brooding like a hen all caught up with her eggs, that's how it was for me. When you're that inside your own heartache, you think it's gonna take something grand to move you. But there was no enormous difference between the one side of the river and the other, but only in the way I decided to open my eyes and see it. Could have been Venice for how much joy was inside me."

In the picture of Eleanor Roosevelt walking toward Nora's family, Nora had the same set to her eyes as she did now. Brown eyes dark as dust storms, eyes sweeping the road clear. Big eyes to take in what was outside and beyond the picture. Seeing past trouble and sorrow all the way to joy, to a woman coming on a hot day in the middle of a thousand other hot days and changing the weather, if only for an hour, and that was enough to understand that change wasn't unthinkable.

"Well," Nora said, "I packed some chamomile and Saint-John's-wort tea up for you. It'll help. Even a brooding hen gets damn tired of sitting on her eggs and has to leave them on their own for a while. Fix a cup of tea when you've been staying in the same spot too long. Let it steep fifteen minutes. Go outside and look for Venice."

I took my left hand out of my pocket, the nine dried beans sat on my palm, and I set my hand in front of Nora. "These are the beans I took when I left. Not seven days ago but twenty-two years. I grow the beans every summer. This year all I could do was throw the beans on top of the old compost pile and poke them in with the toe of my crutch. I didn't think they'd grow. But they did." I dropped the beans onto the counter. Shiny cranberry with pink swirls.

Nora said, "What do you call these beans?"

"Lucky."

"Thanks. I'll plant them next year."

"I'll come back and help you harvest them."

Nora enfolded my hand between both of hers, the cigarette in her mouth sending smoke into her hair, her hands heating mine above the lucky beans.

I rode in the back seat of the station wagon through the silver fog that spilled over from the river. Sunny drove, Del cursed the slowness. Five feet of asphalt ahead of us was all that was visible.

Sunny said, "Del, I ain't going faster than this. Better believe it and settle down. No use in us arriving dead. No use."

I touched the window, the condensation cold. My leg cramping. I missed the feel of Macy's hand on my own, her fingers, the flat of her palm, the motion of her hands, the belief that she could hold me up, that there would be no more falling. I didn't know a thing, not one true thing except that I was terrified that I was like a jack-in-the-box being wound up more and more but the lid never opened. I never popped out.

The fog was an opaque curtain over the car window. A way of keeping everything inside. Of not recognizing the shapes of things, there, off a ways, peripheral. But the fog was not enough to keep me from seeing. A picture: memory of our father in the sunshine, the water hose in his hand, the day breaking a hundred degrees. Our father in his white T-shirt, green khakis with suspenders. Barefoot. Bell and Ray, eight years old, and I was six. Our father putting his thumb partway over the end of the water hose and the water rising into the air in a soft spray. Bell and Ray running back and forth, Bell holding my hand, running me back and forth past the rosebushes that our mother planted. Our father never tiring of Bell and Ray and me singing "London Bridge is falling down." I got too close to the rosebushes and stepped off the grass that our father limed every spring. It wasn't a thorn I stepped on but a bumblebee. Its stinger in my foot. Already, not a cry out of me to provoke or call attention to. But our father saw me let go of Bell and sit on the grass, the bumblebee still attached to its stinger. Our father dropped the hose with the water going and knelt down by me. Said nothing. Took my foot and rested it on his green khakis and slapped the bumble-bee away from its stinger. Our father who looked nothing like me, who called me the sorriest, the stupidest, killed her own mother, I saw how in a moment all the regular, ordinary habits were pushed aside and our father's hands, which knew little about kindness toward me, were soft as that spray of water and pulled out the stinger and rubbed my foot and our father smiled and said, "There you go, kiddo, good as new, better than ever."

Our father. There were brief times of goodness. It only made the bad times worse.

Bell and Ray knew from the start that to understand bad you had to experi-ence some good. They just made sure I never got too much. They wound the jack-in-the-box to the point right before it opened.

Macy

BELL AND RAY knocked on the door. 11:11 p.m. All right. I was game. I opened the door. But not too much. Enough so my head fit through.

"What?" Not hello or come in, pleased as the man in the moon to see you.

"An offering," Bell said. Not hello or may we come in, pleased as hell to see you.

"A blood sacrifice, did you say?"

"Funny," Bell said. None of us laugh.

The cold in the air turned our words to visible gusts. We picked out what we said, careful of how the last word would be the one heard, frozen in the ear. Bell and Ray were in a hurry, but they did not hurry. Their breath in the air was quick. Their words came slowly. All right. I could wait. Patience, my mother said, was nothing more than acting bored. I put on my mother's face. I tilted my head. Wet my lips. Listened for Bell and Ray's blood to come to a boil.

Ray was wearing gloves, green and leather, tight over his skinny fingers. Skinny as Bell's fingers. Her knuckle bones like a mountain range. Little flesh to cover the sharpness. An envelope in Ray's hand. Opportunity knocks.

"Here," Ray said, "time is running out." Not, how time flies or time heals all.

The envelope was not sealed. No time for that. For licking the glue, folding the paper, pressing it closed. No time for me opening it, finding a way in. With my pinky or thumb or knife.

Ray said, "And time is what we don't have."

"Or Dotty," I said.

"Precisely," Bell said.

I could smell her skin, the inside of her wrist. A whole day at the perfume convention and what Bell smelled of was onions. Onions diced and fried in oil. Left overnight in a skillet. She didn't mean to smell like that. Tried her damndest not to. But I'm a nurse. I smelled her troubles. What she concealed under the paper-thin layers.

I folded the flap of the envelope back. Took out the paper: a solid blue like a body of water. Inside the water, a check. One thousand dollars. Pay to the order of: my name.

"What's this?" I said.

"Necessary, my dear Macy," Bell said. "You know where Dot is. We would like that information. Now."

Necessary. Relentless. They had no qualms. A thousand dollars. Ten thousand dollars. What did it matter? They thought I had what they wanted. The wind varnished their ears red. I smiled. The cold in the air was up my sleeves, through the weave of denim. I was as cold as their hearts. I had nothing but lies for them. We were all an arm's length away from Dotty.

"She's between here and there," I said.

"For a thousand dollars, could you be more specific," Bell said.

"No, I can't."

Ray slapped both his gloved hands onto the top of his head and turned to Bell. Shifted, foot to foot. Hurry, he didn't say. "It isn't going to work," he said.

Bell stuck her good hand out to softly touch his arm and could have said, don't worry, Ray. Or she could have reached out her good hand and grabbed his arm hard and said, shut up, Ray. Whatever she said was in a voice that knew everything about him. Everything. How much money was in the checking account, favorite foods, how he took his shoes off, his skin, the feel of his skin, the scars on his body.

Bingo.

"Opportunity," Maybelline once said to me, "really is simply a guess at the right time."

I handed them back the check. "Go fuck yourselves."

Dotty

IN THE CITY the fog thinned. Vapors wandered across the roads, clung to the upper stories of chrome-plated buildings, flattened out like tissue paper on the river. Sunny parked the station wagon in line behind three taxis and a Corvette in front of the Rose Motor Inn. Eight-thirty in the morning and people were hurrying into the taxis and out of the motel as if the day was almost over and they hadn't gotten anything done.

Del said, "Who ya meeting here, anyway?"

"Family." I took the straw hat off my head, slipped it under the straps that held the pillow to my backpack. The pillow from the Hotel Iris that they gave me.

"That's a good thing. Family." Sunny's eyes in the rearview mirror looking into mine.

"Could also be a bad thing," Del said.

"Can't thank you enough for all you did. And your mother," I said.

"Yeah, well," Del said, like that said it all, summed it up.

I pushed open the car door. The air was cold and Lila's blue coat was not warm enough. "Good luck to you."

Sunny said, "Same back to you."

They both glanced at my leg and I looked at it too, as if this would insure that what we wished for each other would come true. I closed the car door. Held my backpack by the handles like it was a suitcase and I was a guest arriving at the Rose Motor Inn. I waved at Sunny and Del driving off. The big leaves of the dieffenbachia waved back out the rear window of the station wagon.

I took a step. Another. I didn't go over how it would be because I didn't know. The wind went right through me into the bones that were mending, the bones that hadn't forgotten about wanting pain pills. I pulled up the collar of the blue coat with the square buttons tight around my neck. I was Eleanor Roosevelt walking into the motel lobby. There was nothing I couldn't do. The desk clerk did not see any of the last seven days: the shaking as my body rearranged its parts, what I kept and what I discarded. He spread his hands out on the desk.

"What can I do for you?" he said. Did not see the shabbiness of Lila's blue coat or my hair's static and oil, the curls weighted down, the ends sticking up. He looked only at his tired hands. It was easy to step right over him.

"The Meyers are expecting me," I said. "Which room are they in?"

He turned a page in the register between his hands. "Yes, and who did you say you were?"

"Dorothy Meyers, their sister."

"Room forty-one, fourth floor to the right of the elevator." He sat down as if the fog had come in with me and wrapped him up and sat him down in the rose-pink-colored chair and he never even knew I was here.

I was in their room. Bell and Ray's. A slight shaking in my leg, a glaze of that old fright, but I was not turning away. From what I saw. From facing them. They were not expecting this at all, for me to walk into their room, right through the door that was not locked because one or the other of them had gotten up to open the door earlier for the complimentary newspaper and they did not bother to relock the door and now I was there.

"Bell. Ray."

And what could they say? Under the blanket and sheet, in the one bed, together. Their arms on top of the blanket. Their collarbones and necks and arms visible. Nothing on—they wore nothing. The newspaper in a scramble across the bed as if it was tumbled within the blanket and sheet.

"We thought," Bell said and lifted her bad hand, but I did not look away from the sight of them together.

"You thought what?" I said. "That I'd be the same pushover as before?"

"Dot," Bell said.

"No, there is no Dot here. You call me what she named me, what our mother named me. Dorothy."

Ray sat up. The scars on his face, those roads of sutures toughened, pale skin led down to the scars on his chest, scars jagged as a child's drawing of a mountain range. "You listen, Dorothy," Ray said and the Dorothy came out like a long spit, "you get out of here and let us get dressed and then we'll talk."

I set my backpack on the tan carpet with the specks of blue. "You couldn't possibly talk your way out of this." I walked over to the white dresser with the drawer pulls of brass and an oval mirror above. On top of the dresser were perfume bottles and I chose the one with the pure white stopper, tapered to a point like a thorn. It was not labeled. Inside, it smelled of snow and ice and sliding and falling. There was no liquid there, just the smell. But I did not fall in.

Bell was on her feet, sticking her arms through Ray's charcoal-grey shiny shirt. But not before I saw the brown nipples, curls of peach-red pubic hair, rib bones, hip bones, all the jutting angles of her thin body. She buttoned the buttons, one-handed, her bad arm hidden in the sleeve. How adjusted she was, as if her bad arm was not bad at all. As if. She threw Ray his pants and a long-sleeved polo shirt. He kept the sheet and blanket around him, swung his legs over the side of the bed and pulled his pants on. Tugged the shirt over his head.

"Now, Dorothy," Bell said, "let's not draw conclusions." She fished slacks out of the pile of clothes on the ottoman and slipped them on. Fuzzy black crushed velvet, zipper on the side. She let Ray's shirttails hang over the slacks.

"You could put on a suit of armor, the both of you, and it would not change what I see. You can't cover it up. You're in a mess, and I don't mean the bed. But what does it have to do with me?"

Bell tipped her head back, shook her hair, and combed it with the fingers of her good hand until it was all in place behind her ears. When she brought her head forward, she aimed her eyes at me. The color of them colder and solidified like ice out of an ice-cube tray.

"Didn't you ever wonder," Bell said, "why Daddy hated you?"

"Oh, come on," I said. "I killed our mother by being born, that's the story, you know it as well as I do."

"Yes," Ray said, "that's the public record." Bell sat on the end of the bed. Ray joined her. Both of them put socks and shoes on. Sat there, the two of them, as if their skin never touched in the bed, under the covers. All these years.

"What if," Ray said, "that wasn't the whole story?"

"What more could there be?" I unbuttoned the blue coat, put my hand on the ache in my hip. The room warm, drapes closed.

"One important bit more," Bell said.

"Can't you see, Dorothy," Ray said, "we're your flesh and blood?"

"But not him," Bell said. "Not Daddy."

Bell's and Ray's spiteful smiles bloomed.

"You're not his child," Bell said.

"Another man's," Ray said.

"Daddy hated you because he had to raise you like you were his," Bell said, "and the man disappeared before Daddy could give you to him."

"Sad story," Ray said.

"Tragic," Bell said.

"But that's why we're here," Ray said.

"To tell you," Bell said, "he's dead. Daddy, that is. You don't have to worry about him anymore. You have to come home now. You have to sign some papers."

"It's only fair," Ray said.

"Don't you agree?" Bell said.

They crossed their legs. Ray put both hands on his knee. Their smiles sharp as whittling knives on their faces. But I was done with all their words. I narrowed my eyes, took a giant step closer to them. They did not see how disarmed they really were. How the secret of our father not being my father did not add or subtract from what was done. Bell and Ray still thinking they had the upper hand. But no, they didn't. I knew which direction I was pointed in. Just like the basket of fruit and ice held out by Eleanor Roosevelt in the middle of a desolate land, I came to change the weather.

"No," I said, "I don't agree. So you say he wasn't my father, but it doesn't change a thing. He *was* our father and you know he made sure I knew I was different from you. Not as good. Kept me waiting for an ounce of kindness. Kept me waiting for the next kick or punch. So he hated me for a different reason. So what? The damage was still done. And you, you're both still believing you can benefit."

"Dot, do you really thing we'd be that cruel?" Bell said.

"We protected you from him," Ray said.

"You're painting the wrong picture," Bell said. "Just ask Macy, she'll tell you."

"Macy knows we're on your side, Dot," Ray said.

"Protect me? Do you ever stop lying for a second? You injured me every bit as much as he did. And Macy is not leverage or a card up your sleeve. You see, it is this simple: you need me or you wouldn't be here. But I don't need you or anything you have to offer. Whatever it is of our father's you want, you can have. I'm just happy as hell that the bastard is dead."

"They need you there," Ray said, "the estate lawyers." His arms crossed in front of his polo shirt.

"Why?"

"Because Momma owned the house and her will is tied to his will. It's complicated."

"Then it's up to you to make it less complicated. A lot less. And without me."

"Dorothy." Bell stood up. The spitting image of our father after he'd hurt me and it was time to pretend he hadn't. "There's a lot in it for you."

"No," I said, "there's a lot in it for you. And you. Right, Ray?"

Bell said nothing. Her eyes didn't even blink. Her bad arm was the only thing that moved, swaying like a tree branch in a breeze.

Ray stood and put his hands in his pockets. "You have no idea what we've gone through. After the accident and all."

"I don't want to know," I said.

Bell said, "You never were more than an infinitesimal dot. Easy to crush and ignore. We can work around you. You won't keep us from getting what we want. You never did. You can go now." Her bad arm swung away from her belly. Dismissing me.

"Not yet. You have something of mine that I want."

Bell stepped closer to me before I could step closer to her, as if this was the game, the mother-may-I, wait for no one to say yes or no. As if she could stop me. We were a hand's length apart. A breath between us.

"What, Dot?" Bell said. As if that was enough to make me fall.

I smiled. "This." I grabbed her good hand and pushed the shirt sleeve up her arm. The bracelet fell to her wrist. The bracelet that I had left in our father's house in my hurry to leave. The bracelet of charms: all apples except for one charm, the silver paint brush with the name *Promise* on the back. I undid the clasp and the bracelet coiled into my palm. My mother's bracelet.

"This is mine," I said. "It never did you a bit of good, did it?"

It was simple to step outside the door and know the weather I brought with me would not change the land in their hearts, but that it did change the land in mine.

Macy

A HAPPY ENDING: IN the shack was where we took our clothes off. Opportunity, there in the flowers put in a soda bottle. Three daisies on long stems, and it's easy to guess the rest. She loves me, she loves me not. I didn't know how the flowers got there. But it was persuasive: she loves me, Dotty said. We placed the blue coat on the floor. Stood on either side of it. I could tell you a story, I said, but it doesn't have any words after a while. Tell me anyway, Dotty said. It doesn't have any buttons, I said, or sleeves or collars or zippers and the shoes are the first to disappear. I took my shoes off, socks, and all the rest of my clothes, standing across the blue coat from Dotty. I said, The story is a mirror. I knelt down and untied her shoelaces. She picked up each foot and when she did, I pulled off her shoes and socks. My hands followed her arms as they raised over her head and I lifted her shirt away. When I slipped her pants down over her hip, I pictured the bones and how they connected. Dotty leaned into my hand. I saw her up on the ladder, slanting into colors and motion. I slid my hands down until her pants were off, added to the pile of our clothes. A mirror, I said, shows us what we don't pay attention to. Look at me and I'll look at you. A happy ending, Dotty said. Yes, I said, a happy ending.

I woke up. I was on the sofa bed, the bedspread pushing into my skin. The familiarity of it all. The uncertainty. I looked to the side of me and Dotty turned over in her sleep as she always turned toward me. Brown eyes opening and in her eyes there was no hardness at all. No grudge. No thought of running away again. It was like before, only it was after. Everything ironed out. Understood. Dotty and me. Is it possible? Dotty said, to live to a happy ending? Yes, I said.

In the driveway I walked around the car and opened the door for Dotty. Offered my arm, my hand. Take it, I said. She slid her hand down my arm to my hand. She was skinnier than when she left. Still walking crooked. Her bones at odds with gravity. Fighting gravity. Each step I thought she would fall. But no. She didn't fall and that was what I wanted for her. Her body relaying the slope of the world to her mind and her mind arranging the world so it made sense. And here she was walking with a different pitch, that's all, a tilt. From the car to the house. Her crooked walking. Each step. With me. The nurse. All my life I tried to fix things. Fix things that might not even be broken. We walked up to the house, Dotty and I. We stopped, a step away from a happy ending. I held tighter to her hand. Dotty said, Don't worry, I won't let go.

We drove over the bridge with the algae growing on the rusted metal, giant lacy blooms. The sky cleared. The rain vanished. All right, I said, what do I have to do to get to the happy ending? Nothing, Dotty said, nothing has changed. We continue, that's all.

I pulled the car over at the top of the off ramp at Park and Fourth streets. 2:09. Dotty opened the door and got in. No one honked even though I had traffic waiting. They saw the happy ending about to happen. The first motion was Dotty's. She kissed me while the stop light turned its colors. Kissed me. Not one iota of hesitation. Like I was the woman she loved. Never mind what came before. Never mind.

A happy ending: I didn't believe in them.

Dotty

FOR AN HOUR I stand. Not moving. Between the gathering rain clouds a quick square of canary yellow sun warms me. The ocean sound of car after car, that ebbing and rush forward as the traffic light changes. My eyes focus on the asphalt next to me, on the potholes and the tires slipping into the holes as cars come off the ramp and pass me on this corner: Fourth Street and Park. But there is no park. Asphalt, with its smell of tar and stone, shimmers. I imagine what it is not: a slippery river with water, iron-rich, violet. Take it down further, to what it was, a thistled hillside with snake grass, deadly nightshade. Down to its granite base, the crookedness of the dirt and rock fractured from earthquakes. All the debris and layers that stay hidden or are maneuvered into another shape, a fancy lie with turn lanes and street signs, easy directions on the surface of things.

The light turns red. The cars inch close to the curb where I wait. They think I am begging. It has everything to do with the way I stand. The stiffness and how I don't smile. With my straw hat at my feet in the folded-over browned grass, I could be asking for money. Most of the drivers want to avoid me. Turn up the radio, check their faces in the rearview mirror. They believe I'm a freeloader, a leech, unconcerned with time, and that irritates them, to not keep to the clock, obey the minute hand, rush with the rush hour. Some stop and throw money, their shiny mouths pinched up with starched words—"Here you go" or "Good luck." I've collected a dollar sixty-three.

Pain in my leg bone sharp scratching and yes, I want a pain pill, a whole handful. Can anyone blame me? One hour standing here, cemented, rooted. Don't even see the cars anymore or the people inside in their hurry, hurry. It does not bother me to be stared at. Go ahead and look: doesn't matter anymore what anyone else sees. I don't mind waiting.

And then she is there. Macy. She stops the car and opens the door on my side. Two cars honk as I get in. I push my pack over the front seat to the back. Macy's hand slides down my arm, over the rough blue of Lila's coat. The light changes to green and then to red and back to green. Macy drives up the hill and turns at the first street and stops the car. The engine still going, the heater rattling. We don't move. Just look at each other until Macy smiles that smile that is all her own, nothing of Lila in it. My hand crosses over the seat to her hand, my lips almost touching hers. Crackled elm leaves skitter along the street. The heels of our hands pushing, fingers tight, heat in our palms. I shake my head.

"Why didn't you tell me," I say, "about Lila."

"Why didn't you?" Macy asks.

I lift Macy's hand to my lips and I talk against her fingers, bones. "I didn't know who she was."

"Neither did I."

I kiss her fingers, wrist bone. Rain begins to click, slow drops, wide apart against the roof of the car and the windshield. The smell of Macy, of wool and starch, her humid skin, of all she hides, the words so ripe in the orchard of what she doesn't say. I look back up into the blue of her eyes: the quarry, the ocean, the sinking, the floating, and I hold her. Her breath in my ear, cheekbone against cheekbone, flutter of her eyelashes, the sureness of her arms. Tears, slow as rain.

She says, "A friend of mine, Maybelline, told me that nothing in the world is simple. I wanted everything in the world to be simple. But it's not, is it? I can't show you the wholeness of love without uncovering what was broken, and that was Maybelline and that was my mother and that is me." Macy pulls back, one hand on the steering wheel, sliding over the ridges, the horn. The other wiping across her eyes.

I turn her face toward me. "Then show me. I just want truth from here on."

"Which version?" Macy asks.

"The one that will land us in New Jersey with everything that kept us from telling the truth."

"And then?"

"We keep going."

The rain quickens. Macy touches my lips with her fingers. "Do you know where?"

"No. Do you?"

"No."

"Then let's just go."

Macy and me. We move as close as we can get and we kiss and inside the kiss it is all blue rain and sun behind the rain and nothing is settled or uncompli-cated. I kiss Macy as if the only thing I know is how all the steps have led us here to this one impossible perfect place.

About the Author

AMY SCHUTZER'S POETRY and fiction are published in *Hurricane Alice*, *Frontiers*, *Feminist Broadcast Quarterly*, *Blue Stocking*, *Fireweed*, *Common Lives/ Lesbian Lives*, and *Portland Review*. She is the recipient of an Astraea National Lesbian Action Foundation Fellowship and a Barbara Deming Fellowship for this novel. She lives on women's land in Estacada, Oregon, where she is at work on her second novel, *The Color of Weather*.

Colophon

The text of this book was composed in Goudy Old Style
with titles in Rosabel Antique and
sections spaced with Minion Ornaments.

Page layout and composition provided by
ImPrint Services, Corvallis, Oregon.